IF I
SHOULD DIE

By Amy Plum

Die for Me
Until I Die
If I Should Die

IF I
SHOULD DIE

AMY PLUM

atom

www.atombooks.net

ATOM

First published in the United States in 2013 by HarperCollins
First published in Great Britain in 2013 by Atom

Copyright © 2013 by Amy Plum

The moral right of the author has been asserted.

A CIP catalogue record for this book
is available from the British Library.

ISBN 978-1-907411-04-5

Printed and bound in Great Britain by
Clays Ltd, St Ives plc

Papers used by Atom are from well-managed forests
and other responsible sources.

MIX
Paper from
responsible sources
FSC® C104740

Atom
An imprint of
Little, Brown Book Group
100 Victoria Embankment
London EC4Y 0DY

An Hachette UK Company
www.hachette.co.uk

www.atombooks.net

For Lucia. Strength. Joy. Love.

Sweet my Love whom I loved to try for,
Sweet my Love whom I love and sigh for,
    Will you once love me and sigh for me,
You my Love whom I love and die for?
—"Mariana" by Christina Rossetti, 1881

PART I

ONE

IN THE DEAD OF NIGHT I SAT ON A BRIDGE SPANNING the Seine, watching a bouquet of crushed white lilies float toward the spotlit Eiffel Tower. I strained to listen for the words I thought I'd just heard. The words of a dead boy—of my boyfriend's ghost. I could have sworn he spoke to me a second ago. Which was impossible.

But there they were again—his words appearing once more in my mind, the two syllables cutting me as sharply as a whip crack.

Mon ange.

My heart hammered. "Vincent? Is that really you?" I asked with a trembling voice.

Kate, can you hear me?

"Vincent, you're volant. Violette hasn't destroyed you!" I leapt to my feet and spun around, searching anxiously for a glimpse of him, though I knew there would be nothing to see. I stood alone on the Pont des Arts. The surface of the water rippled and moved beneath me like the back of a great, dark serpent—the twinkling lights on the riverbanks reflected in its writhing smoothness. I shivered and pulled my coat tighter around myself.

No. She hasn't destroyed my corpse . . . yet.

"Oh my God, Vincent, I was sure she had done it." I wiped a tear from my cheek before a flood of others followed. Just moments earlier, I had given up all hope of ever hearing from him again. I had been positive that he was gone forever, his body burned by his enemy. But here he was. I didn't understand. I choked back tears.

Kate. Breathe, Vincent insisted.

I exhaled slowly. "I can't believe you're here, talking to me. Where are you? Where did she take your body?"

I'm lying dormant in Violette's castle in the Loire Valley. I only became conscious a few minutes ago. As soon as I figured out what she was doing, I came to you. Vincent's words sounded bleak. Hopeless.

My hands shook as I whipped my phone out of my pocket. "Tell me exactly where you are. I'm calling Ambrose—he'll get a group together and we'll be right there."

It's too late for a rescue, Kate. Violette has been waiting for my mind to awake, and now that I'm volant, she will burn my body. When I left, some of her henchmen were stoking a fire while she performed some kind of ancient ritual she claimed would bind my spirit to her once I'm reduced to ashes. I only have a few minutes, and I want to spend them with you.

"It's never too late," I insisted. "We could try to stop whatever it is that Violette's doing. I'm sure your kindred could come up with some kind of distraction. We have to try." Why was Vincent giving up so easily?

Kate. Stop, he pleaded. *Please don't waste the little time I have trying to call Ambrose when there is no way that you can reach me in time. There is* no way, *believe me.*

The force in his voice made me hesitate, but I kept staring at my phone as a lump formed in my throat. If I couldn't do anything, it meant that all was lost. My initial shock was being overtaken by an icy shawl of realization: The boy I loved was minutes away from being burned on a pyre. "No!" I cried, willing the horror to go away.

Vincent was silent, allowing the truth to sink in. I was losing my love—forever. If Vincent's body was destroyed, I would never touch him again. Never feel his mouth against mine. Never hold him in my arms.

But he won't be completely gone. Will he? I had to make sure. My voice came out in a strangled croak. "At least you're volant, right? If Violette had burned you before your mind awoke, you would be gone forever—body *and* spirit."

I wish she had. Vincent's words were bitter. *She said she needed my spirit present in order to perform the power transfer.* A few seconds passed before I heard his voice again. *I think I'd rather be nonexistent than help Violette become powerful enough to destroy my kindred.*

I didn't agree. Vincent still existed, even if his body didn't. The boy I loved so desperately hadn't completely disappeared.

That's something, I thought, feeling a glimmer of hope. And then I remembered, *I will never see him. Or feel his skin against mine as we touch hands. Lips. Never again.* And the hope disappeared.

Fury fought despair inside me. "Why did it have to be you?" I asked. "Why are you the one with the power she's ready to kill for?"

If it wasn't me, it would be someone else.

"I wish it were someone else," I said selfishly. "I want *you* to live." But I knew Vincent wouldn't agree. His whole existence was about sacrificing himself for others. He would give himself in a heartbeat to save one of his kindred.

I looked out over the rippling water and imagined Vincent materializing before me. The soft black of his hair. The sapphire flash of his dark eyes. His tall, solid frame. Vincent's phantom hung suspended over the waves for a moment, glimmering transparently in the moonlight, before dissolving back into my mind's eye.

I don't want to watch her burn my body.

There was fear in his voice. Vincent had experienced many violent deaths, but *this* end was final. I wanted to take his hand. I wanted to touch him. Comfort him. But all I had were words. "Then don't go back. Stay here with me until the end." I tried to sound brave, but I was trembling.

"I love you." I spoke the words, while silently urging myself not to cry. The last thing Vincent needed right now was to see me mourn him.

You are my life, Kate. I have been fighting my destiny to be with you, and after all that struggle I find myself powerless; I can't stop Violette.

I didn't respond. Because if I did, I would scream. My heart felt like it was being wrenched from my chest as Vincent was being separated from me for eternity. The boy who I had given so much to love—who I had gone against my sense of self-preservation to be with—was being taken away from me by a megalomaniac adolescent, and there wasn't a thing anyone could do about it. I couldn't hold it back: I began crying again. But not from sadness. My tears were tears of impotent fury.

Will you pass a message on to Jean-Baptiste and the others for me?

"Of course," I gasped, trying to speak around the boulder of hatred lodged in my throat.

Remind them that since I didn't offer myself voluntarily to Violette, she will not receive my full power. That's the only ray of hope I can see.

Apologize to JB for me. For my disbelief, he continued. *I wish I had figured out what all of this meant while I still had a chance.*

"Yes. I'll tell them." My breath made little puffs of cloud in the frigid air. I rubbed my hands briskly on my arms. Leaping down off the end of the bridge, I strode swiftly in the direction of La Maison, knowing that Vincent's spirit would accompany me. Even if it was too late to save him, I had to tell the others what was going on.

Kate, I want you to know that I awoke the first time I saw you.

I had managed to pull myself together in order to carry out the monumental task of putting one foot in front of the other, but a declaration of love from the boy I was about to lose was too much for me. Tears blurred my vision as he continued.

Something inside me that had been still and silent since my first death all of a sudden sparked and began to live again. I knew there was something different about you, and I had to find out what it was.

"When was the first time you saw me?" I asked, trying to distract myself—to keep myself from breaking down right then and there on the riverbank. "Are you talking about the Café Sainte-Lucie?"

No. He laughed. *I had seen you around our neighborhood—long before the café. We kept crossing paths for weeks before you actually noticed me. And I couldn't help wondering who you were and why you were so tortured—so mournful. I kept hoping your sister or your grandparents would say your name. We just called you the sad girl.*

"Who is 'we'?" I asked, my pace slowing.

Ambrose, Jules, and me.

"Then they must have recognized me that first day in the café," I said, surprised by this new perspective on our story.

His silence was an affirmation. *You've intrigued me from the very beginning. And you still do. You're different. I wanted to spend the rest of your life discovering who you were. But now . . .* His words dissolved and then reappeared with renewed determination.

Kate, I promise I will find a way to get away from Violette and come back to you. Even if it's too late for us, I want you to know I will always be near. I'll always be watching out for you.

Stunned, I froze mid-step. "What do you mean, 'too late for us'?" I asked, feeling like I had been punched in the gut.

Kate, in a few minutes my body will no longer exist. From now on, the only thing I can do for you is try to keep you safe. A human and a revenant—that was a difficult enough challenge. But a human and a ghost? Mon amour, *I would never wish that for . . .*

And that was it. Those were the last words Vincent spoke to me before he was gone, leaving me alone on a riverbank with nothing but the whistling of the winter wind.

TWO

AS I RAN, IT SEEMED THAT THE RIVER WAS RISING up above its banks and invisible waves were lapping at my ankles. Within seconds I felt as if I were moving underwater, battling a powerful current as I fought to propel myself toward La Maison.

Finally I was typing in the digicode and flying through the gate. My stomach twisted with nausea as I threw the door open and looked wildly around.

Gaspard and Arthur were coming down the staircase peering at the pages of a large book held between them. They stopped when they saw me. Shoving the book at Arthur, the older revenant rushed down the steps and took me by the shoulders. "What is it, Kate?" he asked.

"Vincent," I gasped, fighting to catch my breath. "He came to me. But now he's gone."

"Gone where?" he urged.

"Burned," I blurted. "He awoke, came to me volant, and said Violette was about to burn him. And then his voice just disappeared."

Gaspard looped my arm through his, grasping my hand securely. "Get everyone together," he commanded. Arthur was off like a shot, calling together the few dozen Parisian kindred who had gathered at La Maison to wait for news of Vincent's whereabouts.

Gaspard led me through the sitting room and into the great hall. "Your hands are like ice, my dear," he said, seating me in front of the crackling fire and draping a woolen throw around my shoulders.

Even with the radiant heat and warm blanket, I couldn't stop shaking. The flames made me think of another blaze that was burning a few hours south of us. Flames that had taken Vincent away from me—permanently.

I heard footsteps rushing up behind me and found myself enveloped in a couple hundred pounds of muscle. "Katie-Lou, are you okay?" Ambrose asked, his voice harsh with protectiveness. Leaning away, he searched my face. I shook my head numbly and he wrapped me back in his arms.

I stayed mummified against him for the next few minutes while everyone assembled. Jean-Baptiste perched on a wooden stool before the fire, Gaspard stood by his side, and Arthur positioned himself in front of me on the rug. The rest of the revenants fanned out around us, all eyes focused on me. They fell silent as I cleared my throat to keep my voice from trembling.

11

I told them that Nicolas had followed me to the Pont des Arts to deliver Violette's message: She had taken Vincent's body to her castle in the Loire and would destroy it when she "saw fit." And he had informed me of the reason the numa trusted Violette in the first place: She had convinced their chief, Lucien, that she held the secret to capturing the Champion's power and promised to use it against the bardia.

After giving them the message Vincent asked me to relay, I concluded: "And that was all. His voice just cut off like that, in the middle of talking." *Let them believe his message to his kindred were his last words*, I thought. His *true* last words were too personal—not to mention painful—to share.

There was a second of horrified silence before the room erupted. Ambrose dropped me from his bear hug, rose to his feet, and added his voice to the others. "Well, what are we waiting for, people? Let's go storm the castle!"

Jean-Baptiste shook his head gravely, raising his voice to be heard above the crowd. "It's too late." His voice quieted the noisy crowd as effectively as a spoon against a wineglass. "Vincent will be ashes by the time we arrive, his spirit bound to Violette."

"What does that even mean, being *bound*?" Ambrose asked, nestling back next to me. As usual, everyone turned to Gaspard for an explanation.

Now that the commotion had died down, he was back to his tic-y nervous self. He fidgeted with his shirt collar and raised a trembling finger, his wild hair forming an inky halo around his head.

"A wandering soul—a revenant soul that has no remaining

body—is a rare enough thing," he began. "When our enemies succeed in killing us, they destroy our body immediately, and our soul disappears with it. They would have no reason to wait until we are volant to destroy us—trapping us as wandering souls—except perhaps in a case of vengeance against a particular revenant.

"But a wandering soul *being bound* to its captor is so rare that I can think of no examples from recent history. Which is understandable considering the extreme personal sacrifice a numa must make to successfully perform a binding." Gaspard grimaced.

"Extreme personal sacrifice?" I asked, something catching in my throat. His revolted expression was creeping me out.

He was silent for a few unnerving seconds, choosing his words, and said, "They must incinerate a part of themselves with the body of the one they are binding."

"What do you mean? Like their hair or fingernails?" My nose wrinkled in disgust.

"No, it must be flesh and bone," Gaspard said.

Eww, I thought, recoiling from the grotesque image this brought to mind.

"That's not much of a sacrifice," Ambrose said from next to me. "Whatever Violette lops off, it's just going to grow back next time she's dormant."

The older revenant shook his head. "Besides the pain involved in the 'lopping,' as you put it, *that* is the sacrifice: The body part of the numa burned with the revenant corpse disappears forever. In the case of a binding, there is no regeneration."

I leaned closer to Ambrose, fighting the sickened numbness that spread through me. Violette was going to sever a part of her own body in order to bind Vincent's spirit? I knew she had killed him to get his powers. But permanently mutilating herself? Centuries of serving a fate she didn't choose seemed to have cost the ancient revenant her sanity.

"I'll ask him for you," said Ambrose under his breath, and then speaking up said, "Jules wants to know if being bound to Violette means Vincent must obey her."

I hadn't been aware that Jules was with us until then, but knowing he was near, I felt comforted. "If the only reason Violette needs Vincent's spirit is for transfer of the Champion's power," Gaspard responded, "we can hope she will release him once she achieves her goal. But even if she chooses to keep him bound, a wandering soul cannot be forced to act against its will."

Arthur spoke up. "I beg to disagree," he said apologetically. "There *are* historical examples of coercion."

"For example?" Jean-Baptiste insisted.

"There is the account from our Italian kindred that dates back to the Renaissance," Arthur stated. "A numa chief killed a newly formed bardia and bound her volant spirit to him by incinerating his left hand with her corpse. He manipulated her into serving his will by threatening to kill her still-living human family, and became extremely powerful through the strength of his spirit-slave."

"Then it's a good thing that Vin doesn't have any human family left," said Ambrose with a note of triumph. "No mortal bargaining chips for our Evil Empress to use against . . ." Realizing what he was saying, he stopped talking and lowered his face to his hands.

He didn't even look at me. He didn't have to. Because everyone else was.

THREE

"VIOLETTE USING . . . A HUMAN WHO IS DEAR TO him"—Gaspard avoided my eyes—"to blackmail Vincent is, as one would say in modern parlance, quite a long shot. She may not be aware of this ancient story. And even if she is, once she absorbs his power I doubt she will need the servitude of a much-weakened revenant spirit."

His words were meant to comfort me. And they did, to an extent. What he said was rational. But Violette had already used me once to get to Vincent. The thought that she might use me again—this time forcing Vincent to act against his will—was unbearable.

Jean-Baptiste turned to address the crowd. His ramrod-straight posture, chest puffed out and hands behind his back, recalled the Napoleonic military leader he had been centuries earlier. "That's enough talk of hypothetical situations. One of our kindred—my very own second—has been corporeally destroyed. We must act now to save his spirit and to stop Violette from achieving her plans."

With that, he began organizing everyone. Arthur was appointed to lead a contingent to Violette's castle in Langeais. He had lived there for centuries, and could effectively hide a group of spies to keep tabs on Violette's movements. Since Jules was volant, he was to accompany them, enter the castle, and try to contact Vincent's spirit. And Ambrose was placed in charge of defensive strategy against the numa remaining in Paris. "To begin," JB asked him, "could you please see Kate safely home?"

"Home?" I leapt from the couch to face the revenant leader. "No! I want to help. There has to be something I can do."

Jean-Baptiste read my expression. "Kate, my dear, I am not being condescending—I'm being realistic. There is nothing you can do at this time of the night except go home, sleep, and be ready for any updates we have in the morning."

I eyed him skeptically, but he seemed sincere—it wasn't a case of talking down to the weak, powerless human. But I didn't agree with him. There *was* something I could do. Someone I could talk to who might have valuable information about what was happening. And the more informed I was, the more capable I would be to help Vincent.

As JB moved to address the next group, I asked Ambrose to give me a moment. Sitting with my back to him, I found Bran's number on my phone. The call went straight to voice mail. "Bran," I said, speaking softly, "it's Kate." I exhaled and pressed my eyes closed. "Violette told me that her men killed your mother. If that is true, then I am so sorry. But there's something you can do to help us fight the numa. I need to talk to you. Please call me when you get this message, whatever time of the night." I gave him my number and hung up.

Ambrose was waiting, watching me curiously, but didn't pry. As I rose, he gave my shoulders a little side squeeze, and I winced. "Sorry, little sister, forgot about that cracked collarbone Vi gave you yesterday."

"That's okay," I said, leaning my head on his shoulder as we walked to the door. "Pain is actually a good thing. It means I can feel."

Ambrose held my coat for me to slip into. "Okay," he responded to someone I couldn't see, and wrapped his arm cautiously around my shoulders. "Jules wants me to tell you not to worry about anything," he said as we walked through the courtyard and out the gate. "That Violette has bigger things in mind than using Vincent as her puppet and you as bait."

"If that was meant to reassure me, thanks. But the thought of Violette charging up to Paris as a Champion-fueled supernuma doesn't make me feel much better," I admitted.

We walked in silence down the dark street and across the boulevard Raspail. A church bell chimed twice, two low and mournful notes tolling from far across town. One lone taxi sped past us, the busy boulevard empty this early in the morning. It began to rain in a fine mist, and I snagged my hood to pull it up over my hair. When it flopped back down, I left it. The cold needles of rain felt good against my skin. Another reminder that I could feel. That I, for one, still had a body.

We turned onto my street, and I squinted [as] raindrops dotted my eyelashes. "I'm not as conce[rned about Vio]lette manipulating Vincent. That's just a 'maybe.' A[nd what is] definite is that his body is gone, and he can't ever get it ba[ck. He's] stuck as a"—my voice cracked from emotion—"ghost for the [rest] of eternity."

I shuddered and Ambrose tightened his grip. "I know," he said, and the note of despair in his voice showed me all the emotion that his face couldn't. He cocked his head to the side, listened, and then nodded.

"What did Jules say?" I asked.

"He was using language that I couldn't repeat in front of a proper lady like you, Katie-Lou," he admitted.

"About Violette?"

"Yes."

"Good. She deserves it, the evil bitch."

Ambrose laughed and planted a kiss on the top of my head as we stopped in front of my building.

"Jules, will you be able to get close enough to talk to Vincent without Violette knowing you're there? I mean, if he's attached to her . . . or whatever." I asked the air.

Ambrose listened for a second and then said, "He says he'll do his best. But we're pretty much clueless about this whole binding thing."

"If you do talk to him, just tell him that we're doing everything we can. And that I'm not giving up on him," I said in the calmest voice I could manage.

19

ng my hands in his, stooped to look
bit by now, Katie-Lou. And I know
around. But Jules and I will keep
miled. "Girl, I saw the look on your
but I have to agree with him. The
get some sleep so you'll be ready for
."

His words worked like magic on my spring-loaded nerves, and all of a sudden my anxiety turned to a fatigue so deep that I could have curled right up on my front steps and fallen asleep. Ambrose saw it, and his features flooded with compassion. "It's been a long day," he said. Carefully avoiding my hurt shoulder, he pulled me into a big American bear hug. And thank God for it. Sometimes those French cheek-kisses just weren't enough.

Releasing me, Ambrose cleared his throat loudly and rubbed his hands together as if he could squish our grief between his palms. "Okay, little sis," he said. "Call you in the morning." And he was off.

Exhausted, I stumbled up the stairs, my thoughts racing with a million different scenarios of what could be going on in the Loire Valley castle. My stomach clenched painfully as I thought—and then tried not to think—of Vincent's ghost bound to a freshly mutilated Violette. The image made me sick.

I had to do something. My thoughts returned to Bran. As a *guérisseur* to the revenants, he was the only one who might know more than the bardia about their arcane rites. He might actually hold the key to what was happening. *I'll call him again in the morning*, I thought as I opened the door.

I didn't realize I was walking straight into an ambush. My sister and grandmother waited in the sitting room: Georgia snorting as she awoke from where she was draped across one of the couches, and Mamie leaping up from her armchair. She took one look at my face and said, "Okay, girls. Do you want to tell me what this is about? Georgia, you claim that a stranger beat you up, and, Katya, you come home with red, swollen eyes at two a.m. on a school night."

Ignoring Mamie, Georgia crossed the room in a flash and took me by the wrists. Her bruised face was a rainbow of sickening yellows, reds, and purples, one cheek swollen out of proportion. "Did they find him in time?" she whispered.

I shook my head. "No." And the feelings I had been pushing away since Vincent's voice disappeared over the river—the despair I kept trying to shove down over the last two hours in order to function, to string my words together and put one foot in front of the other—careened back up to the surface. "Oh my God, Georgia." I choked and coughed on my tears as she wrapped me in her arms. "He's gone. He's really gone." I leaned my head on her shoulder and began to weep.

"Let's go," Mamie said softly, and shooing us both out of the foyer, directed us down the hallway into my bedroom. Still crying, I peeled off my clothes and pulled on some pajamas. And as Mamie and Georgia settled on either side of me on my bed, it felt like we had time-traveled straight back to the previous summer when I had resolved not to see Vincent again: me sobbing; my grandmother and sister comforting. Only this was a million times worse. Last time it was a breakup, heart wrenching but reversible. This time it was a good-bye. It was forever.

I bent over double and sobbed into my folded arms as they rubbed my back and smoothed my hair. When my tears finally slowed, Mamie asked, "Are you going to tell me or not?"

"What have you already told her?" I asked Georgia, who was gently massaging her bruised jaw.

"All I said was that something bad had happened and we needed to be ready to support you when you got home," she responded, glancing cautiously at my grandmother.

"What is it, Katya?" Mamie insisted. "You act like someone just died." Another sob bubbled up from my chest, and I covered my mouth with my hand to stop myself from full-out weeping all over again. My grandmother's eyes narrowed in confusion.

"We have to tell her, Katie-Bean," Georgia said. "Papy knows already. And you're going to need me and Mamie for support."

"Speak," Mamie commanded softly, and I began. At the beginning.

The next half hour was spent revealing the story to my grandmother, slowly and undramatically, for the least possible shock value. Mamie's expression was wary. She knew I was building up to something bad. But when I got to the point where I discovered what Vincent and his kindred were, she raised her hand to stop me. "That's impossible," she said, as if it were the end of the discussion. "You girls have both gone insane if you actually believe something like that."

"Papy believes it, Mamie," I said. "It was the reason he told me I couldn't see Vincent again."

"He did what?" my grandmother exclaimed. "When did this happen?"

"Yesterday."

She thought for a moment. "That must be why he came to bed so late and was up so early this morning. He was avoiding me. I would have been able to tell something was up." My grandmother met my eyes. "Surely Antoine didn't believe a word of it. He's not even superstitious, for God's sake!"

I took her hand. "I know it's hard to believe. Half the time I feel like I'm living in a really twisted fantasy novel. But, Mamie, try to—I don't know—suspend your disbelief for now. You can talk to Papy about it later. Just please let me finish."

She did her best not to interrupt again. "Yes, yes, I remember. That makes sense now," she said from time to time when I linked the story to something she recognized: my breakup with Vincent (and subsequent makeup); Vincent's outburst about Lucien at our dinner table.

I tried to skip the part where Vincent possessed me to kill Lucien, but Georgia couldn't help herself from filling in the blanks—to my grandmother's horror. By the end her palms were glued to her cheeks and her expression was one of shock and resignation.

"And now the . . . numa, is it?" she asked. I nodded. "They have Vincent's body?"

"They *had* Vincent's body. But they burned it."

I got the words out without choking, but tears coursed down my cheeks as I registered the horror in Mamie's and Georgia's eyes.

"But his spirit still exists? And you can still talk to him?" Mamie clarified.

"I might be able to if he can get away from Violette."

"I always knew she was a depraved munchkin," Georgia muttered, gnawing on a thumbnail.

"What about *your* evil ex-boyfriend?" Mamie scolded her. "After the Lucien story, you'll be lucky if I ever let you date again!" She turned to me and sighed. "Oh, Katya, I don't even know what to say."

"But you believe me?" I asked, watching her face.

"I have no choice, other than believing that the two of you are crazy or brainwashed. Or on drugs," she said in a tone that suggested she might prefer one of those options to the alternative. "And Antoine knew about this?"

"Just since yesterday," I qualified.

Mamie sighed. "I hate to say this, but I don't blame your Papy for banning you from seeing Vincent."

My shoulders slumped, but Mamie held up her palm, cautioning me to wait. "You just told me your story. Please let me respond. I'm trying to think of how to put this without hurting your feelings."

"What?" I asked, as a knot of self-protectiveness formed in my chest.

I watched a series of emotions cross my grandmother's face: pity, indecision, and finally indignation. But then she glanced at my wet, swollen face and her bubble of anger popped.

"Oh, Katya," she sighed. "Even if Vincent and his kind *are* the good guys, it's like telling me you're dating Superman. Who wants their granddaughter to be Lois Lane—constantly threatened by her boyfriend's evil enemies? Instead of falling for a hero, I can't help but wish you loved a normal boy. A nice safe student, perhaps." She looked askance at Georgia. "Even a boy in a rock band would be easier to accept." My sister suddenly found her fingernails of the utmost interest.

Giving me a final squeeze, my grandmother rose slowly and walked to the door. Pausing in the doorway, she folded her arms across her chest and closed her eyes for a moment as if trying to mentally erase everything she had heard in the last half hour. Then, opening them again and seeing Georgia and me sitting there, she sighed.

"First of all, I will call your school in the morning and tell them that the two of you won't be coming in tomorrow. That will give you time to figure out how to deal with what has happened and"—she glanced at Georgia—"to heal.

"Secondly, Katya, I believe your insane tale, even though I've never heard anything like it in my life. Your Papy and I will do our best to be understanding, even if we don't approve. From now on, Vincent and his kindred are an open subject in this house. No more hiding things from us. We are on your side and want to help you make smart, well-informed decisions whether you're talking about bad grades or the undead."

Her nose wrinkled upon the last word. Although she was trying to be matter-of-fact, I knew it was hard for her to get those words out of her mouth. "Okay, Mamie," I promised.

"I'm here for you, darling. This family is familiar with grief. You can always come to me for comfort and know I will understand."

I nodded at my grandmother, and satisfied, she turned to leave. A second later we heard her bedroom door open and shut with a slam. Her voice was audible even through the closed door. "Yes, I can see that you're asleep, Antoine. But you had better wake yourself up, because we have some talking to do."

Georgia and I looked at each other, and even through my tears, I couldn't help but smile.

FOUR

MY SLEEP WAS SO LIGHT I HEARD EACH CREAK OF our ancient building and every car that drove by on the rue du Bac. And even when my mind slipped off into a nostalgia-steeped dream about Brooklyn and my parents, I was halfway listening for Vincent's voice. When I awoke, it felt like I hadn't slept at all, but the clock read eleven a.m. I lay on my bed and stared at the ceiling, unable—no, unwilling—to move.

It seemed like the events of the previous day had happened in another lifetime to another girl. But barely twenty-four hours ago my sister and I had faced off with Violette on top of Montmartre. This time yesterday we had discovered her plan to wield her position as leader of the numa to overthrow France's revenants, using Vincent to accomplish her goal.

She had misled him into following the Dark Way. He had spent a couple of months absorbing the malevolent energy of the numa he killed so that he could withstand the urge to die. For me. It had weakened him to the point that Violette could have easily captured and killed him, if he hadn't preempted her move by charging headfirst into our skirmish and plunging to his death off a precipice. Death for Vincent wasn't permanent. But having his body incinerated was.

A compartment inside my heart that had gradually, over the last nine months, become a huge Vincent-shaped space was suddenly and violently empty. And the rest of my heart's contents—my love for my parents, my sister, my grandparents, my passions for art and books and film—stood cautiously aside, refusing to crowd their way into the hollow space left by my love's disappearance. How could anything—or anyone—replace him?

I was done crying. I could feel it. And as I lay there, I felt a fiery determination begin to fill the void. A resolve to make sure that what was left of Vincent—his "wandering soul," as Gaspard had called it—would be safe.

I sat up cautiously, wincing as I felt a dual pain in the middle and upper part of my chest: grief and my cracked collarbone, both compliments of Violette. Reaching for my cell phone, I saw I had received a text from Ambrose not even a half hour ago. I eagerly clicked to see it, but my heart fell when I saw the content.

Just checking in. No news. Jules still at castle trying to see Vin. Hang in there, K-L.

I was about to put the phone back down when I noticed that there had been a call during the night with no message left. I recognized the number. It was Bran's.

I was up and out of bed in an instant. I stood bouncing nervously on my toes as I phoned him back and was fed directly into his voice mail. "Bran, it's Kate. I saw that you called last night. Call me back."

I tightened the Ace bandage the doctor had given me and, after checking the kitchen and finding a note from Mamie, went to the bathroom to splash cold water on my face. Leaning forward into the mirror, I gently touched the swollen flesh beneath my eyes. Pulling out a concealer stick, I went to work to make myself look normal. A couple of minutes later, I was tiptoeing into Georgia's bedroom where I stood watching her sprawled, snoring form before poking her gently.

"Georgia. Get up."

"Wha . . . Goway," she mumbled, opening one eye before pulling the pillow securely over her head.

"Georgia, it's almost noon. Papy's at his gallery and Mamie went out. I need you to come somewhere with me. But we have to leave before she gets back, or she'll want to know where we're going."

She just lay there, hiding as I poked again. Finally she sat up and tossed the pillow to the floor. "What is wrong with you? Can't you see I'm grievously injured?" Eyes still closed, she lifted her chin to show her face. Her multicolored bruises had now consolidated into half-moons of deep purple and black under her eyes and one cheek was swollen like an apple. My sister looked like a boxer post-knockout. Or a hit-and-run raccoon.

My heart tugged seeing her so banged up, but I knew her

injuries were just surface deep. And there were more important issues at stake. "Georgia, I need you to go with me to find Bran. He might have an answer to what's going on with Vincent."

She fluttered her eyelids for a few seconds, not in a girlie way, but because they were totally stuck together with eye goop. "I think I'm blind," she moaned. I handed her a facial wipe from her dresser and she swabbed her eyes before squinting at me. As soon as she saw my serious expression, she was alert. "Sorry, Kate. Forget about me. What's the plan?"

"Do you remember me talking about those special *guérisseurs*? The healers that deal with revenants? I need you to go up to Saint-Ouen to find one of them with me."

She squeezed the bridge of her nose to wake herself up. "Okay. But it's Friday. A school day."

"Mamie called school to tell them we weren't coming, remember?"

"That's right," Georgia said, still nose-pinching with eyes closed. "So you and I are sneaking out . . ."

"Mamie's gone. We'll just leave her a message that we're popping out for a few minutes."

She let go of her nose and stared at me. "We're going to leave her a message that her two granddaughters who got mixed up in a battle between supernatural creatures yesterday, one of whom has multiple injuries, and the other whose boyfriend was killed, are just popping out unsupervised to . . ."

"Hunt down a member of an ancient family of healers in order to get information to protect my dead boyfriend's ghost."

The corners of my sister's lips curled up. "Right. I'm in." She hopped out of bed and began pulling clothes on. "What do we do if we run into her on the way out?" she called from underneath the shirt she was tugging over her head. I winced as I saw the bruises on her ribs where Violette had kicked her. It wasn't as bad as the contusions and swelling on her face, but she ignored her injuries as she grinned at me.

"We'll tell her we've gone out for bread," I replied.

"The one excuse a French person would never question. Baguettes or die!" Georgia cheered, and we raced out before my grandmother could return.

We were all the way across town before I realized I had left my cell phone at home. "I've got mine," Georgia said, patting her coat pocket.

"Yeah, but Ambrose was supposed to let me know if anything happened." My chest constricted with anxiety. Today was not the day to be out of contact.

"Call him," Georgia offered, holding her phone out to me.

"No, that's okay. We're here," I said, pointing ahead to Le Corbeau's darkened storefront.

Georgia peered dubiously at the old wooden sign with the store's namesake raven creakily flapping back and forth in the staccato gusts of winter wind. "Are you sure this place was actually ever open? It looks medieval," she said, pulling her coat tighter to her.

I rapped on the door window, but it was obvious that no one was in.

"Is that a giant tooth?" Georgia asked, leaning toward the window display.

"It's called a relic. It's probably a dead saint's finger bone or something," I replied, pressing down hard on the door handle. I watched astonished as the door swung smoothly open. "It wasn't even locked!" I exclaimed, and stepped over the threshold.

"Why would they lock it?" Georgia said, following me in. "Who would steal . . . 'an eighteenth-century rosary featuring a sliver of the true cross trapped inside Bohemian crystal'?" she read off a tag, and dropped the beads carelessly back onto their stand. "That's just weird. Man, they could really use a cleaner here. The dust is enough to give you asthma."

We moved deeper into the darkened room, shuffling through the tight space between ancient waist-high statues of saints with knives through their heads and display cases holding contemporary glow-in-the-dark pope memorabilia. My foot creaked on the parquet, and immediately there came a thump from under the floor. "Ssh!" I whispered to Georgia. "Did you hear that?"

"Oh my God," she murmured, her eyes widening in alarm. "They've got a dungeon."

The thumping started again: three evenly spaced knocks from beneath our feet. It sounded like someone was tapping a Mayday code on the ceiling of whatever room was below. Like someone needed help. It could be only one person.

"Quickly!" I ran toward the door that led to the back stairway. Instead of going up to the apartment where I had met Gwenhaël, we headed down toward a rusty door that opened with a grinding creak as I shoved it with my hip.

I burst into a low-ceilinged storage cellar, and was blasted by the sharp stench of dank, mildewed air. In one corner was a gated area, penned in from ceiling to floor with chain-link fencing and protected by a padlocked door. Behind it were stacks of boxes— most likely valuables being stored in the shop's most secure place. And next to the boxes, gagged and tied to a chair, sat Bran.

FIVE

"ARE YOU OKAY?" I YELLED, SPRINTING TO THE cage door.

Bran shook his head, His stick-figure body trembled beneath its bonds, and fresh bruises distorted his face, one eye so swollen that it was only a slit. His face was wet with tears and sweat, and since his mouth was taped shut, he snuffled loudly through his nose in order to breathe.

"Oh, Bran!" I said, covering my mouth in horror.

He had somehow managed to pick up a broom handle, which he had banged against the ceiling when he heard Georgia and me walking above. Now he let go of it, and its hollow clatter against the stone floor broke the muffled silence.

"Do you know where the key is?" I asked, yanking on the padlock.

He shook his head once again.

"Okay, we'll find something to break it off with. Georgia?" My sister stood motionless, staring wide-eyed at Bran. "Help me find something heavy." She leapt into action, rushing to an enormous bronze candelabra propped against the wall. "Perfect!" I said, and helped her pull it across the floor to the cage.

"Tuck it under your right arm," I instructed, and picking up my end, I winced and adjusted my hold as the heavy object sent a shockwave of pain through my collarbone. "We're going to slam the lock battering-ram style from the side. I don't think we can break the padlock, but the ring it's attached to looks pretty rusty. Let's aim for that."

As we backed up a few steps, my eyes met Bran's, and I saw a look of regret as he stared at the candelabra. "This is a really expensive piece, isn't it?" I asked, unable to repress a nervous smile.

He nodded sadly and then shrugged. "Go!" I yelled, and Georgia and I ran toward the lock, smashing it with the sharp end of our improvised bludgeon. The lock didn't budge, but a decorative bronze leaf snapped off the candelabra. Bran winced.

"Let's try it again," I said, adjusting my Ace bandage under my shirt and gingerly pressing my sore shoulder. Then backing up, we ran full force toward the lock, this time smashing the old ring to bits. The padlock hit the ground with a metallic clink and the door swung open. I rushed into the space, and even though it was Bran—odd, scarecrow-looking Bran—I stooped to hug him quickly before inspecting his bonds.

His attackers had used black duct tape across his mouth, as well as around his wrists, chest, and ankles. "I don't want to hurt you," I said, pausing.

He rolled his eyes and nodded as if to say, *Just get on with it.*

I picked at the tape with a fingernail, loosening a corner on his cheek, and then gritting my teeth, yanked it off with one quick motion. Bran's mouth dropped open and he gasped in a few choking gulps of air as tears of pain and relief coursed down his cheeks. He struggled against the bonds attaching him to the chair, but they held fast. "You must hurry, child," he urged me. "They've been gone for hours. They could come back at any moment."

"Who's 'they'?" I asked, leaning in to hear him since his voice came out in a breathless wheeze.

"Numa. They're holding me until the small ancient one arrives to question me."

The small ancient one? I thought, and then shouted, "Wait, *Violette* is coming here?"

"Yes." Bran was trying not to panic, but the urgency in his voice gave his fear away. "Do you think you might . . ." He held up his taped wrists.

"Quick, Georgia. Find something sharp," I yelled.

"Already did," she said from just behind me. I turned to see her wielding a plastic box cutter. She flicked the blade out and handed it to me.

Within minutes Bran was standing up, feebly shaking his legs and windmilling his thin arms to get the circulation back. "My glasses," he croaked. "They fell."

I found his bottle-thick glasses a few feet away from the chair, twisted and cracked. I did my best to bend them back into place and handed them to him. Even though he barely had a slit of an eye to see through, once he had slipped them on, he seemed to transform from a beaten pulp back into his weird, magnified self. He took one step toward me and then collapsed back into the chair.

I rushed to help him. "Are you going to be able to walk?"

"I'm afraid my attackers beat me badly," he responded. "I might need your assistance."

"We should get you to La Maison," I said, draping his arm over my shoulder and pulling him up to a standing position. Georgia held the cage door open for us, and I hobbled with him into the room. "You'd be safe there, at least . . . ," I began. But before I could finish the thought, the sound of the shop's front door opening and closing and the creaking of footsteps on the wooden floor came from above our heads.

"You aren't expecting any customers, are you?" Georgia squeaked, eyes like saucers.

"Quickly, over there!" Bran whispered, nodding across the room to where a child-size metal door sat at the bottom of a flight of ancient stone stairs. Georgia moved to his other side and we speed-dragged him to the door. He fished a key out of a niche in the wall and stuck it in the old lock.

From above us came a voice I immediately recognized. The voice of a young girl. "Where is he?" Violette demanded. There was a bang as the back door slammed and footsteps pounded down the stairway.

"For the love of God, get that friggin' door open!" Georgia hissed, as Bran wiggled the key in the lock. The door popped forward, and we stooped to scramble through the low frame into the dark, cavernous space beyond. I had enough time to see the reflection of a river running beside us before Bran swung the door closed and locked it. We were instantly enveloped by the odor of something sour and rank and the sound of rushing water.

"Take the bar and block the door with it," Bran told me, and shifted his full weight onto Georgia, who staggered a little before recovering her balance. There was enough light spilling through the cracks between the door and its frame for me to see a heavy iron bar above the lintel. I grabbed it and wedged it into brackets on either side of the door frame.

"This way!" Bran said, and Georgia teetered off with him into the dark. Cries of surprise and anger came from the other side of the door.

And then a voice appeared in my head—the one I had been listening for since it disappeared over the river. *Kate, run!*

Vincent was here! He had survived being burned—at least his spirit had. Relief hit me like a tsunami, leaving me dizzy and disoriented. "Vincent, it's you!" I whispered.

I'm bound to Violette, and she's just a few feet away from you on the other side of this door. They don't know which way Bran's gone yet. You better get out of there before they figure it out and break the door down.

Ignoring his warning, I asked, "Are you okay?" My mouth was so dry I could barely get the words out.

The power transfer didn't work, so Violette kept me with her.

She needs Bran to figure out what she did wrong. Now, Kate . . . go.

"First tell me what we can do to help you . . ."

Now!

"Kate, come on!" Georgia urged from a few yards ahead. "What are you doing just standing there?" It took all of my strength to tear myself away from the door—away from the possibility of being near Vincent's spirit—but once I had made up my mind, I sprinted to catch up with my sister and Bran.

"I can't see a thing," I said after a few seconds.

"Me either," Georgia responded. "Here, take him." I propped myself under Bran's right shoulder, draping my arm securely around his waist and helping him move forward. He was so light that, if it weren't for my own injury, I probably could have carried him.

From behind us, a strong light switched on, illuminating the space around us. I glanced back at the glowing rectangle Georgia held aloft. "iPhone flashlight app," she said proudly.

"Quick," Bran urged, and directed us around a corner and down another passageway.

As we struggled forward in the glow of the cell phone flashlight, I took in our surroundings. We were heading down a large tunnel with vaulted ceilings lined with brick. A river ran down the middle, and on either side was a sidewalk wide enough for two people to walk side-by-side. Though I'd never been here before, I knew exactly where we were: the Paris sewers. A network of over a thousand miles of tunnels carrying rainwater, drain water, and . . . yes . . . the sewage of Paris.

"If I see floating poo, I'm gouging my eyes out with this box cutter," Georgia called from behind me.

I ignored her, and shifting my hold on Bran, I got a better grip on him so that we were almost running. Finally, I allowed myself to think about Vincent.

The power transfer hadn't worked. *A very good thing*, I reassured myself. *She hasn't figured out how to drain Vincent of the Champion's power.* But my bubble of hope burst when I remembered that she had still succeeded with the binding ceremony. Vincent's spirit was trapped, unable to leave her side.

And here I was running away from them. I felt like screaming from frustration and rage. Knowing that Vincent was powerless in the evil revenant's hands made me more determined than ever to figure out how to free him.

But first, we had to get Bran to safety. He could hold the key to helping Vincent. It would be hard for the numa to break down a metal door blocked by an iron bar. But almost every building in Paris held an access to the sewers. Once Violette figured out how Bran had escaped, she could be after us in the time it took her to break into the basement of a nearby building.

Bran directed us through the corridors around multiple twists and turns. It obviously wasn't his first time in the sewers—he knew exactly where he was going.

After thirty minutes of half-running half-hobbling beside the fetid water, squeezing through tight openings, and shuffling through low connecting passages, we arrived in front of another locked door. Bran removed a brick to the right of the door frame and pulled out a massive skeleton key. I opened the door with it, and Georgia led him through.

"Lock it from the inside," Bran called. Georgia helped him settle him into a chair, where he sat panting.

I found a lighter and a glass lantern holding a candle. Georgia turned off her phone light after I lit the lamp and the space around us flickered into view. We were in a small room furnished with two cots, a couple of old ratty armchairs and shelves stocked with first aid supplies and canned food. "What is this place?" I asked.

"Old Resistance hideout, made by my grandfather," Bran replied breathlessly. "Since the war, my family has kept it as a safe place. But we never needed to use it as such until last week when my mother hid from the ancient one and her numa. We can't stay long, though. If they know we're down here and come back with reinforcements, they could find us."

"We should take you to La Maison," I said. "But that's in the seventh arrondissement, all the way across town. It would take hours to walk there if we stay in the sewers. And with the shape you're in, I'm not sure you could even make it."

Bran shook his head. "I can't walk much farther. And even if I could, I only know my way around the tunnels under our neighborhood. I could never find my way to the other side of the river."

"So we'll have to go aboveground," I said.

A buzzing sound came from Georgia's coat. She fished her cell phone from her pocket and looked at the screen. "Arthur. Again."

I stared at her. "What do you mean, again?"

"He's been leaving me messages all morning, wondering how I'm doing," she replied with a shrug.

"Why don't you answer?" I asked, incredulous.

Georgia made a face. "I don't want to look too interested. That'll just scare him off." She looked as offended as if I had suggested that she marry him on the spot.

I grabbed the phone out of her hand and answered the call. "Arthur? Yeah, this is Kate. Violette and some numa are after us, and we need your help. We're hiding in the sewers. . . ." I turned to Bran. "Where are we exactly?"

"Under the northern tip of Montmartre Cemetery," Bran responded. "You can tell them to meet us right inside the north gate."

I handed the phone back to Georgia. "He said they'll be here in twenty minutes, and to stay in our hiding place until he texts us." Bran nodded and, settling his head on the back of the armchair, closed his eyes in exhaustion.

"Did he say anything else?" my sister asked, eyeing me.

I rolled my eyes. Even in an underground hideout, at mortal risk of being discovered by evil undead, Georgia was thinking about boys.

"Well, did he?" she insisted.

I sighed. "He asked if you were okay," I admitted.

My sister threw herself onto one of the cots with a satisfied grin and stared dreamily at the ceiling.

SIX

WHEN ARTHUR'S TEXT FINALLY CAME, WE MADE
our way carefully out of the bunker and up some nearby stairs.
Bran directed me to push open a wooden trapdoor at the top,
and we emerged through the floor of a mausoleum, where aboveground marble tombs dominated the small room.

"This is so Buffy it's not even funny," Georgia said, supporting
Bran as I waved curtains of cobwebs out of the way so that we
could exit into the graveyard. Ambrose was waiting by the gate.
As soon as he saw us, he sprinted over and hoisted Bran up in his
arms. "Hurry it up," he said. "It's like numa central around here!"

He bundled Bran into the back of the car, and Georgia and I
packed in on either side. As soon as Ambrose was in the passenger seat, Arthur sped off. "Perfect timing," he said, peering into
his rearview mirror. I turned to see a squad of numa round the
corner of the cemetery wall and push open the gate we had come
through just seconds before.

"Looks like our Evil Empress has got half of Paris's numa trailing her as security," Ambrose commented drily. "We sent Henri and some others to your shop, right after we talked to Kate," he said, eyeing Bran. "But there was no sign of them. The door to the sewers had been smashed through so they could still be down there, weaving their way through toilet-level Paris looking for you."

He shifted in his seat to shoot me an annoyed look. "And who do you think you are? Wonder Woman?"

"I would say Kate's more Catwoman," Georgia commented. "Much cooler. Less derivative."

Ambrose ignored her. "What possessed you to go wandering off after I left you three messages to stay put since Violette and her numa were spotted heading toward Paris? Since when does 'Stay in your house' mean go directly to the location where your enemy is most likely to go?"

"I didn't get your messages," I admitted sheepishly. "I left my phone at home."

He sighed deeply and shook his head in despair. "Gonna get you a cell phone holder that I can chain to your wrist. Vincent would kill me if he knew I let you anywhere near Violette."

"Um . . . Vincent knows," I said.

"What?" everyone exclaimed at once, except for Bran, who asked, "Who is Vincent?"

"The one I talked to you about on the phone last week," I replied.

"The one suspected of being the Victor?" he asked.

I nodded, and then said to the others, "He talked to me when we were standing outside Bran's cellar door."

"What did he say?" Arthur asked, making a sharp turn to avoid a red light.

"He said he was bound to Violette. And that she had come looking for Bran because the power transfer hadn't worked."

"Well, that clears up why the brutes detained me," Bran said. "Although after killing my mother, I don't see why they'd expect me to volunteer to help them."

"Um, I'm guessing that's the reason they beat you up," Georgia pointed out helpfully. "The whole point of coercion is that it doesn't require volunteers."

"Regardless, they would never have gotten it out of me," Bran insisted stubbornly, and then wincing from some unseen injury, laid his head back on the seat and closed his eyes.

"Good man." Ambrose leaned over the seat and patted Bran reassuringly on the knee before turning to Arthur. "Dude, can't you drive this thing any faster?" he urged in a low voice. "Skeletor back there is fading fast."

I watched Bran for a moment, wanting to ask him about Vincent—to see if he knew anything about disembodied spirits. His mother had mentioned family records when I had asked her to help Vincent resist dying. She had told me her line of healers knew some of the revenants' secrets, and she would check their accounts to see if she could help us. I wondered if Bran knew everything his mother had. But seeing his exhaustion and battered face, I knew this wasn't the time to ask.

In a record ten minutes we were entering the gate at La Maison, where a welcoming committee waited by the front door. Jean-Baptiste and Gaspard stood on either side of a concerned-looking Jeanne, who made a rush for the car as we pulled up.

Georgia and I helped shift Bran out, then followed as Arthur and Ambrose supported him, his arms propped around their shoulders. They got him to the front door, where Jean-Baptiste waited. "I'll be fine," Bran reassured his bodyguards, and they carefully set him down as he extended a shaking hand toward JB.

"*Bonjour*," he began, but as his fingers touched the revenant leader's hand, a bright light, like a camera flash, exploded between them, causing everyone around to shield their faces. I blinked several times before the spots began clearing from my vision, and saw that Bran had gone stiff. He let out a deep moan, his head fell forward, and he sank unconscious to the ground.

"Are you okay?" Gaspard yelped, rushing to JB's side. The revenant leader blinked a few times and shook his arm out experimentally.

"What the hell was—" Georgia began, but was cut off by Jeanne, who had leapt into emergency mode. "Up! Get him up!" she commanded, and Ambrose scooped Bran's floppy form into his arms. Carrying him to Vincent's room, he deposited him carefully on the bed. Jeanne was there in an instant, applying cold wet cloths to Bran's head and wrists. Within seconds his eyelids were fluttering open.

"Where am I?" he mumbled. Jeanne handed him his glasses, which had fallen when he had. Pulling them on with shaking hands, he peered anxiously at our faces, looking downright startled when he saw me.

"What is it?" I asked, glancing around to make sure he wasn't looking at someone else. His astonished look—like he didn't recognize me after I had spent the last couple of hours scurrying around underground Paris with him—was freaking me out.

He kept staring for a few seconds, blinking a few times with his non-swollen eye. Then sighing deeply, he said, "Nothing, child," and leaned back into the pillow.

"Are you okay?" Jeanne asked, tucking a blanket around his trembling form.

Ignoring her question, Bran asked, "May I suppose that your residence is safe from the evil ones?"

"You can bet your sweet . . . um, yes, sir," said Ambrose, editing himself. "As long as you're here with us you'll be safe from the numa."

"Safe," breathed Bran. "No one will be safe until the Victor triumphs."

"The Victor?" asked Arthur.

"He means the Champion," I clarified.

Gaspard spoke up. "I am sorry to inform you, dear ally, that the Victor has been captured. He is now in the hands of our enemies."

Bran considered Gaspard's words. "Yes, your Kate has informed me of that," he replied finally. "But Violette doesn't yet have his power. And if she cannot figure out the magic of the transfer herself, she will not learn it from me. That will at least give us some time."

Jeanne stepped forward. "Monsieur . . ."

"Tândorn."

"Monsieur Tândorn, would you like me to call a doctor?"

"*Non. Merci, chère madame*. The brutes concentrated mostly on my face. The rest of me just feels bruised—nothing broken. I'm just very weak. I haven't slept or eaten since they killed my mother."

Jeanne's face took on the look of a dangerous wildcat whose cub is threatened by hunters. I had seen this look before and knew exactly what it meant. The housekeeper's power lay in her ability to take care of her wards. Seconds after she stalked out of the room, I heard pots and pans banging in the kitchen as she planned her assault on Bran's feeble state.

Arthur approached Georgia. "How is your face?" he asked timidly, raising his hand to touch her bruised cheek.

My sister nimbly ducked out of the way. "You know, after that terrifying run-in with the numa, I could really use a mug of strong tea. Do you think you might have any?" she asked coyly.

"Of course," Arthur responded, straightening and transforming back to his usual formal self. He ushered Georgia politely out into the hallway.

As they left, the others followed. Jean-Baptiste lagged behind for a second, looking like he wanted to stay, and then said, "We have much to speak about, Monsieur Tândorn, but I will let you rest. May I pay you a visit this evening?"

"Of course," Bran responded wearily.

"Would you like to be alone, or would you prefer that I stay?" I asked.

"Stay, child," he answered.

I pulled a chair next to the bed and settled myself in. "I was sorry to hear about your mother," I said after a moment of silence.

"Yes," he said. "She was an exceptional soul. A loving mother. A wise woman."

I hesitated before continuing, but he seemed to want conversation. "Did she have time to pass her gifts along to you before she . . . was gone?" I asked.

He took a deep breath and, reaching for an additional pillow, stuffed it behind him so that he was almost sitting. His swollen eye was the color of a ripe plum and the other was magnified by his thick glasses so that it looked like a 3-D chestnut. He glanced at me, squinted curiously, and then looked quickly away again. I fiddled with my hair, wondering if there were cobwebs or debris from the underground passages still stuck in it.

"Yes. Yes, she did," he responded. "I have inherited her healing gifts and am now a *guérisseur* myself."

I smiled sadly, knowing that his newly acquired powers couldn't make up for the loss of his mother. He touched my arm with long bony fingers, and his thin lips curved up at the corners. "It's too bad you don't have a migraine so that I could show you how it works. Although, like my mother, my gifts aren't confined to the mortal realm."

He pulled back his sleeve and showed me a fresh tattoo on the inside of his wrist, the flesh still pink around it. A triangle with flames flaring out from its three edges was enclosed within a circle.

"The *signum bardia*," I breathed. And pulling the gold and sapphire version that Vincent had given me from beneath my shirt, I held it up for him to see.

"We have something in common, child. Both trusted by the kindred. And just look where it has brought us!" He smiled feebly. Letting go of my arm, he laid his head back against the pillow and closed his eyes. It seemed the conversation was over.

"Bran, I've been wanting to ask you about something." He opened an eye and blinked at me, looking exhausted. Now was not the time to quiz him, but I didn't know when I'd have the chance again. "If your mother gave you her gifts, does that mean you have all her knowledge as well?"

"She has told me our stories since I was a child," he responded tiredly.

Feeling a twinge of guilt for pushing him too far, I continued. "Well, she told me a few weeks ago that your family knew secrets about the revenants. And I was just wondering if you knew anything about what the bardia call wandering souls. That's the state that Vincent is in now, since Violette destroyed his body. I wanted to know if there was any way—"

I was interrupted by a knock on the door. Gaspard stuck his head in. "Excuse me, Kate, but you have a visitor."

"A visitor?" I asked, confused.

The door swung forcefully open. Gaspard stepped aside and an elderly woman wearing a pink Chanel suit, four-inch heels, and a look of pure fury walked into the room. Lord help us all, Mamie was in La Maison.

SEVEN

AS MY GRANDMOTHER STRODE INTO THE ROOM, I felt my two worlds collide. The fact that Georgia had been in on the secret for months—had visited La Maison several times—didn't lessen the trauma of someone else I loved entering the dangerous universe of the revenants. Because of me. Now that Mamie was here, I felt responsible for her safety—which from now on was an impossibility; safety and revenants did not go together.

"What are you doing here?" I asked, my voice panicky from both fear *for* my grandmother and fear *of* her.

My grandmother's gaze caught Bran's battered form on the bed, and her eyes grew wider before she fixed me with a burning stare. "When I called your school to give you girls the day off to recover, I did not mean for you to run right back into the danger you so narrowly escaped yesterday. You left me a note that you were popping out and would 'be back soon.' Whatever happened during the hours you were away"—she nodded gravely toward Bran—"I take as a direct betrayal of my trust."

Over Mamie's shoulder I saw Jean-Baptiste hurry into the room. Gaspard closed the door behind him. JB met my eyes and made a zipping motion over his mouth, shaking his head in warning. It was clear he wanted to do the talking.

"*Ma chère madame*," he began. Mamie whipped around to face him. He gave her a polite little bow straight from the eighteenth century, and she reciprocated with a tight nod. Underneath her expensive hairdo and prim suit, Mamie was a force to be reckoned with.

But as I watched my grandmother, I realized that beneath her anger she was actually terrified. And then I remembered how frightened I was when I learned what Vincent was, and my heart went out to her. My grandmother had entered the monster's lair . . . for me.

"*Bonjour*, Monsieur Grimod," she said in a tight voice. "Excuse me for barging into your house uninvited, but I am here to collect my granddaughters."

"Of course, *madame*. But I would have thought that under the present dangerous circumstances, you would prefer for them to be here, under our protection, rather than out in the public world unprotected."

"Unprotected!" Mamie's face turned poppy red. Her gaze shifted to Gaspard, who nodded seriously, agreeing with JB. Glancing back, she shot me her most dangerous look, and then, exhaling between pursed lips, attempted to compose herself.

"Monsieur Grimod, please try to put yourself in my shoes. Last night my granddaughters came home after participating in a violent fight during which both could have easily been killed. Kate's boyfriend actually *was* killed, although I realize that that sort of thing isn't as serious for your kind, your deaths being impermanent," she said crisply.

"But because his body was then *immolated*, he is now floating around as a ghost and being held captive in a castle by a psychotic medieval zombie. The same psychotic medieval zombie who gave one of my granddaughters a concussion and has been sending the other flowers for the last couple of months . . . at our home . . . because she KNOWS WHERE WE LIVE." Mamie's face was now purple from her battle between politesse and her true feelings.

"And now I am being asked if my granddaughter can walk right back into the same situation. Unless I was completely insane, my response to that request would be an unequivocal no."

"But, my dear lady, that is exactly why you should let your granddaughters come to us. Because the case is, unfortunately, just as you stated. The numa know where you live. Violette knows where you live. I would like to offer you and your granddaughters our protection, so it is a very good thing that you are here now and we can talk about it."

Mamie hesitated, then said, "I lost my son a year and a half ago because of a drunk driver. I refuse to lose another family member—or two—for a reason just as meaningless."

"There is nothing meaningless about a battle between good and evil, *ma chère dame*," Jean-Baptiste responded quietly. "And

53

that is the position we find ourselves in right now. Please ... come with me." He held out his arm and waited, ignoring the way Mamie flinched when she finally took it lightly in her fingers.

"We shall retire to the sitting room, where Jeanne will serve us coffee. Or would you prefer tea? If you are amenable, we will send Kate off to join her sister in the kitchen so we can discuss the situation between ourselves."

I followed them into the hallway and Gaspard closed the bedroom door behind us, leaving a comatose-looking Bran alone to rest. "I see you have met Gaspard, my longtime partner," continued JB with a wry smile. "It is his opinion that I am the worst person possible to be charged with explanations, so I will ask him to join us."

I raised my eyebrows in surprise. Jean-Baptiste had just come out of the closet to my grandmother, when I had never heard him mention his relationship with Gaspard to anyone before. It wasn't a secret, but coming from olden times they weren't exactly into the PDA and it was easy to forget that they were together. Hearing it from his own lips was a revelation. It meant that he was trying to show my grandmother that he was putting everything—even his personal information—at her disposal so that she would trust him.

As I was thinking this, JB glanced over and caught my eye.

Merci, I mouthed.

He nodded grimly at me.

"My dear woman, can I just say what a true pleasure it is to have you pay us a visit in our own home," Gaspard was saying, shaking only slightly in his tic-y way as he did a bow/hand-kiss combo that I knew would melt Mamie's heart.

"Katya, do not leave this house," she said, turning to me. "I will join you and your sister when I finish talking to the gentlemen." And holding Jean-Baptiste's arm, she accompanied the revenant couple down the hallway.

I walked into the kitchen to find a tactical discussion about finding Violette taking place over an Italian-themed meal. The sharp smell of garlic hung thick on the air, mixed with the comforting aroma of baked cheese.

"So she hasn't been found?" I asked.

Ambrose shook his head. "Henri and the others just reported back. Once again, she's disappeared."

From beside him, a head turned and familiar green eyes peered up at me. "Charlotte!" I yelled, throwing my arms around her as she rose to greet me. "You came back."

"Oh, Kate. We jumped on a train as soon as we heard what happened." She let Geneviève have her turn squeezing me before returning to her chair.

"Sit next to me," Charlotte said, her hair falling in long wheaten strands around her face. "I am so sorry about Vincent."

"So am I," I said, swallowing to clear the lump in my throat.

I looked down the table at Georgia. "You know Mamie's here, right?"

My sister choked on what she was eating. Arthur leapt up and got her a glass of water. She swallowed a big gulp of it and, coughing into her napkin, gasped, "That is the worst joke you have ever made. You could have killed me." She patted her chest and coughed some more.

"No joke," I said. "She's having a chat with Jean-Baptiste and Gaspard and is coming to get us afterward."

"Holy shit," my sister responded, pushing her plate away.

"You've barely touched your lasagna," Arthur chided softly.

"Not hungry anymore." Georgia wrapped her arms around herself and sat there looking nervous.

Charlotte changed the subject. "Geneviève and I had been talking about coming to Paris ever since your visit."

Not even a week ago, I realized with amazement, Vincent and I had been in the south of France sitting on the cliff overlooking the ocean and talking about our future. Just six days ago he explained the Dark Way to me, and his plan to kill numa in order to resist dying. And now he was gone.

Jeanne came over from where she was preparing a tray for my grandmother, and gave me a firm, affectionate kiss on each cheek. "You'll join us for some lasagna, won't you, Kate?"

"I'm really not hungry. Thanks anyway, Jeanne," I said.

"Nonsense," she replied. She picked up a plate, loaded it with a steaming square of gooey pasta, and set it in front of me.

"Never say no to Jeanne," muttered Ambrose, taking a sizable bite of garlic bread. "Especially over one of her Italian grandmother's recipes. Not that she'll get offended. She'll just take it as a challenge. Watch this." He gestured to his empty plate. "Jeanne, that lasagna was delicious. I'm so full I couldn't imagine having another bite."

"Don't be ridiculous," she said, and bringing the pan over to the table, plopped a giant-size piece in front of him. "With all the fighting you boys will be doing, you need all the calories you can get."

Ambrose lifted an eyebrow and smiled at me in triumph before glancing across the table to Geneviève.

Oh no, I thought. It looked like Ambrose hadn't gotten over his crush on the recently widowed revenant. Which must be breaking Charlotte's heart. She looked down at her food and pretended she didn't see Ambrose's longing gaze.

"How's Charles?" I asked to distract her.

"Oh, he's fine," she said, her face brightening at the thought of her twin. "I mean, I haven't seen him since he ran off to Germany, but he's been emailing or calling almost every day."

"They just got GPS tracking for each other on their cell phones," added Geneviève with a grin.

Charlotte rolled her eyes. "Thanks for letting everyone know about our sad twin-based codependence," she moaned, but smiled. "It's amazing how much he's changed in so little time," she continued to me. "He's always talking about his feelings about 'our destiny' and how we're here on earth to give back to humanity. He and his German kindred left this morning for some kind of spiritual mountain retreat."

She clicked on her cell phone and peered at a digital map showing France and Germany side by side. Over Paris was a blinking red light, and over Germany a green line headed west out of Berlin and stopped with a flashing question mark an inch to the west. "He must not have a signal there because he's not even showing up."

"Yeah, I would say that's pretty codependent," I said with a wry grin.

Charlotte elbowed me playfully, "Oh, stop. No one but a twin could understand. Whatever," she said, and stashed the phone in the pocket of her cardigan.

"A little refreshment for your grandmother and the men," Jeanne said as she bustled out of the kitchen with the tea tray.

Everyone fell into a reflective silence and focused on Jeanne's delicious meal until she returned minutes later. "Status report?" I asked.

"Your grandmother seemed to be holding up well. She didn't look overjoyed, but she was listening to what Jean-Baptiste and Gaspard were saying," Jeanne said, retying her apron.

"Which was . . . ," I prodded.

"They were proposing some kind of plan where you and your sister would be accompanied everywhere you go," she responded matter-of-factly, and then turned to check something in the oven.

Georgia and I shot each other worried looks.

"I know we're waiting for Jean-Baptiste to give us instructions," Arthur said, prying his attention away from my sister. "But we might as well get suited up until he's done talking to Madame Mercier. I have no doubt he'll send us on a scouting trip when we inform him that Henri's team lost track of Violette."

Standing and taking his plate to the counter, Ambrose leaned down to give Jeanne's shoulders a squeeze. "No dessert?" she asked.

Ambrose patted his stomach with both hands. "Naw, I

couldn't, Jeanne. I'm watching my figure." She guffawed as he walked toward the door. "I could use a bit of a workout if we're just hanging out for a while. Swords, anyone?" he called.

"That's an invitation I can't resist," responded Charlotte, and thanking Jeanne for the meal, she followed Ambrose out the door.

"I'm on for a fight!" exclaimed Geneviève, and Arthur stood to join her.

"I'll watch," muttered a paler-than-usual Georgia. I smiled. It was just like her to hide out as long as possible rather than face Mamie's wrath.

"Leave your dishes, dears, and go work off some of that steam," said Jeanne, waving them away from the table and out the door.

"I'll be right down," I called. I was still picking at my lasagna, attempting to move pieces of it around my plate so that Jeanne would think I had eaten.

"I see what you're doing, *mon petit chou*," she said as she stood at the sink with her back toward me.

I laid my fork on the table. "Busted," I replied.

She turned, and her lips curved into a compassionate smile. "You know what? I have something for you. Something that might be a comfort in the hard days ahead."

Taking my hand, she led me out of the kitchen to her room down the hall. It was one she used on the rare occasion when she needed to spend the night, and I had never been inside.

Walking across the carpeted floor, she switched on a frilly lamp and picked up an object sitting next to it. Returning, she placed it in my hand. It was a heart-shaped locket made of crystal and silver.

I fingered the tiny bauble. A sprig of flowers was engraved into the silver side, and I ran my finger over the delicately grooved metal. "Forget-me-nots," said Jeanne, and it felt like a hand clenched my heart and squeezed tightly. Vincent's body was gone, but I would not forget him. Or would I? Would his face start disappearing from my mind like my parents' had, replaced by the images of them preserved in photographs?

I turned the locket over to the crystal side. Through the transparent glass I spotted something dark enclosed within and held it up to the light. It was a single lock of raven black hair.

EIGHT

"IS THIS VINCENT'S?" I GASPED.

Jeanne nodded.

"Where did you get it?" Stunned, I rolled the strange bauble around in my hand.

"The locket is from Gaspard's collection of memento mori," Jeanne responded. "He said I could give it to you."

"No, this," I said, holding it up to indicate what was inside the crystal prison. "Why do you have a lock of Vincent's hair?"

Jeanne thought a moment, and then said, "It'll be easier to show you." She gestured to a corner table that held an assortment of beautifully crafted silver and enamel boxes and candles in simple pierced-tin holders.

"It's a ritual my mother taught me when I took her place. A practice her mother had passed to her. We've always felt a special responsibility for our revenants. It makes us feel better to think we've got some say in their survival. I'm not a religious woman, Kate. But I do say prayers every day for my wards."

I picked up a tiny box from the front of the table and opened the embossed lid. A lock of red hair sat nestled inside the rich blue velvet lining. "Charles," I breathed.

"He's the one I've been thinking of most, recently," Jeanne said, shaking her head sorrowfully. "If ever a boy needed a candle lit for him, it's that one." She touched a box covered in a blue-and-green leafy mosaic. "That's Vincent's," she said. I picked it up and opened the lid to see the empty cushioned interior.

"Now that I've given you my little token of Vincent, I expect you to take over my prayers for his well-being," Jeanne said.

"I will," I promised.

Satisfied, she nodded to the back of the table, where dozens of the delicate boxes were lined up side by side and stacked on top of each other. "Even when they're gone, I can't bring myself to get rid of their boxes. Neither could my mother or even hers."

I shuddered. Those stacks must represent Jean-Baptiste's kindred destroyed by numa.

"Vincent's still here on this earth, sweet girl," she said, "even if only in spirit. You've got to be brave."

Only in spirit. Those words, along with Jeanne's expression of heartbroken pity, drove home the fact that this lock of hair constituted Vincent's only earthly remains. He was a phantom now. Immaterial. What could the future hold for a girl and a ghost? The great big empty space in my chest ached, and would keep on aching, until I could touch him again. *Which will never happen because he's gone*, I reminded myself.

Isn't that what Vincent was trying to tell me when he disappeared? And he had been right . . . except for his conclusion: *I will always be near. I'll always be watching out for you. From now on, the only thing I can do for you is try to keep you safe.*

I pressed hard on my chest, as if that would help the pain go away. In my other hand I clenched the locket tightly. *No*, I thought. *I refuse to accept the scenario Vincent described: continuing my life as if he no longer exists, while he watches over me like a stalker guardian angel. I will not live out that tragedy.*

And, abruptly, my thoughts turned to my parents and the great love they had shared. It had practically radiated from them, rubbing off on everyone nearby, making all around them happy. Filling others with hope.

I could have had a love like that with Vincent. I had felt it. There had been something right about us: It was bigger than just two people in love. When we were together, it had been like one of nature's true and rare beauties; like an impossible beam of sunlight piercing through black clouds, bathing the patch of earth before you in gold. Together, Vincent and I had created something beautiful.

And, with that thought, something hardened inside me. A refusal. A rejection of the fate being shoved onto me. Even though I had no idea what form it would take, I would find a solution. Because a solution must exist.

I touched the crystal locket to my lips. And pulling the cord holding the *signum* Vincent had given me over my head, I added the memento mori locket to the ancient symbol of the revenants and tucked them back under my shirt.

Hearing a knock at the door, Jeanne and I turned to see Gaspard leaning in, his hair sticking out like an explosion. "Ah yes . . . excuse me for interrupting." He averted his eyes as if allowing us to finish in privacy.

"It's fine, Gaspard. I had just finished showing Kate my boxes."

"Yes, yes. Good, good." Gaspard nodded, tugging nervously on the hem of his jacket, straightening what was already ironed to perfection. "Your grandmother is ready to leave, Kate, and wishes you to go with her."

I kissed Jeanne and followed Gaspard to the armory, where we collected Georgia and walked the long hallway to the foyer.

"We're walking to the gallows," Georgia said. "I wonder if she'll ever let us leave the apartment again."

"I wouldn't worry about that," Gaspard murmured, but didn't say anything else.

We found Mamie at the front door, her mood much improved. "So tell me," she was asking Jean-Baptiste, "regarding the portrait of your ancestor that I restored: Was the sitter actually you?"

"*Oui, madame,*" the older revenant acquiesced.

Mamie nodded, studying his face. "Well, even though I know there is magic involved, I must say I am terribly impressed at how well you've kept yourself," she remarked admiringly.

She turned, hearing us approach. "There you are, *mes enfants,*" she said, the stern look returning to her face. "Come along now. We will discuss everything with your grandfather when we get home."

Gaspard held the door open, and Georgia and I stepped out,

Mamie shooing us ahead like a mother hen. Lacing her arms through ours, she turned to say good-bye.

"I look forward to meeting your husband one of these days," Jean-Baptiste said.

"I'm not sure he feels the same way," Mamie remarked with an amused gleam in her eye, "but I will have a talk with him and we will see how things develop. In the meantime, I thank you for your offer of protection. I will be in touch."

"As you wish, *madame*," Jean-Baptiste responded. "You are in complete control of the manner in which things proceed between your family and mine. Just give me the word and I will provide whatever you request."

"*Merci, cher monsieur*," Mamie said, nodding elegantly, and then turning, led us toward the gate.

I knew we were fine when we passed the fountain and Mamie, unable to help herself, lifted a finger toward the angel and his lovely burden. "Did you notice that spectacular example of Romantic-era sculpture, Katya? The diaphanous quality of the woman's dress could only have been achieved by a great master. Surely not Canova himself. But, then again, I wonder. In any case, truly exquisite."

Mamie's fury had passed. I smiled. "Yes, Mamie. I've noticed it before."

NINE

PAPY WAS WAITING ANXIOUSLY IN THE KITCHEN when we walked in, toying with an untouched cup of tea. "It's time for us all to have a talk," Mamie announced before Georgia and I could escape to our bedrooms. She herded us into the salon, gesturing at the chairs she wanted us to take.

I hadn't seen Papy since everything had happened. He glared at me, his features broadcasting anger, fear, and disappointment. "To say that I am furious would be a wild understatement," he said, clutching the arms of his chair.

"I'm so sorry, Papy," I said, meaning it.

He sat there looking hurt for another moment, and then all at once he was like a balloon deflating. He leaned back in his armchair and closed his eyes, his look changing in a second from "force to be reckoned with" to "tired elderly man."

He opened his eyes and focused on me. "When I forbade you from seeing Vincent it was for your own protection. Not so you would throw yourself into the midst of a supernatural battle."

"There were bigger things going on than just me and Vincent, Papy," I explained. "His whole house was in danger and I thought I knew who was betraying them."

"Damn his house," Papy stated succinctly, his anger returning.

Georgia broke the silence. "Vincent's kind of a nonissue now, Papy, having been reduced to basically a ghost."

My chest tightened as she said it. Though I was already fully aware of the situation, it somehow made it worse to hear it stated so directly.

"I told your grandfather what happened yesterday," Mamie clarified.

Papy huffed to show that though he was informed he still didn't approve, but his stern look softened a little.

"Okay," I conceded. "Take Vincent and his house out of the equation. We'll just talk about our house. About me." I steadied my voice. Getting emotional was not going to help my case.

"If you remember, Papy, the numa who showed up at your gallery weren't after Vincent. They were after me, because one of his kindred had informed them I killed their leader. I was sure I knew who had told them. And Georgia and I went to prove it."

"I never thought it was Arthur," began Georgia, but Mamie shot her the stink eye and she shut up.

My grandfather shook his head in disbelief. "Why in the world would you girls take that upon yourselves?"

"Because Vincent didn't believe me," I responded.

"It's true that Kate uncovered the traitor. No one suspected Violette," remarked Georgia.

Papy's old, vein-lined hands curled into fists and pounded the chair's cushioned arms. "The end result doesn't matter. I wanted you to stay away from them, Kate. Not involve yourself even further in their problems."

I could have answered that in a dozen different ways, but felt it was wisest at this point to keep my mouth shut.

Mamie let the ensuing silence settle before speaking up. "Well, you've said your piece, Antoine. And, Kate, you've heard your grandfather. Even though you didn't disobey him in the letter of the law—you didn't meet with Vincent behind your Papy's back—your actions put you and your sister in mortal danger. And, whether or not Violette would have captured Vincent later, your actions yesterday led to his demise."

"Mamie!" Georgia exclaimed, gasping, as my eyes filled with tears. But although they hurt, my grandmother's words only poured kerosene on a flame of doubt that had already been threatening to spark into a full-on bonfire. Though Violette had planned to kill Vincent and overthrow the revenants, everything had come to a head because of my actions.

No one had mentioned it at La Maison. Vincent falling prey to Violette was completely her fault in the revenants' minds. But I couldn't help but wonder how things would have turned out if I hadn't precipitated their showdown. I was going to have to live with that question. And the guilt.

Seeing my face, Mamie rose from her chair and came over to place a comforting hand on my arm. "I'm sorry, dear. I didn't mean to say it like that," she conceded. "But we are all in this mess together now. The numa know who we are and where we live." She paused and turned to Papy. "That's why it seems to me that ordering our granddaughters to stay away from their revenant friends at this point in time would do more harm than good."

"But, Emilie! How can you say that?" Papy exclaimed, rising to his feet.

"Because I have just returned from a long discussion with the head of France's bardia, Monsieur Grimod de la Reynière."

Papy's eyebrows shot up to his hairline. "So that's where you've been!" He stared incredulously at me and Georgia, looking like he couldn't take much more.

Mamie continued as if he hadn't spoken. "And the two of us, along with his companion, a very knowledgeable historian, discussed the most prudent way of moving forward."

My grandfather sank back into his seat with an expression like he had been slapped. "And that would be . . . ," he prompted.

"It so happens that Monsieur Grimod had already set up a system where Kate would be escorted wherever she went. However, yesterday she and Georgia managed to elude that system by leaving school during a time the revenants thought they were safe." Mamie threw me a look of disapproval, but I was already feeling so depressed and guilty that it didn't have any effect.

"He too feels that if the numa had no knowledge of Kate or

Georgia, the best course of action would be keeping them away from the revenants."

Now I was the one who felt slapped. "How can he say that after he was the one who asked me to come back and talk to Vincent when we were broken up?"

"He admitted that to me, Kate," Mamie responded. "He said that it was bad judgment on his part. That he was only thinking of Vincent because he had never seen him that distraught before. That one thinks of one's own child in such circumstances, and that he was remiss to have not considered you and your safety."

Papy gave a kind of harrumphing noise, signaling his displeasure.

"In any case, what is done is done, and we both agreed that at this point you are safer near the revenants than away from them. Actually, we all are. Monsieur Grimod says that at this moment Violette is intent upon war and they should consider any of their allies or contacts at risk, even though it is doubtful that she will maintain an interest in you girls now that she has Vincent."

So. Jean-Baptiste hadn't told Mamie that Violette could use me as bait to make Vincent obey her every whim. That was the real worry as far as I was concerned—the only reason she would be concerned with me in the least.

"Jean-Baptiste promised me that Kate and Georgia will have revenants watching them twenty-four/seven." She turned to us. "Don't worry, girls, you won't even know that they're there."

"He's assigning them both full-time bodyguards?" Papy asked, confused.

"Believe me, Antoine, Monsieur Grimod has a lot of revenants at his service. This will barely put a dent in his numbers. What do you feel about it?"

Papy glanced between the three of us, and then, crossing his arms over his chest, he exhaled a long, sad sigh. "*Ma princesse*," he said, facing me. "I know that Vincent and his kind are here to help humanity. That he's one of the good guys. If it weren't for the fact that being close to him and his kindred put you in danger, I would count it an honor to be associated with them. But your safety means the world to me, and that changes everything in my mind."

My grandfather paused, thinking. "If we asked you to relinquish Vincent and his kind, would you do it?" he asked me.

I couldn't look him in the eyes. Massaging my forehead with my fingertips for a few seconds, I admitted, "No."

"A truthful answer," Mamie said. "Because of that I would rather we collaborate with Jean-Baptiste to keep you safe than to restrict you from seeing them like your Papy did." My grandfather began to disagree, and Mamie put a hand up to signal peace. "Quite reasonably, darling, I don't blame you for it one bit. But that drove Kate into their camp without our awareness."

Papy sat back, defeated.

"Although it is the opposite of my natural inclinations," my grandmother continued, "I feel it is best that you stay under the revenants' protective care—as long as we know where you are at all times." She turned to my grandfather. "Antoine, can you find your way to agreeing with me?"

My grandfather sat there looking miserable. "I don't like it, but it makes sense. There's no question the revenants can protect the girls better than we can. I will agree to this as a short-term plan, but I want you all to know that I feel very much backed into a corner, and that it is not what I wanted in the least."

"We all know that," Mamie allowed, and then turned to us. "Girls, do we have your word that you will not try to shake off your guards like you did yesterday—or leave the house like today, unless you are accompanied?"

Georgia and I agreed.

"Well, then. We have an understanding."

I went to hug my grandmother, and when I leaned over I whispered in her ear, "I'm so sorry, Mamie."

"So am I, dear Katya," she replied. From the troubled look in her eyes, I knew she wasn't talking about my actions. She was sorry that I had lost Vincent, but even sorrier that I had met him in the first place.

TEN

I AWOKE THINKING, *DAY TWO*. VINCENT'S SECOND day as a disembodied spirit, and we were no closer to freeing him from Violette.

Ugh. Violette. Just her name made me sick, a word evoking a tiny, delicate purple flower. Change a few letters, though, and you had "Violent." "Violate." The desire for revenge flared inside me. I wanted to hurt her. To repay her for the betrayal and murder she had inflicted on the bardia and on me.

I swallowed the lump of bitterness in my throat and tasted bile. All my life, I had never really hated anyone. Okay, I had hated my parents' killer—a drunk driver—but she had been an abstract, anonymous person who I never met. Now my hatred had a face. A name. And I felt its venom burning in my veins.

It actually felt good. Because when I focused on revenge, it made me forget my despair. The horrifying emptiness and sorrow I had been feeling—the knowledge that I would never touch

Vincent's hand, face, mouth again, never hear his low voice calling me his pet names—was temporarily submerged by the loathing I felt for the person who had done this to him.

Stop, I commanded myself. Giving in to my hatred wasn't going to do anything for Vincent, only for me. And even if I did manage to pay Violette back, I would still be left with my loss. I had to think beyond my rage.

Yesterday, in Jeanne's room, I had resolved to find a solution. There had to be something I could do. Some kind of secret I could uncover to free Vincent. Maybe even to bring him back. My thoughts raced with possibilities. There could be hope for him. For us!

But as quickly as the thought occurred to me, a come-to-your-senses-Kate reality check snatched away my optimism. Revenants could regenerate injured or severed body parts, but not a whole body. And if there was any way they could, Vincent's kindred would already know about it.

Maybe not, I told myself. Maybe Bran knew something the bardia didn't. At the very least, there had to be a way to free Vincent from his bond to Violette. I was going to try. That resolution propelled me out of bed and into my clothes, and when I looked at my phone and saw Jules's text, I was ready.

I am once again embodied, and able to give you an update. Unfortunately the update is that there is no news. JB thinks it's best if you and G spend the day here. I'm off to hunt for Vincent. Your escorts are waiting downstairs.

I tapped on Georgia's door. "*Entrez*," she called. To my surprise, my sister was awake, dressed, and fully made up. The terrible swelling on her face had gone down, and with the expert job she had done with concealer, all you could see was a few mottled yellow marks along her cheek and jawline.

I nodded at her clock. "Eight a.m. Saturday. Any other day I would think you had just gotten home from your night out. But since I witnessed you in your pajamas last night . . ."

"We're going to La Morgue, right?" she asked. Peering into her dresser mirror, she sprayed some mousse on her fingers and ran them through her hair.

"La Morgue?" I asked.

"I mean La Maison, of course," she said with a wry smile. "Slip of the tongue. All those dead guys, you know."

I shook my head, bemused. "Yes, actually. Jules texted that JB thought we should spend the day there."

"Hmm. I kind of figured he would," she said, applying one last swipe of blusher and turning to me. "So . . . let's go?"

Mamie was waiting in the kitchen. She raised an eyebrow when she saw us come to the table fully dressed. "I take it you have heard of today's invitation to 'La Maison,' as you call it." She set the press coffeemaker on the table and, pouring herself a cup, sat down.

"Your Papy went early to the gallery, and Monsieur Grimod just phoned. We both agree it's best if you girls spend the day in the protection of his house—while Violette is on the loose in Paris, of course," she said.

Her voice was calm, but she was clutching her tiny espresso cup so tightly I was surprised the handle didn't pop off. She knew she was doing the right thing but didn't like it one bit. I gave her a little hug and tossed back a glass of grapefruit juice while Georgia gulped down some black coffee. "Can we take these with us?" I asked, holding up a croissant.

"Of course. I'll walk you girls downstairs," Mamie said, standing and smoothing her skirt briskly before shooing us toward the door.

"Are you going to be okay here by yourself?" I asked. Her exaggerated show of calmness was freaking me out.

"Monsieur Grimod invited me as well, but I would prefer to stay here and work rather than sit around someone else's house all day. He promised to have his people watch our building, just as he has for your Papy's gallery. So don't worry about us," she said.

Ambrose and Arthur were waiting outside our door. "*Bonjour,* Madame Mercier," they called, and she smiled graciously at them. "What polite boys," she said approvingly, and stood at the door watching us until we turned a corner and I lost sight of her.

Arthur offered Georgia his arm, but she pretended she didn't notice, pointing at a movie poster on the side of the news kiosk and chatting with him about the latest Hollywood blockbusters. Ambrose chuckled and winked at me, "Your sister's driving the poor guy crazy." He bit into the croissant that Georgia had given him, devouring half the pastry in one bite.

"Yeah, that's her forte," I commented drily. "So—update. I mean, Jules gave me a no-news update, but give me details of the non-news." I nibbled the end of my own flaky croissant and licked the crumbs off my lips.

"We've been out all night, combing Paris for Violette and company. No luck," he said, looking bothered. "It's like she just disappeared. Jules is still on it, though, along with Charlotte, Geneviève, and the entirety of Paris's revenants."

"Besides you and Arthur," I pointed out.

"And Franck, volant." He gestured to the air above us. "Yeah, the three of us were tagged to watch you and defend La Maison against any 'surprise attack.'" He accented these last two words with finger quotes, obviously annoyed to be left out of the action.

"Well, once we get Georgia to La Maison, I can go with you to join the hunt. I'm sure that with all of the security you guys have, Arthur can hold down the fort."

Ambrose looked doubtful. "Yeah, you might want to ask Gaspard about that," he responded, clearly thinking it was a bad idea.

"So Gaspard isn't out with the search parties?" I asked.

"No. He and JB are questioning Bizarro Man," he replied. "Trying to find a way to detach Vincent from Violette, and pry any other *guérisseur* secrets out of him."

So, JB and Gaspard were thinking along the same lines as I: Bran might know something that could help Vincent. A little balloon of hope inflated in my chest. I felt like running the rest of the way to La Maison, but Arthur and Ambrose acted like we had all the time in the world.

We hadn't walked two blocks when Arthur stopped suddenly and glanced behind us. "Numa," he said. "Franck says that there were two in the park across from the Mercier home. He didn't spot them until they started following us."

"Don't look back," Ambrose said, as I did just that. A pair of young guys in hoodies, looking totally normal except for the colorless numa aura encircling them, were turning out of the park and onto the rue du Bac. They weren't even trying to hide the fact that they were trailing us, and they met my gaze unwaveringly.

"Flight or fight?" Ambrose asked Arthur, smiling widely as he patted the leather sheath strapped to his waist under his long coat.

An elderly woman supported on the arm of a uniformed home-care worker hobbled slowly past us toward the numa. Arthur raised one eyebrow. "With human witnesses? You're not *really* asking me that question," he responded. "Either we walk faster to avoid a confrontation, or we wait to find out what they want."

Arthur and Ambrose turned and pulled together, creating a defensive wall in front of me and Georgia. Just as quickly, the numa turned and crossed the street to walk down a tiny side alley, acting like they had never seen us. But before they were out of sight, one of them turned and, smirking, saluted us.

"Oh-kaaay," Ambrose drawled, staring after the numa in confusion.

"That was a warning," Arthur said. "They only wanted us to know they were there. Let's go." He held his arm out again, and this time Georgia quickly took it. Ambrose wrapped a protective arm around my shoulder, and we walked at a hurried pace to La Maison.

Gaspard met us at the front door. "Franck came ahead to inform us of your visiting party," he said, bustling us all inside. "Who knows what game those numa were playing? We've had no word from—or sign of—their leader."

We walked into the front hallway and Ambrose lurked just inside the door, arms crossed and a scowl on his face, showing his displeasure at being excluded from the action. I knew what he was feeling; I felt the same.

"Gaspard," I said, taking the older revenant aside, "have you discovered anything from Bran that will help Vincent?"

"Unfortunately, no, Kate. But we aren't done discussing the matter."

I felt my little balloon of hope pop and wither. But I wasn't done trying. "I know you promised my grandparents to protect us," I continued. "But I think the best way of doing that is letting me go with Ambrose to join the hunt teams. Two more people could really help the search."

Gaspard began shaking his head, but I continued. "You know I can defend myself now. I'll suit up just in case, though, and promise to stay out of the action if there is any."

"If Kate's going, I'm going, too. I'm sure I can fight just as well as she can," Georgia piped up.

Ambrose stared at her bug-eyed for a minute and then started laughing so hard that he was wiping away tears.

A flush of red crept from my sister's neck up her face. "What?" she exclaimed.

"Sorry, but that's about the funniest thing I've ever heard," he gasped, playfully punching Georgia on the shoulder. "You . . . fighting? Girl, you crack me up."

"In fact, I was going to ask Gaspard today if he would start training me," she said, stubbornly folding her arms across her chest.

That sent Ambrose into another fit of giggles. Seeing how mad he was making my sister, he covered his mouth and turned away.

"I would be honored to train you, my dear," replied Gaspard. "But today is not the day to start. I have more pressing matters to attend to, and Kate must actually come with me." He glanced at me and raised an eyebrow. "Bran has been asking for you in particular, my dear. You seem to be a comfort to him. Since you met his mother, he sees you as a kind of living bond with her."

Arthur spoke up. "If Georgia would accept a lesser master for her first lesson, I would be pleased to instruct her in fight training."

"A very good idea," replied Gaspard, and, turning, he started his way up the staircase toward the library. I began to follow him, but paused as I heard Ambrose cackle, "Now *this* is something I have *got* to see." He clapped Georgia across the shoulders and shook her playfully. "Mind if I come watch?"

"Has this all been decided without my consent?" Georgia said frostily. "I asked for Gaspard. He's the fight master."

A light glimmered in Arthur's eye, and lowering himself to one knee in front of Georgia, he took her hands in his. "*Ma chère mademoiselle*, may I have the sincere pleasure of being the one you choose to introduce you to the art of combat? I would consider it the greatest honor."

She glanced at where I stood watching halfway up the staircase, lifting her eyebrows as if to ask my opinion. I shrugged, stifling a laugh.

Returning her gaze to the ancient revenant on his knee in front of her, Georgia stared doubtfully at Arthur for a moment, and then smiled. "Well, crap. When you put it like that, how can I refuse?" And she lifted him up from his kneeling position and placed her hand lightly on his arm.

"Man, have you got the moves!" Ambrose murmured to Arthur as he followed them down the hall toward the armory.

ELEVEN

BRAN WAS SITTING PROPPED UP AGAINST PILLOWS in Vincent's bed while Jeanne fussed with a tray next to him. "My good lady, I assure you I am perfectly fine," he was saying when we entered.

"You have improved since yesterday, but you're still too weak to get up," the housekeeper insisted.

Bran looked for help from Jean-Baptiste, who was seated by the bed. "Don't expect me to cross Madame Degogue," JB said with a smile, lifting his hands in a gesture of powerlessness. "If she says you stay in bed, then I advise you to do just that."

Bran closed his eyes in frustration and leaned back against the pillows. "Kate is here," announced Gaspard as we approached. He pulled two chairs up to the bed for us.

"Thank you for coming," Bran said, squinting as he looked at me. *Why does he keep giving me such weird looks?* I thought. Bran seemed almost repulsed by me at times, and at others like he wanted to adopt me as a favorite niece.

"Monsieur Grimod, Monsieur Tabard, and I were about to discuss what I know about the Champion, and I wanted you to be here since we are discussing your . . ." He hesitated.

"Boyfriend," I said, filling in the blank for him, and he smiled oddly. There he went again, looking at me like there was something wrong. I combed through my hair with my fingers and, finding nothing sticking up out of it, settled for crossing my arms and fidgeting.

"Yes. Well, we were comparing the bardia's version of the prophecy with the one my family has passed down. It is basically the same." He closed his eyes and began reciting from memory,

> *In the Third Age, humankind's atrocities will be such that*
> *brother will betray brother and numa will outnumber bardia*
> *and a preponderance of wars will darken the world of men.*
> *In this time a bardia will arise in Gaul who will be a leader*
> *amongst his kind . . .*

I was listening to the strange old phrases when all of a sudden I felt another presence in the room. *Kate, you're here!* The words sizzled through my mind like lightning bolts. "Stop!" I yelled. Bran's mouth snapped shut and the three men stared at me. "It's . . . it's Vincent. He's here!" I stammered in shock.

My heart thumped so hard against my rib cage that it actually hurt. "Thank God, Vincent. You got away," I said, choking on my words.

No, my love, I didn't. I only have a minute before Violette draws me back. Speak to the guérisseur *for me.*

"He wants me to talk to Bran," I explained to the astonished men, and I began relaying his message word for word.

"Violette wants to know if you have the secret to the power transfer: the transmission of the Champion's power to the one who defeated him."

"I know there is something about that in my family's records," Bran confirmed, speaking toward a point in the air to the right of my head.

I glanced up to see what he was looking at, but the space next to me was empty. Vincent spoke again, and I translated. "Can you get that information for her?"

"I would need a few days to retrieve it," Bran replied.

And like that, Vincent's voice disappeared.

"What just happened?" Jean-Baptiste looked confounded.

"He said he only had a minute," I explained. "Then Violette was going to pull him back."

"Who was this ghost you were speaking with?" asked Bran, confused.

"That was Vincent."

"I could see him," Bran replied slowly.

"You could *see him*?" I blurted.

"I saw his aura. He was hovering right next to your shoulder," he said, nodding to the space he had been staring at. "Amazing! I actually saw a volant spirit!"

A hushed shock settled over our little group, all of us awed by this apparent miracle, and then, all of a sudden, Vincent was back. *Mon ange, I am here,* his words came.

Bran's eyes flicked back to the space next to my head. "He has returned."

I nodded. "He says Violette will give you three days to find the solution to the power transfer. She is leaving Vincent with us to stay and watch, but will pull him back to her as often as she chooses."

"And *he* is the one whose powers Violette seeks?" Bran insisted.

"Yes," Gaspard affirmed. "As we explained, after murdering your mother, Violette killed him and burned his body in order to get the Champion's power."

Bran leaned back on his pillow. "Well, that explains why the power transfer didn't work," he said softly.

"What do you mean?" Jean-Baptiste asked.

"It's simple. This boy is not the Champion."

Jean-Baptiste, Gaspard, and I stared at one another, speechless. Bran continued, "As my mother and I suspected might be the case, it turns out that I *am* the VictorSeer. The one *guérisseur* from my line who has been chosen to identify the Victor . . . your Champion."

"But how do you know?" I asked, incredulous. "Just last week you told me you weren't certain."

"Ah, but it only just happened," Bran said, smiling weakly and shifting his gaze to JB. "From the moment you took my hand yesterday—the head of the revenants touching the representative of my family of *guérisseurs*—your auras all changed in my eyes."

"So *that's* what happened," JB said.

Bran nodded. "I felt the power possess me, and . . ." He hesitated, choosing his words carefully, "I know quite definitively that I am the one who will identify your savior. And this volant spirit that is with us is not the chosen one. I am sure of it."

"But how—" Gaspard began to ask, but Bran cut him off.

"Don't ask me how, my new friend. I have agreed to help you as much as I can, but there are some secrets I am bound to keep."

There was radio silence in my mind as Vincent began talking directly to Gaspard. "Yes. I agree." Gaspard nodded in response to something he said, and turned to Jean-Baptiste. "Vincent says that, if what the *guérisseur* says is true, we can't let Violette discover her error. The more time she wastes attempting to achieve this fruitless task, the longer we stall her from bringing war to our doorstep."

"But if we stall, won't that put you in danger?" I asked Vincent. The more I saw her in action, the more afraid I was becoming of Violette.

Violette can't do anything to hurt me, he responded reassuringly, but the way he said *me* inferred that Vincent wasn't the only one at risk.

"If we do delay for the three-day period Violette has set, we might have a chance to find the true Champion, now that we have the man who can identify him," JB said, nodding to Bran. "We could call together all of Paris's revenants so that you can see if he is amongst us."

"I will do what I can," Bran said.

"I will tell Ambrose to arrange a meeting of Paris bardia

"immediately," said Gaspard, and bustled out of the room.

"Vincent, does Violette actually hold enough power over you that she can force you to tell her what we are doing if she draws you back?" Jean-Baptiste asked. He listened for a moment and his eyes flicked to me, his expression dark. "She can't compel him to do anything against his will," he relayed. "However, as we suspected, she plans on using something dear to him to do the compelling for her."

Jean-Baptiste was silent for a second, and then said, "I promise you, Vincent. For the next three days we will not let Kate out of our sight."

TWELVE

THE DOOR SWUNG OPEN, AND JULES RUSHED INTO the room. "Just saw Gaspard," he panted. "Is it true? Vincent's back?" He listened for a second, and then practically threw himself on me, talking to Vincent while simultaneously squeezing my breath out. "Oh, man, am I glad we got you back."

I squeaked, "Jules! Oxygen!"

"Sorry, Kate," he said, releasing me. "I'm just happy to see both of you, and you're the only one I can actually touch."

I laughed as I smoothed my scrunched-up T-shirt. "That's okay."

Bran, Jean-Baptiste, and Gaspard began talking in earnest about the prophecy, the Champion, and what could be done once he was identified. Jean-Baptiste looked away for a second and said, "Of course, Vincent. But come back before long. We need to ask you more about Violette and her plans."

"They don't need us right now," said Jules, his eyes sparkling like he had just won the lottery. "Vince, let's go to my room, okay?"

Vincent must have agreed, because Jules grabbed my hand and we were off, down the hall, up the double staircase and through a door next to the one leading to the roof terrace. I stood gawking at a room I had never seen. Jules's room was the attic. But instead of being the dark, musty kind it was suffused with sunlight streaming through a large frosted-glass window set in the ceiling.

Charcoal and pencil drawings filled the room, stacked on every surface and rolled up into tubes along the walls. A bed stood in one corner of the room with more drawings piled on it. The room had a musky, artsy smell, like cologne mixed with paper, ink, and pencil lead.

Jules led me to a garnet-colored velveteen couch under the skylight. "So how are you?" he asked. I paused, not sure who he was talking to. But the way he sat still, listening, I knew Vincent was answering his question.

"And you, Kate?" Jules asked, taking my hand.

"Fine. Thanks for texting with the non-update this morning. The last couple of days have been hellish." I addressed the air. "Vincent, I was so worried about you."

And I you.

His words were like a caress. But they left me wanting more. "Are you okay? Did Violette hurt you?" I asked.

She couldn't do much worse than destroying my body—besides keeping me away from you.

I began to speak, and then hesitated.

What? Vincent asked.

"Does it feel weird to know you're not the Champion?" I asked carefully. "I mean, are you disappointed? Upset?"

There was a moment's silence and then Vincent said, *I couldn't be more relieved, to tell you the truth. If that had been the role fate dealt me, I would have embraced it. Done my best. But it was just one more thing that complicated matters for us. That made our situation even more precarious. So, thinking selfishly, I'm glad to see the title go to someone else.*

Having heard my half of the conversation, Jules jumped in. "I never thought I'd say this, man, but I, for one, am glad you turned out to be just like the rest of us. Otherwise Violette would already be stomping around Paris like some kind of crossbreed numa Hulk. Although the present situation isn't exactly optimal."

We were all quiet for a moment, and then I heard Vincent's words. *I would give anything to hold you right now.*

"Me too," I whispered. Sadness crushed me as, once more, I realized that touching Vincent was something that would never happen again. I wrapped my arms protectively around myself.

Would it be okay . . . Vincent paused. *Could I use Jules to hold you?*

His words electrified me, striking me with conflicting emotions. I didn't want Jules. I wanted Vincent. But my need for him was so great that I was willing to compromise at this point. It just complicated things that Jules's flirting seemed like more than just lighthearted teasing at times. The thought of being physically close to him—like I wanted to be with Vincent—sounded a warning bell in my mind. What if he took things the wrong way?

If I were completely honest, I knew he had feelings for me. Then again, I suspected that he had similar feelings for half the female population of Paris.

Seeing the sudden curve of Jules's lips, I knew that Vincent had asked him the same thing. "So, Kate," he said, raising an eyebrow and suppressing a full-on grin. "Will you accept me as surrogate hugger?" But his smile disappeared when he noticed my expression, and I knew his joking covered the same loss and pain I felt for his friend.

"Will I ever have you back again?" I asked the air.

You have me back, mon ange.

That wasn't what I had meant, and he knew it. I felt my eyes sting with tears. *We have a lot to think about,* came Vincent's words, *but for now let me hold you.*

I nodded my assent, and Jules's body shuddered as if he had caught a sudden chill. And then it was as if two boys were staring out at me. The eyes of my loyal friend and the eyes of my true love both peered from behind Jules's boyish face. Unable to bear it, I looked away and leaned forward into his arms.

It felt like Vincent. The way he squeezed me tightly against himself. I knew his touch; it *was* Vincent. The exact pressure he used as he kneaded my back with his fingers—I knew those movements and they were Vincent's.

And it was my boyfriend's words speaking in his friend's voice as we held each other. "I was so afraid, Kate. I thought I would never see you again. That I would be bound for eternity to Violette and never be able to come back to you. That we would always be separated by a distance I couldn't cross."

My words were like a river, flowing through my lips before wholly forming in my mind. "I missed you. I needed you. I was afraid you were gone." I shifted my hands from the small of his back to his head, lacing my fingers through his hair and drawing him toward me. Pressing my lips to his, I kissed him while tears tripped down my cheeks and onto our mouths. I tasted salt as our kiss deepened.

It was the kiss I hadn't dared to dream of the past few nights. The kiss of finding each other again. Starting soft and growing more passionate, flooding my senses with the body of my love. His soft lips and warm mouth searching, exploring, finding me once again. His hands in my hair and his chest pressed hard against mine. The sound of his staggered breathing as his need for me became tangible through every inch of our touching skin. It felt like we were on the verge of consuming each other, body and spirit. That if we kept pushing toward each other we would actually mesh. Melt into one person.

Then I felt him flinch and I opened my eyes.

And though it was still Vincent looking out at me through the soft brown eyes, Jules was there too. I pulled back against my will, fighting my urge to ignore the facts and drown myself in the fiction. Running my fingers through his hair one last time, I disentangled myself from him and watched as a tremor shook Jules's body. Suddenly there was only one boy looking at me. And it wasn't affection in his eyes. It was pain.

I grabbed his hands and blurted, "I'm so sorry, Jules. I didn't mean to . . . I forgot who you . . ."

Jules pulled his hands from mine, and pressed his palms hard against his eyes. Breathing deeply, he leaned toward me, folding his arms across his chest. "Stop while you're still ahead, Kate, and I can take it as a compliment." He attempted to rearrange his face into a carefree smile.

"No, really, Vince. You can use me as your sex puppet anytime, as long as it's with Kate," he joked. My cheeks burned red with shame. I felt like crying but was too horrified to do anything but sit and watch Jules rise from the couch. He thrust his hands into his pockets and turned away from me hiding his distress. "Seriously, man . . . stop apologizing," he said to the air. Crossing the room, he leaned on the windowsill and stared out through the glass.

I felt like I had parachuted out of a burning plane into an alien landscape: I had no points of reference—not even a clue which direction to walk in order to reach civilization.

After a few silent moments, Jules turned, and his face looked normal again. He walked up to me and ran a finger along my jawline from my ear to my chin, making me shudder. "I need to go," he said softly. "But I don't want you to worry about this. As far as I'm concerned, it's forgotten. I'm glad I was here to help you two reconnect. You both mean everything to me."

But as he left, his voice became gruff. "Where do you think I'm going?" he answered Vincent. "If it's not Guiliana, it'll be Francesca. Or Brooke. What do you care? You just stay here and make sure she's okay." And then the door shut and Jules was gone.

THIRTEEN

"VINCENT?" I CALLED, UNSURE IF HE HAD FOLLOWED Jules down the stairs.

I'm here, Kate, came his words.

I put my head in my hands. "Okay, that was awful."

Was it?

"I mean not awful in the oh-my-God-it-was-amazing-to-feel-like-I-was-touching-you way, but I . . . I couldn't help taking it further. It seemed like it was you."

It was me. It was also unfortunately Jules.

"I didn't mean to kiss him." I curled up into a ball on the couch, wrapping my arms around my knees. I wished I could rewind time by fifteen minutes and do a retake of the whole possessed kissing scene.

You meant to kiss me.

"Yes. You, not Jules. Oh my God, I practically mauled him."

He didn't seem to mind much. And there is the fact that it stopped when it did.

I held my fingers to my burning cheeks to cool them down.

"I am *not* doing that again."

I think that's probably a good decision.

"But then how can we . . ."

Don't worry, mon ange. *Even though that wasn't a huge success . . .*

"'Total fail' is more like it."

There are other ways that we can connect.

"Without actually connecting of course." I paused, my blush flaring to sunburn intensity. "I mean . . . ," I stammered, "I didn't mean in the anatomical sense. Although, yeah, I guess I kind of did." I shook my head. "This is one of the most awkward conversations we've ever had."

That's because it shouldn't have to be a conversation. Not a problem we have to solve. When we have to think practically about things like . . . how a ghost can make you feel like a flesh-and-blood boy could, it kind of strips away the seductive side of things.

I grinned, his words bringing some very interesting images to mind. "And just how does this ghost plan on making me feel like a flesh-and-blood boy could?" I was actually able to get the words out without wanting to bury myself in the couch cushions, probably because I was genuinely intrigued by what he thought was possible.

Well, since we blew my plan A sky high, you need to give me some more time to come up with a plan B. But, Kate . . .

"Yes, Vincent?" I said hesitantly. There was something about his "but" that made me nervous.

Plan A. Plan B. These are only temporary solutions. You and I can't really—Vincent's pause stretched miles—*we can't be together like this,* mon amour. *You can't put up with having a spirit as a boy-friend for long. You need more. You deserve more.*

"I don't want more, Vincent. I want you," I said.

I can't touch you. Can't hold you in my arms. Bring you flowers. Row you down the Seine in a rowboat.

"I don't need that," I insisted.

Kate, you're not listening to me. All I can do is talk to you. He paused. *Can you feel this? Or this?*

I felt nothing.

That was me touching your face and your hair. Don't you see, Kate? I can't be yours in any kind of real way. But what I can promise you is that I will always be here for you, watching out for you, making sure you are safe. And happy.

A tar pit of anger began bubbling deep in my chest. "So you want me to find someone else? A human boy?"

That would be the best thing for you, mon ange. *Someone who is flesh and blood. Who can give you a good life. A normal life.*

"And you're just going to float around like my invisible body-guard and watch me love someone else," I prodded, trying to control my voice.

I'm not saying I'm going to like it. But I can't have you. And I can't leave you. What other choice do I have?

"That is total bullshit!" I yelled. "For one thing, who are you to say what's best for me? Maybe I don't want flesh and blood. Maybe I don't want a normal life. Maybe I still have hope that there is some way of having a life with *you*. Violette found that arcane binding spell. Maybe there are other spells out there that we don't know about. You're giving up before we even start to look for answers.

"So don't go telling me what I'm going to do. What I'm going to feel. Even if you have my heart, I've still got my brain. And I am going to keep using it to find a solution, damn it!"

I sat there fuming, wishing I could see where Vincent was so that I could stare him down. There was silence for a good long moment, and then I heard something that sounded like laughter. "You better the hell not be laughing at me," I growled.

I'm not laughing at you, chérie, came his voice, which sounded muffled by an effort to sound serious.

"You are totally laughing at me, Vincent Delacroix."

It's just that you're so cu . . . I mean incredibly attractive and seductive . . . when you get angry and curse, he replied, stifling serious laughter.

My anger melted in a second, and I couldn't repress a smile. "Vincent, you are seriously impossible," I muttered, and then started laughing myself. I flopped back onto the couch grinning irrepressibly as I heard his laughter bubble forth in my mind.

Stretching out, I laid my head on a cushion and, kicking off my shoes, pulled a cashmere throw up to my shoulders. I waited to see if Vincent would talk first, but he seemed to be fine with just hovering. "Are you still there?" I asked finally.

I am as close to you as I can possibly be.

I hugged the cushion tightly and wished it were him.

Vincent was quiet for a long time after that. I savored the silence, knowing that he was near. When I closed my eyes I could imagine his lean muscular form stretched beside me. After a while it seemed so real, I could almost feel the weight of his arm draped over me and his head nestled next to mine. He was like the ghost lover in one of those tragic Victorian stories. But unlike the swooning, fainting heroines of those tales, I felt empowered by my resolve that tragedy would not be our fate.

FOURTEEN

MON AMOUR, *GASPARD'S ON HIS WAY UP TO GET US.*
They need me now.

The hour we had spent in Jules's room had felt like seconds. After not knowing if I'd ever hear from Vincent again, I needed more time with him. My craving for closeness had barely been met. It was like giving just one bite of chocolate to a starving man.

Vincent read my mind. *I will come to you tonight. I promise.*

"You'd better," I said, wondering how I could be so ungrateful for the miracle of his being here.

It's because you know it isn't permanent, and you're protecting yourself. This answer came from that honest part of my brain that didn't let me get away with things. It was like having my mom live in my head—always ready and willing to provide all kinds of valuable advice, whether or not I asked for it. I knew I should listen, but at the moment I just wanted it to shut up.

I met Gaspard on the stairs and we made our way to Vincent's room, where Jeanne had shooed Jean-Baptiste from Bran's bedside so that he could eat.

As we entered, Bran's eyes flew to the air next to me. He stared at Vincent's ghost for a moment, and then said to Gaspard, "Tell me. Do you plan on attempting a re-embodiment, or will you leave Vincent in this state to aid in the upcoming war with the ancient one?"

Jean-Baptiste and Gaspard stared at him, and then at each other, confused.

I knew it! I thought, my heart racing. I had hoped Bran would have information the bardia didn't, and I had been right. "What's a re-embodiment? How does it work?" I begged.

JB pulled up a chair next to Bran. "I don't think you understand, healer. Vincent's body has been destroyed. How would we give him another? He can't just take over a revenant body; we are bound to our spirits until we are destroyed, and sharing a revenant's body—cohabitation—is harmful to the host's psyche if continued for any substantial period."

He continued in a patient manner, speaking respectfully, but as if he didn't expect Bran to understand how all-things-revenant worked. "As for using a dead human, a volant revenant can possess a fresh corpse—it has been done in exceptional situations—but the possession doesn't stop the body from decomposing at the natural rate. After rigor mortis set in, the body would be useless to Vincent."

Although the image conjured by Jean-Baptiste's reasoning made my stomach turn, I listened intently to understand every angle. Each revenant rule.

Bran blinked a couple of times, and then said, "But I am not referring to a possession. I'm talking about re-creation of his own body."

No one moved. Finally Gaspard spoke. "Healer, we are unaware of this type of . . . miracle. If indeed there is a method for 're-embodiment,' as you call it, then it is not known to our kind. Is this thing truly possible?"

Bran nodded. "Yes. It is. You honestly have no accounts of this in your records? I would have assumed . . ."

"No," Gaspard confirmed. "It seems that the separation of our kind and yours over the centuries has led to a loss in what I am beginning to guess used to be shared information between our groups."

Bran rubbed his fingers across his forehead, and glanced at us doubtfully, as if wondering if he should say more. "My family archives have been fiercely guarded from discovery by those outside our clan as well as by revenants. I always supposed it was so numa couldn't use our information against us. Or against you. But I assumed that the bardia would have much of the same knowledge as we had. At least for such important traditions. Maybe I've said too much. But in this case, I think my indiscretion is warranted."

He cleared his throat and carried on. "The topic of re-embodiment was recorded in one of my family's accounts, written by an ancestor many generations back. It explained that for revenants who are destroyed against their will and trapped as a wandering soul, there is recourse. Their body can be re-created and their spirit introduced into it. I do not know the exact process used. I just know the solution exists."

As the meaning of Bran's words sank in, I felt dizzy. Up to

now, Vincent had been silent. Now he spoke. *Don't get too excited, Kate. This is probably just a legend. A story.*

But I couldn't help it. This faint glimmer of possibility had already banished my despair. There might be a way to get Vincent back. The slimmest of chances was enough to give me hope.

"Do those records still exist?" Jean-Baptiste was asking Bran.

"Yes. They are the same ones that contain the information Violette is searching for. But I must caution you; although I remember my mother reading me one story about re-embodiment, I'm not sure it spells out what must be done during the ritual. It could just be a dead end."

"No matter. Any information at all is more than what we currently possess. We can send someone immediately for your records." JB was already moving toward the door. "Where are they kept?"

Bran hesitated. "Somewhere revenants are not allowed to go," he said, causing JB to stop and turn. His expression fell somewhere between taken aback and furious.

"How about humans?" I asked. "I'll go."

No, Vincent said. I ignored him and kept my eyes on Bran.

"My dear, we are trying to keep you out of danger, not throw you into the middle of it," said Gaspard.

"Actually, since Kate holds the *signum bardia*, she would be allowed to enter my family's archives," Bran said thoughtfully. He rubbed his stubbled chin as he considered.

"Vincent tells me that he forcefully objects to the possibility of Kate going on her own," Gaspard said, holding up a cautionary finger.

"You could have her accompanied to the entrance if you are worried about her safety," Bran offered, "but once inside, I assure you she will be perfectly safe."

"I'm going, Vincent," I said to the room. "If there is even the slightest possibility we can get you back, there's no way you will stop me."

But, mon ange, he said.

"No! I will not listen to you. Jean-Baptiste, will you send someone with me?"

"Of course, dear girl," he responded immediately.

"Bran has promised I will be perfectly safe once inside, and I'll have guards until I get there. You can't say no to that. And even if you do . . ."

Okay, Kate! You win, Vincent conceded. *But I'm going with you, too.*

Satisfied, I turned to Bran. "When can I go?"

"You will have to wait a few hours—until nightfall. The entrance is in a place that is all too visible during the day." Although Bran had made it clear that a revenant couldn't enter his family's archives, he seemed grateful that I had volunteered. *He trusts me*, I realized, the thought filling me with inexplicable delight.

"I'm dying of curiosity. Where is it?" I asked. I knew Paris like the back of my hand, and couldn't imagine where that type of secret place would be hidden.

"It has been in Paris since Roman times," Bran responded, "and was built as an offshoot of the dwellings of the regular *guérisseurs*—those healers who dealt with humans, I mean. Where would a Roman soldier likely go for healing and relaxation?" he quizzed me with a tired smile.

"To the Roman baths," Gaspard and I responded together.

Bran nodded. "My family's archives are located in a cave beneath the Roman baths, underneath the Cluny Museum." And with a smile he added, "Hidden underneath one of the city's busiest neighborhoods: the Latin Quarter."

"I will fetch Arthur and Ambrose," Gaspard said. "If you could brief them on the access to your family's archives, we will send them to guard Kate." He turned to me. "Perhaps you would like to replace Arthur in your sister's fight training?"

Now that we had a plan, I wanted to get started . . . not waste the next few hours waiting for nightfall. *Come on*, I heard Vincent say. *I would hate to miss a chance at seeing Georgia with a sword.*

"That's because there's no possible way she can chop any of your body parts off," I said, feeling buoyed by Vincent's joking mood. Although he wasn't letting on, he must also hope that Bran's family secrets contained a solution . . . or at least a clue . . . to escape his disembodied state.

"I, however," I continued, "am in grave bodily danger. Georgia with a sword . . ."

. . . might be dangerous enough to actually be of some use against the numa, Vincent said, the voice in my head trailing off in a chuckle as we headed downstairs to the armory.

FIFTEEN

"VERY WELL DONE," ARTHUR SAID AS HIS SWORD clattered to the armory floor. Georgia smiled and, placing one hand on her hip, circled her sword in a victorious flourish, causing Arthur to duck to avoid grievous bodily injury.

"Hi, Katie-Bean!" she yelled, spotting me coming down the stairs. "Guess what? I totally rock at sword fighting! Just wait till all those haters see me do this—" she said, lunging in a crazed Three Musketeers move, forcing Arthur to skip nimbly out of the way.

"Vincent's back!" I announced, powerless against the wide smile spread across my face. "Or at least his ghost is. Violette's freed him for three days."

"Oh, Kate, that's wonderful!" Georgia squealed and, dropping her sword, ran over to throw herself on me. "And even better," I continued, once she stopped jumping up and down and let go of me, "Bran has heard of wandering spirits like Vincent getting their bodies back. I mean, it's a story that he heard a long time ago, but they're going to start researching it right away." I didn't mention that I was going to go in search of that story in a couple of hours. Georgia would definitely want to join me.

"That's very good news," Arthur commented. "I can't wait to talk to Vincent myself."

"I just sent Ambrose up to the library to meet with Jean-Baptiste," I told Arthur. "Your 'presence is required,'" I quoted JB.

"Please excuse me," he said to Georgia, bowing slightly.

"Only if you promise me more . . . ," she said with a crooked smile. Arthur promptly turned bubble-gum pink and choked on whatever he was about to say. "More sword lessons, that is," Georgia said, her smile widening as she saw him sputter.

"It's urgent," I prodded.

"Yes, of course," said Arthur. He left at top speed, taking the steps two at a time.

"So where exactly is our lover boy?" Georgia asked.

"Upstairs talking to JB and Gaspard," I said. "Revenant business."

"Then do you wanna practice with me?" Georgia asked, posing her sword tip on her toe, and then recoiling as it went through her shoe. "Ouch!"

"Um, yeah. They're sharp. Why don't you practice with one of the blunt-tipped practice epées," I asked.

"Oh, please," Georgia said. "I'm not a complete wimp."

"Well, I'm not a complete idiot," I said and, opening the wardrobe, got out my hard-to-slice Kevlar workout suit. "If I'm getting anywhere near you with a sword, I want protection. I won't be able to do much, though, with my battle wound," I said, touching my collarbone.

"Don't worry, I'll go easy on you," Georgia said, slicing wildly at the air while I suited up and chose a weapon. As I approached, she got into starting position, her lightweight sword held in her right hand as she leaned forward, left knee bent.

"You've got good starting form," I encouraged her. Taking it very slowly, with exaggerated moves, I let her swipe at my weapon while shuffling forward and back, following her own clumsy movements.

"You see?" Georgia said after a few minutes, breathing hard with effort. "Arthur said I was a natural. I'm just as good as you are, and you've been training for months!"

I shook my head, and with a quick lunge I swung lightly—careful not to put weight on my injured shoulder—hitting her sword near the hilt and sending it flying through the air. As it clanged off a wall and onto the floor, Georgia righted herself and put her hands on her hips.

"What the hell was that?" she cried.

"Georgia, you're not good—yet. Arthur only said that because he's got a major crush on you."

My sister looked hurt.

"That doesn't mean you won't get better if you keep training," I quickly added as I registered her expression.

Her smile returned. "More," she said, and walked over to pick up her sword.

"Georgia," I said, moving my sword from one hand to the other and back, enjoying the feel of its weight in my palms. "What's this all about? The fight training, I mean. Is it just a ploy to get nearer to Arthur? Because I can promise you that's not necessary. He's already totally into you."

"Of course not. I don't need to make a fool of myself to attract a man," my sister said, looking defensive.

"Really?" I said, biting my lip so I wouldn't laugh. "How about that Southern accent you put on whenever cute guys are around?"

Georgia waved her free hand in the air as if to say, *Oh, that— that's nothing.* And then her shoulders slumped. "Honestly, Kate. Getting whopped by a crazed zombie tween left me feeling extremely vulnerable. Not to mention weak. And those are two qualities I genuinely despise."

My heart warmed. This was the side of my sister that made me feel I would follow her not only to Paris but to the end of the world. Complete with all of her party-girl, don't-take-life-seriously, sometimes-maddening qualities. Because I knew this side of her too. The side some people never saw—the one defined by her strength, goodness, and loyalty.

"*That* is an excellent reason for fight training!" I said, and her smile was back in a second.

"So you think you can take me on with your *Kill Bill* sword-fighting skills?" she teased.

"Just go easy on me," I laughed, and raised my sword.

In the end, I didn't have to sneak away from Georgia. Knowing Mamie wouldn't approve of her going out, but unable to stand being separated from her friends, my sister had invited them to come to our house. By five o'clock Arthur was walking her back to the apartment, and forty-five minutes later, he, Ambrose, Vincent, and I arrived at the Cluny Museum of the Middle Ages.

"Perfect timing," I said, walking up to the gates and reading the sign. "Closing time, five forty-five p.m."

The museum was housed in a massive fifteenth-century abbey that took up most of a city block, and had been built next to first-century ruins of Gallo-Roman baths, an ancient ancestor of today's spas. Crumbling walls extended three stories above grassy grounds, the ceilings and floors having disappeared centuries before. High up on the walls, monumental arches in red brick spanned the white stone, tracing the outlines of the palatial rooms the Roman soldiers once wandered through, moving from thermal pool to frigid bath to sauna.

In the hazy darkness of early evening, the abbey looked like a haunted castle and the ruins around it like its unearthed dungeons. I was suddenly glad for my armed escort. As if sensing my thoughts, Ambrose smiled and patted the hilt of the sword he wore under his coat. "See any numa in the area, Vin?" he asked and, apparently satisfied with Vincent's answer, relaxed a little.

You look nervous, mon ange, Vincent told me.

"Nervous? Me?" I said. "Never." Which was a total lie. I was about to go into a cave, deep down in the earth. I had never told Vincent about my claustrophobia. I hadn't needed to.

Going down into the sewers hadn't bothered me. We were in wide man-made spaces just below street level. But Bran's cave was sure to be different—it threatened to reach right back to my childhood fear and paralyze me once I was in its depths.

My family had visited Ruby Falls in Tennessee when I was a kid. At one point the guide turned the lights out to show us how dark it was in a place sunlight never touched. I freaked out, and once we got outside, it took an hour for my mom to calm me. Since then, even the thought of spelunking made me break into a sweat. But I wasn't about to admit that to Vincent. A little claustrophobia didn't matter when much more important things were at stake. Like his very existence.

I wiped my forehead with my palm and tried to appear calm.

"The healer said the entrance was at the southwest corner of the monument," Arthur said, pointing through the gate to one side of the ruins.

"How are we going to get in?" I asked, eyeing the twenty-foot-high cast-iron fencing running the perimeter.

"Never fear, Zombie Man is here," quipped Ambrose, and wrapping his hands around two of the bars, he began pulling at them, as if he was stretching them apart. He let go after a second, turned to me, and winked. "Just kidding," he said. "Bending iron bars is, sadly, not in my superhero résumé. I suggest we try that instead." He nodded toward a small iron door closed with a padlock. Just behind it were steep steps leading down into the ruins.

"Probably the caretaker's entrance," I said as we approached it.

Arthur took out his key chain and fumbled through the keys until he found a tiny silver lock-picking tool. In a second the padlock was off. After waiting until no passersby were watching, we slipped through the door and down the stairs into the grassy area, hiding in the shadows until we were sure no one had seen our illegal entry.

It was chillier among the ruins, as if by descending into the ancient maze of open-air rooms we had actually traveled to another place and time. Like Siberia in mid-winter. I drew my coat more tightly around me and led the way through the dark maze, heading in the direction Arthur had indicated. A minute later, we were standing in a completely unremarkable corner at the juncture of two fifteen-foot-high walls. There was no door carved into the side. No suspicious cracks in the walls. No sign of a passageway of any sort.

"How about using that volant future-sight ability, bro, and telling us where to look," Ambrose said. After a second, he nodded and said, "Vin says that in a few minutes Kate is gone and we're here waiting for her, but he can't see where she went or anything about how it happened. There must be some weird *guérisseur* juju goin' on around here blocking revenant powers. Which means we must be in the right place."

My spine tingled as I wondered just how powerful Bran and his people actually were. They seemed so . . . ordinary. Especially his mother, who had looked like any other little old lady knitting in front of her fireplace.

"Well, I guess we gotta do things the hard way," Ambrose said. He dropped to his knees and began feeling around on the ground, knocking at places where the grass had worn away. "There doesn't seem to be a trapdoor or hollow space," he said.

Arthur and I took opposing walls and began feeling our way along them with our fingertips.

"What was it exactly that the *guérisseur* told you?" Arthur asked as he worked.

"Same as what he told you," I responded. "He just said that the entrance was in the southwest corner of the ruins and that I could enter by using my *signum*." I pulled the pendant out from my shirt, and the little crystal memento mori clinked against it as I pulled them over my head and held them up.

What's that you're wearing with the signum? Vincent asked immediately.

"It's a lock of your hair," I responded. Arthur and Ambrose glanced at me quizzically but returned quickly to their work. For the hundredth time I thought how weird it must be for them to constantly have volant spirits around and only catch the part of conversations that were directed at them. "Jeanne gave it to me," I continued self-consciously.

As I turned the *signum* in my fingers, the light of the streetlamp above flashed on the gold and reflected off something shiny embedded in the wall. I leaned forward to take a better look. Something metallic was set into the stone and completely covered in white dust, making it invisible from a few feet away. I brushed it off to uncover a golden *signum bardia* the size of my own.

"That's our girl," Ambrose crowed.

Be careful, I can't see anything in the future from this moment forward, Vincent told me.

"I will," I promised, and glanced to Arthur, who leaned

forward, inspecting the *signum*. He stepped back and nodded his go-ahead.

"Let's see what this baby does," Ambrose said eagerly.

I held my pendant up and pressed it against the symbol on the wall, my cabochon sapphire depressing a button in the center as the encircled triangle slotted snugly into place. Arthur, Ambrose, and I stood, watching for any sign of movement. "Well, that felt very Indiana Jones-ish," I said after a pause. "So what happens now?"

At that second, the ground rumbled slightly under our feet, feeling as if a Métro train were passing directly beneath us, and a section of the wall swung forward into the dark. Ambrose's eyebrows shot up. "Awesome!" he exclaimed.

Not awesome. At all, I thought, peering into the pitch-black space behind the door. Noticing a flashlight hanging from a hook on the wall just beyond the opening, I tentatively reached through to detach it and quickly pulled it out. Flicking it on, I pointed it down the passageway.

A narrow tunnel carved into the stone appeared in the yellow beam of artificial light. It went straight ahead a long ways, then sloped downward at a steep rate until it turned to the right and disappeared. My chest tightened with anxiety, and I started sweating again. This didn't look like a cave. It looked like a tomb.

I don't want you to go in there alone, Vincent said.

"Yeah, well, I wouldn't mind if you came along," I admitted, wiping a clammy hand on my jeans. *Who knew that palms could sweat this much?* I thought.

I just tried to enter, and I can't. It's like there's an invisible wall blocking the door that burns when I touch it, Vincent said.

"Vincent says he can't get in," I said. Arthur placed his hand on my shoulder. "We should probably inspect this initial passageway before you enter. I'll give it a go," he said gallantly. As he stepped into the black tunnel, a bright light flashed before his head. He leapt back, yelping in pain and rubbed his face frantically. Something smelled like roasted marshmallows.

"Let me see!" I said, and pulled his hands from his face. "It singed your eyebrows and the front of your hair!" I exclaimed.

Ambrose's face was red from suppressed laughter. He gave up. "Oh, man," he sputtered, tears leaking from the sides of his eyes. "You should have seen your expression."

Arthur's cheeks grew as red as Ambrose's, but he wasn't laughing. "You try," he challenged.

Ambrose patted his short-cropped hair protectively. "The 'do is sacred," he said, and leaning cautiously back, he reached his arm through the doorway. An orange spark flew from the end of his index finger. "Ow!" he yelled, and stuck the burned finger in his mouth.

"See," Arthur said, looking mollified.

You can't go in there, Vincent said.

"I was able to reach in for the flashlight, so it looks like I actually can," I said. "And I guess I'm *going to*, if you saw that I had disappeared with your future-sight or whatever."

But, Kate, he said as I walked unscathed into the mouth of the cave. I was enveloped by a musty wet-chalk odor. It smelled like the tunnel had been recently excavated, although the walls and ceiling were blackened by centuries of torch soot.

I glanced back to Arthur and Ambrose, who watched me from as near the door as they dared. "Should we close the door to the cave?" I said, pointing to the *signum* that was still stuck in the wall.

"No!" they said together.

"We're staying right here. No one can get in," Ambrose reassured me.

Be careful, came Vincent's words, sounding as if he was already yards away.

I shined the flashlight into the dark, swallowed hard, and before I could talk myself out of it, set off into the tunnel.

SIXTEEN

AS THE PATH DESCENDED, THE TUNNEL GOT smaller, and soon I was hunching over and bending my head to clear the ceiling. The increasingly tight space made me more and more anxious. The farther downward I walked, the heavier the pressure grew inside my chest, until it felt like my lungs were going to implode.

Finally, I couldn't go any farther. My heart beat so hard that I felt it pounding in my ears. I leaned back against the tunnel wall and slid down into a crouch. Clutching the flashlight in a death grip, I attempted to talk myself out of a full-blown panic attack.

"Close your eyes and imagine being somewhere else," my mom had said to me, deep inside the mountain at Ruby Falls. *Okay, Mom*, I thought. *Where else can I be?* And suddenly, I remembered the roof terrace on top of La Maison, where Vincent had taken me last month. Stretched out around us had been a panoramic view of Paris by night, the city sparkling like it had been decorated with a million strings of Christmas lights.

Vincent had kissed me there—in that most romantic of spots. We had rolled around on a sun bed kissing and laughing and—for a few blissful moments—forgetting that fate conspired against us. For a short while we loved each other without caring about anything else. It was on the rooftop that Vincent told me he loved me. That he couldn't imagine a life without me.

I felt the cold winter air on my face, and Vincent's finger brushing my lips, outlining my mouth before he leaned in and touched his lips to mine.

Then, in my fantasy, he disappeared and I was alone on the roof. The delicious warmth was gone—suddenly and violently— and the coldness of the winter night stung my face and hands. And suddenly I remembered our situation in the here and now: Vincent's body was gone and his spirit was bound to a madwoman. And I was within mere yards of something that might help him.

My eyes snapped open and I stood back up, hunching over into an old-lady shuffle to make my way down the narrowing passageway. There were so many twists now that the flashlight illuminated only the few feet ahead of me. I was so deep that the rock walls were damp against my fingertips.

As I turned a curve, my foot landed against a pile of rubble, sending a stone flying forward. It disappeared around a corner and the echo that returned—of a dozen stones skipping across a vast hollow space—told me that I had finally arrived.

Ducking beneath a low shelf of rock, I suddenly found myself in a cavern the size of an Olympic swimming pool and maybe four times my height. I aimed my flashlight around the walls and located the massive wooden torches lodged in either side of the door. Pulling out the lighter Bran had told me to bring, I lit first one and then the other. *I just lit a torch*, I thought, immediately storing that nugget in a bizarre-things-I-have-done compartment of my brain that had been rapidly expanding over the last year.

As the flames flared to life, I coughed from the smoke and inhaled a deep gulp of stale cave air. The dark stone surface of the cavernous room danced in the flickering light of the torches, making it appear even more otherworldly.

The walls on either side of me looked like massive honeycombs. These were stacked on top of one another all the way up to the ceiling. I counted a few rows and estimated there were around six hundred in all.

The doors were painted with letters and flowers and organic swirly shapes that looked like tattoos. They all had one thing in common: In the center of each door appeared a hand with little yellow-and-orange-teardrop shapes at the tip of each finger, as if they were shooting out flames.

The doors closest to me on the left-hand wall looked ancient, all crumbling stone with only vestiges of their painted designs. Their condition grew better the farther down the room they were, until at the far end the doors were made of wood instead of stone and the paint looked less decrepit.

The wall facing me at the end of the hall had none of the

half-moon-shaped doors, and was instead covered completely in wall paintings. Next to it, at the far end of the wall to my right, the painted doors began again, these looking almost new. There were only a few rows of brightly painted doors and then they stopped, leaving rows and rows of long empty holes stretching toward me.

I ran my fingers against the mouth of the one nearest me and, shining my flashlight inside, knew immediately what it was: a tomb. I had seen the same style of funerary niches in several Roman ruins I had visited around France. The Romans had carved holes horizontally into rock walls and laid their corpses to rest inside.

I shone my flashlight cautiously around the room before stepping farther in, scanning for booby traps. And then I remembered who had sent me: Bran would have warned me of anything I needed to watch out for.

I was in his family's secret "archives" as he called it. *More like mausoleum*, I thought, although one *could* consider it an archive of bodies. Reassured that Bran would never put me in danger, I turned off my flashlight and stuck it in my bag.

In the gleam of the torches, I saw, at the far end of the room, a table holding stacks of books and shining metal objects. That was what I was here for—Bran had told me the books he needed were among them. As I walked farther into the room, I noticed that the final door on the right wall had been decorated with fresh flowers: roses and lilies and white lilac.

As I came closer, the odor of fresh paint mingled with the fragrance of the flowers. This door had recently been decorated.

Something strummed painfully in my chest as I neared it. Even before I was close enough to read the letters carefully painted across the bottom of the door, I knew what they would spell.

❦ Gwenhaël Steredenn Tândorn ❦

Bran's mother. He must have buried her here just a couple of days ago. I knelt down to look more closely at the ground-level tomb and admired the carefully painted hand-with-flames and decorative tattoolike swirls around it. Bran was no artist, but he had obviously spent a lot of time and care creating his mother's memorial. I spotted a small card tied in with the flowers, and held it between my fingers. In tiny spiderlike script, I read, "This is for you, Mom. I will miss you every day."

My heart tugged. I brushed away the tear that ran down my cheek. I knew exactly how Bran felt. For me it wasn't as fresh a wound, but it was one that would always bleed. I missed my parents. And even though I had finally stopped thinking of them every minute of every day, when memories did come the pain returned full force.

"Good-bye, Gwenhaël," I whispered, and, standing, walked toward the lone table. I spotted the books that Bran had mentioned on the left edge of the tabletop: a stack of red leather-bound tomes. But before I reached them, I paused, my eyes drawn toward the paintings covering the entire surface of the end wall. They reminded me of a place I had visited in Florence with my mom— the Basilica of Santa Croce. Just like the walls of that church's multiple small chapels, this wall had been divided into strips of separate scenes and placed row on row, like a comic book.

In the basilica the panels had been filled with pictures showing stories from the Bible or of Italian saints, each chapel decorated by a single artist. Here, the panels were all painted by different artists—in different styles, and seemingly from different periods. The peeled and fading paint of the upper levels suggested that they were the oldest, so I began there, reading the images as stories like my mother had taught me.

The first panel reminded me of the amphora I had seen in Papy's gallery, showing two armies of naked men fighting one another, the soldiers wearing what looked like ancient Greek helmets. One side was led by a man with a golden red halo that flared out from his head like flames. The enemy army's leader had a halo that looked like a cloudy haze of bright red blood. A couple of figures in the corner of the frame were hovering over dead and mutilated bodies and holding their hands over them, as if they were healing them. Their halos looked like little sparks of fire—five sparks above each head, like the flames above the hands painted on the tomb doors. *This must be the symbol for the* guérisseurs, I thought.

The next image reminded me of the medieval paintings of saints being martyred. Men dressed like priests, with big pope-like hats, stood aside watching as soldiers killed a group of people with swords. Their victims were bound hand and foot to wooden stakes, and had the same gold and red haloes as in the previous image, while others had round yellow haloes—the typical ones you see in religious paintings. Under the gold guy was written "bardia," the red had "numa," and the round halo "bayata."

Behind them, in the distance, a flame-haloed *guérisseur* stood outside a cave in which huddled a group of the three types of haloed beings. The story was pretty clear: the revenants and the "bayata," whatever they were, were being persecuted by the Church, and the healers were helping to hide them.

The revenants must have experienced a whole history alongside humankind that we were completely unaware of. I stood there in awe, transfixed by what this meant. Supernatural beings had been living among us since the beginning of time . . . or at least for a long, long time. And scenes from this secret parallel history were depicted clearly before me. The magnitude of this discovery made me feel very small and insignificant . . . but also very lucky.

I eagerly moved to the next panel, which depicted the cave I was standing in. Workers, all with the five flames over their heads, were digging the tombs and painting the walls, while a woman in long white robes held her hands out, shooting beams of silver in all directions. Within the beams were painted stars, moons, suns, flamed hands, and the *signum bardia*. I guessed this was some type of magical *guérisseur* casting a spell on the cave that would allow some to enter, but keep the revenants out, as had been demonstrated so dramatically (and hilariously) outside. I wondered what other magic protected this cave, as there were symbols I didn't recognize floating in the woman's silver starburst.

I suddenly thought of Vincent, Ambrose, and Arthur waiting

outside the cave for me. The longer I stayed the more worried they would get. I checked my cell phone. I had left them forty-five minutes ago. And of course there was no signal, so I couldn't call to let them know I was fine. I knew it was time to go, but couldn't resist looking at a couple more pictures before leaving.

My eyes skipped back up to one of the ancient scenes; this one from the Roman period, judging on the characters' togalike robes. In the center there was a figure curled up in a fetal position inside a big round tub. It was life-size, but had no hair or facial features and looked more like a rough sculpture of a woman before the details were carved in.

Around the figure stood several people, both bardia and *guérisseur* judging by their auras, each taking part in a different activity. One had cut his arm and was bleeding into the tub, another was bending over the curled-up figure's head, a third seemed to be casting a spell over it, and a fourth stood to the side holding a torch and a vase. They were obviously performing some sort of magical ritual, but I couldn't imagine its purpose.

Underneath the image was an inscription in Latin, and I was thrilled to discover that I could decipher a couple of the words. *Argilla* must mean "clay," since the word was *argile* in French. And I knew that *pulpa* meant "flesh," close to the French word for "octopus"—an animal made of flesh with no bones. Unable to translate the rest, I looked around for another scene to study. *Just one more*, I thought, starting to feel anxious about getting back to Vincent and the others before they went apoplectic with worry.

My gaze fell upon a picture near the middle, probably because it was the most beautifully painted. Some *guérisseur* artists were obviously more talented than others. With most, the objective seemed to be getting the message across instead of demonstrating the artist's skill. But this one could have been painted by Raphael or Michelangelo, the sumptuous beauty of the characters being this painter's goal.

In it, a group of numa with red auras stood across a small stream from another group of golden-aura bardia. One of the numa was wading through the clear flowing water as he crossed over to the bardia's side. A female bardia stretched her hand out to him. The numa in the water had a bloodred halo, but unlike those of his kindred, his aura was laced with veins of gold. *Is he some kind of crossbreed revenant?* I wondered. Or maybe like the bayata, was he another supernatural being altogether? I had so much to learn—an idea that simultaneously thrilled and scared me. I couldn't wait to find out more about Vincent's kind, but was leery of what type of creepy things were waiting to be discovered along the way.

As I hurried to scoop up the stack of books Bran had indicated and stow them carefully in my bag, I wondered about the things I had witnessed. How many other humans knew of this cave? Besides the actual *guérisseurs*, not many, I was sure. I felt awed—overwhelmed—by my inclusion in this group. Just a normal girl from Brooklyn standing in a magical cave underneath the bustling activity of one of the world's major cities. *A girl who is anxiously awaited by three undead guys outside the door of the cave*, I remembered and, staring longingly back at the paintings I hadn't had time to look at, I made a split-second decision. Grabbing my phone again, I lifted it to take a photo of the wall.

I can study them back in the safety of my own room, I thought. But it wasn't until I pressed the camera icon that I remembered, in a flash of panic, the magic protecting the cave. Would it incinerate my phone? Would it incinerate *me*? When nothing happened, I breathed a sigh of relief and headed quickly toward the door.

Picking up a tool that looked like a giant candle snuffer hanging by the door, I used it to extinguish one of the torches. As I moved toward the other, I noticed that this wall was painted in comic-strip style like the wall facing it. But, judging from the characters' clothes, these paintings were the most recent; all from the last couple of centuries.

I flicked on my flashlight before snuffing out the second torch. And as the flame began to die, I noticed the painting located just above the door. It was of a group of men in uniforms decorated with swastikas, standing in front of a giant map. In the middle of the group was a mustached man with slicked-down hair, who I recognized immediately. And just as the torch extinguished, I saw that the men around him—Hitler's advisors—all had red haloes.

SEVENTEEN

JEAN-BAPTISTE WAS WAITING FOR US AT THE door when we returned. "From your triumphant expression, I trust your mission was a success, Kate?" he asked anxiously.

I patted my bag and smiled widely. "I've got the goods."

He breathed a sigh of relief. "Wonderful. Come this way. Bran and Gaspard are waiting in the library."

"We're good too, JB," Ambrose muttered, "thanks for asking." He turned to Arthur. "How 'bout a workout?"

Arthur shook his head. "Thought I'd do some research. Don't you ever get tired of fighting?"

"Don't you ever get tired of being an egghead?" Ambrose riposted, but when Arthur looked hurt, he laughed and mock-punched him in the arm. "Just kidding," he said. "I love your books. Especially that one with the guy. And the girl. Yeah, that book was great," and he walked off toward the armory.

"Do you need me, or can I check in with you once Bran's had

time to look through the books?" Arthur asked Jean-Baptiste.

"I'm sure we'll be calling on your expertise very soon," JB said, excusing him.

"See you later," Arthur said, tucking his hair behind his ear and giving me a wink before wandering off toward his room.

"How was your visit to the archives?" JB asked eagerly as we walked up the stairs. "Did you see them too, Vincent?" he asked, and then stroked his chin thoughtfully. "Interesting. Guarded by *guérisseur* magic. How fascinating. Kate, what did you think of them?"

"The place was amazing," I responded. "I've never seen anything like it in my life. I feel truly lucky to have been there."

"You *are* truly lucky to have been there," he said wistfully. The fact that a mystical treasure trove of supernatural history existed a half hour's walk from where he lived—one that he would never be able to see—seemed to be eating JB up. And I was sure Gaspard felt the same. Once again, I was awed that Bran trusted me enough to send me on such an important errand.

Bran and Gaspard were ensconced in a corner of the library, deep in conversation. They turned as they heard us enter. "Kate," both said at once, and Bran said, "And Vincent," looking at a space so close to me I might as well have two heads.

I pulled the stack of books from my bag and set them on the table before the men. Bran's face lit up, as he ran his fingers lovingly over the cover of the top one. "I've never seen them all in the same place, outside the archives. My mother used to bring them home one by one to read them to me. And the only time

I visited—just a couple of days ago—I was otherwise occupied." He suddenly looked sad.

"I saw your mother's tomb," I said softly, pulling a chair to the table and sitting beside him. "It was beautiful."

"Thank you, child," Bran replied, looking consoled. "I'm glad you went. It could well be your only chance."

"You never visited your family's archives before this week?" Jean-Baptiste asked, astounded.

"No. Only the active *guérisseur* in the family is allowed within. That is why my mother brought the books to me, one at a time, as is the custom." He glanced at the volumes. "I figured that today was a day for breaking rules."

"Who actually wrote these volumes?" asked Gaspard. He appeared to be using superhuman restraint to resist leaping upon the books and devouring their contents.

"My ancestors," Bran replied. "The *guérisseurs* in my family have been wielding their art for many generations. Although the active Tândorn *guérisseur* has maintained a continual presence in Saint-Ouen since medieval times, the nonpracticing rest of our clan lived in Brittany and were farmers.

"Like most peasants at the time, my ancestors were illiterate. They passed their stories from generation to generation, memorizing volumes full of accounts of their dealings. In the nineteenth century, the first Tândorn who could write took it upon herself to copy out the family's oral history. Three of these books"—he nodded toward the volumes—"were written by her. There have only been seven or eight *guérisseurs* since her, and they added their knowledge to the last two books."

He shuffled through the stack and pulled out one of the oldest-looking volumes.

"This is the one I remember containing the information the ancient one seeks: they mention a Vic . . . Champion-to-conqueror power transfer. This is an account from a foreign source, of course. As you know, there has never been a Champion in France."

Gaspard leaned toward me and added, "Champions have appeared throughout history in other spots of the globe. Whenever the threat of numa has grown too great in an area, a Champion seems to arise."

Turning the pages slowly and scanning each one, Bran stopped at a passage filled with tiny scrawl in brown ink that looked practically illegible from my vantage point. "Yes, here we are. An account from a *guérisseur* who had traveled with a caravan from India and met one of my ancestors."

"Stop looking into the future, Vincent," Jean-Baptiste said. "Why on earth would it scare Kate if it's not even a possibility?" He turned to me. "Vincent doesn't like what Bran is about to read and requested that we wait to discuss it until you are gone."

"Thanks a lot, Vincent," I said, feeling peeved. "Overprotective much?"

Sorry, mon amour, I heard him say. *There are some stories I don't think are completely necessary for you to know. Especially when they involve me.*

"I think I can decide for myself what will upset me," I countered. "Please, Bran, go ahead."

129

Bran scanned through the story and then encapsulated it for us. "The story took place in medieval India under the Tanwar Dynasty. This Champion was destroyed and his spirit cast into an animal that was killed and eaten by his numa captor. It was thus that the Champion's power was transferred into the numa. It took an army of bardia to bring him down, and only after he had used his multiplied powers of strength and persuasion to conquer an entire city.

My throat tightened. "Okay, I'm not upset, but I am disgusted," I said, my stomach turning. "Vincent, is that what Violette tried with you? The animal bit?"

Yes, he replied, while Gaspard nodded. Vincent had obviously already told him the story.

"What happened?" I asked.

Kate, it's really not important, Vincent pleaded. *Not that I don't think you can take it. It's just that . . .*

"Tell me."

Violette forced my spirit into the body of a rabbit, which she then killed and ate raw. But sometime between the killing and the eating, my spirit left the animal.

"What would have happened to you if it had worked? If you had been the Champion?" I asked Vincent.

Bran responded for him. "Violette would have absorbed Vincent's spirit, which would have been combined with her own. His identity would have been intertwined with Violette's and his power added to hers."

But, obviously, that didn't happen, Vincent rushed to say.

My head hurt. A dull burn behind my eyebrows, like when I crunched on ice. I raised my hand to cup my forehead and felt tears sting my eyes. The very idea of Vincent's and Violette's spirits intertwined made me sick.

It's okay. I'm here now, Vincent said consolingly.

"But when Violette jerks you back to her, what will you tell her? That she did the right thing, but it didn't work since you aren't the Champion?" I asked.

"No, he's going to lie," Jean-Baptiste said. "We will concoct some type of bogus ceremony for her to try on him in order to stall her a bit longer."

Bran added his two cents. "Stalling isn't actually going to solve anything. He's still bound to her, and will remain so until one of two things happens."

"And those would be . . . ?" I asked.

"Until Violette is destroyed or Vincent is re-embodied."

I'll kill her. Gladly, I thought, my fury making me even more nauseous. However, realizing that my slaying a revenant protected by a numa horde wasn't the most probable outcome, I settled for practicality. "Then let's find this account of the re-embodiment," I urged.

"I remember my mother reading it to me when I was still a child. I haven't actually seen it myself, so I have no idea which of these books contain the story," Bran admitted. "I'll need to work my way through them until I find it."

"I'd be happy to help," I offered. I reached for one of the books, but withdrew my hand when I saw his expression.

"I'm sorry, child, but these texts are full of my family's secrets," Bran said. "I have sworn to protect them and show them to no one."

My heart sank. If Bran read through all of these books by himself, it could take a long time. And time was something we couldn't afford.

"Do you mind if I wait here until I have to go home?" I asked.

And do what? asked Vincent. *Watch him turn pages? You'll be bored and you'll drive him insane.*

"There's a lot here to keep me occupied," I responded, gesturing at the walls of books. "I don't want to go home yet."

"You are welcome to stay," Bran responded, to my relief.

"Vincent and I are going to take this opportunity to chat," Jean-Baptiste said. "I need to know everything you can tell me about Violette and her plans."

I'll be back, mon ange, promised Vincent.

Bran spent the next hour carefully studying his books, while Gaspard hovered nervously to one side. He was more tic-y than usual, wringing his hands and trembling as he watched Bran work. I suspected his nervousness was due to the fact that he was in the presence of a wealth of arcane information that he couldn't actually touch. The thought of what could be written in the books was enough to fill me with wonder, and I wasn't a hyper-anxious nineteenth-century historian. Under the circumstances, I felt he was holding himself together quite well.

I spent the time reading a grisly account of pre-Columbian Aztec kings who used revenant Seers to find newly formed bardia. They forced them to serve as immortal bodyguards by threatening their loved ones. When the king died, their bardia slaves were immolated with them. Although I shuddered at the horror of it, the story's disturbing content made me see our own situation in a different light: Things could be worse.

Finally Charlotte peeked her head through the door. "Your grandmother called to ask you to come home for dinner. Jean-Baptiste asked me to walk you back," she said. "He's still interviewing Vincent about Violette. There has been no numa activity since this morning, and since Violette is waiting to get something from us, JB feels you're all safe staying at your house tonight."

"But what if . . . ," I began, looking pleadingly at Gaspard.

"We will call you the second we find anything," the older revenant promised me.

"Violette gave Vincent three days," I said, letting myself feel the panic I pushed down every time I looked over and saw Bran moving at a snail's pace through his texts. "That means . . ."

"Which leaves two days and eleven hours. Yes, dear Kate, I am just as aware as you are of our time constraints," Gaspard reassured me, laying a comforting hand on my arm. "But since there's nothing you can do to help at the moment, you might as well go home to your grandparents."

I gritted my teeth and turned to leave the room with Charlotte. I hated feeling powerless. It's not like I was helping out much just sitting around the library. But being at home with my grandparents wasn't going to do anything to help.

As I gathered my coat and bag, it suddenly occurred to me that Papy may have come across examples of re-embodiment in his research. That thought lifted my spirits enough that I left without arguing further.

As we exited La Maison's courtyard and headed toward my house, Charlotte turned and waved to a couple of shadowy figures positioned at the end of the block. Two bardia fell in step, keeping a block behind us. JB was keeping his promise to guard me carefully.

A couple of bikers raced by dangerously near as we crossed the street. I laced my arm through Charlotte's and squeezed her close to me.

"So what do you think about that re-embodiment thing?" she asked. "The whole house is buzzing about it. Do you think it could be true?"

"I think that if there's even a microscopic chance that it's true, I'm going to make sure we try every known way of testing it."

She nodded. "Hopefully the *guérisseurs'* books will have something useful in them."

"If not . . . or even if so . . . I'm going to see if I can't dig anything else up. My grandfather has read an awful lot on mystical topics, you know, including a few revenant texts."

"Hmm . . . ," she said doubtfully.

Why does no one believe a human can help the bardia? I thought, frustrated. I changed the subject. "So what's it like to come back to La Maison with Ambrose there?" We crossed the bustling boulevard Raspail. It was a freezing third week of February and the shop windows were full of light summer clothes that I couldn't even dream of wearing as I pulled my thick coat tight around myself. We stopped in front of one display.

"You should really try something like that," Charlotte said, nodding toward a short, waistless lingerie-style dress that the mannequin wore over skin-tight jeans.

"Um, that might actually happen in another lifetime. And you are avoiding my question," I responded, pulling her away from the window and onto the crosswalk with me.

Charlotte shrugged in defeat. "It's hard. Ambrose's eyes never leave Geneviève. When he hasn't been guarding you, he's been trailing her."

"So that's why he was itching to join the hunt for Violette this morning," I said, putting two and two together.

"That and the possibility of a good fight." Charlotte smiled.

"Has he said anything else to you about her?" I asked.

"No, only that one time after we arrived in Villefranche-sur-Mer. He must have spilled everything during that confession, because he hasn't mentioned her since."

I threw my arm around Charlotte in a side hug as we approached my street.

"But you know, Kate," she said as we stopped in front of my door, "I'm doing okay about it. And I'm not just saying that flippantly. When I saw you and Vincent get together after he had been alone for so long . . . well, that gave me hope. And watching the way he treats you made me realize that maybe I had set my sights too low. After chasing someone who didn't give me the time of day . . ."

I raised my eyebrows.

"Okay, that's not exactly true," Charlotte confessed. "Ambrose loves me . . . but like a sister. I just see how Vincent anticipates your every desire and tries to make it come true for you. How, when he sees you walk into a room, it's like he's transformed into this person who is bigger and better than the one he was just minutes before. I want to be that for someone. I think I deserve it. And I'm not going to pine away for a guy who feels that for someone else."

The weight in my chest and the razor-sharp pangs of sadness returned full force with Charlotte's reminder of what things used to be like with Vincent. *And could be again*, I reminded myself. I couldn't give up hope, especially now.

"So until my own chivalrous knight shows up," she continued. "I've decided to live a full life and be happy with my lot. Which is already pretty damn good: It's not like every girl is granted immortality and charged with saving human lives."

She winked at me with this last comment, and I could tell that it wasn't just bravado. She really meant it. I threw both arms around her and kissed her cheek. "Fate's brought you this far, Charlotte. I don't see why it wouldn't end up giving you your heart's desire."

EIGHTEEN

PAPY WAS SETTING THE TABLE WHEN I GOT HOME. Hearing me close the front door, he glanced up anxiously. "Oh, good, you're home, *princesse*," he said.

My grandmother popped her head out from the kitchen. "Has the healer discovered anything?" she asked. "Georgia caught us up on today's goings-on."

"No," I said, shaking my head. "Bran is studying his family records. It's a lot of material, and he won't let anyone else look at it."

"Understandable," Papy said, nodding sagely to himself. "Are there still guards outside?" he asked.

"Yep. There are two bardia sitting in the park across the street, watching the building," I confirmed. "And Charlotte walked me home."

"It feels like we're under lockdown," Papy commented a bit begrudgingly. "A couple of them followed me home from work today, too. I'm not actually sure we need all of this security. You girls do, of course, but it's not like they have any interest in me or your grandmother."

"Just be glad for it. With all of this strangeness, one can't take too many precautions. And whatever is going on, we still have to eat," said Mamie from the kitchen, before yelling, "Georgia. Your sister's home. Time for dinner!" She appeared carrying a tray with a huge steaming puff pastry shaped like a fish. "*Saumon en croûte*, served with carrots in curried butter," she announced.

"Mamie, that's gorgeous! Did you make it?" I asked, the combined odors of the baked pastry and steaming salmon making me realize how hungry I was.

Mamie made her tutting sound. "I worked all day, dear Katya. This was made by Monsieur Legrande," she said, referring to the fine food boutique down the street. "But I'm sure he made it with love." She winked.

"I'd eat it even if he made it with lust," announced Georgia as she entered the room, "although picturing a lustful Monsieur Legrande . . . ick." She wrinkled her nose.

Papy rolled his eyes. "*À table*, everyone."

"Any word on the research, Katie-Bean?" Georgia asked as she sat down, but it was just a formality. She knew I would have phoned if anything important had happened.

I shook my head.

"Well, even though a solution hasn't been found, you must be relieved that Vincent is free for a few days, at least," Mamie said, setting the dish down and skirting around the table to wrap

138

me in her arms. "And that healer seems to know a lot about the revenants. He'll find a solution, I'm sure," she said soothingly.

We took our places around the table, and after Mamie wished us a *bon appétit*, everyone tucked into the delicious food.

"I was actually wondering if you had come across the topic of re-embodiment," I mentioned, hoping that Papy would latch on to the topic without much prompting. My bet paid off. I could see his thoughts racing.

"Re-embodiment," he said. "Infusing a spirit into an inanimate object. Now that's an interesting idea." He tapped his chin. "I mean, there is the symbolic re-embodiment in the Christian Eucharist—transforming the communion wafer and wine into the actual body and blood of Christ. Which was probably based on the Egyptian 'divine bread' ritual performed by the priests of Osiris. But I can't think of an example where there was a re-invention of a body and then possession with a soul."

"How about Frankenstein?" suggested Georgia with a helpful expression.

"Georgia. Shush," urged Mamie, spearing a carrot and placing it delicately in her mouth as if demonstrating for Georgia what she should be doing instead of spouting out disturbing ideas.

"No, I mean it. That's an example of a body that was created pretty much from scratch, and then electrocuted to give it a spirit."

"I think that the electrocution part just animated the reassembled body parts," debated Papy. "It didn't give the monster a soul."

"I distinctly remember him playing by a river with a little girl and crying," insisted Georgia. "You can't cry if you don't have a soul."

"Um, can we pull the conversation away from horror movies and back to real life?" I asked, posing my silverware on my plate as I watched Georgia pop more salmon in her mouth. The idea of sewn-together body parts apparently didn't affect her appetite. "I doubt the revenants are going to reassemble a Vincent-shaped body and then wait for a lightning storm to shock him into existence," I said.

"Wouldn't have to," responded Georgia, holding her fork up to make her point. "Nowadays you could probably do it with defibrillators."

I squeezed my eyes shut in frustration.

"Georgia?" Mamie asked.

"Yes?"

"Please shut up."

"Okay." My sister shrugged as if to say we would regret not having listened to her.

I turned to my grandfather. "Although Monsieur Tândorn remembers his family's records mentioning something on the topic, I thought I'd ask you anyway, since you're my resident expert on every strange bit of mythical lore under the sun."

Papy nodded at me, acknowledging my words, but still lost in his own thoughts. "There is the whole concept of the golem in Jewish folklore . . ." And he was off throwing out bizarre stories that he theorized might have fact buried within the fiction. The rest of us listened—me rapt, Mamie and Georgia trying to follow but losing interest before we finished dessert.

After dinner, I followed Papy to his study, where he sat down behind his desk and began stuffing tobacco into the bowl of his pipe. He waved at me to close the door—ostensibly so that Mamie wouldn't know that he was smoking, but we both knew she was fully aware. This charade was a symbol of his gratefulness that she allowed him to carry on with his not-so-secret vice.

"So tell me more about what this *guérisseur* said about 're-embodiment,'" he requested.

"Well, the way he mentioned it, it was as if he expected the revenants to know about it. He said it was used for revenants who had been destroyed against their will and who were trapped as wandering souls."

"It must be an extremely rare occurrence, since you would think that if numa attacked a bardia, they would burn them immediately in order to destroy both body and spirit." He lit the pipe and puffed on it until the flame caught. "Unless they had some nefarious plot like Violette's."

"That's exactly what Gaspard said."

Papy thought for a moment. "How old is the oldest of the Paris revenants?"

"Jean-Baptiste is Napoleonic. Jeanne said he was two hundred and thirty. But Arthur, the one who was Violette's protector, is something like five hundred."

"And he wasn't aware of this re-embodiment possibility?"

"No," I responded.

"So, if none of the revenants are aware of it, that must mean that the story predates the year 1500. How long is Bran's lineage?"

"Well, the book that the numa stole from your gallery—*Immortal Love*—mentioned his family, and that dated from the tenth century."

"Hmm. This line of *guérisseurs*, who happen to be specialists on revenants, have been passing down their family secrets since at least the Middle Ages. No wonder both the numa and the bardia wanted to get their hands on them. They must possess a veritable wealth of information."

He puffed on his pipe for a few seconds, and then leaned back in his chair and eyed me. "What we can deduce is that if this process of re-embodying wandering bardia souls actually exists, it fell out of revenant lore and oral history well before the sixteenth century. So we are looking for ancient examples, which falls within my area of specialty. I certainly don't recall coming across anything like this in direct reference to revenants, but I will begin to put my mind to it."

I watched my grandfather jot down a couple of notes onto his leather-edged blotter, and felt overwhelmed with gratefulness. I hadn't specifically asked him to help. But he had jumped right in and taken on the task. Because he loved me.

And he also loved a good treasure hunt, his treasure of choice being esoteric knowledge of ancient things. Like revenants. Whatever it was, I was glad he was on board.

"Thank you, Papy," I said, walking around the desk to hug him.

"Don't worry yourself, *ma princesse*. But tell me as soon as you know what is in the *guérisseurs'* account so I can start my research with as much information as possible."

"I will," I promised, and left my grandfather alone in a cloud of pipe smoke and musings about immortality.

NINETEEN

I SAT IN BED, WAITING TO FALL ASLEEP BUT unable to keep my mind from wandering back to La Maison and the library where Bran searched for a way to give Vincent a body. I wondered if he would look the same, and quickly decided that I didn't care. To be able to touch him, see him, have him back . . . I didn't care what he looked like as long as he was flesh and blood.

I distractedly picked up a book from the stack next to my bed, and seeing the title, I smiled. *The Princess Bride*. I had read it three or four times. Minimum. I had gotten it out a couple of weeks ago for a certain reason. And stuck here with no other recourse but to obsess about something that was out of my hands, any distraction was welcome. I let the words of "S. Morgenstern" draw me away from my reality into someone else's fairy tale.

I had gotten to the sword fight with Inigo Montoya, which contains my favorite-ever fight-scene repartee, when my thoughts were suddenly interrupted by the words, *What are you reading?*

I snapped my book shut and sat up in bed. "Holy cow, you scared me," I said.

I'm sorry, mon ange. *I thought you'd be expecting me.*

"Well, I was hoping you'd come, but wasn't sure if you'd remembered that promise—after all of the archives excitement," I admitted, squirming.

How could I forget wanting to see you? he asked, and his words were like a hug. *Um, Kate—why are you shoving that book under your blanket?*

I sighed and pulled it out, holding it up to the air and flapping it around since I didn't know where he was.

He laughed. *Don't tell me you're still trying to win our longest-running argument.*

"The book *is* better than the movie, Vincent. I just think that because you read it in English, you didn't get the irony or the dry humor."

Don't tell me we're going to argue about this while I'm volant and you've got the book in your hand. Talk about an unfair advantage.

I ignored his plea for a time-out. "The movie doesn't have Fezzik's and Inigo's backstories," I insisted.

The book doesn't have Billy Crystal playing Miracle Max, he rebutted.

"Touché," I mumbled, unable to argue with that point, "but this debate is not over."

It's a date.

I smiled. Placing the book on my bedside table, I sat up on the bed and crossed my legs, as if I were having a chat with a real person who sat right in front of me. At least I could pretend.

I focused on a framed picture on my dresser taken of me and Vincent on my last birthday. In it, we're about to leave for our rowboat date, and the two of us are smiling like idiots. Something pinged painfully in my chest like a snapped rubber band.

"I can't believe we're even talking about this," I said wistfully, "when this morning I didn't know if I would ever talk to you again."

I know what you mean, he responded. *But talking books with you is actually one of my favorite activities.*

I smiled, remembering the epic book conversations we used to have. We agreed on almost everything except book-to-film adaptations, in which case I almost always preferred the book and Vincent the movie. "I am guessing that if you are here arguing with me about twentieth-century fiction, there hasn't been any progress back at La Maison?" I asked.

Nope, Vincent said. *Bran's going through the books, page by page, to make sure we don't miss anything important. There is just as much, or probably more, about cases of migraines and fetus gender prediction than there is about revenants. But he's worked his way through two of the five books. Pity he has to sleep, but I took the opportunity to pay my love a visit.*

I leaned back against my headboard. "Vincent, do you think that this re-embodiment thing has a chance of working?"

Honestly, I think that if it actually existed, we would have heard of it before.

I nodded, outwardly agreeing, but inwardly determined to

search every possibility. I agreed with what Mamie had said. My story with Vincent wasn't going to end this way.

You should sleep, Vincent said.

I lay down and pulled the covers high over my shoulders, closing my eyes. "Tell me a story," I said.

You want a bedtime story? Vincent asked, laughing.

"Yes. Something that will keep me from worrying. To distract me."

Okay, he said. *There's a story my mother used to tell me when I was a little boy. It changed a bit with each telling, but I can give you the essentials.*

"Perfect," I said, already feeling sleep creep over me. Today had been exhausting, and I had no clue what tomorrow would bring.

It starts with a knight who has a dream in which he sees a beautiful lady dressed in blue, lying asleep in a boat traveling down a river. A voice tells him that the lady exists, that she is his true love, and that if he searches long and far he will find her. It also warns that if he attempts this journey, he will face danger and possible death on the way. When he awakes, the knight saddles up his horse and begins his quest to find her.

And with Vincent's story materializing word by word in my head, I fell into a deep and dreamless sleep.

I was awakened the next morning by the same voice that had lulled me to sleep.

Bonjour, mon amour.

"Mmm," I said, rolling from my side to my back and attempting to open my eyes. "Did you leave or have you been here this whole time?" I asked.

I went back home. And I know it's early, but I thought you should know . . . Bran has found something.

My eyes popped wide-open and I sat straight up in bed. "What? What did he find?"

A story. You should come over and hear it for yourself. It's a really old story, but it sounds credible and may give us some clues.

As he spoke I had clambered out of bed, put my jeans on, and was struggling with a wadded-up top.

You have time to find some clean clothes, my love, came Vincent's words.

"No time!" I said, and then dashing over to my dresser, swiped my deodorant stick under each arm. "Okay, time for complete necessities," I allowed. "And this shirt is clean, just not folded."

Right, Vincent said, laughing.

Mamie was already up and having her coffee. "Bran, the healer, has found something. I need to go."

"Okay, Katya," she said, looking worried but bustling to the hall closet and grabbing her coat. "Just let me see you downstairs and make sure someone's there to accompany you." I didn't tell her that Vincent was already here. It would have taken too long to explain, and maybe even freaked her out that he had been in my bedroom, invisible.

Two revenants I had seen at the New Year's party appeared out of nowhere when we stepped through the door. Mamie kissed my cheeks and said, "You be on your way. Your Papy left early for his shop. Let him know what was discovered as soon as you can. He really wants to help." She tried to look hopeful.

When we arrived, Gaspard was waiting for me at the door of the library. "Come on in," he said excitedly. "Vincent told me you were on your way." He led me to where Jean-Baptiste sat with Bran, who was pointing to a section written in a tiny scratching script in black ink.

"Ah, here's Kate," Bran said, as Jean-Baptiste stood and pulled out a chair for me. The *guérisseur* looked up at me and did the painful squint he had been doing ever since the numa punched him. I had begun to get used to it, but it still made me feel uncomfortable. "I've already given a summary of this to Messieurs Tabard and Grimod," he said, "but I can read it to you word for word if you wish."

"Please do," Gaspard said, picking up a pencil and taking notes.

Bran began speaking in a spooky monotone—as if he were reading a spell—and followed along with his finger as he read.

"'The Tale of the Thymiaterion, as recounted by a member of a group of flame-fingered *guérisseurs*—'"

"What's that mean?" interrupted Gaspard.

Bran peered up at him, confused. "A thymiaterion? I have no idea."

"No, no. I know what a thymiaterion is. It's a type of ancient incense burner. What does 'flame-fingered' refer to?"

"Flame-fingers. It's what our kind are called, the *guérisseurs* who deal with revenants."

That explains all the hand paintings in the cave! I thought.

Bran continued, "'*Guérisseurs* from Byzantium who fled the Plague and were now itinerant.'" He looked back up at us. "From the order that these tales were transcribed, I would suspect this refers to the Black Plague. Which means the mid-fourteenth century."

"Yes, yes," said Jean-Baptiste impatiently. "Please continue."

"'Just before the Plague, a group of bardia from Italy moved to Constantinople, bringing a valuable Etruscan treasury with them. Soon after, a powerful numa named Alexios killed the bardia chieftain, Ioanna, and bound her to him. Ioanna's kindred destroyed Alexios, thus freeing her spirit from its bond to her numa captor.'

"'Ioanna's kindred sought out the flame-finger Georgios, to conduct a re-embodiment, telling him that the process had been conducted several times, ages before. He resisted, not knowing what he could possibly do. They instructed him that a giant bronze thymiaterion in their treasury was to be used, and that the object itself held enlightenment. Instructed by ancient symbols carved into the object, Georgios conducted the ceremony and reunited the wandering soul with a man-made body that became as her own.'"

My heartbeat accelerated. This meant there *was* hope for Vincent! I felt light-headed and had to restrain myself from leaping up and hugging everyone in the room. Instead, I calmed myself and listened harder. I didn't want to miss a single word.

"'We asked the travelers what became of the magical object. They told us that during the siege of their city the thymiaterion was smuggled out with the rest of the bardia's trove, which had since been plundered and scattered throughout the land.'

"'Thus was the story given us by flame-finger Nikephorus—previously of Constantinople but now a wanderer—transcribed as it came from his very mouth. We marveled at the fantastical story, and some disbelieved it. But my grandfather, who had not yet passed his gift to my mother, said that he sensed it was true. That this power was one of our own.'"

Bran carefully placed a piece of paper on the book to save his place. "So you see, my memory did not fail me. I knew I had heard of re-embodiment."

And? I thought. I glanced at the others, who seemed to have the same reaction. We were all waiting for more.

Jean-Baptiste lowered his face to his hand and massaged his temples. Then, clearing his throat, he said, "And just to reconfirm. This is definitely your only record of re-embodiment—the fourteenth-century account of a band of itinerant bardia."

Bran wrinkled his brow and looked defensive. "Well, my family seemed to think it had merit, because this was one of the tales that was kept and passed along, and one which my own mother pointed out to me as describing one of our powers, even if it was rarely used. But it seems that the instrument itself—the thy . . . whatever it is—is essential for the task we would be undertaking."

My heart plunged. "So, just to clarify, we are looking for a giant incense burner that was lost over six hundred years ago," I said, trying not to sound incredulous.

"I would suppose that more than one of these objects existed," Gaspard responded carefully. "If it was, in fact, an important

151

magical tool in the ancient times, I would guess that several were created. It wasn't as easy to fly across the globe to a convocation of kindred, but there was communication between widespread revenant cultures. Information did manage to spread globally between revenants."

An ancient legend about a magical incense burner. That wasn't exactly what I had hoped for, but at least it was something. Determined not to let my disappointment show, I took my notebook from my bag and jotted down some notes, asking Bran a couple of questions to clarify. Gaspard gave me a curious look.

"I thought my grandfather could follow up on any leads you find with his own resources," I said.

Gaspard frowned. "Not to disrespect your grandfather, my dear, but I doubt he would be in possession of anything that our extensive library would not already have."

"Well, I found the copy of *Immortal Love* in his gallery, which is what led me to finding Bran and his family in the first place," I countered.

"That is true," Gaspard conceded, "but I honestly don't think you should trouble your grandfather with this. With our resources here we should be able to turn up the information needed, if it exists at all." He waved his hand to indicate the size of the library.

"Why are you reluctant to have me include my grandfather in this research?" I asked him point-blank.

Gaspard umm-ed and ah-ed for a second, and then Jean-Baptiste cut in to save him. "We aren't used to including humans in our dealings except on a support level," he said in an apologetic tone. "Maybe that is shortsighted on our part, but our insularity has a purpose: survival. It's just what we're used to. This isn't to say we don't respect your grandparents and value their trust."

I nodded. "But now we're in a race against time to find the information, right?" I stood and tucked my notebook into my bag.

Gaspard nodded.

I grabbed my coat. "So, with your permission, I'll work with my grandfather to see what we can find." I began walking out the door, and then turning, gave them a competitive grin and said, "Beat you to it!"

TWENTY

"YOU SAY IT WAS A GIANT THYMIATERION," PAPY confirmed. "Ancient Greek?" He flipped through an auction catalogue as he launched questions at me. We were ensconced in the back room of his gallery, sitting between life-sized statues of gods and warriors.

"No, Bran said the bardia came from Italy," I replied, checking my notes.

"Ah, Etruscan then," Papy said, replacing the catalogue and pulling out another.

"Yes, that's what he said—Etruscan," I confirmed. "When Constantinople was under siege, they snuck their treasury out, hid it, and it was later plundered."

"I wonder what exactly they mean by 'giant,'" Papy said, opening a two-page spread of ancient objects for me to see. "This is an example of an ancient Etruscan thymiaterion." He pointed to a picture of a red clay chalice. Its stem was shaped to look like a man who was holding the cup's bowl on his head.

"They were used to burn incense during religious ceremonies, and were usually only around a foot or two tall. You can find them made in limestone, clay . . ."

"This one was bronze," I said, showing him the scribbling on my notebook.

Papy thought for a bit. "Something like that would be a major object. Museum quality. I haven't come across anything like it in my own dealings, but between the world wars there were entire collections of museum-quality objects coming out of the Middle East and being sold on the art market—under quite *iffy* circumstances. The unacknowledged fact was that they were the product of plundered graves.

"I don't know if any of these collections involved revenant artifacts . . . if they did, the revenant collectors would have made sure all mention of them were taken out of the public records. But the first place I would start looking is in the auction records from those years."

"Do you have any?" I asked.

Papy turned and walked to his bookcase, running his finger along the spines of some old books, and then pointed to one. "Let's see, here is 1918." He moved down two shelves and stopped at another book. "And here is 1939."

My jaw dropped open. The section he was pointing to comprised about fifty books. "Are those records by any chance on the internet?"

Papy gave an amused smile and shook his head. "Tell you what.

I'll take the ones in German and leave you the catalogs in English and French."

We worked all morning and into the afternoon. After a few hours Papy had interrupted my work saying, "You realize, *princesse*, that we are just working on a hunch. We might not even find anything."

"I know, Papy," I had replied. "And you don't need to help me if it takes a long time."

Papy said, "*N'importe quoi*," a phrase that means, "Don't be silly." And though he got up to make some phone calls and show one lone client around the gallery, he spent the rest of the day working side by side with me.

We checked in with Mamie at one, and Georgia arrived a half hour later carrying a picnic basket with lunch for the three of us. Hanging her coat on the outstretched arm of a marble nymph, she sat down and pulled over a volume, flipping through the pages until she reached an illustration. Angling it away from Papy, she held up a page showing a nude statue of Perseus holding Medusa's head.

I lifted my eyebrows, waiting.

"Nice package," she commented matter-of-factly, and then flipped to the front of the book with a faux-studious air. I tried to hide my laughter from Papy, who was looking at us quizzically.

"So, what are we looking for?" my sister asked with a straight face, and once I explained, she got straight to work.

From time to time, one of us would find something. An

unspecified Byzantine collection of bronze objects. An ancient incense burner. Papy would have a look, and then shake his head, saying that he knew that collection or that piece, and it couldn't be associated with our thymiaterion.

But a couple of hours later, when I found "Ten Important Etruscan Objects, unearthed in Turkey," Papy sat up and studied the entry more carefully.

"'Includes bronze temple objects: statues and incense burners, engraved with unidentified mystical symbols,'" he read. "'Several items of massive size. Part of a hoard discovered outside Istanbul. See also lots forty-five and forty-six.'" He read the descriptions of the other two lots, and then checked the back of the book for the insertion that listed the successful bidders.

"I think you've found something here, Kate," he said, glancing up from the book. I tried not to get too excited, but my blood felt like it was buzzing through my veins when I saw Papy's face light up.

"This is a major collection that I have never heard of. And probably for a very good reason: Once it was bought, it must have been hidden away. Also, the buyer is only listed as 'an anonymous New York collector,' so it could possibly refer to one of our secret collectors of revenant subject matter."

He sat thinking for a moment, and then closing the book he rose to his feet. "It's worth following up on. I know only one New York collector of antiquities living at that time to whom this might refer. His son took over his collection and has long been one of my clients in Manhattan. Besides collecting antiquities, he has me contact him when I have anything even remotely referring to revenant lore. 'G. J. Caesar' is what he calls himself, which is obviously an alias."

"Why?" asked Georgia.

Papy looked at her. "I would assume that the G. J. stands for Gaius Julius . . . Caesar, as in the Roman general and statesman."

"I knew that," Georgia said lightly.

Papy shook his head. "I don't even have a phone number. A couple of decades ago, I used to send descriptions and photos of the objects that might interest him to a post office box. Now, of course, he has email. But I doubt he would answer me if I inquired about an object already in his collection. Our contact has been limited to buying and selling."

"Well, where do you ship his purchases to?" I asked. "If we have a mailing address, we could probably look up his phone number. That is, if he is even listed." Hope was filling me like helium. I felt buoyant. Like I was ready to go to New York and track the guy down myself. So far this was just a lead, but it was the only one we had.

"He has his own shippers pick up the objects," Papy said. "I'm afraid this is going to be a bit of a dead end, unless I do something I've been putting off for the last couple of days."

"What's that?" I asked.

"I'll need to meet Monsieur Grimod," Papy said. "And if things are as urgent as you say, I should go ahead and do it now."

"Well, Kate and I better go with you!" Georgia said quickly. She snapped her book shut, jumped to her feet, and began putting on her coat, throwing me a look that said she had been waiting all day for a reason to visit La Maison.

I already had my coat on and was halfway to the door. "I'll call to let them know we're coming," I said, pulling my phone out of my bag. As I began dialing, it rang.

"You were about to call?" Jules said from the other end of the line.

"How did you know . . . ?" I began.

"Vince is here with me, in full fortune-teller mode," he responded. "And, yes, you can come over. I'll let JB know you're on your way."

TWENTY-ONE

FOR TWO SECONDS AFTER JB OPENED THE FRONT door, it looked like we might not make it over the threshold. I'd never seen my grandfather uncomfortable in a social situation, but Papy's jaw was clenched so tightly that I was surprised he was able to wrench it open again to say, "*Bonsoir.*" But he finally managed to speak, and the two men tipped their heads to acknowledge each other before giving a formal handshake.

"Kate. Georgia," Jean-Baptiste greeted us and, then stepping out of the way, said, "Please, Monsieur Mercier, come in." He gestured toward the staircase. "We might as well proceed directly to the library."

"They look like they should be going to a steeplechase or a musty old man's club instead of to a library to discuss the re-embodiment of my immortal boyfriend," I whispered to Georgia as we followed them into the foyer.

"Maybe that's what old guys discuss in their leather chairs

while puffing their cigars," she responded with a grin. "And here we were imagining it was the stock market or property prices."

The sitting room door opened and Arthur stepped into the foyer. "*Bonjour*, Georgia," he said, striding eagerly toward us. He took her hand and was about to lift it to his lips before remembering which century he was in and opting for cheek-kisses instead. "How are you?"

Georgia lifted her face up for inspection. "Better, wouldn't you say?" she asked.

"Yes. You look . . ." He was going to say "beautiful." I could tell. But he stopped himself and said, "Much improved. I'm glad you're healing."

Georgia smiled flirtatiously at him and said, "That sure was sweet of you to call to check up on me this morning and leave me those messages. I'm sorry I couldn't phone you back. I'm really trying to take it easy. To recover my health, you see."

"Of course!" Arthur exclaimed, jamming his shoulder-length hair self-consciously behind his ears. I noticed that he hadn't shaved, and that he was wearing black jeans and a T-shirt instead of his regular button-down and suit pants. I had to smile. Arthur was making an effort for my sister.

"I didn't expect you to phone me back," he said. "I was just checking in, you know. But why don't you come back to the kitchen with me and I'll get you something to drink. Did you have lunch? Are you hungry?"

As they walked through the door to the hallway, Georgia threw me a backward glance, wagging her eyebrows in victory before turning back to him. I could barely restrain myself from cracking up. Georgia was the queen of games. And she was obviously playing this one very carefully.

Mon ange, came a voice in my head.

"I was wondering where you were," I said, following Papy and Jean-Baptiste up the double staircase.

I can tell you've discovered something—your cheeks have gone all rosy. Which, I must say, suits you, mon amour. *Would it be out of place for me to tell you how utterly ravishing that makes you look?*

I touched my fingertips to my cheeks and felt them flush even redder. "Yes, that is completely off-topic," I chided jokingly, but his compliment made me feel radiant. As usual.

What did you find? he asked, amused.

"Some old auction catalogue with a sale that *might* have contained our thymiaterion."

Well, that's more than Gaspard and Bran got. They couldn't find anything resembling the object itself, and extended the search to anything else that might bear the symbols referred to in the story. Ones that would explain how a re-embodiment is performed.

"Did they have any luck?"

None.

I walked into the library to see my grandfather shaking hands with Gaspard and then with Bran. The four men assembled around a table, and Jean-Baptiste held out a chair for me.

Papy began by placing the auction catalogue on the table. He told them that if the thymiaterion wasn't already in a museum or other major public collection—which it couldn't be, because he would already be familiar with it—then it must be in a private collection. He explained about the flow of Middle Eastern antiquities into the antiques market between the wars, and his theory that the piece was moved from Turkey to a European or American collection during this period.

He tapped the book with his index finger. "I own all of the records from the major auction houses during that time, and in one of them Kate found a sale that might refer to the object we seek."

He said we*!* I thought, marveling once again that my grandfather was joining forces with revenants—for me.

Papy opened the catalogue and showed them the reference, then flipped back to the buyer list. "If a purchase of this nature was made for a museum or a major collector, the name would be listed. Instead, this important collection went to an anonymous buyer."

He turned to JB. "I am guessing that this library contains several books that were purchased from me."

"You would be guessing correctly," Jean-Baptiste confirmed, just the slightest flicker of discomfort crossing his face as he revealed yet another of his secrets to an outsider.

"Then perhaps you know who the other members of this worldwide confederation of secretive revenant-themed buyers would be."

"I would certainly know some of them," Jean-Baptiste affirmed.

"Well, there are only a handful of important antiquity collectors based in New York. And only one of those who I know to contact if I find a revenant-related object. I feel that the buyer who bought this auction lot might have been the father of a long-time client of mine based in the city."

Jean-Baptiste watched him, waiting.

"But I have no way of communicating with this collector, who goes by the pseudonym 'G. J. Caesar' except by email. And I doubt he would respond to a request from me concerning something already extant in his collection."

As soon as Papy said the name, a shadow fell across Jean-Baptiste's features, and I could tell that he was steeling himself for something unpleasant. Gaspard must have felt it too, because he made a kind of hiccupping noise and then began fiddling with some papers.

Papy continued, undaunted, "That alias seems to ring a bell with you. I had hoped you would carry out the commission and ask if the piece is in his collection. He would surely be more open to sharing information with you than he would with me."

There was a long, uncomfortable moment in which Jean-Baptiste seemed to wage an internal battle. Finally, he stood and said, "I may know the man to whom you refer, but I don't have his information easily accessible. Give me a day, Monsieur Mercier, and I will see what I can produce."

"That seems reasonable," Papy responded, glancing at me. I was shaking my head.

"We have less than forty-eight hours left," I urged, "and Vincent says we're not even sure that Violette will respect that offer. She could drag him back sooner."

"I know exactly how much time we have left," Jean-Baptiste responded, stony-faced. "I just need a little while to think."

Gaspard's fidgeting intensified, until he looked like he was about to blow a fuse. Rising to his feet, he faced his partner. "Jean-Baptiste, time is of the essence here. It is time to let bygones be bygones. I refuse to allow you to spend the day debating whether or not you will speak to Theodore. Fifty years is long enough for a dispute. Now, get on the phone and call him."

"I might not even have his correct number anymore," Jean-Baptiste countered.

"Vincent just updated the Consortium's information in the database last month. I have no doubt he's listed there," Gaspard said, hands clenched tightly by his sides.

My mouth dropped open. Gaspard was never this assertive— except for the personality transformation he underwent when he had a weapon in his hand. Jean-Baptiste seemed equally surprised because he stood there staring coldly at Gaspard before turning on his heels and stalking out of the room.

Who is this Theodore? I wondered. I had never seen Jean-Baptiste act like this before—not to mention Gaspard *react* like this before. There must be some serious bad blood between the two revenants, and I was burning with curiosity to know why.

Everyone sat uncomfortably for a moment, until we heard Jean-Baptiste's voice come from his bedroom across the hallway. He was speaking to someone on the phone. Gaspard cleared his throat as if to muffle the noise and give JB privacy.

After a tense moment, we heard the sound of a telephone

slamming back into its set, and footsteps stomping back to the library. Jean-Baptiste appeared, his face a mask of composure but its mottled reddened tone belying his true emotions. He avoided looking at the rest of us and spoke directly to Gaspard.

"Theodore, indeed, has a five-foot-tall thymiaterion with mystical symbols engraved around the pedestal, including the *signum bardia*. He knows of two others extant in the world: one in China and one in Peru, so he can't be sure that his is the one that was mentioned in the *guérisseur*'s tale. But he assumes that that doesn't matter as long as they were all created for the same purpose.

"He said that he never discovered its use, but he's excited by the theory that we are proposing—that it was created to facilitate a re-embodiment."

"Did he offer to bring it to us?" Gaspard asked.

Jean-Baptiste shook his head. "He said it would take weeks to get the customs clearances to take an object like that out of the country."

My heart leapt to my throat, and I blurted out, "Then we have to go there!"

"That is what he suggested," Jean-Baptiste confirmed, turning to me. "Bran must take his family's records. And a revenant must accompany Vincent in case he needs to inhabit a corporeal body while the process is attempted."

"Surely you should go," urged Gaspard. "The head of France's bardia should represent, since it is in a way as much a diplomatic mission as it is a—"

"I will not," Jean-Baptiste interrupted angrily, before visibly calming himself and continuing. "You made your case for my contacting Theodore, and rightfully so. But that is the extent to which I will be involved. You do not know what you are asking, Gaspard."

Jean-Baptiste tilted his head slightly, listening, and then said, "In any case, Vincent has made up his mind. He wants Jules to accompany him."

"Then Bran and Jules should prepare to leave," Gaspard said.

"I'm going too," I stated, my eyes flickering to Papy as the words left my mouth. I lifted my chin, preparing for his refusal.

"I am not letting you fly to New York with two men I barely know," Papy said, scooting his chair back abruptly. He looked like he wanted to grab me and leave the house running.

"Then it's decided," JB dictated. "Monsieur Mercier will accompany his granddaughter. Bran, you will want to prepare your things. Gaspard, please let Jules know of his appointment and call our pilot. You will all leave tonight." And he turned and marched out of the room.

Papy and I stared at each other in shock while Gaspard walked over to the phone and began dialing. Bran scooted off and began assembling his books, as if nothing out of the ordinary had happened.

Finally Papy unstuck from his frozen position and, taking me gently by the hand, said, "I don't care who he is or how much power he holds. Monsieur Grimod will not make decisions for me regarding my own granddaughter."

"Papy, I have to go with them. You've got to understand that," I said, not pleading but simply stating it as a fact.

"Kate, this could be dangerous," he said.

"How dangerous could it be? It's a trip to New York on a private plane, a visit to an antiquities collector, some ceremony that involves Vincent—not me—and then we're back again. In fact, it's probably safer for me to be *out* of France—and away from Violette and the numa—than *in* it."

Papy stared around him, at Bran, eyes like an owl's, as he glanced up from his books at us. At nineteenth-century Gaspard, holding the telephone inches away from his ear, as if it were a dangerous object from the future that just may infect him with progressiveness if it touched his head. "How can we trust these people?" he asked, resisting.

"They're better than the alternative, who have actually threatened us," I reminded him softly, and in my mind corrected that to *threatened me*.

"But . . . school—" he began, in a last attempt to dissuade me.

"Is out for the week," I responded. "Remember—winter ski break starts tomorrow. Papy, listen. If this works, Vincent will regain his body. I have to be there for that. If it doesn't, then at least we will be face-to-face with this antiquities guy, who might be knowledgeable enough to know of another solution. Just think, you'll be able to meet this client you've been dealing with for decades."

I could tell that Papy had already thought of that. He was tempted by the possibility of meeting the mystery collector and getting a glimpse at his collection. But this desire was overshadowed by his worry for me.

Jules bustled into the room, looking like someone was pushing him. "Vincent informs me that I'm leaving ASAP for New York?" he said, looking around at us, confused.

"Yes. Go pack," Gaspard said, hanging up the phone. And Jules was off—no questions asked—back out the door and up the stairs to his room.

Gaspard came over and looked Papy in the eye. "Your decision, sir?"

Papy took a deep breath, glanced at me, and then said, "My granddaughter and I will go."

"You will need this, then," Gaspard said, and handed Papy a small wooden box. Inside was a gold chain looped through a pendant: A flat gold disk engraved with the circle, triangle, and flames. "It is yours to keep, to signal to others that you are trusted by us."

"I recognize the symbol," Papy confirmed.

"If you wish to return home and pack a bag, a car will be waiting outside your building in two hours," Gaspard stated, all business. "I will ask Arthur and Ambrose to walk you and your granddaughters home." My grandfather nodded his assent and Gaspard left to find Georgia and our revenant guardians.

"Do you have one of these, too?" Papy asked, as he looped the chain over his head and tucked the pendant into his shirt.

I hesitated, but heard Vincent's voice say: *You can show him.*

I pulled mine out and Papy's eyes grew wide at the dollar-coin-size gold disk. He reached out tentatively, fingering the edging of bright gold pellets and studying the flame-shaped design around the triangular sapphire. "You have been wearing that . . . out on the street?" he asked, his voice tremulous.

"Well, yes. I mean, underneath my clothes," I said. His expression made me feel like I had done something crazy, like running naked through the streets of Paris.

Papy struggled to contain his awe, muttering, "I'm not even going to tell you what that is worth, *princesse*. How rare that piece is. Because if I did, you probably wouldn't dare wear it again."

I heard Vincent chuckle in my mind, and I smiled. "It's just a *thing*, Papy."

"Yes, Kate. A *thing* that guarantees you the revenants' protection. But it also serves as a symbol of what you mean to them. And if they chose this particular *signum* to represent your value—to display the care they are investing in you—I couldn't come close to competing with the protection that I myself can offer. It means you're priceless."

My grandfather smiled at me tenderly and gave my hand a squeeze. "I'm officially outclassed, *princesse*."

"It's not a contest, Papy," I said, smiling. "It's a group effort. And now you're one of the group."

Papy took my arm and led me out of the room. "Then let's get this show on the road."

TWENTY-TWO

WE LEFT PARIS FROM CHARLES DE GAULLE AIR-
port at eight p.m., and through the magic of minus-six time zones
arrived at JFK Airport at ten in the evening. I barely slept—
whether from anxiety or excitement, I couldn't tell. Probably the
two. Papy and Bran both dozed off as soon as we were in the air.
Jules talked quietly to Vincent in the back of the plane and, after
a while, settled in with a book.

A driver was waiting for us at arrivals with a handwritten sign
that read "Grimod." Piling our luggage onto a cart, he ushered us
to a waiting limo outside. Snow lay inches thick on the ground,
and an icy wind made me pull my coat tighter as I dodged ice
patches on the sidewalk.

We were silent on the ride into Manhattan. I felt a strange
numbness as I watched the twinkling city lights grow closer
through the limo window. And it wasn't only from the lack of
sleep and jet lag. It was because I was back.

Back to where I had grown up. Back to where I had lived for sixteen years—my entire life—with my mother and father, gone to school, learned to drive, kissed my first boy. This place was fact and Paris was fiction. So why did everything feel so surreal? I had an inkling that my numbness was covering something else: distress, perhaps. Or maybe reawakened pain I wasn't ready to face.

Bran peered out the window with wide eyes, taking in the vista with slack-jawed awe. He let out a little gasp when the spot-lit Empire State Building came into view. Papy asked, "Is this your first time to America?"

"It's my first time out of France," Bran responded, unable to tear his eyes from the sights outside.

"How about you?" I asked Jules, who was leaning back against the headrest, watching without emotion as our limo crossed the Manhattan Bridge high above the East River.

"The farthest I've been is Brazil," he said, swinging his eyes lazily over to meet my own before shifting them back away. He had been acting differently ever since the Kiss. Distant. He sat as far away from me as possible on the trip to the airport and on the plane. Normally he would have been by my side chatting his head off with both me and Vincent.

He was obviously avoiding me. Understandably so. I had barely seen him since Saturday—two days ago. There was a definite sense of discomfort between the two of us. I deeply wished it would go away and things would return to normal. I loved Jules. Just not in *that* way. But being Vincent's best friend, he would always be a big part of my life.

My mind slipped back to the scene in his bedroom, as I tried to see it from the outside. From my point of view, it had felt like I was kissing Vincent. My eyes were closed and that's what I had seen in my mind. But now the picture that came into focus was of me in Jules's arms, the two of us holding each other in a desperate attempt to get closer.

Glancing up at Jules, I saw that he was watching me, and my cheeks ignited as I banished the image from my mind. He held my gaze—he knew what I was thinking, I could tell—and then closed his eyes and laid his head back against the seat.

Kate, are you okay? I heard Vincent say.

"Yes. Just tired," I responded, and then glanced quickly at Papy. He was trying not to look annoyed: Hearing me talk with Vincent volant freaked him out. He claimed it was rude to carry on a conversation that others couldn't join, but I knew it was really because he hated seeing his granddaughter talk to the air.

The limo driver headed north on Park Avenue and turned left when we got to the eighties. Driving to the end of the block, he stopped in front of a stately apartment building facing the Metropolitan Museum of Art. "We are here," he said in a heavy Russian accent, and got out to help us with our luggage.

A uniformed doorman bustled out the front door, meeting us on the sidewalk and bringing our bags inside. He tucked them all behind a counter, and turned to face us with his hands clasped behind his back. "Mr. Gold is waiting for you. Please show me the tokens of your association."

"Tokens?" I asked, confused.

"You are a part of Mr. Gold's club, are you not? I need to see proof of your membership."

"The *signum*," Jules prompted.

"Oh," I said, and pulled the necklace from underneath my shirt. Papy did the same, flashing it at the doorman, and Bran pulled back his sleeve to show his tattoo.

The man showed no surprise at our strange "tokens." Bowing slightly, he said, "Thank you. This way," and held a gloved hand out to indicate the elevator.

He didn't ask Jules for a token, I thought, as the doorman pressed the button for the top floor. I studied him more closely and realized with surprise that he was a revenant. But my shock wasn't because Mr. Gold had hired kindred to guard his building—it was because I had actually been able to tell what he was.

The weird special effects I had noticed around the numa were reversed in this man's case. The inch of space around him was packed with more vibrancy and color than the rest of the air, whereas numa sucked the color out of their surroundings, leaving them with a colorless penumbra.

I glanced at Jules. He had the same vivid nimbus around his body. I had spent so much time with him and the others that I just didn't notice it with them. Now that I was a part of the revenants' world and was aware that supernatural beings existed where I never would have expected them before, I was paying more attention to who was human and who was not. In the case of the doorman . . . not.

He's one of us, Vincent said, confirming my deduction.

174

We got off the elevator, followed the man down the hallway, and stopped in front of a door. He unlocked it and ushered us into an apartment. "Mr. Gold will be right here. He asks that you make yourselves comfortable." And with that he closed the door, leaving us to examine our surroundings in awe.

The apartment was massive and modern, all white walls and hardwood floors with floor-to-ceiling windows and barely any furniture. Stone pedestals held ancient pottery and metal objects: A Greek mask in gold. A bronze Roman helmet. A finely sculpted marble hand the size of a refrigerator. I had seen things like this in museums, protected under heavy glass. But here they were within arm's reach, tastefully arranged under gallery lighting that made them glow like jewels.

Papy's sharp intake of breath indicated that he was just as impressed as I was. Even Jules straightened a bit as he took his hands out of his pockets and went up to touch the exquisitely carved marble shoulder of a nymph. Bran just stood gawking with his regular astounded look, his magnified eyes taking in every inch of the room.

The door opened again, and in stepped a young blond-haired, blue-eyed man in a white suit. He bowed slightly. "Theodore Gold," he said.

"But you're the doorman!" I exclaimed. He was barely recognizable without the uniform and hat. *The perfect disguise*, I thought. *No one looks a doorman in the face.*

"Yes, I'm sorry about that," the man said with upper-class, posh-sounding diction that sounded nothing like the strong

Jersey accent he had assumed as the doorman. "I value my privacy, and prefer not to depend on others for security. I would rather screen my own guests than risk the outcome of someone else's error. Although you had a revenant with you"—he nodded toward Jules—"he could have been brought here under duress, used as a hostage if you wanted to get to me."

"I take it you are Jules," he said, greeting him with European cheek-kisses. "Welcome, kindred."

"I'm Kate," I said, and held out my hand for an American-to-American shake. Mr. Gold gave me a warm smile, and to my relief didn't ask for a clarification of why I was there. I didn't really feel like launching into an I'm-the-wandering-soul's-girlfriend conversation.

Bran was next. "Your tattoo tells me that you are the healer Jean-Baptiste spoke of. I have read of your kind. It is truly an honor to meet you."

He turned to my grandfather. "You must be Monsieur Mercier. Gaspard phoned to inform me of your—and your granddaughter's—connection to the Paris kindred." So, he knew.

That's one less thing to explain, Vincent said to me.

"You read my mind," I whispered back.

"I am Antoine Mercier," my grandfather confirmed in his beautifully accented English. He peered at the revenant with a mixture of suspicion and curiosity. "But are you Theodore Gold IV? *The* Theodore Gold? Author of *The Fall of Byzantium*?"

The man smiled. "Yes, that was my work."

Judging from Papy's expression, he might as well have just met the pope. "But you are so young! I am in awe that I am actually meeting you. Your grandfather's book on Roman-era pottery is like my own personal bible."

Amusement flashed across Theodore Gold's face. "Actually, Theodore Gold Junior was also me. As was Theodore Senior. I do try to change my writing style each time to make the whole necessary charade a little more convincing."

Papy just stood there gaping.

Mr. Gold laughed and patted Papy on the shoulder. "Well, I am honored to have fooled someone as well versed in the field as yourself, Monsieur Mercier."

My completely unflappable grandfather was still rooted to his spot. "A revenant," he said. "There is only one Theodore Gold. The whole dynasty of eminent antiquity experts is . . . one person. And you are the G. J. Caesar I have been selling pieces to for the last few decades?"

"I think I may have actually bought a piece from you before that under Theo Gold Junior's alias, Mark Aurelius, before I passed the collection down to myself," Theodore pointed out helpfully.

"May I sit down?" Papy asked, the color having drained from his face.

"Please," said Mr. Gold, gesturing toward a couch. Set before it was a low table with bottles of sparkling water and a platter of mini-cheesecakes.

"I wasn't sure if you ate on the plane," he commented as we all sat. "Now, we have much to talk about. May I guess that the volant revenant I sense is the bardia Vincent that Jean-Baptiste mentioned?" He waited and then nodded his head. "Good. So from what I am told, you are looking for a giant thymiaterion with instructional symbols engraved into the stem."

Bran explained about his family's records, and retrieving the book from his bag, he read the passage aloud.

Mr. Gold looked impressed. "Incredible. It certainly is tempting to ask to see the rest of the book"—he paused as Bran shook his head—"but I realize that the information it holds must be confidential. I trust you are giving us all of the details you have on the matter?"

Bran nodded. "I've gone through my family's entire records, and this is the only mention of re-embodiment."

"Fine," Mr. Gold said, clasping his hands together. With his timeless look and white suit, he reminded me of a young Robert Redford in the seventies version of *The Great Gatsby*. Or a character straight out of an Edith Wharton novel: handsome and wheaten haired, with that tanned just-stepped-off-the-yacht look that very wealthy people have.

"I understand that time is pressing," he was saying, "and that Vincent can be called back by the traitor at any time. How long has it been since she let you go?" he asked. "Yesterday before noon," he repeated, looking at his watch. "It's eleven p.m. now, so in six hours or so we'll be coming up on two days, Paris time. Well, let's hope she doesn't feel like yanking you back sooner. We will need all of the time we can get to decode the symbols."

He tossed back the rest of his glass and stood. "And on that note, we should be going."

"Where?" I asked, as we all rose from the table.

"Why, to see the thymiaterion," he said.

"It isn't here?" I asked, glancing around the room.

"No, I only keep a few of my favorite objects here. The world's most complete collection of revenant-themed art happens to reside across the street."

"At the Metropolitan Museum of Art?" asked Papy, incredulous.

"Yes, my dear man," responded Mr. Gold with a wry grin. "At the Met."

TWENTY-THREE

"I'VE NEVER VISITED THE MET AT MIDNIGHT," I whispered as I followed the others to a side door, far from the main entrance's grand stairway.

Has that been a lifelong dream? came Vincent's words.

"A whole museum of paintings to myself, yes," I answered. "A museum full of ancient objects at night, though, has a sky-high creep factor." I shivered, recalling a frequent childhood nightmare in which the statues in Papy's gallery all came alive.

Mr. Gold took out a set of keys, opened a first set of doors, led us through a second set, and then past a seated security guard. He began reaching into his pocket for ID, but the guard just nodded and waved him by.

"This way," Mr. Gold said. We crossed a cavernous room filled with ancient pottery perched on stands and protected under glass cases. In a dark corner of the room, we piled onto an open service elevator. Our host waited for the doors to shut tight, fitted a key into the elevator's control panel, and pressed a button for one of the subbasements.

As we rode the car down, I couldn't help but ask, "So how did you get a key to the museum? And access through the employee's entrance?"

"I *am* an employee," said Mr. Gold, as we exited the elevator. "I am officially the head curator of antiquities, but I'm not around very much. If the same staff sees me over long periods of time, things would seem rather . . . questionable, wouldn't they?"

We trailed behind him down several low-lit corridors, and stopped before a double door with a sign marked ARCHIVES. Gold typed a code into a keypad and inserted another key into the lock.

"Securing a substantial donation to the museum—to the tune of several hundreds of millions of dollars—unsurprisingly convinced the museum to give me private access to this entire area." He opened the door and flicked on a light switch.

Before us was an enormous warehouse-size space, beautifully decorated with scattered columns and frescoed walls. Everything was individually spotlit, with additional lighting glowing from panels in the walls and floor. I shivered in astonished delight, and glanced at Papy to gauge his reaction. My grandfather looked like he had died and gone to antiquity-dealer heaven.

This was the secret collection of revenant art. It must have held thousands of objects ranging from small pieces of jewelry mounted in cases against the wall to giant marble statues of heroes carrying massive weapons and wearing nothing but the *signum bardia* on cords around their neck.

"You are three of the only humans to have visited this important historical collection," Mr. Gold said with a wry smile. "Although I occasionally have revenant visitors drop by on appointment. How much do you know about revenant history?" he asked me.

"Vincent has told me some stories. And Gaspard has mentioned things from time to time. But my overall comprehension is probably pretty lacking."

You're being modest, Vincent said. *I happen to know you've read everything you can get your hands on.*

I didn't respond. The less Mr. Gold thought I knew, the more he would tell me.

We walked slowly toward the other end of the large hall. Though Jules, Papy, and Bran were looking around as we walked, they were all listening in on our conversation.

"Well, considering the project we are about to undertake, it would be useful to give you a quick history of both revenants and our *guérisseur* friends." His voice took on a storytelling pitch, and I could tell he had told this tale before, although I guessed it was to new revenants, and not to human outsiders.

"Ever since man existed, there have been bardia and numa. But in ancient times they were worshiped as heroes and reviled as demons. Both lived among humans as either their guardians or, in the case of numa, dangerous but effective allies for men who sought power at any cost.

"Before modern medicine, healers, known in France as *guérisseurs*, were much more common and well respected among their fellow men. Since *guérisseurs'* powers developed in accordance to the needs of the communities around them, a small percentage of them developed powers to help revenants with their own specific requirements."

Bran stopped looking around and began paying full attention to Mr. Gold's story, drinking in every word.

"Like the bayati—humans with paranormal abilities who were later called saints—revenants around the world began being persecuted with the rise of major world religions. In Eastern countries some were able to hide themselves among mortal holy men and shamans. But not in the Western world. It was at this point—after being hunted and destroyed on a massive scale during the fourth century—that revenants withdrew from the mortal world."

This fit in with what I already knew, and explained a lot of what I had seen in the flame-fingers' archives. I began to wonder if the word "archives" didn't apply as much to the images as they did to the few books and objects I had seen. The wall paintings explained the story Mr. Gold was telling in a much more memorable way.

I drank in every word as he continued. "In order to facilitate the revenants' disappearance from human awareness, the bardia launched a concerted campaign to hide revenant-themed art and literature that was common enough in the Roman times and before. The numa were on board with this, having lost just as many of their own number in the religious persecution."

Mr. Gold stopped in front of a statue of a man lying on a bed. Hovering over him was a woman with a tattoo identical to Bran's etched into her forearm. She was passing her hands over the dead-looking man.

It's probably a dormant revenant, came Vincent's words, and I nodded, agreeing.

"As *guérisseurs* became increasingly scarce," Mr. Gold continued, gesturing toward the statue, "the number who possessed gifts aiding revenants diminished, and revenants' knowledge of them fell out of the common use. I, however, am in possession of some ancient tablets that spell out some of the gifts of these *guérisseurs*." He turned to Bran. "You can see our auras, can you not?"

"Yes," Bran affirmed. "The practicing *guérisseurs* of my family can see both human and revenant auras. It is easy to distinguish between the two."

He glanced at me as he said this, and I smiled. "I remember your mother saying that Jules had the aura of a forest fire," I said, thinking back to the different haloes depicted in the cave's wall paintings.

"Yes," Bran said. "That is their defining trait to us. Which is indicated in the symbol of the *signum bardia*." He pointed to the flames on the marble woman's tattoo.

"You can diminish a young revenant's need to die," continued Mr. Gold.

Bran nodded. "Apparently that is true, but my late mother was not able to find instructions to the actual procedure in our family records."

Our host considered this.

"Why would that be useful for a revenant?" Papy asked.

"Some revenants fell in love with humans and desired to age

at the same rate as their partners," explained Mr. Gold matter-of-factly. Jules caught my eye and grinned, while out the side of my eye I saw Papy stiffen. I didn't dare look at him, wishing Mr. Gold would skip on to the next part.

"There is also the fact that in ancient times, when the population of the world was smaller, revenants who lived in unpopulated areas might not often find the occasion to rescue humans. They could visit *guérisseurs* to ease their pain."

Mr. Gold held his hand up to count off *guérisseur* gifts. "See auras, pacify the need to die . . . and then there is, of course, dispersion," he said, displaying three fingers.

"What is that?" Jules asked.

Mr. Gold met Bran's eye and the healer shrugged. "I haven't heard of it."

"In our case, not important," Mr. Gold concluded. "And the fourth and final gift—as far as I know—is re-embodiment. It was noted in ancient records, but examples are extremely rare.

"Until Jean-Baptiste mentioned it on the phone this morning, I hadn't even heard it referred to in contemporary times. And without his suggestion, I would have never guessed that the mysterious symbols on the side of our incense burner had anything to do with it. Now . . . I wonder."

He rubbed his chin contemplatively before turning and leading us farther into the room. "Unfortunately, the knowledge of the actual procedure has been lost with time"—he glanced over his shoulder and gave Bran a significant look—"at least to us revenants. Which is why I am glad you are here, *guérisseur*."

TWENTY-FOUR

"AH, HERE IT IS: OUR THYMIATERION," MR. GOLD said as we approached a large bronze piece that looked like a giant golden chalice. Its rim was level with my chin and its bowl was just as big in diameter: A children's blow-up pool could fit inside.

Engraved flames licked the entire surface of the stem, which was as wide as my waist. And circling the stem about halfway up was a series of saucer-size circles, each engraved with a different object.

"As you can see, there are seven symbols," explained Mr. Gold. "The first one in the series is the *signum bardia*, which was my indication that this was a revenant-associated piece. And the last in the series, if you follow the circle around to the left of the *signum*, obviously represents fire," he said, indicating a circle with a single flame etched inside.

"A knife with drops of blood," said Papy, gesturing to another medallion, "and next to that a fan." He pointed to a symbol of a stick with a spray of feathers attached to one end.

"This looks like some sort of vase or pitcher," I said, touching an image of a pottery vessel with two handles on the sides.

"An amphora or a pot," Papy said.

"That is the symbol of my kind," said Bran, pointing to a circle showing the same hand as was painted on the cave tombs: palm-side forward, fingers spread, and a tiny flame above each finger.

One symbol was left. It was an open box, its slablike lid slid to one side. "What's this one?" asked Jules, who had been watching silently.

"A box," Papy said and shrugged. "I don't recognize it as one of the typical ancient themes."

Bran had taken a pencil and was copying the symbols into his book. "The *signum* and the flame-fingers' symbols must indicate that the object was used in a ceremony including both revenants and my kind," he said. "That taken into account, we are left with five symbols in this order: the pot, the knife with blood, the fan, the box, and the fire."

"How about water, blood, air, space, and fire?" I asked, tracing the symbols with my finger.

"Historically, the earthen pot symbol stands for clay or earth," Mr. Gold said. "Blood might take the place of water as a liquid. So it's only the box that doesn't fit in with the four elements."

Bran looked thoughtful. "This reminds me of something. Something that is on the tip of my tongue, but I can't quite reach it." I glanced at Papy hopefully.

"Why don't we leave you to think?" suggested Mr. Gold. "Or

you can take a walk around the room and see if something else doesn't jog your memory."

Bran nodded distractedly, and sat down on the floor right there where he had been standing and stared at the giant incense burner as if he expected the answer to fall off it into his lap.

Papy excused himself and began wandering excitedly from piece to piece, mumbling facts and dates as he went along. Jules was mumbling too, but in his case I could tell his murmurs were part of a conversation. "Theodore," Jules said, "Vincent and I were just saying that you looked familiar. Have we met you before?"

Mr. Gold smiled. "Yes. I was in Paris just before World War Two. September of 1939 it was. I came over to help with the evacuation of the Louvre Museum's collections. My French colleagues and I packed all of the artwork and shipped it to various locations in France to protect it from the invading German army. It was during that time that I met your leader, Jean-Baptiste."

Although this sounded like a private conversation, I was intrigued and had inched closer to listen.

Jules nodded. "Vincent is saying he wasn't yet in Paris. Have you been back since then?"

A shadow crossed Mr. Gold's face. "Actually, yes, I returned to France a few years later, when your Paris bardia were in a full-scale war against the numa. A few of us Americans came to your aid. I was the only one of my kindred who was not destroyed."

"That's it," Jules said. "You were one of the Americans living in JB's house in Neuilly."

Mr. Gold nodded, his expression grave.

"Vincent tells me you and JB have been in a bit of a spat since then. Not that that's any of our business," Jules said, instantly looking like he regretted having blurted out Vincent's words.

Mr. Gold looked truly troubled now. He thrust one hand into his pocket and rubbed his forehead with the other. "Yes. There were some . . . unfortunate events that occurred—" he said hesitantly, but his words were cut off by a cry from Bran.

"I've got it!" he exclaimed. We all hurried back to where he was hopping excitedly around the thymiaterion, tracing the symbols with his fingers as he chanted something. His huge eyes swept our little group excitedly. "It's a nursery rhyme that my mother taught me, and that her father had taught her."

"Please," urged Mr. Gold, "proceed."

"It goes like this," Bran said, and then began chanting in a singsongy way:

Man of clay to man of flesh
Immortal blood and human breath
Traces to the spirit bind
Flames give body ghost and mind.

"'Flesh' and 'breath' don't rhyme," muttered Jules.

"It rhymes in ancient Breton," Bran responded drily. "You see, the pot is clay, there is the blood, the fan stands for breath, and then flames, of course," he said, and then, pointing to the box, admitted, "but I still don't know what this is for."

"What does the poem mean, exactly?" I asked.

Bran's expression went from excited to gloomy in a second flat. "Unfortunately, I have no idea."

TWENTY-FIVE

"'CLAY TO FLESH,'" I REPEATED, MY THOUGHTS suddenly percolating with a memory that I couldn't quite place. And then I remembered where I had seen those words. "There was an inscription in Latin under one of the wall paintings in your family's archive that mentioned *argilla* and *pulpa*," I said to Bran. "It showed this curled up figure lying in what I thought was a tub . . . but now that I've seen the thymiaterion, I'm sure that's what it was! You must know the one I'm talking about," I urged.

Bran shook his head. "During my one visit, I stayed long enough to lay my mother to rest and take account of the books and objects there. I didn't have time to study the paintings."

I suddenly remembered the photo I had taken. "I took a picture of it with my phone," I began eagerly, and then seeing the dark look on Bran's face, I hesitated. "I'm sorry. But I wasn't going to show it to anyone else."

He considered this but still looked upset.

"Well, let's have a look," said Papy.

As I fished through my bag, my mood plunged. "It's in my suitcase back at Mr. Gold's house," I said. "In any case, I took a photo of the whole wall. I doubt the inscription would be legible from the distance I got the shot."

"Do you remember any other details from the painting?" Mr. Gold asked.

"Yes," I said, looking to Bran for his approval.

"Go ahead, child," he said, sighing. "I can allow the divulgence of my family's secrets in an emergency like this."

Reassured, I said, "From what I can remember, there was a flame-fingered *guérisseur* in it, as well as several revenants, and it looked like they were carrying out a magical procedure. There was definitely fire—someone holding a torch. And a revenant had cut his arm and was bleeding into the bowl."

"I think I have a couple of funereal urns with the same type of image," said Mr. Gold, rubbing his chin. "There are so many mystical ceremonies whose meanings were lost with time. The urn in question displays one of several that I've always wondered about." Buzzing with excitement, he led us away from the thymiaterion toward a table holding several dozen stone containers, each the size of a mailbox.

"These are the ancient Roman version of funeral urns, used to store the deceased's ashes after a cremation," he explained. "Here's one showing what I suspected was a golem, which would fit your description of a curled up figure," he said, pointing to a container carved with a creepy-looking scene.

"Golems!" Papy exclaimed. "Kate and I were just talking about golems the other day. That makes complete sense!" he said.

We gathered closer to inspect the carving. Almost identical to the wall painting in the *guérisseur* cave, it showed a doll-like figure with no hair or features curled up in a circular bowl, the same size as the bowl of Mr. Gold's thymiaterion. Next to it, a figure with a fiery halo cut her arm with a knife and let the blood drip upon the doll, where it spread in a puddle around the hunched-up golem. Another woman—this one with no halo—leaned over with her mouth next to the figure's head. Her lips were puckered in an "O" shape and seemed to be blowing on the golem's face.

Beside her, a man held his hands above the creature's legs. Five flames flickered above his head as well as the end of each fingertip, and above his hands hovered a cloud of fire. A fourth figure with no visible halo stood behind them holding a box in one hand and a flaming torch in the other.

"It looks like a step-by-step guide on how to give a wandering soul"—I pointed to the fiery cloud—"a body." My heart was racing so fast I felt like I was going to have a heart attack if I didn't calm down. We might have actually found our answer!

I think you might be right, came Vincent's words. From his breathlessness, he sounded just as excited.

Bran started bouncing around nervously. "Just looking at that image is awakening something in me. Something primal. I believe we're on the right track."

I glanced at Jules, and saw that his sullen look had been replaced by one of hope. Meeting my gaze, he shuffled over next to me and squeezed my hand. "I thought we were on a wild-goose chase," he whispered. "Not that I minded, free trip to New York and all. But now I think . . ."—and the way his eyes were lit up with excitement I could finish his sentence for him—*this could actually work.*

"'Man of clay,'" quoted Bran, who was closely inspecting the urn with Papy and Mr. Gold. "I'm thinking this means we must shape a golem like this one out of clay and lay it in the thymiaterion." He pointed to the bathtub-shaped thing on the relief, and I noticed for the first time that it was lifted up off the ground, perhaps at waist height to the standing figures. The woman breathing on the figure was standing on a box in order to reach.

"'Immortal blood' means a revenant must pour his blood onto the clay man," Mr. Gold added, pointing to the bleeding bardia.

"That would be me," volunteered Jules, squinting doubtfully at the image. "Looks like a hell of a lot of blood there." He looked around at us. "No problem, of course. Just a comment," he said defensively.

"I can do the breathing part," I said. I had felt pretty useless up to this point, so I jumped at the chance to be involved.

"And it seems that I will be transferring the aura of Vincent into the clay body," Bran concluded, looking up from the box to a spot in the air right next to my head. *So that's where he is,* I thought with a thrill. *He's been next to me this whole time.*

"I'm guessing the golem must be lit by fire," commented Mr. Gold. "It comes last in the list of symbols on the thymiaterion, and would explain the torch he's holding," he said, indicating the man in the background.

"We still have the mystery box," stated Papy, pointing to the other hand of the torch-bearing revenant.

"What could it be?" I mused.

"Boxes can represent all sorts of things from temptation to empty space to imprisonment," Papy said, glancing at Mr. Gold, who nodded his agreement.

"I hate to interrupt all of the deep thinking going on here," Jules commented, renewed purpose animating his voice, "but Vincent has just reminded me that we're working within a pretty tight time frame here—which ends whenever our illustrious enemy decides to click her fingers and call his spirit back. Let's start on the mud sculpture and get this show on the road."

"Right," said Mr. Gold. "It's lucky the thymiaterion is here in the museum. The restoration studio on the next floor has a supply of clay. Jules can help me bring down some boxes on a hand truck."

"But what about the box symbol?" I asked.

Mr. Gold pulled a heavy set of keys out of his pocket and began searching through them. Finding the one he was looking for, he looked up and met my eyes. "Without a clue as to what the box represents, we're going to have to take our chances and work without it."

"But...," I began, and then stopped as I heard Vincent's words: Mon ange, *we're running out of time.*

As our group scattered, I couldn't help thinking more about the mystery box. Even if we had all the "ingredients," I wondered if the ritual would really work. We were flying by the seat of our pants here. Using only guesswork, how could we hope to succeed

194

at something this complicated?

I pushed my doubts aside. This was our only hope. What could it hurt to try?

It was almost two a.m. before we were finally assembled in a circle around the thymiaterion. Although the collection was pretty well isolated from the rest of the museum, Mr. Gold was worried about lighting something as large as the golem on fire. He had been scuttling around, shutting off all the smoke detectors he could find.

Papy and Bran had been busy plundering the museum's reference books while I helped Jules and Mr. Gold with the clay. My grandfather joined us now with a look of frustration. "I could find no lead on the box symbol," he said regretfully. Taking his appointed place, he picked up the torch Mr. Gold had assembled out of a broom handle tightly wound with kerosene-soaked cloth at one end. Jules struck a match and carefully lit it, and it ignited so violently that both he and Papy staggered back a step in surprise.

The flaming torch cast long shadows, animating the army of statues stationed around the room. The clay man lay curled up inside the bowl of the incense burner, smooth-skinned and bald-headed.

Mr. Gold had formed the hands and feet in simple paddle shapes, pointing out that the golem carved on the funereal urn had no fingers or toes. But Jules had a fit when he saw it, and insisted it be as realistic as possible. He said it offended his artistic sensibilities to see his friend represented in such an unflattering manner. He went to town on the whole thing and when he was done it resembled Vincent in a slightly generic fashion. Although the figure was strange-looking, it seemed fragilely human, like a sleeping child. And the thought that Vincent's spirit might enter it and bring it to life moved me in an almost visceral way. I reached out and brushed its cool, smooth surface with my fingers.

Bran had taken off his glasses. He said that the kind of sight he needed didn't require them. Without them he seemed frailer, more human and less cartoonish. He looked like any middle-aged man, although he had managed to keep his pitch-black hair, and his face looked scarily gaunt now that his eyes weren't magnified. "Are we ready?" he asked, glancing blindly around the room.

"Vincent, are *you* ready?" I asked.

I couldn't be more ready, my love, he said.

I nodded to the others.

"Then, please proceed," responded Mr. Gold.

Bran raised his hands over the lip of the chalice and positioned them above the golem's legs, focusing his gaze on the air above it, where I suspected Vincent was. He stood that way for a minute or so, and then glanced over at Jules. "Go ahead," he urged.

"Aren't you going to say anything?" asked Jules, confused.

"Like what? An incantation? I'm a healer, not a sorcerer," huffed Bran.

"Okay then," Jules said, sounding nervous. He draped his arm over the side of the chalice and brushed it with the dangerous-looking sculpting knife. Gritting his teeth, he glanced at me.

I raised my eyebrows.

"What?" he said defensively. "Okay, I don't mind getting hurt for someone else, but I'm not used to self-mutilation."

"I could step in as your replacement if you'd prefer," offered Mr. Gold.

Jules shook his head. "Vince, you owe me big-time for this one," he said. Then, sucking his breath through his teeth, he cut swiftly and deeply into his forearm. Holding it over the clay figure, he let the blood stream over it while uttering a string of colorful curse words.

I stepped onto the top rung of the stepladder that was pushed up against the cup. Leaning over, I pursed my lips and blew a breath of air like I was throwing a kiss toward the clay man's mouth.

You're so sexy when you breathe on me, the words came.

I sputtered. "Stop making me laugh, Vincent, or you're going to come back to life with no lungs." *If this bizarre ceremony even works*, I thought. I tried to force the pessimism out of my head and blew another breath toward Clay Vincent.

"And now the fire," said Mr. Gold. Jules and I drew back as Papy stepped forward and touched the flaming torch to the clay.

"Now is probably not the best time to point out that wet clay doesn't light," muttered Jules as the flames sputtered where Papy touched the blood-drenched mass. Then—all of a sudden—the fire took on a life of its own and my grandfather jumped back as the body began to burn.

"It's working," I gasped, my heart racing as I leaned back to avoid the flames.

"I can see his aura expanding and rising up into the room," Bran said excitedly. "Now it needs to come down and inhabit the body," he said, placing his hands as close to the flames as he dared.

"Come on, Vince, let's do this thing," murmured Jules, as he grasped his wound to staunch the flow of blood.

Kate, I heard.

"Yes, Vincent?"

Something's wrong.

The fear in his voice made my blood run cold. "What?"

Something's happening. It's like I'm in little particles that are all flying away from each other. It's wrong. I'm disappearing.

"STOP!" I yelled. "Something's going wrong!" I leapt down off the stepladder and grabbed the bucket of water that Mr. Gold had insisted on having handy, in case the fire got out of control. I flung the water over the top of the chalice, and the flames extinguished with a long hissing sound.

"Vincent!" I yelled. "Are you still there?"

"What happened?" Bran asked. He looked dazed.

"Vincent said he was disappearing. That he was spreading out."

"Dispersion," said Mr. Gold. Bran whipped his head around to face the revenant. "Dispersion of wandering souls. The third gift of the flame-fingers. You said you'd never heard of it. Well, I think we just figured out how it worked."

TWENTY-SIX

"WHAT THE HELL IS DISPERSION OF WANDERING souls?" I asked, my voice shrill with panic. I was shaking and felt like I was going to throw up. "What just happened to Vincent?"

Papy appeared by my side and wrapped his arm around me protectively.

"There were two ways to treat wandering souls," I heard Mr. Gold say. "Either re-embody them or disperse them. Not all of us revenants deal well with living forever. In modern times, some even opt for suicide. But *guérisseurs* in ancient times were said to possess the gift of letting a bardia's spirit go while it was volant, essentially dispersing it to the universe."

"So Vincent's just been . . . dispersed?" I choked out as tears flooded my eyes. "How do we get him back . . . from the universe or whatever?" I was so paralyzed by fear that I couldn't even feel my body. If Papy hadn't been supporting me, I might just have fallen over.

No, mon ange. *I'm still here*, came Vincent's voice. It was weak and came in through my brain waves as barely a whisper.

"Oh, thank God. He's still here," I announced. My tears flowed unchecked and I sank down to sit on the floor, resting my head on my knees. I felt like I had been picked up, shaken, and dropped to the ground, my shock and relief were so intense.

Papy fished his handkerchief out of his pocket and leaned over to hand it to me.

Bran staggered backward and sat down on the ground and Mr. Gold joined him, putting an arm around his shoulder and saying, "It's okay, Monsieur Tândorn. He's still here."

Jules stooped over to sit on the ground next to me, holding a towel to his arm. Seeing the blood, I forgot about my own distress. "Let me help you," I offered, and grabbing the first aid kit Mr. Gold had set aside for the purpose, I cleaned and dressed his wound.

"Well, that was a huge success," Jules said, taking in big gulps of air. "Not only did I undergo massive blood loss, but I almost had a heart attack."

"We're not giving up," I said, ignoring the horrifying thought that was endlessly looping in my mind: *You were* that *close to losing Vincent forever.* "We just have to figure out what we did wrong. I'll bet it has to do with the box symbol. We're missing something."

Papy spoke up. "I realize that we are in a terrible rush, and necessarily so. But now that we know how perilous this procedure can be, wouldn't it be better to break for the night and rethink everything in a calm fashion?"

Everyone agreed. It scared me that the more time went by, the more likely Violette was to call Vincent back. But plowing ahead without additional information was too dangerous.

"You okay, bud?" Jules said to the air, and listening, he gave a weak smile. "He says it's the second time in the last few weeks that he's been on the brink of permanent destruction. He's getting used to it."

Trust Vincent to have a sense of humor at a time like this. I knew he was just trying to make the rest of us feel better. He must have been scared out of his wits.

I thought for a moment, then turned to Mr. Gold. "I'd like to see if that quote under the wall painting is visible," I said. "It was longer than the verse Bran quoted. Maybe that would hold the clue."

"I've booked you rooms at a hotel a couple of blocks away," he responded. "But if you want to use my computer to download and magnify the image . . ."

"I have my laptop with me," responded Papy. "We can have a look in the morning."

"As for you, Jules, I alerted a house of our kindred located in Brooklyn that you would be staying," Mr. Gold said. "I thought you'd prefer that to a hotel, since I was told you met several of them a few years ago at the London convocation."

Jules nodded weakly. "That sounds perfect."

"Good. Then I'll phone a doctor to meet you at their house to stitch up your arm."

As we left the museum, Mr. Gold hailed a taxi for Jules.

Then, stopping first at the apartment to get our luggage, Bran, Papy, and I followed Mr. Gold down the street to a small hotel on Park Avenue.

I was so tired by this point that I felt like I was sleepwalking. Now that the urgency of our task had passed, my body was suddenly aware that it had been awake for a day and a half. I stumbled into the hotel room, ripped my clothes off, and fell into bed.

Vincent stayed with me for the night, whispering an earnest *Je t'adore* as I fell asleep, and greeting me with *Bonjour, mon amour* when I opened my eyes in the morning. I glanced at the clock on the nightstand. It was barely six a.m. and I was wide-awake.

Have I ever told you how cute you are when you sleep?

I moaned and rolled over, pulling the covers over my head. "I don't feel cute. I feel jet-lagged," I said sleepily, and then remembering what happened the night before, I sat up, instantly alert.

"The question is . . . how do *you* feel?"

If I had a body, I would say "weak." But it's more like I feel very scattered. Not together. I guess you could say "faded."

"Oh my God, Vincent, that really scared me last night. I almost lost you."

But you didn't, he insisted. *I'm still here. And we'll figure this out and try again.*

I knew he was trying to comfort me, but all I could feel was fear. If we tried again and he dispersed . . . , well, that would be the end. Which wouldn't be fair. Because we were just beginning.

I knew we couldn't last forever; my own mortality put a limit on the time we had together. Eighty years—or whatever the life expectancy was now—had always seemed like a nice long time, before I met immortals. Not now.

There were so many things Vincent and I hadn't done. More than ever, I wanted to connect with him. To hold him in my arms, be held by him, and get as close as two people possibly can. To give him all of myself and take what he gave me. But that wasn't even an option now. And, judging from the way things went last night, might never be.

Vincent quickly changed the subject, as if he could see my black thoughts. *Your grandfather and Bran are already having breakfast in the café downstairs. They slipped a note under your door.*

"Not much use for a note when they could have just left a message with my immortal answering service," I said.

Very funny.

"Turn around. Or leave. Or whatever," I said, throwing the covers back and rearranging my T-shirt. "I have to get dressed."

I'm not looking, Vincent assured me.

"Yeah, right," I said, self-consciously ripping my T-shirt off and pulling some fresh clothes out of my suitcase. "How many times have you seen me naked?" It was something I'd always wondered but never had the chance to ask.

I'm a gentleman—Vincent said—*not a stalker. I always let you know when I'm in the room.*

"How many times?" I insisted.

I swear to you, Kate. I would never take advantage of my situation like that. Maybe a bit old-fashioned of me, but I don't want to see you until you invite me to.

I couldn't help but grin. Vincent was so chivalrous. I doubted that most boys my age would have passed up an opportunity to see a girl naked—if the girl was sure never to find out. Chivalry: one of the advantages of dating a teenager who had been around since the olden days.

There was a silence. *Not that it hasn't been tempting.*

"Vincent!"

Can I look now?

"Yes, I'm dressed," I said.

Do you know the phrase "Un rien te va"? Vincent asked me.

"No," I confessed.

It means you look good in anything. I think you look even sexier first thing in the morning than when you've spent time beautifying.

My smile took up my whole face. "I think that's about the nicest thing a boy has ever said to me."

Just saying what's true, Vincent said.

"You're lucky I can't jump on you right now," I commented.

I disagree, he said.

I had felt a yearning for Vincent's body before. But never when he wasn't there to touch. And now I wanted to touch him more than ever. To be touched by him. Maybe that was because it wasn't possible, but I had a feeling that it was more than that. We had waited to make love because I hadn't felt ready yet. But this brush with death—with Vincent's eternal disappearance—had made me realize that that kind of connection with Vincent was what I wanted. If I was given the chance again, this time I would choose yes.

Trying to clear my head of impossible dreams, I picked up my purse and the room key and began heading out the door when I suddenly remembered my phone. I hadn't even taken it out of my suitcase when I arrived because I wasn't sure I had international service. Plus . . . who was I going to call?

"Wait a second, Vincent. I'm just going to check that picture," I said, sitting back down on the bed. "I don't even know if it turned out, since the cave was so big and my flash was pretty weak."

I clicked on the camera icon, and there it was: the last picture I had taken. It had worked. Although dark around the edges where the flash hadn't reached, the middle of the painted wall was clearly visible . . . I expanded the image with my fingertips . . . *and* in focus!

"Oh my God, Vincent? Do you see?"

Yes! he said. *It's hard to read at this size, but if we loaded it onto your grandfather's laptop, I think it would be legible.*

"Let's go, then!" I said.

Papy and Bran were sitting behind empty cups of coffee, studying a piece of paper. Seeing me arrive, Papy poured a cup from the pitcher on the table and set it on the place setting next to him.

"No time for coffee!" I said. "The picture from the cave. It worked! We need your laptop, Papy."

My grandfather handed me his room key and I was back with the laptop in minutes. Plugging my phone into it, I waited a second until the image popped up, then selected the painting with the re-embodiment and cropped everything else out.

"The image is very similar to what was on Theodore's urn," Papy agreed.

"Can we see the words more closely?" Bran asked, leaning in toward the computer.

I zoomed in, and the inscription filled the screen. As Papy began translating it from the Latin, Bran scribbled it down on the piece of paper.

A man of clay is only mud
Until his brother spills his blood.
Mortal breath will animate
The dead's own ashes re-create.
Once these elements combine
The cooling flames will entwine
Spirit with inanimate form
For wandering soul to be reborn.

"The dead's own ashes? Does that mean Vincent's ashes?" I asked, a cold wave of alarm washing through me.

"That's what it seems to suggest," Papy said. He cleared his throat and looked uncomfortable. "Is there any way for us to get Vincent's ashes?"

"I seriously doubt it," I said. "It's been days since Vincent was burned." I felt sick. I couldn't believe we had come this far only to run into an unsolvable problem.

"Maybe Violette kept some of his ashes. For some sort of

use?" Bran suggested doubtfully.

No, I heard Vincent say. *To both suggestions. I was there afterward. And I saw one of Violette's people sweep my ashes into a bag and dump it in the trash. It was one of the more horrifying things I've experienced.*

I transmitted this to Papy and Bran, and they both fell silent.

"Ashes," I said, thinking it through. "That must be what the symbol of the box represents."

Papy nodded. "And do you remember the carved image on the side of Theodore's funereal urn? The man with the torch held a box in his other hand. It makes sense. Ashes were kept in stone boxes—such as the boxlike urn presenting that very re-embodiment scene."

I chose a muffin from the bread basket and munched in silence while the men studied the picture. "Bran, what was your poem again?" I asked.

He turned the paper over to show the verse already transcribed onto the page: That's what he and Papy had been studying when I arrived. I read it out loud:

Man of clay to man of flesh
Immortal blood and human breath
Traces do the spirit bind
Flames give body ghost and mind.

I studied it for a minute and said, "Where Papy's poem mentions 'ashes,' Bran's mentions 'traces.'"

"Well, I translated the original Breton word as 'traces,'

but it also means 'remains,'" Bran said, interest flickering in his eyes.

"Ashes. Remains," I said, my brain working at double speed. "The ceremony needs something of Vincent to bind his spirit to the clay figure. Otherwise his spirit is dispersed."

And then it hit me. "I have something!" I shouted, rising to my feet and tugging at the cord around my neck. From under my shirt, I pulled the pendants that I never took off: the *signum* and the memento mori that Jeanne had given me. The men looked at me quizzically as I held the locket toward them. "It holds a lock of Vincent's hair."

Adrenaline coursed through my veins, making me want to sprint back to the Met, dragging Papy and Bran with me, to try the ritual again. I couldn't believe I had been wearing the missing puzzle piece around my neck for the past few days.

"Where did you get that?" Papy asked.

"Jeanne gave it to me. She keeps locks of hair from all of the revenants in her care in these little boxes."

"How strange," remarked Bran.

"Her mother did it and her grandmother, too. It's, like, a family tradition."

Papy pounded the table in excitement. "Which, quite obviously, started because of something like this," he said. "Jeanne didn't even know what she was doing by keeping the custom going, and perhaps neither did her mother or her grandmother. But somewhere along the way, a revenant keeper began that tradition in case remains were needed for this re-embodiment procedure. Fascinating!"

"So we found it!" I said, touching Papy's hand and willing him to come with me. "We found the solution. We better get over to Mr. Gold's to let him know."

"I have his number," said Papy. He took out his cell phone and began dialing.

Within a half hour we were all standing around the burner again, Jules having taxied over from Brooklyn the moment Mr. Gold called. A big exhaust fan was sucking up the smoke from the torch. Now that it was daytime, Mr. Gold was concerned that passersby on the street above or in the museum, once it opened, would smell the fire. The whole mess from the water mixing with the clay the day before had been cleaned up during the night. I suspected that was Mr. Gold's work.

I sat down next to Jules, who was looking distinctly green.

"Are you okay?" I asked.

"I'm not that excited about cutting my arm open again," he said, using a tiny scissors to carefully clip the stitches he had been given the previous night. "Vincent's worth it—of course. But I'll try to slash the same place so I won't have two major wounds to manage until I'm dormant in a couple weeks."

"How was last night with your New York kindred?" I asked.

"Good," he said, eyeing me with an expression that said he didn't feel like talking about it.

"Did you know anyone at the house?" I persisted.

"Yes. There were a couple of guys who came to Europe for a convocation about ten years ago." He sighed and looked back down at his stitches, clipping another of the tiny black threads. "It was actually really nice. They had set out a whole welcome-to-America party for me, which kicked off as soon as the doctor sewed up my arm and lasted until I left this morning."

"I was out like a light," I admitted. "That's got to be one of the huge perks of zombiehood: no jet lag."

Jules smiled. A real Jules smile. It was nice to see.

"All right, we need to move now, people, before the first employees arrive," prompted Mr. Gold.

"Joy," remarked Jules drily. He stood and extended his good arm to help me up.

I took my place on the stepladder and peered over the rim of the thymiaterion at Clay Vincent. Jules stood on my right, and Bran directly across from us while Papy readied himself with the torch. A nervous hush settled over our small group. Bran had spread his hands out, and Jules was just lifting the knife when I heard Vincent say, *No!*

"What's happening, Vincent?" I asked. Everyone froze.

Violette's pulling me back. I feel myself being tugged away from here.

"Fight it, Vincent!" I urged.

"What is it?" Mr. Gold asked.

"Violette is trying to get him back!"

"Is he still here?" yelled Papy.

"Yes, but I can see him being pulled upward—though it seems he is resisting. We must proceed quickly," said Bran, and spread his hands above the clay form.

Opening the locket, I pulled the lock of hair from inside and stood there, wondering what I should do with it. Then, making a split-second decision, I pressed it securely into the side of the clay man's shoulder with my thumb.

I didn't see Jules slit his arm a second time. I couldn't watch. But there he was, bleeding profusely again on top of the golem, as I bent forward to blow lightly upon the face. I saw Bran reach up toward Vincent's invisible-to-me aura. He made a motion like he was grasping it and pulling it down toward the clay man.

Kate, Vincent's voice came. *I don't know if I can fight . . .*

His voice disappeared. "Is he still here?" I cried, looking wildly across the cup at Bran.

Bran peered upward and shook his head. "No. He's gone."

Papy lowered his torch. Mr. Gold stood next to the bucket of water, looking helpless. Jules lowered his bleeding arm to rest on the rim of the thymiaterion and raised his other hand to his forehead.

I couldn't believe it. We were so close to bringing Vincent back, and Violette chose this crucial moment to reclaim him. A hatred like I had never felt before set my entire body aflame. She would not do this. Violette would not take Vincent away from me. This would not be the end. Fury and shock from what had just happened forged together like iron in my chest. Fueled by something bigger and older than I—something primal—I commanded, "Come back, Vincent. *Now!*" My voice echoed through the cavernous room.

And then, so loudly it was like a megaphone positioned next to my ear, I heard, *I'm back. But not for long. Do it quickly!*

"He's returned! Go!" I shouted. Papy stepped forward and held the torch to the clay figure. As the air around it exploded into blue flames, Jules jumped back and I fell from the stepladder to the ground.

"Vincent! Don't let go!" I yelled, scrambling back to my feet. My heart pounding violently, I grabbed the side of the metal cup and heaved myself up to watch. The flames blazed higher, forming a giant fireball, which then erupted with a loud whooshing noise like a great wind, leaving tiny blue flames licking over and around the body like a paraffin burner.

Bran stretched his hands tentatively toward the fire. "Cold. The flames are cold, like the 'cooling flames' in the inscription you found, Kate," he said, looking up at me. "It must be working."

As he spoke, the edges of the clay man began shimmering, like air does in intense heat, and the lumpen form gradually became more manlike. "Something's happening!" I cried. I was paralyzed by shock and hope. "Please let it work. Come back, Vincent. You have to come back," I whispered, pleading.

Red clay became olive-toned skin, and the bald head became waves of raven black hair. The face that Jules had carefully sculpted became a real nose and mouth and eyes, closed as if in sleep. But it lay there, still and unmoving, until, focusing on the air just above, Bran yelled, "Come, bardia spirit, inhabit this body!" He made one final sweeping gesture, as if pulling the aura downward, and touched his fingers to the body's side.

The eyes flew open and Vincent took a great gulping gasp, as if trying to swallow all of the oxygen in the room.

"Vincent," I said, my heart in my throat.

His eyes flew to mine. He reached toward me, and I took his hand and pressed it to my cheek. His skin was burning hot, like with a fever. I kissed his fingers, and his skin smelled like fire and rain-soaked earth. Like the boy I thought I would never touch again.

TWENTY-SEVEN

IT WASN'T UNTIL JULES AND MR. GOLD HAD helped Vincent down out of the thymiaterion that we realized we had forgotten one essential element for resurrecting a spirit in a brand-new body. Clothes.

This was a first for me. The most I'd seen of Vincent up to now was post-workout with only a towel around his waist. But noticing Papy look pointedly at me, I turned around and crossed my arms, waiting until the others wrapped a silver packing blanket around him before throwing myself on him.

"Kate," he said, staggering a bit, and then pulled me tightly to him and kissed the top of my head. I held my mouth up for a real kiss and his lips were like a revelation. Like our very first kiss, only a hundred times better. Vincent smiled weakly at me, and then his eyes shut as his head fell forward and he collapsed in my arms. Now it was me staggering, as I found myself holding all of his weight.

Jules rushed over to help me lower Vincent's unconscious body to the ground. I held his head on my lap as Mr. Gold checked his blood pressure. "How stupid of us," he chided, "We should have planned to have food and water here for him. He's probably in a state similar to awakening from dormancy—terribly weak and in need of nourishment. Let's get him home quickly."

"We can't take him out on the street naked," Papy said.

Jules pulled off his T-shirt and I helped him shuffle it over Vincent's arms and head. Pulling on the sweater he had set aside while he was bloodletting, Jules said, "Give me your keys, Theodore. I saw some workmen's overalls in the restoration studio where we got the clay."

Within ten minutes we were making our way out of the giant hall, weaving up and down passageways until we reached a tiny service door where there was no guard to witness an unconscious Vincent being carried between Jules and Mr. Gold. We managed to get him across the street and into Gold's building with only a few curious looks from early-morning passersby.

Once inside the safety of the apartment, Jules and Mr. Gold laid Vincent down on one of the living room couches. "Oh. I'm bleeding again," Jules said simply, staring at the blood coursing from his arm. Our host was off in a flash, and returned with a linen bandage. He wrapped it tightly around Jules's wound before leading him to another couch and persuading him to lie down.

Vincent was breathing but still not conscious. Bran sat down next to him and studied his paper-white face. "His aura is very weak," he commented.

"Quickly. Get some sustenance for Vincent. Kitchen's that way," Mr. Gold barked from Jules's side. Papy and I bustled down the hallway and began combing through an impeccably clean all-white kitchen in search of food and drink. I grabbed a tray off the counter and loaded it with a bowl of almonds, a few bananas, some jars of French yogurt, and a loaf of whole-grain bread, and Papy added a carton of orange juice and bottle of water from the fridge.

When we got back to the living room, Mr. Gold was on the phone, telling his doctor to come immediately; that it was an emergency. I sat down on the couch next to Vincent and, propping his head forward with one hand, poured some water through his lips. As soon as the liquid hit the back of his throat, he sputtered and sat up, opening his eyes and looking around wildly. "Where am I?" he asked, and then seeing my face, he immediately relaxed.

And finally, now that the crisis was over, it was as if a switch had been thrown and the room erupted into a frenzy of joy. "We did it!" Mr. Gold exclaimed, breaking into a funny celebratory jig. "Thank the gods," Jules said with a look of overwhelmed relief, and flopped back onto the couch.

Papy started clapping, which encouraged Mr. Gold to add a little kick to the end of his dance, before running over to Bran and clasping him in his arms, patting his back firmly. "*You* did it!" Mr. Gold cheered.

Bran stood there looking shy, but his eyes shone in victory. "I can't believe it!" he said. "My first action as a *guérisseur* was a re-embodiment of a revenant spirit. If only my mother could have seen that."

"The whole line of *guérisseurs* before you would be proud of you, and those who come after you will speak of this event with awe," Mr. Gold said.

Bran managed to look fiercely proud while at the same time like all he wanted to do was go somewhere to hide.

I just sat there beaming with joy and relief, my love brimming over as I touched Vincent's face and stroked his hair. "How do you feel, *mon amour*?" I asked, stealing his nickname for me.

"My sight's really blurry," he said, blinking. "We're back in Gold's apartment, right?"

"Right," I confirmed. "We are back in Gold's apartment and I'm touching your hair and looking into your eyes and hearing your real voice and . . . I can barely believe it." As I leaned forward to brush my lips against his, my heart felt like it would burst.

"I'm no doctor, but I assume he needs more sustenance than kisses," teased Mr. Gold.

Blushing, I held the glass of water for Vincent as he drank deeply, then scooped some almonds from the bowl and poured them into his hand. Popping them into his mouth, he laid his head back on my lap as he chewed, never taking his eyes off me. He clutched my hand like he was afraid of being swept back into the ether. Using my free hand, I gave him a banana and more water, and some color started showing in his cheeks.

After waiting a little while, Bran asked, "Can you talk?" He and Papy had pulled chairs next to Vincent's couch and watched him with curious stares.

"Maybe you should wait," I suggested, but Vincent squeezed my hand. "It's okay," he said.

"So what exactly was happening when the ancient one tried to pull you back to her?" the *guérisseur* asked.

Vincent stared up at the ceiling, trying to remember. He exhaled deeply. "I was there above you, just kind of hovering," he said. "Then all of a sudden, I was pulled up and swept over the city toward the Atlantic Ocean. And then I heard Kate's voice," he said, shifting his gaze to me, "and suddenly I had the strength to slow the motion down, then stop it, and move in the opposite direction until I was back with you."

"Maybe the great physical distance between you and Violette reduced the power of the bond," suggested Papy.

"Maybe," Vincent said. "She couldn't have known I was halfway across the world when she called me back to her."

"In any case, you're back," said Mr. Gold, leaving Jules's side. "And we have achieved something that hasn't been done—to my knowledge—for centuries. A groundbreaking event in the freshly renewed relationship between the bardia and the flame-fingered," he said, directing this last statement to Bran.

"Thank you . . . all of you," Vincent said, looking around the room, "for your help and"—he looked at Jules—"for your devotion." I would have cuddled up to him then and there if my Papy hadn't been sitting right across from us. Also, I was afraid of breaking him. He was so weak.

"No need for thanks," Mr. Gold said. "We're all in this together. Now we must plan for your recovery and assess when you will be strong enough to return to Paris. But, first things first." He picked up the phone and dialed. "Gaspard," he said after a short wait, "yes, Theo here. I have very good news."

Do you want to talk? Mr. Gold mouthed to Vincent, who nodded and took the phone from him.

"Gaspard? Yes. It's me."

An exclamation of surprise was audible from the other end of the line.

"I hope you mention my extreme sacrifice," yelled Jules from across the room.

As Vincent began recounting the story to Gaspard, Papy took the opportunity to make his own call. "Emilie *chérie*, the reembodiment ceremony that I told you about last night? Well, we tried it again just now, and it worked." He smiled broadly at me. "Yes, we're all extremely relieved. Of course you can talk to her."

Papy handed me the phone, which I took with one hand because I wasn't letting go of Vincent for a second. "Darling, what wonderful news!" exclaimed my grandmother. "When will you come back?"

"A doctor's on his way now," I said as the doorbell rang. "We're just waiting to see how long it takes for Vincent to be strong enough to travel, and we'll be back."

As I spoke, a man with a doctor's bag walked in. I wasn't surprised to see he had the bardia-aura thing going on around him: I had doubted that Mr. Gold would ask a mortal doctor to tend to Vincent.

They shook hands and the doctor headed over to Jules first. "Didn't I sew this up yesterday?" he asked with consternation.

"Yeah, well, let's just call it 'repetitive stress disorder,'" Jules replied, then winced as the doctor gave him a shot near the wound site.

"I better go, Mamie," I said.

"I'll be sure to tell Georgia your news, and we can't wait to see you and Vincent back here at home. Give him a big hug for me."

I hung up the phone, bemused. A hug for Vincent—from Mamie? That gesture in itself reminded me of how much she loved me. I couldn't stop the smile that spread across my lips, and seeing it, Vincent smiled back at me. But since he hung up with Gaspard, there was something else in his eyes: worry. I was about to ask what Gaspard had told him when the doctor interrupted.

"So what do we have here?" he asked.

Vincent raised an eyebrow at Mr. Gold, who responded. "Vincent here was dormant following quite a violent death, and didn't receive sustenance for a good while after awakening."

Not completely a lie. I suspected that the re-embodiment story wasn't something Mr. Gold wanted to spread around. Who knew what ties Violette still held in the revenant world? It had only been a few days since her treason had been uncovered.

I got up so the doctor could sit and take Vincent's blood pressure. Bran moved across the room and began making notes in one of his leather-bound books. *Adding a groundbreaking event to the flame-finger records,* I thought.

Mr. Gold and Papy stood next to a window talking. "During the time we must wait for Vincent to recover, I would be delighted to return to the museum and show you the collection in more depth, now that we don't have more pressing issues on our minds," Mr. Gold was saying as I walked up to them.

"That would be an honor that I could not pass up, Theodore," Papy said.

"Please call me Theo. You too, Kate," he said, winking at me.

"Only if you call me Antoine," said Papy, and grasped Theo's arm warmly.

"You'll be fine," I heard the doctor saying to Vincent. "But I would strongly recommend bed rest for the next couple of days."

"Two days?" Theo said.

"Two or three," the doctor clarified, folding his instruments and putting them back into his bag.

Vincent waited until Theo closed the door behind the doctor before speaking. "That won't be possible," he said, trying to sit up.

"Why not?" Theo asked, looking surprised.

Vincent leaned his head back on the couch pillow and said in a weak voice, "Because back in Paris, war has begun."

TWENTY-EIGHT

"WHAT IS THAT SUPPOSED TO MEAN?" ASKED Theo, horrified. He strode over and sat at the foot of the couch.

"Gaspard just informed me that numa have been arriving in Paris in large numbers. Our kindred from all over France have reported them leaving their own cities and heading toward the capital. There hasn't been a sign of Violette, but no one questions the fact that she's orchestrating an offensive against the bardia." Vincent's voice was fading.

"All right. I will call Gaspard back to get more details on the happenings in Paris. But you would be of no help in this state. You have got to recover before we can even think about putting you on a plane." Vincent didn't even try to fight Theo. He didn't have the energy.

Jules had sat up upon hearing Vincent's announcement. Theo asked, "How about you? Are you feeling better?"

"Still weak, but nothing a good sandwich couldn't cure," he

said, although he looked a bit woozy to me. Theo picked up the phone and placed an order at a deli and then phoned Gaspard to inquire about the state of affairs in Paris. Fifteen minutes later, we were all digging into an assortment of enormous sandwiches, crispy dill pickles, and salty potato chips.

Vincent stopped after a couple of bites. "I'm too exhausted to eat," he told me. "Although I don't want to take my eyes off you for a second, I'm going to need to rest, *mon amour*," he said, his eyes blazing as he touched my cheek with his fingertips.

I twirled a lock of raven hair in my fingers and smiled at him, feeling like seventeen years of Christmases, birthdays, and wishing on falling stars had all been combined into this one moment. I was the luckiest girl on earth.

"Feel free to use my bedroom," offered Theo.

"Too exhausted to walk, too. Couch is fine," responded Vincent. And then he turned over on his side facing the couch back and closed his eyes. I covered him with a blanket Theo had brought in, then left my chair next to the couch to join the others at a table near the window.

"Tell me what happened with Violette," Theo was asking Jules, who launched into the story starting at the moment Violette and Arthur had moved into La Maison and continuing until I discovered that she had been betraying the bardia all along and was now the leader of the Paris numa.

"She told Kate, here," Jules said, nodding at me, "that her plan was to overthrow Jean-Baptiste and his kindred using the force of the numa and the stolen strength of the Champion, who she believed was Vincent. She had been priming him for destruction—had convinced him that following the Dark Way would help ease the pain of resisting death, when it was actually weakening him to the point that she could easily defeat him."

"And you are sure that Vincent is not the Champion?" Theo asked Bran.

"One hundred percent," Bran affirmed, holding up a dill pickle and studying it carefully before nibbling off one end. He grimaced and placed it as far away from him as possible on his plate.

"How can you be so sure?" Papy asked, but then looked abashed at having barged in on a supernatural discussion.

Theo shook his head. "You now bear our *signum*, Antoine. You participated in the most mystical revenant ceremony I've ever witnessed. And your daughter is the beloved of a bardia. You have a right to ask questions."

"Thank you," said Papy.

"It's because of his aura," Bran answered. "He has the revenant aura, which the flame-fingers describe as 'an aura like a forest fire.' But our prophecy says that the Victor's aura 'blazes like a star on fire.' Vincent's aura is no different from that of Jules. Or your own," he said, nodding to Theo.

"So how do we know that the Victor is even here?" Theo asked.

"He is not here. He is yet to come," Bran said, pushing his plate away with a curt gesture.

"But weren't you going to let Jean-Baptiste parade all of Paris's bardia in front of you to check?" I asked. "Why would you do that if you were sure the Victor wasn't yet here?"

Bran shrugged. "That was *his* suggestion, not mine. And he seemed very determined."

"But *how* do you know the Victor is coming?" Theo insisted.

"Because I'm the VictorSeer. I wouldn't have become so if there wouldn't soon be a *victor* to *see*," Bran replied testily.

A silence settled on the room as everyone stared at Bran. He fidgeted uncomfortably.

"How do you know you're the VictorSeer?" Jules asked, leaning forward on his elbows and clasping his hands together.

"I felt it happen when I touched your leader's hand. At that point, I received the gift. I know I have it just as clearly as my mother knew she didn't have it," he said simply, like it was the most obvious thing in the world.

"So that's how *you* know the Champion is coming during your lifetime," I said. "But why was Violette so sure he was coming soon?"

"The revenants' prophecy is the same as that of the flame-fingers," Bran responded. "It's the revenant calendar's Third Age, and has been since the Industrial Revolution. So she's obviously been waiting since then. She must have thought she saw the Champion's characteristics displayed by Vincent."

"My ears are burning," called Vincent from across the room. "As is my throat. Could I have some more water, please?" I leapt up and pulled the coffee table with the refreshments on it closer to Vincent's couch so it was within reaching distance.

The men stood and Theo began clearing the table. "We should

really leave Vincent to rest in peace so that he will heal as quickly as possible," he said.

"I want to stay with him," I insisted.

"Of course, my dear," reassured Theo. "But would the rest of you like to join me for a more expansive tour of the revenant collection at the museum?"

Papy and Bran quickly agreed, but Jules walked back to his couch and flopped down on it. "Now that my bloodletting responsibilities are over, I think I'll stay here too," he said, closing his eyes.

Once the other men were gone, I sat watching Vincent for a while. His breathing was shallow, and although I knew he wasn't sleeping—couldn't sleep . . . until his next dormancy—it seemed he wasn't quite here either. I left him to rest and went to dig through Theo's bookcase, settling for a coffee table book about Edith Wharton's New York. I wasn't surprised in the least when I saw mention of a Theodore Gold being one of Wharton's circle, and smiled when I spotted him among a crowd of people at a society ball, wearing tails and a top hat.

I kept checking on Vincent, but after a couple of hours, when he hadn't budged, I put my book aside and went to look out the windows. I heard movement from the other side of the room and turned to see Jules watching me from his couch.

"What?" I asked, suddenly feeling self-conscious.

"Oh, nothing," he responded. "Just that you come all the way back home and spend your whole time here cooped up in an apartment. Kind of depressing, isn't it?"

"Well, I did see a secret collection of supernatural-themed art hidden in the basement of the Met. That's not too bad," I retorted with a mock frown.

"Wanna take a walk?" Jules said, pushing himself up off the couch and walking toward me. "It's my first time in New York, and if I don't pass out from blood loss, I'd like to see a little bit. Would you do me the honor of being my tour guide?"

"But I shouldn't leave . . . ," I began.

He took my hand and pulled me toward the door. "Vincent will heal faster without you hovering around worrying over him. Right, Vince?" Jules called as he grabbed our coats.

Vincent murmured, "Show Jules New York, Kate, or I'll never hear the end of it," and pulled the blanket higher around his head.

"See?" Jules said to me, and opened the door to the hallway. "Rest up, man," he called back to Vincent, his voice now completely serious. "We just got you back. Now we need you to get stronger."

TWENTY-NINE

"WE'RE ONLY LEAVING VINCENT FOR A COUPLE OF hours, right?" I asked as we got onto the elevator, suddenly afraid that he might disappear while we were gone.

"Is that long enough to take me up the Empire State Building?" Jules asked.

I studied his face to see if he was joking. "You really want to go to the Empire State Building?" I asked. "The most touristy thing to do in New York City?"

He nodded sheepishly. "I know. But how can I miss it? I saw the original *King Kong* in 1933 and have been wanting to go ever since."

"So your interest is purely from a cinematic history point of view," I teased him.

The elevator doors opened and Jules held his hand out gallantly to allow me to step off first. "There's that," he said, once again confident, "as well as the fact that I've always dreamed of standing at the top of the Empire State Building with a beautiful girl."

By the time Jules and I got back to Theo's apartment everyone had assembled for dinner. Vincent had propped some cushions behind him and was now sitting up. "For you!" I said, holding up the enormous bag of clothes and shoes we had bought at Macy's after we were done playing tourists.

"A special present for a special recovering dead guy," Jules jibed, visibly relieved to see that his friend looked stronger after just a few hours. "We thought you might want to change out of those overalls at some point, and I'd like my T-shirt back."

"Just as soon as I take a shower," Vincent said. "I keep picking little bits of clay out of my hair. No joke." He ran his fingers through his black locks and grimaced.

He sounded like old Vincent again, not feeble Vincent who looked close to death this morning. "Have you eaten?" I asked, sitting next to him on the couch.

"Don't care about food. Come here," he said, and taking my face in his hands firmly kissed my forehead and then my lips, scanning the room as he did so to see if Papy was looking. He was. So the kiss was short and sweet. "More later," he whispered.

"You should stay here tonight, Vincent," said Theo, who was spreading an impressive array of take-out menus in front of Papy and Bran. "Even though you're feeling stronger, I don't think you should move to the hotel until tomorrow. And I've scheduled your plane to leave the following morning."

"We're here another day and a half?" Vincent asked, surprised. "I really think Jean-Baptiste will need Jules and me before then."

"Actually," Theo said sternly, crossing his arms, "this morning on the phone, Gaspard told me that Jean-Baptiste won't allow you to return before then. He says he needs you to be strong, not to come back in an enfeebled state. He asked me to personally guarantee your health, so I'm afraid I have to put my foot down."

Bran held up a few menus and announced, "I am intrigued by the menus for"—he peered more closely at them—"Fat Sal's and Burritoville. And what is this food called . . . bagels?"

Papy, Bran, and I returned to our hotel after dinner, crashing before nine p.m. We were all exhausted from the day's events. And, in my case at least, jet lag was rearing its ugly head.

When we arrived at the apartment the next morning, Theo and Vincent were waiting for us. "What took you so long?" Vincent murmured as he nuzzled my neck. "You could have had breakfast here."

"I didn't actually eat," I said, laughing and then shivering as he brushed my ear with his lips. "Papy and Bran did, but I used the extra half hour to sleep in. I would have come earlier if I knew you were up."

He drew back and smiled at me. "I've been up all night."

"I didn't mean awake," I said, rolling my eyes. "I mean up and *about*. You look totally normal again. How are you feeling?"

"I feel great. Seriously. I would have been able to go back to Paris today. But Theo insists I stick around another twenty-four hours just in case. And there's also the fact that I'd love to see a bit of your hometown while we're here." He brushed my hair back behind my shoulder. "You look beautiful," he said.

"Must be the New York air," I responded, feeling my cheeks redden.

"Then, pollution suits you well, *ma chérie*," he replied.

"Jules offered to walk the city with our kindred today. And Antoine, Bran, and I are off to the museum again," Theo announced. Turning to Vincent, he asked, "Are you sure you want to go out today? I can give you my extra set of keys if you need to come back to rest."

"Thanks, but I might as well go ahead and check into the hotel," said Vincent, hoisting the Macy's bag and grabbing my hand as we all walked out into the hallway.

"Well, you have my number if you need to reach me," Theo said, locking the door behind him.

Papy and Bran looked downright gleeful about spending another day in the museum, and I could tell from their conversation that Theo was enjoying the unprecedented opportunity to show the collection to "outsiders."

As we stepped out the door, Theo said, "We'll meet for dinner at the end of the day. See the restaurant on that corner?" He pointed to an Italian restaurant one block down. "How about eight p.m. there? But I want you to go back to the hotel and rest at some point during the day," he ordered Vincent.

Vincent took my hand and led me in the opposite direction from the men. "First stop—hotel," he said. He was bursting with energy, bouncing on his toes and playing with my hair as we walked.

"So you don't want to stay out in Brooklyn with Jules and your kindred?" I asked slyly.

"And be a whole borough away from you?" he said, scrunching his eyebrows with a mock-horrified expression. "Are you trying to kill me all over again?"

Once at the hotel, Vincent booked a room and then held up the bag of clothes. "I'll just drop these off and we'll go somewhere to eat. I feel like an enormous home-cooked meal, like you see in all of the American movies."

I laughed. "It's called comfort food. And I know just the place."

THIRTY

A HALF HOUR LATER AND ABOUT SEVENTY BLOCKS south, we sat in one of my favorite old haunts, the Great Jones Café. Vincent was finishing off a plate of Yankee meatloaf smothered in gravy and I had a bowl of Louisiana jambalaya that was spicy enough to make my nose run. Which helped cover up a crying jag that suddenly overtook me, until I choked trying to swallow my food.

Alerted to my tears, Vincent set down his fork and took my hand. "Kate. It's over. I'm here now. Violette can't reach me anymore."

"I know," I said. "But until the second you started breathing, I really didn't know if I'd see you again. I had hoped, but I didn't believe . . . if you know what I mean."

Vincent's lips curled into a smile. "I do know. But you had enough hope for both of us. Now stop thinking and eat your mush—or whatever that is."

I laughed, and—like that—I had let it go. I was able to push the horrific past and unsure future aside and focus wholeheartedly on enjoying the present. With my living, breathing boyfriend.

"This is *so good*," Vincent said, taking a bit of jalapeño cornbread. "I didn't know if I'd ever eat again, and I can tell you, taste buds are something you really miss when you don't have them."

I laughed. "So you missed food. What else did you miss?"

He raised one eyebrow and giving me a sexy grin, put his fork down on his plate. "I missed this," he said, running his fingertips up and down my arm, making me shudder.

"Yeah, I kind of missed that too," I said, trying to look nonchalant as I took a sip of iced tea.

"Just kind of?" Vincent teased.

"Okay, a lot," I admitted with a sly smile.

"Let's get off the topic of me, and my former inability to satisfy your lust." My mouth dropped open and he laughed. "No, really. What's it like to be back in your hometown?"

"Well," I said, considering the question. I put my glass down and crossed my arms, glancing around the room and absorbing my surroundings. "It's actually incredibly surreal. I've been away for a year and a half, but it seems like a lifetime. I don't feel like the same person anymore. Life in Paris is my reality now. It feels like life in New York was a dream. I feel . . . disconnected."

Vincent placed his hand upward on the table. I unwrapped my arms from my torso and placed my hand in his. He rubbed my palm with his fingertips. "What can you do to reconnect?" he asked softly.

"I had been thinking about that," I confessed. "There was

something I had considered doing. But you don't have to come with me if you don't want to."

I told him it what it was, and his eyes widened. He leaned back in his chair and shook his head in wonder. "And it only took my resurrection to convince you to do this."

"I've actually been thinking of it for a while," I said. And getting out my phone, I made the call I had imagined making for months.

An hour later, we were standing on the front stoop of a Brooklyn brownstone. The door flew open, and my friend Kimberly stood there motionless with a wild look in her eyes before screaming and throwing herself on me. "Kate!" she squealed. "I never thought I'd see you again!" We stood there squeezing the life out of each other for a good minute before she let go and stepped back.

Wiping tears from her eyes, she glanced up at Vincent. "Well, well. Who do we have here?" she asked.

"I'm Vincent," he said, reaching out to shake Kimberly's hand.

"Uh-uh. I don't think so," she said, planting her hands on her hips and peering at him skeptically. "Are you the reason Kate has been ignoring her friends ever since she got to France?"

"No, he's the reason I had the guts to reconnect with you after all this time," I answered for him.

"Well then," she said, breaking into a smile. "You get more than a handshake!" She flung her arms around him and, while clasping him in a death hug, peeked around his shoulder and mouthed, *Oh my God, he's gorgeous!*

"I like your friends," Vincent said, taking my hand as we walked down a side street lined with stately trees and brownstone homes—each nestled behind its own tiny yard.

But Vincent wasn't looking at our surroundings. He was studying me with an unfamiliar glint in his eye.

"What?" I asked.

"Oh, I'm reveling in the fact that I just witnessed a side of you I hadn't previously seen: Historical Kate. What you were like before I met you."

I smiled, watching our feet tread the same pavement I had walked along for . . . ever since I began to walk. "My friends liked you too," I responded. "But that was pretty obvious."

"I'm not sure they'd feel the same if they knew what I am," he replied.

"Trust me, it wouldn't make a difference to them," I said, looking up to gauge his expression.

Vincent raised a skeptical eyebrow.

"I mean, once they got over their shock and horror, of course," I said with faux-seriousness.

We had spent the afternoon going from one friend's house to the next, until we had amassed a posse of six and then adjourned to a local café—our favorite old hangout. I didn't even have to worry about Vincent feeling left out. He was so polite and interested in everyone that my friends fell all over themselves to include him, adopting him immediately.

It felt like I had never left. And at the same time, everything had changed. My life was in France now, with my grandparents. And Vincent.

"Do you think you'll come back?" Kimberly had asked. And for the first time, I actually tried to imagine it. I realized with sadness that, besides my friends, I had nothing else to come back for.

When Vincent and I finally left, everyone promised to come visit—if their parents let them—during the summer. But as soon as my friends were gone, my mind switched from their world—a world of homework and proms and college applications—back to my own. One where my safety was at risk because of an evil undead medieval teenager. For the hundredth time, I had the weirded-out feeling that I was living in a novel. In a scary, suspenseful story that I couldn't guess the end of for the life of me.

"It's here," I said, as we stopped in front of a pretty brownstone, three blocks from where we had left my friends. I stood before the gate and stared at my home. The house I had grown up in.

After my parents' death, my grandparents hadn't wanted to sell our childhood home, so they were renting it until Georgia and I decided what to do with it. But the previous renters had moved out the month before, and it was empty, the windows dark.

I had wanted to come. Now that I was here, I wasn't sure I wanted to face the material evidence that my family—as it had been—was no more.

"If you don't want to go in, you don't have to," Vincent said softly, sensing my hesitation.

Encouraged by his calm, strong voice, I opened the latch on the cast-iron gate and pulled him into the yard with me. But instead of climbing the steps to the front door, I headed to a teak bench against the garden wall. I sat down and pulled my knees close to my chest, hugging them to me.

Leaning back, I closed my eyes and was transported to the yard of my childhood. The same smell of wet stone and wood. The background noise of cars driving on the busy avenues at either end of my street. I was ten again and completely engrossed in *Anne of Green Gables*, curled up on my bench: my very own time-and-place machine.

"*Mon ange*, scoot up just a bit," I heard, and I opened my eyes to see Vincent standing above me. I wiggled forward, and he wedged himself into the bench behind me, easing me back to lean against him and wrapping his arms around me. And sitting there cocooned in Vincent's body, I felt safe enough to revisit my memories and say one last good-bye to my parents.

THIRTY-ONE

ON THE WAY BACK TO THE HOTEL, VINCENT AND I stopped at a bookstore and spent the next half hour loading up on English-language books. It was the perfect break between the emotion of visiting my home and the formality of dinner with the rest of our group.

When we arrived at the restaurant, Theo was sitting alone at a table in the corner. I sat down across from him. "So where is everyone?" I asked, as Vincent took the chair between us.

"Your grandfather and Monsieur Tândorn send their excuses—they were too tired to join us. And Jules decided to skip dinner and stay with our kindred," explained Theo. "He'll meet you tomorrow at the airport."

As soon as our food was in front of us and the server had left, Theo got down to business.

"To be completely honest, Vincent, I asked the others not to come tonight. I need to talk to you privately, and I assumed you would wish Kate to be with you."

Vincent seemed curious but not alarmed, though I had warning bells clanging all over the place in my mind. What could Theo possibly need to say to Vincent that the others couldn't hear? Judging from the secrecy and his troubled expression, it wasn't a mere "congratulations on being alive."

Theo picked up his napkin and wrung it anxiously for a moment before smoothing it on his lap. He avoided our eyes as sweat beaded on his brow. Finally he spoke. "I promised Jean-Baptiste I wouldn't talk to you about this, but I cannot send my French kindred into a war with the numa without getting this off my chest."

He took a deep breath and began. "I told you I came to Paris after World War Two when you and the numa were battling."

"Yes," said Vincent. "You were the only one of your American group to survive."

"That is correct," affirmed Theodore. "And the numa-bardia conflict ended just before I left." He leaned forward, clutching his hands together and resting his elbows on the table. "What do you know about how that was concluded, Vincent?"

"Well, we inflicted greater damage on the numa than they did us. They called for a ceasefire. Jean-Baptiste passed an order that we were not to purposefully hunt the numa down. It would be seen as aggravating the situation, which could result in another war flaring up. He recently revoked that order after Lucien ended the peace treaty by breaking into our residence and trying to destroy me."

Theodore eyed him for a moment, as if deciding whether Vincent was telling the whole truth, and then nodded. "That is the tip of the iceberg. What actually happened is not quite that cut-and-dry, unfortunately. It was Jean-Baptiste who was in fear for your numbers, not the other way around. When he felt that your kindred were at risk of being decimated, he went to Lucien to broker a peace agreement—letting the numa name their terms."

Vincent raised an eyebrow and looked skeptical. "JB . . . made a deal with Lucien?"

Theodore nodded. "Jean-Baptiste didn't want any of you to know what he was doing, so he took me—an outsider—to act as his second. To this day, none of your kindred, not even Gaspard, are aware of what happened during that meeting."

A chill crept up my spine, as my thoughts traveled from, *A peace agreement with the numa. What's wrong with that?* to *Negotiations with the enemy kept secret from one's kindred. Not so good.* It was hard to believe that Jean-Baptiste would meet with Lucien and hide it from his kindred. He must have been truly desperate to save them from destruction. But still . . .

"I didn't know where Jean-Baptiste was taking me until we got there," Theo continued. "He swore me to secrecy afterward, saying that the survival of France's revenants depended on my silence. I left France that same day and haven't been back to Paris since. When Jean-Baptiste phoned me earlier this week, I hadn't spoken to him for decades."

Vincent sat back, looking like he had been slapped. "I'm sorry, Gold. I just can't believe that."

"It must somehow ring true to you, because you're not angry. Or defensive," Theodore stated, studying Vincent's face. "I think you do believe it. You just don't want to."

Vincent lowered his head to his hands. "What were the terms of the agreement?" he asked, without looking up.

"Both sides agreed that their permanent places of residence would not be attacked."

Vincent looked up and eyed Theodore doubtfully. "But the numa don't keep permanent places of residence."

"Yes, they do. That was the other part of the agreement. As the party declaring defeat, Jean-Baptiste surrendered several of his properties to Lucien. The house in Neuilly. Several apartments in central Paris. An entire apartment building in the République neighborhood."

No. It couldn't be true. Jean-Baptiste giving his properties to the numa. Not only letting them live in his homes, but . . . hiding them? I could understand making concessions in order to save his clan, but giving shelter to the enemy and not informing his own people? That went way beyond mere negotiations. That felt more like treason.

Vincent looked as upset as I was. He took his napkin off his lap and crushed it between his hands. "That's not true," he said, shaking his head in denial. "He rents those out."

Theodore smiled sadly at Vincent. "Who takes care of those rentals? Does he ever send any of you to check on the places?"

"No, he manages those properties himself," replied Vincent hesitantly.

"And when Jean-Baptiste retracted his ban on wantonly

killing the numa, did he mention that that was where they might be found?"

"No," stated Vincent, hanging his head in defeat. "Those would be the last places we would look."

"Quite understandably, he hasn't wanted you to know about his deal. It's his pride on the line. He's gotten too far into this mess and can't get out without bringing shame on himself. And on the phone the other day, he said that he expected me not to bring up 'old business.' Which I haven't until now. But I can't in good faith let you return to Paris oblivious of what was done.

"It's not the danger of the numa having secret safe houses that bothers me. It's the fact that you will be following a leader who has double dealt behind his own people's backs. Who has not laid all of his cards on the table for his own people to see—despite the danger it could bring to them." Theo picked up his water glass, took a drink, and then set it firmly on the table.

"A leader who makes secret deals with the enemy should not be in the position of making decisions for his kindred at this crucial moment. If Violette is determined to overthrow the Paris revenants—with the Champion's power or without—she is a great danger. And you will need someone you can all trust with your lives to lead you in this fight."

He leaned forward until Vincent met his eyes. "I know that Jean-Baptiste is like a father to you," he said. "But I charge you, Vincent Delacroix, with relaying this information to your kindred. Otherwise, when the time comes and the battle begins, their blood will be on your hands."

THIRTY-TWO

WE SAID OUR GOOD-BYES TO THEODORE, PROMISING to update him on events in Paris, and then walked back to the hotel in silence. Vincent was deeply disturbed by what Theo had told him, and I could tell he was going over every detail of the conversation. "Are you okay?" I asked as we entered the hotel lobby.

Vincent squeezed me to him and kissed the top of my head distractedly. "Yes. I mean, no. It's just hard to imagine Jean-Baptiste hiding something like this from us for so many years. It makes me feel like I never really knew him."

"He was just trying to protect you all," I said, playing devil's advocate, but not really feeling it.

"I know. But the way he did it, and the fact that he's been offering the enemy his protection without informing us . . . I just don't understand."

"I'm sorry," I said, taking both of his hands in mine, and searched his face until he met my eyes.

"No, *I'm* sorry," Vincent said. "You don't need to worry about this. And I can't do anything about it until I get back to Paris. But you need to sleep if we are leaving first thing in the morning." Vincent leaned down and lightly brushed his lips against mine, awakening a million tiny butterflies inside me. "I'll walk you to your room."

I smelled them before I turned on the light. Lilacs. A huge spray of white lilacs in a vase on my bedside table. Their beauty and perfume transformed my plain hotel room into a scene from a Pre-Raphaelite painting. I looked up at Vincent. A mischievous smile stretched across his lips.

"How did you do this?" I exclaimed. "I've been with you all day."

"I passed a note and some money to the front desk earlier," he confessed, looking exceedingly proud of himself for pulling off the subterfuge. "You've told me you love the scent of lilacs. I thought it might bring you sweet dreams tonight, since I won't be able to hover around whispering Pablo Neruda poems to your subconscious mind."

I took a deep whiff of their clean floral fragrance. Vincent leaned on the door frame, beaming with pleasure. "Do you want to come in?" I asked.

He shook his head and gave me a crooked smile. "I didn't rent a room for nothing. I haven't forgotten the south of France and your reasonable but maddening request to wait. And in the light of that: You. Me. Beds. Bad idea. I'll just take these"—he scooped up a couple of paperbacks from the bag—"and be on my way. Anything to keep my mind off the whole Jean-Baptiste saga until

I get back to Paris and can actually do something about it."

"What *will* you do?" I asked, not really caring anymore about Jean-Baptiste. All I could think about was Vincent standing there with his tousled hair and broad shoulders half in and half out my hotel room. My body was thrumming with a mixture of resolve not to tempt him too far and desire to throw myself upon him before he could get away.

"I haven't decided yet," he responded, rubbing the back of his neck worriedly. Obviously Vincent's thoughts weren't on the same level as mine. Or else he wouldn't even be able to speak right now, much less strategize. I knew the decision I had made in the south of France wasn't going to hold much longer.

"Well, good night." I threw my arms around his neck and gave him a long, slow kiss. In it was all of the day's emotion, both the miracles and the mundane.

I almost lost Vincent, and now I had him back. And not only him, but my life. My former life from before I pushed it away. And now my past and my present were joined and I was beginning to feel complete.

Vincent seemed to understand the meaning behind the kiss. It was in his smile as he touched my face and then my hair with his fingertips. It seemed to cost him as much effort as it did me to pull apart, because after one last hasty kiss he practically sprinted out of the room, pulling the door shut behind him.

I changed into an oversize T-shirt and sat on my bed, turning things over in my mind: the way I had almost lost him. And could again. The fragile nature of human life: One minute we're here and the next we're gone, like my parents. And the desire to be closer to Vincent. To love him with more than my heart and mind.

My feelings from that morning returned full force. My resolution to actually *do* something if I was able to get Vincent back. I had told myself I was ready. That it was time. Now that it was possible, did I still feel the same? I realized that, yes, I knew what I wanted. This time I was a hundred percent sure.

I grabbed the vase of lilacs and my room key, and hoped no one would see me sprinting with the flowers down the hallway in my T-shirt and undies.

Up one flight of stairs and I was there, standing nervously in front of Vincent's door. I knocked. He opened, a bemused expression on his face. "To what do I owe this surprise visit?" He looked at the lilacs and then back to me, confused. "You decided you didn't like the flowers?"

I pushed past him into the room and placed the flowers on a low table. "I don't want to be apart from you anymore," I said.

Vincent smiled sadly and closed the door behind him. "I know exactly what you mean," he responded. "Five days as a wandering soul, unable to touch you and thinking it was permanent . . . I feel like never letting you out of my sight again." He threw himself down on the bed and patted the spot next to him. "You can stay here tonight."

"No, I mean I don't want to be apart from you. I want to be with you. Really with you." I had to force myself to say the words. My voice shook because I was afraid he was going to say no.

That this wasn't the time. That we should wait until things had calmed down.

But I had made up my mind. We were going back to Paris the next day, and Vincent and his kind would be facing a danger that could possibly destroy him. Again.

He propped himself up on his elbows and sat there for the longest time, watching me with an expression that I couldn't read. "If you're still too weak, we can be careful," I offered, wondering if that's why he was hesitating.

Grinning, he shook his head, and pushing himself up from the bed, he walked to me. With only inches separating us, he looked into my eyes. It felt like he was reaching deep inside my mind, furthering the connection between us. Heart. Mind. And then body. It was the next step and it was now.

Vincent's lips curved up slightly. He leaned down just as I reached up, and we met in between, our lips touching first and then the rest of us, pressing deliciously against each other, pulling the other as close as possible, needing, giving, weaving a tapestry of our bodies. Of our selves.

THIRTY-THREE

I AWOKE TO THE SENSATION OF VINCENT'S LIPS on my forehead, and opened my eyes to see his face above mine. "*Bonjour, ma belle,*" he said in his low sexy voice.

I squinted around, not knowing where I was for a moment, and then the hotel room came into focus around me. *Oh my God.* I was in Vincent's bed. And it was morning. I had spent the night in Vincent's bed. And last night we had . . .

My skin lit with a fiery flush, and an unstoppable smile possessed my face. I leaned forward and, letting the covers drop, threw my arms around Vincent's neck and squeezed him against me.

He laughed and pulled back so he could look me in the eyes. "Was that hug for last night?"

"I love you," I answered.

He pulled me back to him and whispered, "And I adore you, Kate Beaumont Mercier. With a love I never thought I could feel.

With all my soul and every inch of my body. Which, by the way, is now marked by you forever."

"What do you mean?" I asked. He turned to show me a bluish tattoolike mark on his shoulder. "What is that?" I touched it, mesmerized.

"Isn't this where you pressed the lock of my hair into my clay doppelgänger?" he asked.

I looked more closely. The mark had a circular pattern to it and was the size of . . . "It's my thumbprint!" I exclaimed, holding my thumb next to the mark.

Vincent grinned. "That's what I thought. Very cheeky of you; you not only brought me to life, but you marked me permanently as yours."

I grabbed him and pulled him down to the mattress. Perching above me, he leaned forward to place an extra soft kiss on my neck just beneath my ear. I shivered and said, "You *are* mine."

"I've got no argument with that," he conceded, smoothing my hair back from my face with his thumb. "But I do have the very unfortunate news that in exactly twenty minutes we are meeting your grandfather in the lobby."

"Hmm, grandfather," I said. My brain suddenly left the deliciousness of being in bed with Vincent and was gripped by more unpleasant things. Like how I was going to pack and dress in under a half hour.

With lots of running and leaping about, I somehow made it, and in twenty minutes we were climbing into the back of Theodore's limo. Bran did a repeat performance of the gaping-out-the-window routine that he did on the way in. Papy busied himself with transferring all of the photos he had taken of Theodore's collection the previous day from his camera to his laptop. I laid my head on Vincent's shoulder and dozed off, waking as we pulled up to the airport's private plane terminal.

As we assembled on the sidewalk, I saw Jules step out of the passenger side of a car parked in the drop-off lane in front of us. He headed straight for Vincent with an expression like his best friend was the last person in the world he wanted to see. "Vince, man. We have to talk," he said, and the two of them walked a short distance away.

Papy and Bran made their way into the terminal with the luggage, but I didn't follow them. I had a terrible feeling in the pit of my stomach as I watched Jules explain something and Vincent stumble back a step, as if Jules had just stabbed him in the gut. Jules kept talking, folding his arms tightly across his chest, as if he too were in pain.

I looked over at the car that had brought Jules. The bardia driver was just sitting there with the engine idling: What was he waiting for?

I walked in their direction. Something was very wrong.

"You're being an idiot!" Vincent suddenly yelled, and thrusting his hands into his pockets, he stalked off, slamming the revolving door to the terminal so hard with his shoulder that it ground to a halt before starting back up with a metallic screech. Jules just stood where he was, watching me approach with a pained expression.

"What's going on?" I asked.

"I'm not going back," he said simply.

"You're staying here in New York?"

He nodded.

"But why?"

Jules massaged his temples. "Something's come between me and Vincent," he said.

I stared at him, confused. "Well, I'm sure you can work it out."

"No, actually we can't work it out, Kate," he responded, gritting his teeth. "There is no possible way of working it out. The only way to salvage this is for me to walk away and leave you two to . . ."

"Leave *us*?" I asked, incredulous. "What does this have to do with me?"

He lowered his head, breathing shallow breaths. Holding himself together. When he looked up, pain was written across his face as clearly as if it were spelled out in giant letters.

"Do you really have to ask me that, Kate? Can't you tell?"

"No," I said, and then suddenly understood. My mouth dropped open, and I shook my head in denial. Jules was my friend. He couldn't be in love with me. He had a dozen beautiful girls at his beck and call. Girls who weren't attached . . . to his best friend. "You can't . . . you can't be leaving your kindred for . . . *me*."

He sighed and looked toward the gray winter sky, as if praying for something to swoop down and carry him far away. When he looked back at me, his eyes were glassy. He reached forward to take my hand.

"Kate. I'll say it like this. Vincent is my best friend. There's not a person in this world I'm closer to. But for the past year, I have betrayed him in my heart every single day because I want for myself what he loves the very most."

I squeezed his hand tightly to fight the numbness paralyzing me. My eyes stung, but no tears came. "I don't know what to say, Jules. I . . . I don't . . ."

"I know you don't feel the same, Kate. That you never have. Never will. And I would rather not live with that reality being pushed into my face on a continual basis. Because, believe it or not, though I die for people on a regular basis, I'm not a masochist."

His sad smile hit me like a fist. "Oh, Jules," I said, and threw my arms around his neck.

"There's nothing else to say," he murmured, pressing his face into my hair. And then he let go, walked to the waiting car, and drove away without looking back.

"Are you okay?" I asked.

We were halfway across the Atlantic Ocean and Vincent hadn't said a word. He wrapped his arm around my shoulders, pulled me to him, and kissed the crown of my head.

Leaning my head against his shoulder, I said, "I'm really sorry about Jules."

Vincent sighed. "Half of me hates him for falling in love with you. And the other half thinks, 'How could he help it?'"

He pushed my hair back from my face. "What I can't believe, though, is that I honestly didn't see it coming. We could have talked it out before it got to this. But I thought that Jules was flirting with you just like he does with any other pretty girl."

His expression changed from frustration to worry. "You don't feel the same for him, do you?" he asked, his voice dropping an octave.

I shook my head. "No. I mean, I feel close to him. And to be honest, the attention was flattering. But, as you said, I thought he was like that with everyone. For me, he's the boy I love's best friend. And a good friend of my own even apart from that. But I don't have room in my heart for two."

Vincent looked relieved.

"Are you mad at him for leaving you at such a bad time?" I asked.

"No. One revenant won't make a difference to the outcome of a battle. And he swore that if ever I needed him he'd be on the first plane to Paris."

"You didn't tell him about JB, did you?"

"No," Vincent admitted, meeting my eyes. "And I'm not going to. If Jules needs distance, it wouldn't be fair to tell him something that would pretty much oblige him to come back."

He took my hand and raised it to his lips, and then pressing it to his chest, he laid his head back against the seat and closed his eyes.

"I'm sorry you lost your best friend," I said. "I hope he'll get over it and come back."

In the softest of voices, Vincent said, "So do I."

THIRTY-FOUR

IT WAS TEN P.M. WHEN WE ARRIVED IN PARIS. Ambrose and Charlotte were there to pick us up. "I thought I'd never see you again!" squealed Charlotte as she threw herself on Vincent.

"Looks like you're not rid of me yet." He squeezed her tightly.

"Man, it's good to have you back," said Ambrose, clapping him on the shoulder before turning to greet Papy and Bran. He scanned the doors behind us. "Where's Jules?"

"He decided to stay in New York for a while. Said he could use a change of scenery," Vincent said, throwing me a warning glance as he gave his kindred the same story he told Bran and Papy on the plane.

"He ditches now? When Violette's plotting Paris domination?" Ambrose asked, looking confused. When Vincent nodded, the big revenant just shrugged. "Jules in New York? Man, he is going to have himself a ball." He shook his head at the thought. "Here, let me take those," he said, picking up a couple of suitcases.

"Did you have a good time?" Charlotte asked, joining me as we headed toward an enormous SUV. "I mean, did you get to do anything else besides re-embody Vincent?"

I smiled. "Yes, actually. I went to see my old friends."

She grabbed my arm and started jumping up and down. "Hurray! That's fabulous news, Kate! One step back into the world of the living," she cheered, and then quickly added, "I mean . . . not that you absolutely *have* to include humans in your social circle. But it made me sad that you had cut ties with everyone from your former life."

"I know," I said. "I actually feel like a huge weight has been lifted."

"Well, you're glowing," she said. "It looks like the trip back home was good for you."

I grinned and hugged her tight.

Once we were on the road, Ambrose and Charlotte caught Vincent up on news. We had been gone for three days, but it felt like weeks.

Although Vincent told his kindred all about Theodore Gold and our experience in the Met's crypt, he didn't bring up the subject of JB. So I had to wait until we were alone, saying good-bye at my front door, to ask about it.

"What are you going to do?"

"Talk to JB on my own," he said with an uncomfortable shrug. "See what he has to say."

"Good luck," I said, and leaned up on my tiptoes to kiss him.

"I hope you're not too lonely tonight," he whispered, and gave me a wink that made a whole swarm of bees start buzzing in my belly. I closed the door behind me, and heard him say through the glass, *"Bonne nuit, ma belle,"* before turning and disappearing from view.

During the night everything changed.

I was awakened by the repeated ringing of my phone. Finally I picked it up and saw that Georgia had called four times. I dialed her back.

"What is important enough to wake me in the middle of the night?"

"It's ten a.m., Katie-Bean."

"Not in New York it's not."

"Listen. I'm over at La Morgue. You have to get over here. Now." My sister sounded breathless.

"What's going on?"

"When I got here for my fight training, Gaspard was gone. He and Jean-Baptiste took off. As in left town. For good!"

"No!" I gasped, sitting straight up in the bed.

"Yes."

"I'll be right there," I said. Jumping out of bed, I dialed Vincent's number as I threw some clothes on.

"Mon ange. You're up." He sounded so calm, I wondered if my sister had been mistaken.

"I just got this freaked-out phone call from Georgia, who claimed that JB and Gaspard have left."

"Yes, I was going to tell you myself, but I thought you'd want to sleep in. Clearly Georgia didn't agree."

"Well, here I am, wide-awake. You can tell me now," I said, wedging the phone between my shoulder and ear while I pulled my jeans on.

"Trust me—it's not an over-the-phone kind of conversation," he replied. "I'll send Ambrose over to get you."

I left a note for Papy and Mamie telling them where I was going, and raced down the stairs. Ambrose was already there, standing outside my door discussing something serious with Geneviève when I emerged. "You've got to tell me what happened!" I said as they fell into place on either side of me.

"No can do, Katie-Lou," Ambrose said, scanning the streets for signs of numa as we made our way to La Maison. "With news this big, Vincent's going to want to tell you himself."

I wanted to push him for info, but didn't know how much Vincent had revealed to his kindred. Would he try to cover for JB? Or had he told the bardia about their leader's betrayal?

We arrived to find a house full of revenants. It felt like a flashback to one week ago, when Paris's kindred had assembled to await news of where Violette had taken Vincent. But instead of the grave atmosphere of the previous gathering, a feeling of shock hung heavy in the air. Some faces showed disbelief and others bitter disappointment, and people were talking in whispers.

Ambrose led me upstairs to the library, where Vincent waited. As soon as the door shut, Vincent's stiff pose relaxed. Shoulders slumping, he wrapped his arms around me and buried his face in my hair.

"What happened?" I asked. Not knowing how to comfort him, I combed his tousled black locks back from his face.

"I confronted him. And he confessed. It's exactly how Theodore explained it. JB made a deal with Lucien, and has been paying for protection ever since in the form of his Paris properties."

"Oh, Vincent," I said, my throat clenching as I saw how upset he was.

"He said he only did it for us. That he felt we were on the brink of defeat. That the losses we had taken were too drastic and he wanted to protect the kindred that were left: his chosen few family members, among them me, who he thought was the Champion. He thought I would rise up and lead the kindred to a final defeat and that his compromise would be justified in the end. He admitted that after a few decades he regretted it, but he was in too deep and couldn't bring himself to tell us about it."

"I'm sorry," I murmured, wrapping my arms back around him.

"You should have seen Gaspard," Vincent continued, running his fingers distractedly up and down my spine and nuzzling my hair. "I think he was hurt the most, discovering that JB had hidden something from him for all those years. But he stuck with him. They've gone into self-imposed exile, and JB named me the head of the bardia," Vincent said flatly.

I drew back to look him in the face. "What?" I exclaimed.

"He named me head and Charlotte my second."

It shouldn't have felt like such a shock. Vincent had been Jean-Baptiste's second. It was a foregone conclusion that he would one day become leader. But so quickly? And I hadn't even considered that Charlotte might be next in line of bardia hierarchy.

"Charlotte?" I asked, glancing at Ambrose, who stood blocking the door with his massive frame. He cracked his knuckles and unleashed a sly smile.

"Well, it wasn't going to be me. I like to pick fights, which unless you're Attila the Hun isn't considered the healthiest leadership characteristic."

Turning back to Vincent, I asked, "Are you okay with this?"

His expression was troubled. "I have no choice," he responded. "Someone must begin assembling our troops. If Violette hears about the sudden change in command, she'll take the opportunity to strike before we can get ourselves organized. And we've just gotten word of where she is, so the time to act is now."

"What can I do?"

"Keep the details to yourself. I have only told our Paris kindred that JB chose to leave. And Kate . . . please stay close. Not only do I feel better knowing you're within the safety of these walls, but just having you nearby gives me more confidence." These last words were in an almost-whisper.

As I watched him, my heart felt like it was expanding—blowing up like a balloon. I brushed his rough, stubbly cheek with my fingertips. "You were made for this, Vincent," I said. "Champion or not, you will have everyone's support. I've seen how the others respect you, and they will follow you to the very end."

Vincent smiled ruefully. "Okay, Ambrose, you can tell everyone to come in," he said.

A dozen or so of Paris's most important bardia filed in—a fraction of the people I had seen downstairs—and sat in rows of chairs before the library's fireplace. Vincent and Charlotte took two chairs facing them, and I grabbed a comfy leather club chair in the back.

Vincent briefed everyone, asked the revenants to call up every contact they had, and ordered them to arm themselves and wait at the ready. I almost choked when he explained that Violette had been spotted coming and going from the Crillon Hotel for the last few days. Trust her to choose the place where heads of state and movie stars stay as her headquarters. She wasn't about to join her minions in hiding out in the catacombs or caves under Montmartre or, as we now knew, JB's protected residences throughout Paris.

Vincent called upon one of the revenants to speak. The woman reported that she had news from Bordeaux that the numa had emptied from the city and were said to have headed to Paris. Others spoke up with similar news from other French cities, confirming what we had heard while we were in New York.

"Violette is obviously trying to force things to a head," said Charlotte, speaking for the first time. Although she was dressed in her regular tomboyish jeans and T-shirt, she had tied her blond hair back into a chignon, making her look older than her fifteen years.

"It isn't surprising. This *is* the Third Age that the prophecy specified—in fact, over a century has passed since it began," said Bran, who I hadn't noticed sitting on the far side of the group. "It is high time for the Champion to manifest. He will come, whether Violette orchestrates a situation that necessitates him to appear, or whether he is already here."

"What does your prophecy say?" asked Charlotte.

"I compared my text with Gaspard's: the bardia's version and that of the flame-fingers are basically the same." He scrabbled through his book, lifted it a couple of inches from his eyes, and read:

In the Third Age, humankind's atrocities will be such that brother will betray brother and numa will outnumber bardia and a preponderance of wars will darken the world of men. In this time a bardia will arise in Gaul who will be a leader amongst his kind.

He will possess anterior powers of perception, persuasion, and communication and preternatural levels of endurance and strength. His aura will blaze like a star on fire. He will lead his kind to victory against the numa and they will be conquered. This will usher in the Fourth Age, which will be an era of peace before the clouds of hatred once again gather over the earth.

The revenants began whispering between themselves. "It sure sounds like you, bro," remarked Ambrose from his position by the door.

"Our Monsieur Tândorn has assured me that that honor is not mine," Vincent responded, and then addressed Bran. "Among all of our kindred you have seen, you have not identified him?"

"No," responded Bran.

Vincent began handing out orders, placing the bardia present in charge of their lower-ranking kindred downstairs, as well as those who hadn't yet arrived. One team was given the responsibility of watching the Crillon, and others were divided into a spy network throughout Paris and its environs. People began to stand, and I made my way over to Bran.

"Hello, dear Kate," he said, instinctively reaching toward me, and then awkwardly withdrawing his hand. I smiled. He was like a ghost, so slight and withdrawn that he felt somehow intangible, and avoiding human touch seemed to be right in line with his otherworldly aura.

"You look tired," I said.

He shrugged. "This is my first experience with jet lag. Of course, those who do not sleep are not affected," he commented wryly, inclining his head toward Vincent, "which is quite unfair. Speaking of sleep, if I'm not needed I think I'll go take a nap," he said with a yawn, and shuffled out of the room behind the others.

I felt an arm twine around my waist and turned to see my sister. "So . . . was it worth waking up for?" she asked.

I nodded. "Thanks, Georgia."

"I hear your boyfriend's the king of revenants now. Does that make you the Queen of the Dead?"

I rolled my eyes. And then noticing Arthur standing behind Georgia, I said, "Hi."

He gave me a broad smile and tucked his blond hair behind his ear. "Thanks for bringing Vincent back," he said. "Now that he's once again corporeal, I feel a little less guilty about having been Violette's stooge." Leaning over, he gave me cheek-kisses and his stubble prickled my skin.

"Ow," I laughed, rubbing my face. "Excuse us, please," I said to Arthur. "We need a sister-to-sister chat."

"Of course," he said, making an effort to smile at me but unable to keep his eyes off my sister.

Catching Vincent's gaze, I mouthed, *Do you need me?* He shook his head. I pulled Georgia over to a secluded corner of the library where no one could hear us, and we flopped down on armchairs in front of a window. I pressed my cheek with my fingertips. "How do you not get razor burn?"

"Because I'm playing hard to get," my sister responded.

"What? You haven't even kissed him?" I stared at her while she smiled beatifically. I eyed her suspiciously. "Who are you, and what have you done with my sister?"

"God, Kate, you make me sound like a total slut." But the way she said it sounded like she considered it a compliment. "He's *medieval*. I figure I should act like one of those maidens from his time and protect my innocence."

I burst out laughing. "Georgia, you really like this guy, don't you?"

"Yes, and now that Violette has replaced him with someone else, I feel like I'm no longer her Public Enemy Number One."

"Violette has *replaced* Arthur?" I repeated. "What are you talking about?"

"Well, Arthur says that every time she's been spotted, she's had the same numa guy with her."

"That would be Nicolas," I said, waving my hand. "He was Lucien's second. That's not news."

"No, silly," said Georgia. "I'm not talking about fur coat guy. This is another numa. A really young one. Like adolescent. No one's ever seen him around before. They think he's either new or one of the recent imports from another city. Whatever, Violette doesn't go anywhere without him."

"That's creepy," I admitted.

"Yeah, he's like her prepubescent lapdog."

I wrinkled my nose, and Georgia nodded, agreeing with my sentiment.

"Anyway, that leaves Mister Hunky Medieval Author Guy all for me!" She lifted her eyebrows and got comfortable in her chair. "But my adventures in boyland aren't important. What I really want to hear is . . . what was it like to be back in New York?"

It was dark when Ambrose dropped me off at home. Georgia had won her freedom and went out with some friends for dinner— friends who were probably unaware that they were being trailed by Arthur and another guard-revenant.

I let myself in. "Mamie? Papy?" I yelled, throwing my coat over the hall chair. The apartment was unusually silent. Most nights at this time Mamie was getting dinner ready and jazz or big band music accompanied her cooking. I hesitated in the dining room, feeling a little creeped out.

"Back here in my study," came Papy's voice.

Breathing a sigh of relief, I hung up my coat and headed back to his office. My grandfather was sitting in his favorite position, tucked in a corner in an old leather armchair with his lit pipe in one hand and a book in the other.

"Where's Mamie?" I asked, perching on the edge of his desk.

"On a house call," he replied, puffing a stream of smoke as he spoke. The room filled with the citrusy odor of Papy's pipe tobacco, a smell I always associated with him.

I glanced at the marble clock on the mantel. "At seven p.m. on a Thursday?"

"It's a foreign client, in town for a few days. Your grandmother's gone to their hotel to inspect a painting they have out on approval from a Parisian art dealer."

"She went to someone's hotel room?" I asked doubtfully, picking up a glass paperweight and inspecting the iridescent beetle trapped eternally inside. "I can't imagine Mamie meeting a client in a hotel."

"Not just *any* hotel. The collector is staying at the Crillon, so Emilie felt it was worth it," Papy replied, looking back down at his book and thumbing through the pages.

The paperweight crashed loudly against the hardwood floor, breaking into splinters and releasing its prisoner, who lay gleaming in the lamplight.

Papy leapt up from his chair, the alarm on his face echoing mine. "What is it, Kate?" he asked.

"The Crillon. Are you sure?"

"Yes. Kate. What in the world is the matter?"

"Violette is staying at the Crillon," I said. My voice sounded like someone else's, hollow, as if I were hearing myself from the outside.

"Violette?" my grandfather asked, confused.

"Violette. The medieval revenant who destroyed Vincent."

"No," Papy gasped, suddenly looking his seventy-two years.

From across the room came a string quartet ringtone. Papy strode over to his desk chair, reached into his coat pocket, and pulled out his cell phone. His hand shook as he held it up to see the caller's name. He raised the phone to his ear and sank down into his desk chair with a sigh of relief. "Oh, Emilie, thank God you're there. Kate and I were . . ."

His face suddenly changed, and as he listened, the blood drained from his face. "What? No! But how . . ."

I could hear the tone of my grandmother's voice through the earpiece. It was careful—measured and slow. Papy hung up the phone and lifted his eyes to meet mine.

I shivered, as if a gust of air had just rushed through the study and clasped me in its frigid fingers.

"Violette would like to speak to you and Vincent at the hotel. She's keeping your grandmother as a guarantee that you will show."

THIRTY-FIVE

OUR ARGUMENT TOOK ALL OF A MINUTE. PAPY didn't want me to go. I didn't want him to go. In the end, we both dashed out of the apartment, throwing our coats on and running down the stairs, too rushed to wait for the ancient elevator.

As usual, there were no taxis in sight. "How about the Métro, Papy?" I asked him.

"And risk a delay? No, thanks. It's almost as fast by foot," he responded. We resorted to speed-walking down the rue de Bac. The chilly March air and glowing lampposts lent the scene a false sense of security—as if all was right with the world—when in actuality we were on our way to a meeting that threatened to end with someone getting hurt. Or worse.

My phone rang. I fished into my pocket for it, and saw it was Vincent. "Where are you going?" he asked. I spun to look behind me, but didn't see anyone following. "I asked, where are you going—without revenant escort?"

"Vincent, I'd rather not tell you."

"What is that supposed to mean?" he asked, sounding more angry than hurt. "Two bardia from Geneviève's house are following you and your grandfather. They called me to check in—said you guys took off at top speed without even waiting for them."

"Well, if they're following us, then they'll keep us safe. Why are you calling me?"

"Kate, what is going on?" Vincent asked, sounding alarmed.

"Violette has . . . she has Mamie at . . . They're at the Crillon. Papy and I . . . we're going there." I was trying to speak clearly, but our hurried pace mixed with panic about Mamie made my words come out all garbled.

"Why didn't you call me and tell me that? I would have come with you."

"No, Vincent! Don't come. We don't need you," I said, choking back panic.

There was a split second of palpable shock, and then: "Violette wanted me to come, didn't she?"

I didn't respond.

"Kate, you can't go. At least tell me you'll wait until I get there," he said. I could hear he was moving quickly while holding the phone to his ear.

"My grandfather and I will be there in about fifteen minutes. Tell Geneviève's people to accompany us, but we don't need you," I said, trying to catch my breath. Papy walked with a fast gait on a regular day. Tonight I was practically jogging to keep up with him.

"Ambrose, Charlotte, and I will meet you in the Crillon lobby," he insisted, ignoring my request. "Don't go up to the room without me."

I didn't respond. I heard Vincent cursing on the other end as I hung up. Pocketing the phone, I sped up to match Papy's pace. We had to get there before Vincent could join us. Violette's plot to lure him to her by kidnapping his girlfriend's grandmother was transparent. I wasn't going to let her win the fight this time. Papy and I would find some way of saving Mamie without Vincent having to sacrifice himself again.

Within ten minutes we were crossing the Pont de la Concorde and entering the grand square. Papy threw himself into the oncoming traffic, and I held on to his arm to minimize the chance of one of us getting hit. We made it intact to the entry of the museum-like building housing the Crillon Hotel, and slowed as we passed under the monumental stone entryway and through the glass doors.

"Where do we go?" I asked as we glanced around the sumptuous lobby filled with giant flower arrangements and lined with marble columns. And then I spotted two men walking toward us from a far corner of the room. "Okay, here come the numa," I said.

"How do you know they're numa?" Papy looked at me quizzically.

"Can't you see that black-and-white kind of fuzziness around them? Like an aura where all of the color has been sucked out of the air."

"No," he said, peering at them and then back at me worriedly. *I've been hanging around supernaturals too much*, I thought, just as Vincent, Charlotte, and Ambrose strode through the door, suited up in their black leather battle gear. Papy's eyes widened, but the hotel staff just glanced at them blithely as if they had seen it all before. Add the two similarly dressed numa, and it looked like a rock band was throwing a party in a hotel suite.

Vincent made a beeline toward me. "Are you okay?" he asked.

"Yes," I said, glancing worriedly toward the advancing numa, "but I didn't ask you to come."

Vincent ignored my protest. "Kate, don't say anything about me not being the Champion. If Violette hasn't figured it out, that's the one card we can still play."

The numa shot the bardia lethal glares as they neared. "Please, follow us," said the shorter of the two. I saw a flash of silver from underneath his long black coat.

"Only you two," said the second one, nodding to Vincent and me.

"I am coming with them," said Papy in a voice that indicated they would have to forcibly restrain him from following.

"Ditto," said Ambrose. Charlotte slid her hand down her waist to show the outline of the weapon hidden beneath her duster.

The numas' eyes flicked to each other and then toward the desk staff and back to us. "You can accompany us as far as the suite, but you're not going in," Shorty said finally.

They turned and led us past an elevator bank to a stairway, insisting we go first. Our group climbed two flights of stairs, and emerged into a long corridor with scarlet silk lining the walls and gold sconces lighting the passage.

At the end of the hall, a numa with salt-and-pepper hair,

wearing an expensive suit and a silk cravat, stood outside a double door. It was Nicolas. He stiffened as he saw the size of our group. "She'll only see the two," he said, nodding imperiously toward Vincent and me.

"We couldn't make a scene in the lobby," explained one of our escorts.

"And we can't all stand around here in the hall, now can we?" said Ambrose with a wicked smile. "Being a public place and all."

"You will guard them in the suite's antechamber," hissed Nicolas, giving the numa a look that promised trouble once he had them on their own.

"So, Nicolas," said Vincent as we followed him through the door. "Once Lucien's right-hand man, now you're playing second to an adolescent?"

Nicolas stood aside to usher us into a small entryway-like room with chairs and coat and hat racks. He smiled sourly at Vincent. "In *my* world, being second involves much less responsibility. And risk. Why, just look at you—you're once again in danger, saving an old lady, while Jean-Baptiste is safe and sound back ruling the castle."

Charlotte's and Ambrose's gaze shifted toward each other and then back to Nicolas. The numa didn't know about JB's departure. At least we had that going for us. Violette wanted Vincent because she still believed he was the Champion. But if she discovered he was also the new bardia leader, who knows how she would use that to her advantage?

"Sit," commanded Nicolas, gesturing toward the chairs. "Not you," he said to Vincent and me. Opening a door that gave onto another long corridor, he gestured for us to pass through.

"I will not stay out here while my wife is inside," insisted Papy.

"Oh yes, you will," said one of the guards, shuffling off his coat to show a belt equipped with several knives and a sword in scabbard, superseded by a shoulder strap holding a gun. My grandfather frowned.

"If all goes well, your wife will join you momentarily," said Nicolas.

"And my granddaughter?" Papy asked, raising his chin to show that he was not afraid.

"I'll be fine, Papy," I urged. "Just don't do anything to upset them."

Nicolas followed us closely through the door. I heard Papy's protests cut off by a gruff command of "Sit down, old man!"

And suddenly I was so furious I felt like going back and challenging that guard. My anger chased my fear away, at least temporarily. I spun to face Nicolas. "You won't hurt my grand-parents," I said, telling not asking.

"Besides serving as bait, they are of no use to us," responded Nicolas as he prodded me to continue. "The door to your left," he indicated.

Vincent turned the knob and, instead of holding it open for me as he usually would, strode first into the room.

"Ah, there you are." I heard Violette's little-girl voice before my eyes found her, sitting with my grandmother at a table set for tea. In front of Mamie, a full cup of coffee and a plate of pastries sat untouched.

"Kate!" she gasped when she spotted me, but though she was trembling, she didn't make an effort to rise. I spotted her hands curled into fists beneath the table and could tell she was trying to control her shaking. The same indignation rose inside me seeing my strong grandmother reduced to the state of a panic-stricken hostage. I wanted to rush Violette and throttle her then and there, but restrained myself as I noticed there were other people in the room; two numa bodyguards stood against the wall directly behind us, their arms folded across their chests as they monitored the scene.

Violette took a sip from her cup before lowering it to the saucer. "It's so good to see you again, Kate," she said, rising from the table. At her waist, a jeweled knife handle glittered atop its leather scabbard.

"And you, Vincent. How surprised I was when my sentries told me you were all back in one piece again! I can only imagine you figured out the secret of re-embodiment, a method we scholars have been searching for for centuries. How clever of you." She looked at him hungrily, as if she wanted to snatch the details straight out of his head.

"It was the *guérisseur*, wasn't it?" she said as she advanced. "He must have had the information. I can't imagine Gaspard would have neglected to inform me of such an important discovery."

Vincent ignored her question. "Let the woman go, Violette."

I still couldn't figure out why Mamie hadn't moved an inch, until I saw that someone sat just behind her holding a sword to her back. It was a boy. He must have been thirteen. His longish, light brown hair swept down over his eyebrows, nearly hiding his dark brown eyes. The monochrome numa aura outlined his body. A young numa. This must be Violette's new companion.

She saw me staring at him. "Louis, you can let Madame Mercier go. Manners maketh man, as they say. And even though we are no longer officially 'man,' we still have our code to follow, don't we, Vincent?"

"You are still bardia in body," Vincent said, "but in your mind you are already numa. Therefore you have no code and I have no faith in your words. Let me escort Kate and her grandparents safely away from the building and then I will return."

"Yes, please let my granddaughter and me leave," pleaded Mamie, now standing.

Violette's civilized demeanor exploded, shattering into a million glass shards. "You will all do exactly as I say!" she screamed, her eyes narrowed. Everyone froze and stared at her. The bodyguards unfolded their arms and took a step in our direction before receiving a glare from Violette that stopped them in place.

She pressed a hand to her chest, and closing her eyes, she sighed. Then, in a voice little louder than a whisper she said, "Nicolas, dear, escort Madame Mercier out."

Louis took my grandmother by the arm and walked her quickly past us, handing her off to Nicolas. He whisked her into the hallway, closing the door behind them. I caught a whiff of her gardenia perfume as she passed, and my chest clenched painfully as I wondered again if any of us would get out of this alive.

"Now. Where were we?" said Violette, and turned to us. "Oh yes, Kate and Vincent. It is time for us to conclude some unfinished business." She strode toward us, snakelike in her smooth predatory movements.

"You," she said, pointing at Vincent, "belong to me." And for the first time I noticed something strange about her right hand. It looked disfigured. Unbalanced. A thread of panic ran its way down my spine as I saw what was wrong: Her little finger was gone. Where the knuckle would have joined it to her hand was an angry red scab with black stitches poking out of it. That was the flesh-and-bone sacrifice she had made to bind Vincent to her. Uselessly. I stared at the amputation and wanted to vomit.

"I never belonged to you," Vincent responded, each word dripping contempt. "You used Kate and her grandparents to get me here. Now you've got me, and unsurprisingly, you've got a fire"—he nodded toward the blaze burning in the stone hearth—"and apparently you figured out what you did wrong last time. So let Kate go and let's get on with it."

Violette nodded to the bodyguards. They stepped forward and each took Vincent by an arm. He looked toward me, eyes pleading for my compliance, as he let them grab him without a struggle.

Vincent was *not* going to sacrifice himself to save me. A red-hot poker of fury pierced my heart and propelled me as I lunged toward him. "Vincent. You can't! Not again." My head jerked forward as I felt strong hands grasp my arms from behind. I whipped around to see that the boy, Louis, was my captor. And he was stronger than he looked. His eyes flicked to mine, and barely moving his lips, he said in an almost inaudible voice, "I'm sorry."

His words confused me, but I turned quickly away as Violette stopped inches from Vincent. She held the knife under his chin while he stared defiantly into her eyes.

"Take me instead of him," I insisted.

Lowering the knife and taking a step backward, she switched her gaze from him to me and laughed. "Now, tell me, Kate. Besides the pleasure it will give me to kill your boyfriend . . . again . . . before your eyes, why in the world would you imagine I'd want *you*?"

I struggled against Louis's grasp, and thinking quickly, I spat, "I could be your first human kill. Isn't that how it works? You could be a numa like you want to be. Just don't kill Vincent again. Let him go and take me instead."

"Well," said Violette, an amused expression crossing her features as she glanced behind me to meet Louis's eyes. "Now, isn't that a charming gesture? One might even say a *self-sacrificing* offer. How benevolent of you, Kate.

"You were right, Vincent," she said, focusing her attention back on him. Her lips curved into a sick smile. "I *did* figure out what I did wrong last time." Her eyes studied his face, and she tilted her head girlishly to one side. "I chose the wrong Champion."

And, lunging forward, she plunged the knife into my chest. Her movement was so fast that I didn't know what had happened for a full second, until I looked down and saw it sticking out of my torso, still clenched in her tiny, porcelain-white fingers.

Then, grabbing the hilt with both hands, she pulled the blade in a quick upward motion, and I only had time to look toward Vincent and see the terror in his eyes before a rushing sound erased his scream and the darkness drowned me.

PART II

THIRTY-SIX

I'M SO THIRSTY. MY MOUTH FEELS FULL OF SAND, but my lips part and I realize it's my swollen tongue that is choking me. I wrench my eyes open, but I am sightless. My lungs want to explode. And then my throat releases and I am gulping air, frantically inhaling it into my burning chest.

A hand takes my chin and holds it roughly as liquid is poured into my mouth and spills over my lips. But I am able to swallow, and the presence keeps feeding me until my mouth closes and my head settles back. My consciousness ends there.

I am cold, though I sense a fire close by. My body feels like it has been frozen solid and is now defrosting, sharp needles stabbing the entire surface of my skin. My muscles cramp painfully and I feel my arm jerk up to my chest, the joints in my fingers spasming, clenching my hand into a claw. I still can't see, and my mouth is parched. I hear footsteps and the hand is back, feeding me water—I can taste now.

Something brushes my lips and forces its way past my teeth. I bite down and taste the sweet juice of a fig and feel its pulpy texture fill my mouth. I swallow and take another bite, desperate to get the food inside my cramping belly. The fig is followed by walnuts. Three. I swallow them, and then immediately turn my head to the side and vomit them up, retching past the point of emptying my stomach. Retching and crying and shaking violently. The hand waits until I'm done, wipes my face, and starts over. Water. Fig. Three walnuts. This time I keep it down. The footsteps walk away and my mind shuts down once again.

I hear water lapping close to my head. My eyes fly open. I am staring at a wooden ceiling. I can see. I try to sit up, but something restrains me. I pull my head up far enough to see that I am bound to a bed by cords. I am dressed all in black . . . no, not black. Dark red—my fingertip brushes against my leg—and crusty. With horror, I realize that my clothes are saturated in my own dried blood.

Feeling panic, I try to get my bearings. The wall next to me is painted metal. I swing my gaze across the sparsely furnished room and out a window across from me to see an expanse of water stretching to a riverbank.

I'm on a boat. Tied to a bed.

"Ah, she's awake," a voice says, and I crane my head to see Violette walk into the room. Behind her, Louis stoops to get through the low door.

I recoil as they come into view. Something has happened to my vision. The colorless inch-wide aura I used to see around numa has disappeared and instead there are mistlike crimson haloes encircling their heads. Inside me, something new screams that numa are near. As if I didn't already know. A nauseating fury overcomes me and I shudder and taste bile.

They stand above my head, upside down, staring me in the face. Louis looks worried and Violette triumphant. "Welcome to the afterlife," she says.

I stop straining against the cords and gape at her. I try to speak, but my throat makes a croaking noise.

"This is so fascinating!" she says, clasping her hands together. "I've never witnessed an animation before. It never actually interested me until now."

I don't understand what Violette's talking about for a minute, and then—suddenly and sickeningly—I do. She stabbed me, I remember. But did I die? No, I couldn't have. Violette has kept me alive, suffering and on the brink of death, so she can continue to torture me.

I struggle against my bonds, kicking and straining—uselessly, I know—but I am furious and the fight makes me feel better. I whip my head toward Violette and try to form words with my bone-dry mouth. "You . . . are . . . ," I rasp.

"Yes, dear?" she says, beaming. "I am what?"

"A . . . psychotic . . . bitch," I manage to say, pouring all of my hatred and fear into my words, willing them to hurt her with every drop of energy I still possess.

"Aww. Isn't that cute," she says, laughing delightedly, and

sweeps out of the room with Louis following closely behind. "And how appropriate as Kate's first words as a revenant," I hear her comment as she shuts the door behind her. "Shows she's got spunk! This will be more fun than I thought." And her voice fades as they walk away.

I lie there, stunned. What is she talking about? Me—a revenant? I can't be. But after a moment, I push aside the doubt and let myself consider it.

Not only would I have had to possess that mystical revenant predisposition or gene or whatever, but I would have had to die saving someone. Violette tried to murder me. I didn't sacrifice myself for anyone.

And then, with an icy chill of realization, I remember the scene in Violette's room at the Crillon when I offered to be her first human kill—for her to take me instead of Vincent. What had her words been?

I hear them as clearly as if she were standing in the room next to me. "Now isn't that a charming gesture? One might even say a *self-sacrificing* offer. How benevolent of you, Kate."

Violette tricked us. She planned the whole thing so that I would die for Vincent. But why?

I check my body to see if I feel differently—and I do. It's in the way my heart beats more slowly and the sluggish pace that my blood pumps through my veins. But that could be because I'm dying. Bleeding to death.

No, something else has changed. Though I am weak and parched, it's like there's a sun—a flaming ball of white-hot energy—inside me that's radiating through my pores. There was my body's response, a painful physical reaction, when Violette and Louis entered the room that warned me numa were near. And then, there are their auras. The colorless penumbra I saw around numa before I died has been replaced by haloes of red mist, just like the *guérisseur* artists had presented around numa in their cave paintings. I see auras like they did. I have changed. I am no longer human.

"No!" I manage to scream before my voice gives out. I yank at my bonds again, kicking and pulling and thrashing my head around, until I finally give up and begin crying. No, not crying, sobbing. Weeping. The tears run down the sides of my face, and I try to lift my hands to wipe them away before remembering that I am bound.

Something pinches my arm. Hard. I open my eyes to see Violette's face hovering above mine. "It seems you passed out," she says in a practical voice. "A typical symptom of animating after such a violent death."

"Why are you keeping me here?" I growl. I wish I could get my hands free so I could gouge her eyes out with my fingernails. "You used me as bait to get to Vincent—he was standing right there in front of you. What could you possibly want with me?"

"Why?" she repeats, tapping her chin with her finger. "Because you, Kate, are the Champion. And I, Violette, want your power. It's as simple as that." She turns to Louis. "Get the Champion some more water, please. We can't have her dying off before she comes into her true power." Louis leaves the room.

I had thought through every possible response she might give me, but this is one I had not expected. I stare, incredulous, as Violette pulls up a chair to the bed and sits down next to me.

She's lost it, I think. *Though she was questionably stable before, all of this power has driven her completely insane.* "You're crazier than I thought," I say.

"Well, now, that would be one point of view," she responds. "Another would be that I am very shrewd. Observant. Discerning, even. You see, my gamble that you were a revenant has already proven correct. And if Vincent isn't the Champion, which became all too clear when the power transfer failed so miserably"—she unconsciously rubs her amputated finger with her other hand, eyes narrowing when she remembers it's not there—"then there was a very good chance that it was you."

I gape at her, uncomprehending, and she huffs impatiently. "The prophecy says that the Champion has anterior powers of communication, persuasion, and perception. I didn't understand that until I considered the word 'anterior' as meaning 'before becoming a revenant.' Having the gifts while you were still human.

"Thinking of it like that, the communication part was obvious. I thought Vincent was special for communicating with a human while he was volant, but it was the other way around. You were the one who was special."

She scoots her chair around so she can watch my reaction as she speaks. "You had the kindred at La Maison eating out of your hand, including Jean-Baptiste, who doesn't deal with any human he doesn't have to. Vincent went against his better judgment to see you, and you wormed your way into the hearts of the rest of Paris's revenants. I would call that *anterior powers of persuasion.*

"And then I remembered that the night before our little scuffle up on Montmartre, Vincent had asked me if you could possibly have begun to see numa's auras just from spending time with revenants. I told him no. But if you had a heightened sense of perception, that would explain it."

She smoothes her hair back, looking extremely pleased with herself. I want to tell her exactly what she can do with her ridiculous theory, but she isn't done talking. And I need to hear it all.

Folding her arms across her chest and tapping an index finger against her fight-toned bicep, she says, "And then there's the all-important fact that the *guérisseur* Gwenhaël told my men, under great duress I admit, that the Champion was he who killed the numa leader. I knew Vincent possessed you to kill Lucien, but it was you who threw the knife.

"Once I stopped focusing on Vincent and thought of you, it all clicked. And so you see, here we are. I'm not a *guérisseur* or a Seer so I can't tell if you have the Champion's fabled 'star on fire' halo. Therefore, I'll just take my chances and destroy you once you're fully animated. How do they say it now . . . no skin off my nose?" Realizing what she's said, she rubs her amputated stub again and forces a smile. "And don't forget, you offered yourself to me. You gave me the Champion's full powers."

No, I think again. *She has to be wrong.* But I remain silent, unwilling to give her the satisfaction of knowing how much she has shaken me. When I don't respond, Violette stands and walks over to a table sitting next to the hearth and, leaning over, begins scribbling something in a notebook.

I close my eyes and think about what she's just told me. I don't believe her. I can't. How can I be the Champion? The Champion is some kind of undead superhero. *Okay, so I fit one of those qualifications*, I think, pain ripping through me as, once again, I acknowledge that I am . . . *undead*. A tear rolls down my cheek just identifying myself with that horrible word, but I fight to pull myself together. I have to think.

Every time Bran talked about the Champion, he used the pronoun "he." The prophecy he read us used the word "he." That has to mean something, doesn't it? Everyone seemed to think the Champion was a man. Wouldn't Bran have said it differently if he knew I was the Champion? *Not necessarily*, I think. He might not have known. I wasn't even a revenant then.

And then I remember. It was immediately after the big event—when he touched Jean-Baptiste and became the VictorSeer—that he began regarding me strangely. I was always checking my hair around him, wondering what he was looking at. But what if it hadn't been my hair he was focusing on? What if it had been my aura? *It was a kind of weird squint*, I think with dawning horror. If my aura is as bright as a "star on fire," no wonder he squinted every time he looked my way.

My thoughts begin racing, each realization stinging me like

a crazed hornet. There was his insistence that the Champion wasn't here yet. He didn't even want to look at the other bardia to verify. *It was because he thought it was me.* There were the sideways glances when the subject of the Champion arose. And his willingness to let me visit the flame-finger archives.

And then I recall his words when I returned from the cave with his books. "I'm glad you went," he had said. "It could well be your only chance." Why would he say that? Bearers of the *signum bardia* are allowed to enter. But revenants aren't. He knew I was a latent revenant. And he knew I would soon be the Champion. Bran had known this whole time.

Shock hits me like a tidal wave, roaring in my ears and sending me spinning and crashing in its wake. I lie there powerless to do anything but watch the girl who is determined to destroy me.

"Any other questions?" she asks, snapping the notebook shut and slipping it into her jacket pocket.

"What did you do with Vincent?"

"He is of no value to me anymore," she says testily. "I would have killed him along with you, but I didn't want to risk your sacrifice. You offered your life for him. I wasn't sure you would become a revenant if you failed to save his life. So I left him in the hotel."

I close my eyes in relief. *He's safe.*

"Yes, you rest," says Violette, walking back to the bed and standing directly over me. "It'll be at least another day before you regain your strength. Although, as you can see," she says, glancing at the cords binding my body, "I'm not taking any chances."

She begins walking toward the door. "Violette?" I call, craning my head so I can see her.

"Yes, Kate?" she asks, looking curious.

"I hope I'm not the Champion," I say, my voice dead calm now, "because I would hate to give you any additional satisfaction. But if I am, I hope you have to chop off an entire hand this time and eat a raw cat in order to absorb me. And I hope you choke on it."

Her creepily calm demeanor finally shatters. Making a noise between a growl and a scream, she stomps over to the bed and slaps my face as hard as she can. Then, spinning on her heels, she races out of the room, slamming the door behind her.

I lay my head back down and taste blood in my mouth. And smile.

THIRTY-SEVEN

THE DOOR REOPENS ALMOST IMMEDIATELY, AND
Louis enters with a tray. Although his raised eyebrows hint of
curiosity as to what just happened between me and his mistress,
he says nothing. Setting the tray down, he wordlessly pours a
glass of water. He lifts my head and helps me get some of it down
before replacing the glass and feeding me an orange segment.

My fury slowly cools as I study him for the first time. I see
what must have been an awkward boy of thirteen or so, before
he took on the deceptively charismatic facade that is part of the
revenant transformation.

As Vincent explained to me last summer, when revenants animate, they become more physically alluring than when they were
human. It is their superstrength: People are attracted to them,
and thus more prone to trust them.

In the bardia's case, this is a good thing—more lives saved. But
in the numa's case, it is to their victim's peril. When the numa

want to be scary, they sure as hell are. But when they are in con-man mode, they can be as poisonously charming as Lucien was when he tricked my sister into falling for him.

What could this boy have done at such a young age to animate as a serial betrayer? I wonder.

Louis avoids my eyes as he stands to go. And although I know he's only following Violette's orders, I thank him as he leaves the room. He pauses in the doorway, looking curiously back at me before shutting the door and leaving me alone with my thoughts.

Time passes snail slow and my limbs ache so much that tears leak from my eyes. I'm not crying; it's just my body's response to the intense pain. Which makes sense: My dead human tissue is coming to life again. I shudder with horror. Vincent didn't tell me this part of his story.

He didn't tell me a lot of things. Because he never thought I would be in this situation. Neither of us suspected me of being like him. Although, now that Violette has enumerated the reasons, I realize we should have seen it. If there hadn't been the belief in Vincent's being the Champion clouding the issue, we probably would have.

And if we had, well, things would have been different. We wouldn't have had to deal with the issue of my mortality and his living forever. Because I had the chance to become immortal. That's the cruel irony: Now that I have the possibility of spending eternity with Vincent, someone is going to take it away from me. Is going to kill me—again—and burn my body.

Just let her try, I think, my rage making me feel all-powerful. I struggle violently with my bonds, convulsing like a madwoman in my despair, but the only result is bleeding arms.

I measure time with the beat of my slowed-down heart and the change of light outside the boat's window. It must be mid-morning when Louis enters the room and begins the feeding routine again. Eating and drinking while flat on my back is difficult, to say the least. But I am so famished that I manage to chew and swallow everything he gives me—and keep it down.

"How old are you?" I ask finally.

His eyes widen, and then narrow. His jaw clenches and he shakes his head. Quickly folding up the tray, he leaves the room.

I close my eyes and try to relax, but every muscle in my body is jumping. I am desperate to move, but only my feet and hands are free to rotate. So I work them. And then I flex my fingers and toes and try to relax. There's nothing else I can do, besides imagining what my family must be thinking right now. They believe I'm dead. They are mourning. Once again. My heart actually physically hurts as I picture them, so I cast the image out of my mind and begin thinking of escape.

I study the locks on the windows and memorize the layout of the room. I don't know what I'm capable of, so it's hard to strategize. I wish I had asked Vincent more questions about revenant powers.

And what if I *am* the Champion? What was it that Vincent told me . . . besides the "anterior powers" that Violette had described. Strength. Endurance. I wonder if I have superpowers. I strain against the bonds again and nothing happens. They don't snap like threads. Okay . . . I'm not the Hulk. I can only hope the endurance part is right. Because if not, being tied to this bed is going to drive me insane.

As the sun outside the window reaches the zenith—*midday*, I think—my desperation grows. Violette said that my strength would be back in a day. I have to get out of here before then. More than my fear of being killed again is my determination not to be her key to becoming a Champion-fueled supervillain and wiping out the bardia.

I remember the story about that numa who absorbed the Indian Champion's power and the destruction he managed to wreak before he was stopped. Violette doesn't need any more persuasion to tempt people to follow her. And add, I'm just guessing, more than double a revenant's strength, endurance, and all that, she could have Paris under her control in no time at all. Not to be comic-book-hero dramatic, but if I have the fate of Paris . . . and eventually France or even beyond . . . resting on my shoulders, I better the hell find a way to get out of here.

Louis is back, doing the whole silent nursemaid routine once again. But this time, I'm determined to get him to talk.

"I know you're not supposed to speak to me. But I'm guessing you're not much younger than I am. And I'm also guessing you might not want to be here."

I watch the practiced blankness of his expression drop for a second, as his eyes meet mine, and then he puts the mask back on and continues to feed me. But I have seen what I was looking for: sadness. Despair.

I swallow the bite of apple he's feeding me and think of what to say. Where are those supernatural powers of persuasion when I need them? I decide to tell the truth. "I never asked for this, Louis. I don't want to be the Champion. I don't even want to be a revenant. I just want to go back to being a normal human girl and never see that scary medieval freak again."

Louis freezes, not knowing what to do. My anger seems to make sense to him, but my honesty leaves him confused. I can see that what I said touched something in him.

Standing, he walks to the door and shuts it carefully, and then comes back to sit next to me. "She doesn't want me to talk to you," he whispers. "I'm supposed to tell her the second I think you're trying to persuade me to help you."

"Well, I guess that's normal if she believes I have enhanced powers of persuasion," I say. "She must trust you a lot to leave you alone with me."

"Trust?" he guffaws. "Why do you think she's here on this boat, never more than a few yards away from you?"

My nose is running, and the one thing I want more than anything else in the world is a Kleenex. I sniff a few times, trying to wipe my nose on my shoulder, and Louis jumps up to get a towel and dabs at my face.

"Thanks," I say. And then something occurs to me. "Back in the hotel room . . . why did you apologize when you grabbed me from behind?" I ask as he folds the towel and places it on a side table.

He watches me from across the room. Deciding. Then squeezing his eyes tightly shut, he rubs his forehead worriedly. "I was almost fourteen when I died—just a few months ago," he says in a voice so tight it sounds like his throat will burst.

Exhaling, he walks over to me. "I didn't mean to kill anyone. Okay, yes, I did. But I was just temporarily . . . insane I guess. I hated the guy so much for what he had done to us and my mother." He shudders and shakes his head. That's all he's going to say about his past.

"I'm just . . . I'm sorry about all of this. I don't want to be this way. She found me and made me her favorite, and all I want to do is die. But that's not even possible for me anymore."

I don't know what to say.

"I have to go," he says, and begins to leave the room.

"Wait!"

"What?" he asks, turning to me.

"Thanks."

"For what?" He looks suspicious.

"For talking to me. For wiping my nose. Just . . . thanks."

"I didn't do anything," he says, narrowing his eyes. And turning, he leaves, shutting the door behind him.

I lie there, staring at the ceiling. Louis is like Violette. A freak of nature. He must have become a numa by accident, the same way she became a revenant. And now he is doomed to be her partner, at least until she gets bored of him. Which, for Arthur, took about five hundred years.

THIRTY-EIGHT

A MOMENT LATER, I FEEL ANOTHER PRESENCE IN the room.

Kate, it says. I am used to hearing a voice inside my head, but for the first time it's not Vincent's. I scan the room, searching for the source of the voice, but see nothing.

"Who is that?" I ask in a freaked-out whisper.

It's Gaspard, says the voice. *And apparently you don't have to speak out loud. I heard your words before you spoke them. How terribly convenient.*

I can't help smiling. He sounds the same in my head as in real life. *What are you doing here? I thought you and JB left Paris.*

We did. But Jean-Baptiste saw your aura all of the way from Normandy, and insisted on coming back. Everyone's been searching for you. Jean-Baptiste followed your light and led them all here. I must say, my dear, you look absolutely ghastly. Dried blood caked all over. You're practically . . . zombiesque.

I ignore his remarks on my appearance. *How are my grandparents? And Vincent?*

They're all fine. Ambrose and Charlotte got your grandparents safely out of the Crillon and then went back in and rescued Vincent.

I breathe a sigh of relief. *So where are we?*

The houseboat you are imprisoned within is just outside Paris, moving westward, says Gaspard. The voice disappears for a moment, and then is back. *How strong are you?*

I don't know, I admit. *How long have I been here?*

Violette killed you almost four days ago, Gaspard says. *I can't stay for long. She and her men will sense that I am here. Vincent doesn't want to try a rescue attempt until he knows you're strong enough to fight on your own. There's no way to creep up on a boat in the middle of the river, but we don't want to give Violette the time she needs to destroy you.*

His voice disappears again for a good few minutes, and then he is back. *Vincent says, and I quote, "Be strong, mon ange." He says you should do your best to get free, but stay where you are and pretend you are still bound. I will come back in a few hours to check on you.*

Gaspard? I say.

Yes.

I'm a revenant. I realize it's the understatement of the century, but somehow saying it out loud makes me feel better.

I know. It seems that you're actually a bit more than a revenant, dear Kate.

I inhale sharply. *How do you know?*

Well, firstly, your aura is like nothing Jean-Baptiste has ever seen before. It's like a homing beacon for his Seer capabilities. And then, once confronted, Bran confessed. He's known this whole time, but was bound by his people's rules not to pronounce you Champion before you actually became such.

My hunch was right. Bran had known. I can't decide whether I am grateful or upset with him for not letting me know. But then again . . . maybe he had tried with all of his little hints. In the only way he could "legally" let me know. I had just been blind to it.

Just be careful, Kate, Gaspard continues. *I'll be back to check on you.*

So. My state—both revenant and Champion—is now common knowledge among the bardia. They all know. *Vincent* knows. I'm not sure how I feel about that. There is a pang in my heart as I wonder if this will change the way he sees me now. He told me more than once that he would never wish the revenant destiny for me.

Well, none of that will matter if I can't get out of here. My body will be ashes and my spirit absorbed into Violette, strengthening her. Making her unstoppable. Just the thought of being a part of her sets me into action. I work on my bonds, moving my hands back and forth and picking at the ropes. All I manage is rope burn and more bleeding. I feel like screaming, but now that I'm in contact with the others, I don't want to draw more attention to myself than is necessary. I lie back on the bed and wish I could sleep.

After what seems like forever, Louis is back with another tray.

This time he leaves the door open behind him. Lifting my head to help me drink, he places slices of fruit and nuts in my mouth and waits for me to chew and swallow.

I sense that he hates this guard work. There's something about the way his jaw clenches when I occasionally wince in pain. And the way his eyes dart to my face every few seconds to gauge my reactions. I've been feeling an emotion from him that I finally realize could be sympathy. I have a sneaking suspicion that he would rather be anywhere besides here, helping me grow stronger so I can be destroyed.

I take a chance that my hunch is right. "Louis, please help me get out of here," I whisper.

He acts like he doesn't hear me and pops a hazelnut into my mouth. I chew and swallow and wonder if there is a trick to this persuasiveness thing. Focusing on what I want from him, I picture him getting up, closing the door, and then untying me. I concentrate all of my energy into that little film reel in my head, watching him go through the motions I want time after time. I feel another nut against my lips, and my eyes pop open to see his gaze flicker quickly away from me as I take the food from his fingers.

He stands and walks toward the door. I am crushed by disappointment. He is my one chance: Unless I get superstrong superfast, there is no way I'm getting out of here on my own. As I watch him leave, I see something that I haven't noticed before. Within his bright red aura something gleams, like tiny filaments of gold. I blink a few times, wondering if lying on my back for so long is giving me eyestrain, but when I look again, the golden glint is still there.

As if he feels me watching him, Louis pauses. And then he turns and comes back. Carefully avoiding my gaze, he leans under the bed and yanks on one of the cords. It bites into my arm as the rope twists against my skin. I am petrified with alarm, wondering what he is doing.

Without looking back, he takes out a single key and leaves it on the windowsill before leaving the room, shutting the door loudly behind him.

What just happened here? I ask myself. I lift my head to look down at my hands. He has turned the cord around leaving the knot right next to my fingers. I lay my head back down and close my eyes in relief. Then, summoning all of my strength, I prop myself up and begin working the knot with my fingernails.

It's a simple knot, but it has been tied so tightly that I have to actually unravel some of the cord using my thumbnail as a knife. I hear footsteps approach the door and freeze, lying back down so that if someone peeks in they might not see anything amiss. The footsteps walk away, and I throw myself into the task harder than before, ripping the skin on my thumbs to loosen the cord. Finally I feel the knot release and I tear the cord free.

There are three more cords holding me down: across my shoulders, upper legs, and feet. I work these for the next few minutes, each being easier than the last now that I have more mobility, and finally I am free.

I consider waiting for Gaspard, but it feels like hours since he left. I could drape the ropes back around me, pretend to be tied up in case Violette returns. But if it comes to fighting her, I'm not sure I can win. I have no way to judge my strength.

Though I don't feel up to a fight, I do feel desperate enough to move my limbs. Maybe even to attempt an escape. Curious, I touch my chest, pulling my shirt apart where Violette's knife sliced it. I am covered in a thick layer of dried blood, so it is hard to see the knife wound. I run my fingers over my breastbone, where the blade entered. It is smooth. There is no wound. Not even a scar. I shiver and goose bumps raise on my forearms.

If I had any remaining doubts about my mortality, they are now gone. I am undeniably supernatural.

I swing my legs over the side of the bed and sit there, feeling the blood rush into my thighs. The pins and needles return with full force. I try to stand, but slump immediately to a sitting position until finally I can feel my toes. I stay like that for another moment before trying to stand again. Then I limp painfully across the room to the window.

Picking up Louis's key, I slip it into the lock. It fits, and I turn the handle carefully, teeth clenched, trying my best to avoid making noise. I push the window open slowly—an inch at a time—and after nothing happens, dare to stick my head out and look down. There is a six-foot drop to the main deck. No one is in sight.

I shake out my arms and legs, trying to get my circulation going before easing a still half-limp leg through the window and following it with the other. I hang over the side with my elbows and then ease myself down until I'm holding the window ledge with my fingertips and drop silently to the deck.

Or at least, that's what I attempt. My blood-encrusted Converse make a kind of crunching sound as they hit the wood, and the impact—one I could normally spring back up from—has me crouching, unable to straighten myself because my long-unused leg muscles have seized up.

I'm stuck there for a full three seconds, my heart beating like a drum, panicky that Violette will appear in front of me before I can get safely into the water. *Be calm and think*, I urge myself, and scan the space around me for anything that can be used as a weapon.

Just in time. As I push myself, with effort, into a standing position, I feel a hand clamp down on my shoulder. I look around to see one of the numa guards from the hotel scowling down at me.

THIRTY-NINE

"HEY!" THE NUMA SHOUTS. BEFORE HE CAN ALERT the others, I grab a metal oar attached to the wall next to me and swing it as hard as I can against his head. I am still weak, but seem to have hit him in the right spot, because he releases my shoulder and staggers backward just as another numa arrives on the deck and starts toward me.

"What is going on?" I hear Violette scream, and then I am diving off the boat's deck into the frigid water below.

I swim with determined strokes toward the shore. If I am the Champion, it definitely hasn't made me any stronger. I am tired and weak, but panic moves me quickly through the water. I thank my lucky stars that I was already a good swimmer when I was human.

When I was human. My chest constricts, and I falter in my stroke. I'm a monster. *No, you're a revenant,* I correct, urging my body forward.

I hear a splash in the water behind me. And then another. I assume that the numa guards are chasing me, but I don't take the time to look back. I struggle through the water, my muscles searing with pain, heading straight for the riverbank.

Suddenly someone else is in my head. Gaspard. *Kate, I am leading the others to the point where you are coming ashore. The numa will reach land before the kindred get to you. You will have to fight.*

Can your future-sight tell me if I will win? I ask, fighting to maintain my speed.

No, I can't see that.

Another few minutes and my feet touch the ground. I surge out of the water onto the shore. There are no buildings around, so we must be near one of the national parks outside of the Paris city limits. *No one to see me. No one to call to for help,* I think. *It's just me against the numa.*

Without looking back, I stumble forward, dripping and waterlogged and leaving a trail of bloody water behind me. Searching for anything I can use as a weapon, I grab a broken tree branch, snap it off, and strip it of its twigs as quickly as I can. It is almost the same size as the quarterstaff I trained on with Gaspard, although quite a bit heavier.

I turn to face the water and am thrown for a moment. The two men swimming in the water have the same creepy red halo of light shining around them that they did on the boat. But now that they're farther away, the red is illuminating the inky water beneath them and shooting straight up into the air like a beacon.

I blink. The light subsides while my eyes are closed, but it flares back up when I focus on them again. As they approach, the light grows dimmer, until they are upon me, charging up out of the water and the beacon disappears, leaving only the misty red haloes.

I don't have time to consider what the strange optical illusion means right now. Gaspard was right to warn me: They are so close that if I run, they will quickly catch me. And I have no idea where I am. No sense of direction. It would be too easy for me to get lost trying to find a way out of the woods.

Only five seconds elapse between the time I arm myself and the moment they are upon me, and I spend this flash of time furiously peeling bark away from one end of my stick.

I try to strategize as I watch them approach. Panic engulfs me as I see their lumbering forms and realize I have no idea how to take on two numa at once . . . with only a stick. *Don't think. Just act*, I tell myself. I breathe deeply and try to put myself into the zone—the frame of mind I've learned to slip into after months of fight training with Gaspard.

I don't have time to concentrate. My fingers are bleeding, and a shard of wood is stuck painfully beneath my nail. But the pain helps me focus. Stumbling slightly from the weight of the branch, I swing up and smash it against the shoulder of the first numa to reach me.

He isn't ready for the blow. Caught off balance, he stumbles and falls heavily onto one shoulder, crying out in pain as it dislocates.

The second of my attackers is upon me, and I swing awkwardly again, unused to such a heavy staff. It hits him low, striking his shins, but he is better prepared than his kindred. Though he staggers, he keeps his balance. He lunges for me, and I skip aside, letting him plow by before he turns and charges me again.

My enemy on the ground is back on his feet. I have two numa upon me at once, but I am ready, feeling the rhythm of the fight now. Everything I learned comes back to serve me, and I am in control.

I wait, balancing the stick horizontally in both hands, watching the attacker facing me. It seems that the two numa have no strategy besides rushing me individually. As Gaspard explained, one of the numa's greatest weaknesses is "anarchy in warfare." Unless they work under a strong leader, it's every numa for himself. I take advantage of this and focus on one at a time.

My enemy roars and runs for me, and I hit him squarely in the shoulder with the blunt end of the stick. As he falls back, I spot the other numa charging me from behind. Pulling the sharp end of the stick forcefully backward, under my arm, I wait until he is three feet away and thrust it through his chest.

Oh my God. I feel wood pass through flesh and am sickened, my throat spasming in an all-too-human reaction. *Don't think about it,* I urge myself. If I take the time to feel, I'm dead. Again.

The numa's eyes pop wide and he lets out a cry that is more like a groan as he places both hands around the rod protruding from his chest. I jerk the stick backward out of him, and he falls to the ground.

Bringing the bloody end around, I swing the rod back toward

my opponent at the level of his head. He reaches up and grabs it with both hands, wrenching it from my grasp. But his hands slip on the blood covering the staff and, fumbling, he drops the rod to the ground. I am too close for him to bend down and get it.

Furious, he roars. Raising his fists, he pulls back his arm to punch me. I strike first, bending low to my left, below his punch trajectory, and kick out with my right foot, planting it squarely in his chest. He stumbles back a step, but lunges low and is able to grab the improvised quarterstaff.

Swinging it like a baseball bat, he lands a powerful strike to my upper back, sending me flying forward. As my face hits the ground, I feel my cheek grind against dirt and rocks, and lie there, bleeding and unable to breathe. I push myself onto my hands and knees, gasping and choking and spitting dirt and blood. My breath has been knocked out, and I see stars and wonder how long I have before I pass out. I hear the numa coming up behind me, and scrabble forward, trying to get away. He catches me by the hair, grabbing my wet, straggly locks with one hand, and uses it to pull me to my feet. With the other, he holds the sharpened end of the rod to my face. With an expression like he will immensely enjoy what he is about to do, he draws my head back to ram it onto the staff point.

In the split second before I die, I see Vincent's face before me once again. He's on the quay of the Seine, standing in the sun, hands thrust into his jean pockets, giving me that crooked smile that I now know means, "I love you." *I love you, too*, I think, and my fear disappears as I gulp one last breath of air.

But before the stake meets my face I hear a twanging noise, and the numa is knocked off his feet to the side, landing heavily upon the ground. He twitches once, but the arrow lodged through his temple killed him before he even fell.

"Kate!" Vincent calls, and then he is clasping me against himself so tightly that I can feel his heart beat against my chest. Gasping for breath, I lean against him for support and let him take all my weight as I revel in the fact that *he is here*. Finally, he lets go and smoothes my wet, straggly hair off my face so that he can see me. He brushes the dirt and blood off my face with his fingertips. The emotion in his eyes makes my own cloud with tears.

"You're alive," he finally manages to say.

"Not really," I respond, my chest still heaving with exertion, and then can't say anything else because he is wrapping his arms around my shoulders, pulling me to him.

"I didn't think I'd ever see you again," he says. And he takes my face in his hands and kisses me.

It is tender. It is deep. It is my first kiss in my new incarnation . . . since my heart stopped and started again. I am undead, and yet Vincent is kissing me, and my worries that he wouldn't want me this way—that this would somehow change the way he felt about me—dissipate.

I kiss him back, pushing aside the rest of my fears and doubts and sorrow about what has been lost and abandoning myself to the pleasure of touching him again.

Drawing back from Vincent, I turn to see Charlotte standing nearby with a bow in her hand and a mischievous smile on her face. She's glowing. Not just in a happy kind of way—the air around her body is actually glowing a golden red, and around her head is the halo of the bardia, "an aura like a forest fire," as Gwen-haël had put it.

I glance at Vincent. He's the same: golden haloed and the air around his body shimmers like flames. *This is how I see now*, I think with amazement, and wonder if I'll ever get used to seeing my friends glowing and my enemies oozing red mist.

That is . . . if I live long enough. I remember that, though my immediate goal of escape is achieved, we are still in the middle of a numa-bardia war. Violette's not going to let me dance away from this without wreaking vengeance. *She'll try to get me back*, I think with a twinge of anger.

Charlotte pipes up: "Sorry for interrupting you two, but Violette's boat is long gone and the others are waiting for us back at the cars."

Vincent nods at her, and then pulls me in to give me one last kiss. He takes off his coat and wraps it around me, and pulls out his phone. He tells someone we're on our way and instructs them to pick up the bodies of the numa for burning.

Charlotte takes me by the hand. "I know that now's not the time to talk about this. And you're going to have all sorts of decisions to make and things to figure out, but . . ." Tears spring to her eyes and she drops her bow and throws her arms around me. "Welcome, kindred."

FORTY

FOUR VEHICLES AWAIT US AS WE WALK OUT OF the clearing toward the road. One is an ambulance. As we approach, two revenants in paramedic uniforms pull a stretcher out of the back and head into the woods in the direction we came from. "We're taking ambulances everywhere we go now," comments Vincent, nodding to them as we pass. "No numa bodies are left behind anymore. We're trying to clear out the city."

"How's that going?" I ask. I know he's trying to make conversation so as not to have to talk about Things. Whether it's because he's not ready, or he thinks I'm not ready, or because there are others around, I'm not sure. But I don't mind playing along since I'm actually dying to know what happened while I was gone.

"Not well," he responds. "We ambushed a few of them in JB's residences, but word spread fast and they evacuated the rest. Now it's like we're starting from scratch, with no idea where to look."

"And violence in the city is getting worse by the day," Charlotte interjected. "According to JB's police connections, since Violette left La Maison and became numa chief—full-time, that is—suicides have more than tripled, reports of child abuse and domestic disputes have skyrocketed, and the suburbs are exploding with gang violence. The more numa pour into town, the more incidents of violent crime are reported. We can't even begin to keep up."

"And you've been spending your time looking for me?" I ask, aghast.

"Of course," Charlotte says, as if that goes without saying. She walks ahead, leaving Vincent and me alone.

He pauses, staring at the ground for a moment. "You know that Bran identified you as the Champion?"

I nod.

"It makes sense," he says, his eyes showing concern mixed with something I can't quite place. Is it fear? He wraps an arm securely around my shoulders as we arrive at the car.

Ambrose and Geneviève leap out and envelop me in a sandwich hug. "You just about scared me out of my wits, Katie-Lou," Ambrose says.

He leans back and takes a look at me. I glance down and realize how I appear: covered in blood—my own and the numa's—matted with mud, dark stains on my clothes that even a swim through the river didn't manage to wash out, a knife slash through my T-shirt. I hold up my hands; where my fingernails don't already have dried blood crusted beneath, fresh blood oozes.

"Zombie chic," he concludes. "Only a Champion could pull it off."

"You better watch out, Ambrose. I might just fry you with my eye beams if you piss me off," I say.

He eyes me doubtfully. "You can do that?"

"Honestly," I admit, "I have no idea what I can do." I force a laugh, and Ambrose squeezes me to him again.

"You're going to be okay, little sis," he murmurs, and carefully tucks me into the backseat.

Vincent has been giving instructions to the driver of the first car, and now he returns and says, "Let's go!" He settles next to me while Ambrose takes the wheel.

"I'll ride with the others," says Charlotte as Geneviève climbs into the front seat. I notice Ambrose's eyes follow Charlotte as she jogs to the car in front of ours and jumps inside. Clenching his jaw, he guns our motor and spins the car out onto the road, doing an illegal U-turn to head in the opposite direction.

"Steroid rush?" asks Vincent drily.

Ambrose holds up his hands in denial. "This body is a hundred percent natural."

"Hands on the wheel," prods Geneviève.

"Thanks, Mom," Ambrose retorts. "Do you know exactly how long I've been driving?"

"Wow. Great to be back," I try to joke.

Vincent leans over and whispers, "How do you feel?"

"I'm okay," I say, and then realize that I'm not. I've been trying to hold myself together for so long: to keep myself safe . . . to escape Violette. I've let myself reason through what happened, but couldn't afford to let myself *feel* it.

But now that I'm out of immediate danger and under the protection of my friends . . . *my kindred* . . . I am suddenly overwhelmed by the events of the last few days and begin to tremble. Vincent takes me in his arms and holds me securely. After a few minutes, my shaking calms, but my teeth chatter and tears stream down my cheeks.

Geneviève turns to me and she places a steadying hand on my knee. "It takes most of us a while to come to grips with our new existence," she says, her voice steeped in compassion. "Normally you would have time to acclimate to becoming a revenant before being tossed into the middle of things. I cried for two weeks after Jean-Baptiste found me and helped me animate. And it was months before I was mentally ready to face my destiny."

"I assume Violette won't allow me any coping-with-newfound-immortality time?" I ask.

"No," Vincent says. "We figure that the only reason she has postponed a direct attack on us is because she wanted the Champion's power first. Now that you've escaped her, she won't wait long to make her move."

He doesn't want to say it. To call me the Champion. That's what the look of fear is about. Vincent doesn't want to think of me that way. I don't want to think of *myself* that way. It's too bizarre, and I don't even know what it means. I feel like an unpinned hand grenade—about to explode but having no idea whether I'll fizzle or blow up everything in the vicinity.

"Are we ready?" I ask, forcing that subject to the back of my mind.

"Our first priority was finding you," Vincent says. "Now that you're safe"—his voice catches on the last word—"now that you're with us, we will plan our next move."

I lean my head against the seat, weighed down by the scope of what is ahead. "We have to protect my grandparents and Georgia," I say. "They'll be the first ones Violette goes after now that I've escaped."

"They're already at La Maison," says Ambrose, glancing at me in the rearview mirror. "Charlotte and I took them there from the Crillon. Besides returning to their apartment to get things they needed, they haven't left our house."

I hadn't doubted that Vincent would take care of my family, but feel immense relief knowing that they are safe inside the bardia's walls. And then something occurs to me and my stomach ties itself back into knots. "Do they know . . . about me?"

Vincent turns my hand over and rubs his fingers up and down my palm. "I told them."

Tears spring to my eyes, and I pull my hand away from Vincent to wipe them away. "How . . . what did they do?" I ask, my voice breaking.

Vincent's eyes meet Ambrose's in the mirror.

"After getting your grandparents outside, I went back to the hotel room," Ambrose explains. "Vincent had been roughed up and knocked unconscious, and Violette and all her numa had left with your body. I smuggled him out of the hotel and back home. When he came to, he told us what had happened."

"When Bran heard the story," Vincent says, "he went

apoplectic and confessed that he had known you would become the Champion. You already had the 'star on fire' aura, and it was so bright he couldn't even look straight at you.

"I went from thinking you were dead to being informed that you were, not only a revenant, but the Champion, within a matter of moments," Vincent says, lowering his voice. "I went from mourning you . . . to relief that you weren't gone forever . . . to realizing this meant that you were out there somewhere being prepared for another death by Violette. If I hadn't had to keep my wits together and organize the search for you, I would have gone crazy."

"He was in major shock," Ambrose interjects as if Vincent's story needs backup. "I've known the man for almost a century, and I've never seen him so out of his mind. Arthur and I actually had to restrain him so that he wouldn't hunt Violette down by himself."

For a few minutes, the only sound is tires against asphalt. "I broke the news to your grandparents," says Vincent finally. "And like me, they hung on to the hope that you had survived."

Thinking of my family's pain, I close my eyes and rest my head on Vincent's shoulder.

Ambrose takes over the story. "JB showed up a couple days later, saying there was some crazy-ass revenant-in-the-making light like nothing he'd ever seen—visible all the way from Normandy."

"That's how we were sure you had animated," says Vincent. "We hoped we would find you before Violette destroyed you. Kate, your grandparents are just going to be glad to see you again.

Don't worry about anything else."

"I'll call now." Geneviève takes out her phone.

"I can't . . . I can't talk to them," I stammer. "Not on the phone."

"Don't worry," Geneviève says. "I'll have Jeanne break the news. That will probably be easiest for them." She makes the call, and I hear the housekeeper answer.

"We've got Kate," Geneviève says. "She's alive. And . . ." She pauses, considering how to put it. "She's one of us now."

I hear the sound of Jeanne's relief explode from the other end of the line in a jumble of emotional French syllables before she hangs up.

"Can we have some music?" Vincent asks. Ambrose switches the radio on and repositions the rearview mirror, and Geneviève turns around to give us privacy.

We lay our heads against the seat back and look at each other. Neither wants to be the first to speak.

Looking down, Vincent picks some dried mud off my hand with his fingernail and says, "Although this isn't what I wanted for you, it's better than the alternative. Your being immortal is better than your being dead."

"I know," I respond, closing my eyes and exhaling deeply. When I open them his face is next to mine. His fingers stroke my wet hair, smoothing it down. "Let's not talk about it now," I whisper. "If we survive these next few weeks, we'll have as long as we want to figure it all out."

He nods. Leaning forward, he kisses my cheeks, my forehead, my eyes, my lips.

"Mon Kate, qui était à moi, qui n'est plus à moi," he whispers as he kisses me. And then he says it in English. "My Kate, who was mine, who is no longer mine"—he tiredly rubs his bloodshot eyes—"because now you belong to fate."

FORTY-ONE

AS WE DRIVE INTO PARIS, THE SKY CHANGES FROM cotton candy pink to cantaloupe. Thin red beams appear amid the white lights of the city that begin to flicker on as twilight approaches. They look like lasers pointed into the clouds, and I wonder if the carnival has returned to the Tuileries Gardens.

We turn a corner and the Seine appears, and upon seeing it, my heartbeat steadies like it does every time I see the river. It is a blue flag of continuity for me, symbolizing the continuous flow of time in an ageless city. Comforted, I take Vincent's hand in mine and close my eyes until we arrive at La Maison.

The gates swing open, and I see three figures seated on the side of the fountain. They stand as we drive into the courtyard, and I leap from the car into their arms.

"Oh, Katya," says Mamie, pulling me to her and wrapping her arms around my neck.

"*Princesse*," Papy says, encircling the two of us in a hug.

"Are you okay?" Mamie asks, her eyes searching my face.

"I'm fine, Mamie. I just had a fight with a couple of numa. But I won," I say, attempting a smile.

"We were so worried, Kate," Papy interjects, and something catches in his throat. With a stiffness that sounds unnatural for him, he says, "Nothing matters except the fact that you are here now." It sounds like something he has practiced. Like he's trying to convince himself as he says the words.

I see his distress. He is hugging me—the old Kate—while recoiling from the idea of hugging the new me. The undead me. I don't blame him. Hopefully we'll both be able to get used to it with time. *If we have the time*, I think, remembering that we are going into war and nothing is certain.

Georgia stands quietly until my grandparents let me go. Her eyes are swollen and red, and it looks like she hasn't slept in days. "Kate," she murmurs. After seeing my mournful Papy, it breaks my heart to see my sister like this.

"You don't look any different," she says, hesitantly touching my cheeks with her fingertips. "And you won't ever look any different from this, even when I'm old. Even when I'm dead." She smiles mournfully. "I don't know why I'm crying. I should be cheering, 'Huzzah, death!'" She rotates her finger in a halfhearted celebratory circle. "You're immortal now, for God's sake."

"Not if Violette has anything to do with it," I respond.

She studies me for a moment, and then I see a little spark of life flash behind her pale green eyes. "She obviously hasn't seen our sword fighting skills," she says, smiling with effort. "We're just going to have to give her hell." And taking my hand, she leads me into the house.

Vincent follows us, walking beside my grandparents. Jeanne waits inside the foyer. She brushes tears away, gives me a silent hug, and then motions toward the sitting room. "Jean-Baptiste and Gaspard are waiting for you," she says, and then, glancing toward Vincent, adds, "They will be leaving right afterward."

My grandmother and grandfather pause, unsure if they're invited to join the meeting, but I can tell they don't want to leave my side. "Come with me," I say. Jean-Baptiste rises to his feet as we enter, and it is strange to see him acting like a guest in his own home.

Hello, Kate, says Gaspard.

"Hi," I respond out loud, for the benefit of the others.

Even if I couldn't see it ahead of time, I knew you'd win against those brutes, he says with pride.

"Thanks to your training," I say, "and Charlotte showing up at the right moment with a well-aimed arrow."

Jean-Baptiste gives me the *bises* and then puts his hands on my shoulders as he inspects me. "You look the same. Eyes, cheekbones, lips, hair . . . ," he says, balking a bit when his gaze reaches my straggly mud-blood-and-river-water coiffure. "None have been altered. Becoming one of us hasn't changed you a bit. Incredible."

"Why would Kate change?" says Vincent, grinning. "I was ready to follow her to the ends of the earth when she was human. She doesn't need anything extra to convince humanity to lay their lives in her hands."

Now that the conversation is turning supernatural, I glance back at my grandparents to gauge their reaction. Papy is staring longingly at the door, and Mamie is fidgeting and looking extremely uncomfortable. Georgia raises an eyebrow at me. I can tell that she too feels this conversation isn't making anything easier for my family.

"So," the older revenant says, "our very own Kate is the Champion. When I saw the light you gave off from inside that houseboat, I knew something special was happening. Imagine my astonishment that it was you, my dear. Under my nose this whole time, when I had believed that Vincent was the chosen one." He peers closer at me and touches my cheek.

"It all makes sense in hindsight," he continues. "At least now I can forgive myself for letting you into the house the day you discovered Vincent dormant. Being persuaded by a teenage girl is one thing. But being persuaded by the Champion . . . well, I can handle that."

"I'll try to take that as a compliment and not a dis, Jean-Baptiste," I say, smiling.

"That makes one thing I can forgive myself for," he admits, a shadow falling across his features. "My kindred have much more to pardon. Which is my cue to go. Shall we, Gaspard?"

"We never asked you to leave," Vincent says, blocking the door.

"I know that," Jean-Baptiste replies. He grabs his cane out of an umbrella stand and taps Vincent's leg gently with it. Vincent pauses and then steps aside. JB walks past us into the foyer and stops under the elephantine chandelier.

"But I should not be here"—the bardia's former leader continues—"in the middle of a black and white war, diluting the good side with my grayness. The fact that my intentions were good doesn't excuse the sin I committed to win my kindred's protection. And in the end, it did no good. Gaspard and I must go. *Au revoir*," he says, and steps out the door.

This feels wrong. Vincent doesn't want them to leave, and neither do I. "Wait," I call. Jean-Baptiste hesitates. "I want you to stay," I say. He turns and peers at me. "I don't agree that it would be better for your kindred that you go," I continue. "You've been their leader for centuries, and now they"—I hesitate and then, taking Vincent's hand, continue—"*we* are facing a great danger. Stay and help us."

"My dear, haven't you been listening to me?" Jean-Baptiste says sadly. With one finger, he adjusts the ascot at his neck, as if it's suddenly tightened. "With what I have done, it is better that I not lead my kindred into battle."

"You don't *have* to lead them," Vincent interjects, letting go of my hand and stepping toward JB. "You named me leader and I accepted the role. But just because you aren't leading doesn't mean you can't stay and stand with us against Violette. I want you to stay. *We* want you to stay."

The stiffness in Jean-Baptiste's pose loosens a little, and sighing, he walks over and places his hand on Vincent's arm. "My boy, I will consider. Give me an hour or two to think about things."

Vincent nods solemnly, and Jean-Baptiste turns and walks out the door.

À bientôt, Gaspard says to me.

"I hope to see you soon," I respond. Vincent closes the door, and I turn to face my family. My sister wrinkles her nose. "What, Georgia?" I ask.

"I don't want to ruin the gravity of the moment, or anything, but . . ." She pauses and glances at my grandparents, bracing herself for their disapproval. "If you don't take a shower stat I just may puke. Eau de zombie is *not* a good scent for you." I try not to laugh and kind of hiccup instead, and finally Georgia starts to smile.

Papy shakes his head. And suddenly in the place of my strong, capable grandfather stands a tired old man. He gives me a hug, patting me on the back, and then withdraws. "I love you, Kate, and I am indescribably relieved that you are not gone forever. But I can't talk about what has happened to you—or what will be happening. You'll just have to excuse me. Give me time."

"Let's go to the library, Papy," Georgia says, and putting an arm around his shoulders, she leads him up the stairs.

Mamie waits until they've disappeared before she speaks. Tenderly touching my face as if reassuring herself that I'm actually here, she says, "All I want to do right now is take you home and lock the doors and stay inside for the next few weeks protecting you from the world. But I realize that that isn't our reality anymore. We can't even go home. In fact, from what Bran tells us, you will be the one protecting us."

"Mamie, I promise I won't do anything unnecessarily . . ."

"Shh, Katya. Stop right there." She gives me a sad look. "Like your Papy, I don't want to think about it either. The idea of your being in danger is one I can't face. But you need to know that we support you and love you just the same as we did before. We'll figure out the details later."

She gives my cheek a firm kiss before releasing me. "Jeanne has promised me tea," she says simply, and heads through the door into the back hallway.

"Are you okay?" Vincent asks, now that we're alone. He is being overly careful, waiting for me to make a move. Watching to see what I want.

I hold out my hand and pull him out of the wide-open foyer into the privacy of the sitting room and close the door behind us.

He strokes my matted hair with his fingers and looks me up and down. "Charlotte's assembling everyone for a meeting, and you and I both need to be there. Not that I don't think you look beautiful caked in mud," he says, smiling, "but . . . before you see everyone you might want to take that shower your sister suggested."

"Eau de zombie?" I ask with a smile.

"You actually smell fine," he says, grinning. "Eau de river water's more like it."

"Do I have time for a shower?" I ask, pulling him closer until his face is inches from mine.

"A little," he responds.

"How much time?" I ask.

He swallows. "Enough for a shower. Not enough to do what you're thinking about," he responds hoarsely.

"Ten minutes," I say. "Let's just take ten minutes."

He glances at my lips and presses his eyes shut. When he opens them, his expression is one of longing. "Kate, I don't want ten minutes. Ten minutes isn't enough. I want days. If we start something now, I'm not going to want to stop. They'll have to drag me out of your bed to go to war."

"A kiss, then?" Before I can finish asking, his lips are pressed to mine. I hold his head in my hands and kiss him like I've been longing to.

I lose sense of myself. I lose track of time. All that exists are me and Vincent and the experience of loving each other.

Eyes closed, forfeiting vision to increase sense of touch. Eyes open, staring into wells of blue flecked with gold. Eyes closed, the pressure of his mouth against mine consuming me. Eyes open, watching his lids narrow with desire. Eyes closed, feeling his body hard against mine. Knowing that time is not ours today, and wondering if it ever will be.

As my bathtub fills with hot water, I fold my arms across my chest, hugging myself as I wander the circumference of the bedroom Vincent has appointed for me. I peer at the collection of precious objects and admire the paintings until I start seeing a pattern.

A painting of the Pont des Arts. A tiny red wooden rowboat set on a bookshelf next to a crystal Eiffel Tower. A pair of antique opera glasses. A vintage postcard from Villefranche-sur-Mer. A matchbook from the restaurant where we ate brunch in New York.

I near a small cubist painting hanging near the window, about the size of a hardcover book. I lean in to admire the tiny refracted scene of a glass sitting on a café table, and when I see the signature, I inhale so sharply that it sends me into a coughing fit: Vincent hung a Picasso in my bedroom.

And then I reach the antique footed bathtub and notice for the first time that there is an enormous vase stuffed with branches of white flowers standing on the floor beside it. And my brain suddenly registers the delicious perfume I've been smelling ever since I walked into the room: It is lilac.

FORTY-TWO

"I HEAR WHAT YOU'RE SAYING, BUT I DON'T agree," Charlotte says.

Vincent cuts in. "According to our sources, dozens of numa have arrived in Paris over the last twenty-four hours. We have no idea where they're assembling. Our raids on Jean-Baptiste's rental properties two days ago succeeded in taking out eight numa. But that small victory cost us, since they immediately evacuated his other apartments. Now we have no idea where to find them. So if anyone has a productive suggestion"—he eyes Charlotte, who holds her hands up in surrender—"please feel free to voice it."

I can't focus. I have been feeling progressively stronger as the hours pass, and the last thing my body wants to do right now is sit through a long meeting. I'm actually kind of craving a jog around the neighborhood. Which is pretty strange for me.

My eyes stray to the library's window while Vincent and the others pore over a map of Paris spread across a table. I can't help strategize anyway. I don't know anything about Paris's numa or where they've been spotted. After trying to be interested for a half hour, my brain gives up and I let my thoughts wander.

I notice Ambrose sitting to one side, obviously as distracted as me. But his gaze isn't out the window. Geneviève sits just across the table from us, as alluring as the day I first saw her with Vincent in La Palette: long platinum blond hair, eyes so light they are almost gray.

I look back at Ambrose and follow his line of sight back to the object of his attention: not Geneviève but Charlotte, with her long wheat-blond hair and rosebud cheeks. She bites her lip as she draws a line on the map from one mark to another. And I see him flinch as she glances up at him and then, with equal attention, at each person around the table as she explains the strategy.

I walk over to sit next to him. "You look kind of distracted, Ambrose," I whisper.

"Yeah, well, I'm not much into planning. I'm mainly here for the muscle," he responds, managing to rip his gaze away from Charlotte. He flexes a bicep and winks. "They just use me for my body."

I laugh and want to hug him, but control myself. "So, it's nice having Geneviève and Charlotte back, isn't it?"

Ambrose's eyes shoot back to Charlotte and he nods. "She's changed, hasn't she? Charlotte, I mean."

"Um, besides growing her hair long she doesn't seem to have changed much to me," I say, trying not to smile. "Why?"

"It's just that she seems so . . . in charge. I mean, she's always had her act together, but ever since she's been back she's seemed more confident or something. And now that she's Vincent's second . . . I guess I've always thought of her as a little sister. You know, the huggable kind you want to take care of. But now that I see her working with him and taking control . . . I mean . . . the girl is *fierce*."

Ambrose's face shines with respect and a sort of curious awe, and I have to restrain myself from jumping up and cheering for the fact that it has finally happened. He has finally noticed what was right under his nose. The question is—does she still feel the same for him?

I lean my head on his shoulder and gaze around the room, feeling a deep sense of joy in knowing my fate is irrevocably tied to these people I love. Once again my attention is caught by a light outside the window. "So is there some kind of neighborhood party or French festival going on?" I ask Ambrose.

His brow creases. "No," he says. "Not that I can think of. Why?"

"It's just those red lights that I keep seeing. Like that one right there." I gesture toward the window.

"I don't see any lights," he says, squinting out the glass.

"See, there it is again. There are two."

He looks skeptical. "Uh, nope."

"Oh, come on, Ambrose. It's like two red lasers pointing straight up into the sky, just at the end of the block. Don't tell me you can't see them."

Ambrose takes my hand and leads me to the window. "Just where do you see them?"

"Right there," I say, pointing to the two very obvious lights. "In fact they're a lot bigger than lasers. They're like flame-colored columns . . . ," I say, my words faltering as I have a flashback to the riverside. The lights are the same color as those I saw projecting from the two numa who were chasing me. The light I saw when they were a little ways away that disappeared when they got closer.

Something clicks. Heightened powers of perception. Can I see something the others can't? "You don't see it?" I ask Ambrose once more.

He scans the darkened vista outside the window and then looks at me, worried.

"I think I've figured out how we can find the numa," I call toward the table, and everyone turns my way.

Ten minutes later, the entire group is outside on the street facing two of Violette's sentries. Charlotte steps in front of them, her hand on the hilt of the sword hidden beneath her coat. "What are you doing here?" she asks.

One of the numa dares respond. "Keeping watch," he says simply, his eyes narrowing as he spots Ambrose standing behind Charlotte scowling and looking twice his already-imposing size.

"Where is your leader now?" asks Vincent.

"Even if I knew, why would I tell you?" the numa responds.

"Because we might spare your pitiful afterlives and let you go," growls Ambrose.

"No, you won't," the numa says defiantly, and he and his companion swiftly draw their swords.

Ambrose leaps in front of Charlotte. "You're right. I won't," he says, and rams his sword forcefully through the numa's chest. A second passes before he lets the limp form drop to the ground.

The other numa is down almost as quickly, and Vincent wipes his sword on the man's coat before returning it to its scabbard. "Let's get them off the street," he says.

I shudder as Ambrose swings one of the bodies over his shoulder. Two bardia accompanying us pick up the other corpse between them and head toward La Maison.

The danger gone, I drop back and follow them. But something feels wrong to me. It's not like my kindred killed the numa without provocation. They were armed and wanted to fight. But there is still an unsettled feeling in the pit of my stomach. It isn't pity— it's something else. Unable to pinpoint my emotion, I focus on Charlotte, who walks up behind Ambrose.

"You know, there *is* such a thing as holding people for questioning," she says crisply.

"Yeah, see, I kind of forget that in the heat of the moment," he replies, flashing her an apologetic smile. She shakes her head impatiently and runs to catch up with Vincent, who is opening the gates.

Ambrose meets my eyes. "Like I said, she is *fierce*!" he says, shaking his head in awe.

FORTY-THREE

OUR GROUP LOOKS OVER THE CITY FROM THE vantage point of La Maison's roof terrace. Paris once again reminds me of a great lady. Tonight she wears a black velvet dress and pearls flash from her buildings' windows. But for me, the vista is slashed by flaming red lines. A few on our side of the river appear as thick as columns, whereas the ones far off in the direction of Montmartre are as thin as crimson threads.

"How many do you see?" Vincent stands by my side holding my cold hand in his warm one.

"A lot."

"Like a few dozen?" he asks.

"Like more than a hundred," I respond. Silence falls over our little group as everyone studies the horizon for something they cannot see.

"They're not all in one place," I continue. "There are a group down that way," I say, pointing toward Chinatown. "Others over there, on the other side of Bastille." I indicate a forest of red beams far to our east. "More up toward Montmartre."

Vincent studies the ground at his feet for a moment, and then turns to our group. "We need more bardia," he says. "If we count all of our kindred in and directly around Paris, we aren't more than forty. We can take the numa little by little, as long as they don't group together. But if they do, we're lost. Who else can we ask to join us?"

"Jean-Baptiste said that he and Gaspard will join us as soon as Gaspard reanimates early this morning," Arthur says.

"Won't it take him a while to recover?" I ask.

"No," Arthur responds. "He wasn't injured when he went dormant. We old guys are up and on our feet practically as soon as we awake. It's you newbies that have a harder time in the morning," he says with a grin.

Arthur's in a really good mood for us being on the brink of warfare, I think, and wonder if it is because we will soon fight Violette, or something else . . . like my sister, for example.

"I put in a call to our New York kindred a few hours ago," Vincent admits, reaching back for my hand. I look up at him in surprise. "Jules?" I ask hopefully.

"No, I talked to Theo Gold. But he was supposed to pass the message on. I asked that Jules bring a contingent here as soon as possible."

The others nod doubtfully. In the time it would take for Jules to bring a group over from New York, the war could already be over.

"It's been over a week since I talked to Charles, and I've left him a million messages telling him we need him," Charlotte says. "I tried to contact him again today. No response. He and his hippy-dippy in-touch-with-their-feelings kindred are probably still up in the mountains, meditating on leaves or something. I'll keep trying, but they'll never get here in time if we engage today." She is trying to sound lighthearted, but I know she wants her brother by her side if she is going into battle.

Vincent nods. "Okay, I'm putting out a call to all of France's revenants. Anyone else you know within driving distance, please contact. This is going to go down in the next twenty-four hours. If we wait any longer, their forces can only grow and their defenses become stronger. We have to strike first. And we'll start tonight while they're still scattered and in small groups."

People pull out their cell phones as they head down the stairs. Vincent puts his arms around my waist, presses his lips to my forehead, and leans back to look me in the eye. "Are you going to be able to do this? You don't even need to fight. If you can just lead us to the groups that will be enough."

"Believe it or not, I am dying for some action. I feel like I could sprint a whole marathon."

"That wouldn't surprise me in the least," Vincent says, his lips forming a smile. "But you're not feeling weak? You haven't even been fully animated for a day."

"I feel totally wired," I admit, bouncing up onto my toes. Taking his face in my hands, I pull him close and kiss him.

"Yeah. I'm kind of feeling the same myself," he says with a sexy grin. "Let's just try to hold that thought until we defeat the numa."

We kiss again and his expression becomes serious. "I really don't want you in the heart of the action, Kate. Even though you're strong, you're also new. And, yes, as a revenant you are hard to destroy. But don't think for a second that Violette has given up on capturing you. You are her prize, and every numa out there will be trying to bring you back to their leader."

I nod. "I understand."

"Just because you're the Champion doesn't mean you have to act like one," Vincent says with a ghost of a smile.

"The prophecy says I will lead you to victory," I tease.

"If you lead us to each of Paris's numa, I would say that more than qualifies," Vincent allows. "But victory can be measured in lots of ways. Whether any of us will survive this war isn't at all sure. I want to see my kindred safely through without loss of life. Especially yours."

Bran is waiting for me when we step down through the trapdoor. "Kate!" he exclaims, and reaches out as if he wants to hug me, before changing his mind and dropping his arms by his sides. I hug him instead, his skinny frame floppy in my arms.

"I am sorry, my dear, but I can't look you straight in the face. Your aura was already hard to look at when you were human. Now it blinds me." He averts his eyes and looks at the floor behind me.

"Bran, why didn't you tell me before?"

"What might have happened if I had? You could have put yourself in harm's way just to discover if I was right. Or perhaps Jean-Baptiste would have. He is a good man, but was desperate to have the aid of the Champion."

Bran tries again, unsuccessfully, to look me in the face. "Now we know why. He needed someone to help him get out of this mess he had gotten into. To destroy the numa so he would no longer be bound to his shameful bargain."

I touch his arm thoughtfully. "Do you know what my powers are, Bran?" I ask.

"I have no information besides what is contained in the prophecy. But you already performed one of your most important roles: You single-handedly reunited the flame-fingered with our bardia wards after centuries of being lost to each other. That role in itself saved your Vincent. Once I master the gifts of ease of bardia suffering and dispersion, our continued alliance in the future can only be beneficial."

With effort, he shifts his eyes to look straight into mine. His face takes on an unreadable expression: something between sadness and hope.

"Be careful, Kate," he says. And leaning forward, he gives me an awkward back-patting hug.

Charlotte is waiting in my room when I arrive. She has brought my fighting gear up from the armory, and is already dressed in hers, ready to go. She sits beside a low table helping herself to a tray of food. I pop a cheese *gougère* into my mouth and savor its flakey goodness as I pull up a chair. "I'm ravenous!" I admit.

"When's the last time you ate?" she asks.

"On the boat. Violette was feeding me so that I would get my strength back and fully animate. Looks like that worked a little too well for her!" I think back to the strange, sad numa boy, Louis, and something tugs inside me.

Charlotte munches on an apple slice, looking pensive.

"What are you thinking about?" I ask.

"Ambrose," she responds. "He's been acting really weird lately."

"Weird good or weird bad?" I ask, popping a melon ball into my mouth.

"Weird freaky," she replies, looking troubled. "He keeps watching me. I wonder if he questions JB's decision to name me as second. Maybe he's waiting for me to slip up or something."

"Hmm," I say, unable to keep my lips from crooking up at the corners.

Mercifully, there is a knock on the door and Arthur sticks his head in. "Fifteen minutes," he says. My heart skips a beat and I realize that I'm nervous. The other times I fought, the fight came to us. I've never had time to think about it in advance.

"Man, he's got it bad for your sister," Charlotte says after he's gone. "But she is really playing it cool."

"It could be because Papy and Mamie would completely freak if they thought that another of their granddaughters was falling for a revenant."

Charlotte shrugs. "Your grandparents are involved now, whether or not they want to be. You're one of us—it's not like they can just pack you up and take you home."

I think about Mamie and Papy and their response to seeing me: joy and relief mixed with horror and despair. My heart aches. Will they ever be able to look at me the same as they did before?

I change the subject. "How does it feel to be Vincent's second?"

"Like I was born for it. Like I've been waiting for this role for the last fifty years." She smiles. "It's time for you to get suited up. I'll wait for you in the foyer." She stands and turns to go.

"Charlotte?"

"Yes."

"Please don't leave."

She looks at me curiously, and then comes over to put her arms around me. "This is scary, isn't it?" she asks.

"Yep."

She gives me a squeeze and then walks over to the bed and picks up a pair of leather pants. I shuffle out of my jeans and take them from her.

"Violette's timing really sucks," she says. "You shouldn't have to jump right in like this before you even have time to test yourself. But we're going into it together. You, me, Ambrose, Vincent, and the rest of our kindred. We never work alone. You will always be one part of a whole. Together we can win this fight—I am sure of it."

Charlotte's courage is contagious. As I pull on layers of protective clothing, I begin to feel emboldened, and a sense of purpose sparks my will. I am bardia. Whether or not I feel capable, I was made for this.

FORTY-FOUR

IT IS ONE A.M. WHEN WE LEAVE. I AM GLAD IT IS late. My grandparents will have no idea I'm gone. Hopefully we'll be back before they wake up and they won't have the time to worry.

The closest small grouping of lights is just north of us, where I see three clear red beams shoot into the night sky. We cross the Carrousel Bridge and walk through the Louvre's courtyard, passing the sparkling crystal pyramid, and back out through the monumental archway.

Vincent walks beside me, checking from time to time to make sure the others are keeping up. We are followed by five groups of highly armed revenants, and heading toward three lone numa. So why is my heart thumping so hard?

Finally we turn down a small side street and I nod toward a large open gate halfway down on the right. "The lights come from inside there," I say.

"I know that passageway," says Charlotte. "It's covered with a glass roof and lined with shops on either side. The shops will all be closed, but there are apartments above them on the second floor."

"Okay," says Vincent, and phones the group behind us. "Arthur. Our targets are inside Passage du Grand Cerf. Bring your group to the rue St. Denis side and secure that exit. Have the other groups guard the street. And call the ambulance to meet us here. We will have three corpses to pick up."

"We're just going to trap them and kill them?" I ask Vincent as we approach the arched gateway.

"Kate. They're numa. They are murderers. And if we don't kill them, they will kill us."

I nod, but I still feel strange about it.

All of the shopfronts are dark, but a few lights are on in the second-floor windows. As we approach, one of them flickers off and footsteps can be heard coming down the stairs. A door in the middle of the passageway opens, and two men step out. Their shoes click hollowly against the black-and-white tiles.

"Stay here." Vincent waves me back as he and the others stride quickly forward. The light catches the men's faces: It is Nicolas and Louis. *Violette's second and her favorite in the same place at once!* I think. We have stumbled into something important.

Seeing the young numa, I can't help but follow Vincent and the others. Once I get within a few yards of them the red beacons extinguish, like they did when the numa got close to me on the riverbank, leaving only the misty red auras. *I don't see golden beams shooting up from the bardia's auras*, I realize. *There's only one reason a Champion would have this gift: to hunt numa.*

I see the flickering gold inside Louis's aura, and it seems to me like a tiny bit of hope has materialized as light and is struggling to free itself from the cold crimson glare. Something tugs at my memory, and I try to think where I have seen this before. And then it comes to me: the *guérisseurs'* archives. The painting of the numa with the gold in his aura—the one crossing the stream and being received by bardia. *That scene is about redemption*, I realize suddenly. I think back to how Louis had seemed sympathetic to me on the boat, and had helped loosen my bonds. He actually helped me escape, which, even considering my persuasiveness superpower, is kind of incredible for a numa to have done. The color of his aura must mean that he's like the numa I saw in the painting. Is it possible for some numa to change their destiny? To change sides? Vincent told me it wasn't, but what if he was wrong? Violette crossed over to the other side—what's to prevent a numa from doing the same?

"Nicolas!" calls Vincent, and the numa spin and draw their swords.

"Please don't tell me you all were just popping by for some late-night shopping," says the older numa drily, though he is unable to hide his shock.

"No," says Ambrose. "Just doing a little tidy-up-the-neighborhood work, and thought we smelled some trash in here."

Nicolas ignores him, keeping his gaze on Vincent. "So you are the bardia's new leader? I would think you'd be more interested in hunting down our leader than chasing after her second-in-command."

"There were three of you. Where's the other?" Vincent asks.

Louis's eyes flicker toward the apartment they just came from. And then, realizing what he's done, he nervously grasps his sword in both hands as if he can protect the door from all ten of us. "Watch that door!" orders Charlotte, and Ambrose stations himself in front of it, sword drawn.

"Would you like to die fighting, or should we stand here all night chatting?" asks Vincent, and the revenants on both sides of the passage draw their swords.

I see the fear on Louis's face, and my heart goes out to him. *You don't want to be here, do you?* As soon as the words cross my mind, his eyes widen, and he looks around as if trying to locate a volant spirit.

No, I think with disbelief. Did I just communicate with Louis? Could I contact the mind of a numa? Only one way to find out. *Louis, this is Kate. You told me your secret. And I want to save you. Are you willing to side with us? To turn your back on the numa and help the bardia?*

He stands there confused until he locates me standing behind Vincent and Charlotte. He looks me straight in the eyes, his own widened in fear.

Do you want to escape the numa? Will you come with us? I ask again. Nothing. *Well, DO YOU?*

"Yes!" he yells. Dropping his sword, he puts his hands up in the air.

"What the hell are you doing?" asks Nicolas, looking Louis up and down.

Vincent catches my arm as I step past him. "Kate! What . . . ," he begins.

"Amnesty," I say to the numa. "I'm offering amnesty to both of you, if you agree to abandon your kind and come to our side."

Nicolas begins laughing but keeps his sword at the ready.

"Kate, what are you saying?" hisses Charlotte. My kindred look at one another in shock.

"I am saying that, like anyone, they deserve a second chance before being slaughtered. That maybe, if given the opportunity, they will walk away from what they are."

"Kate," Vincent pleads, "that isn't even possible."

"Violette was a bardia and she became numa. It must be possible," I insist.

"That rule was written in our texts. It was never actually tried—as far as we know—until she did it. But it can't go the other way. That . . . that is unthinkable."

"You know," Nicolas says, "I think your Champion here has a point." And he begins to lower his sword.

"Freeze right there," says Geneviève with a permafrost voice, taking a step closer to him. "Don't you dare move."

Keeping his eyes on me, Nicolas ignores her and squatting carefully down, he lays his sword on the floor. Then, straightening, he spreads his hands before him, showing us that they are empty. "I have been waiting for this day. The day when someone finally asked me what I wanted."

Louis draws his breath in in surprise and stares openmouthed at his fellow numa.

"And finally, it took the Champion to ask the right question. Do you think I like working for Violette, that miserable, obsessive, self-absorbed ex-bardia?" He looks from one incredulous face to the next. "Of course not. So when asked if I would rather die in her service or join you—help you defeat her—my response is . . ."

And his hand moves inside his coat and back out so quickly that I don't even know what has happened until I look at Geneviève and see the knife sticking out of her neck. She makes a gurgling noise and crumples to the ground. Ambrose roars and leaps toward Nicolas, who dips down and retrieves his sword.

As they begin fighting, Vincent rushes forward and throws Louis to the ground, pinning him there with his foot. He lifts his sword over the boy's back, ready to thrust it through his chest. "Let's see you try the same trick from that position," Vincent growls.

As Charlotte goes to Geneviève's aid, I rush past her to Vincent. "Don't," I cry, grabbing his arm.

My resolve wavers for a second as I see Charlotte lower Geneviève's dead body to the ground. I turn back to him. "Vincent, you have to believe me. I know what I'm doing is right."

He squeezes his eyes shut. Arthur's group is running toward us. Making a split-second decision, Vincent yells to them, "We're taking this one alive."

"What?" Arthur is incredulous.

Vincent moves his foot off Louis's back, and Arthur bends down to jerk the boy to his feet. "Who is upstairs?" Vincent demands.

"Just . . . just another numa," Louis stammers. "We were dropping off weapons for Violette. He is in charge of arming those who are arriving in town."

Vincent and Arthur fling the door open and run up the stairs. A yell comes from inside the apartment. Sounds of fighting begin and just as suddenly stop.

I look over and see that Nicolas is now down, his body a heap under a fur coat, lying in a puddle of dark blood.

An overhead window flies open and Vincent leans out. "We got him, but he was on the phone. Call the other groups and let them know that enemy reinforcements may be on their way."

"Enemy reinforcements are already here," comes a voice from behind us. A dozen numa stand in the passage's opening.

FORTY-FIVE

I HADN'T SEEN THEM COMING. I KICK MYSELF FOR not being more attentive, but my focus had been on saving Louis and not on protecting my own. I glance around to see how many we are. Ambrose, Charlotte, Vincent, Arthur, and the four revenants in Arthur's group. With me, that makes nine. Ten if Louis fights with us.

The other groups, another fifteen bardia, are somewhere on the outside. Or at least, they were. Either they have already been defeated or they can still come to our aid. In any case, at the moment we are outnumbered by double. But for some reason, this doesn't scare me. It just feeds my determination.

Breathing deeply, I draw my sword and bounce on my toes, adrenaline sizzling in my veins. *I am ready for this,* I think, and run at the first numa I see, attacking before he can get to me. I catch him by surprise and slash at his sword arm before he can lift it. He drops his weapon and crouches down to recover it. As he stands, I lunge. My sword pierces his chest. I drive it deeply in and then quickly pull it out.

He stares at me, eyes bulbous. Grabbing his chest, he coughs up a small stream of blood and then falls forward, his sword clattering to the ground beside him.

I can't believe I just killed someone. I expect to feel sick like I did at the riverside, but instead I feel exhilarated. It's us against them: bardia versus numa in a fair fight. *Death in this case serves the larger good*, I tell myself. But with a pang of realization, I know those words are to comfort the old Kate. New Kate has more numa to kill.

Charlotte is fighting like a madwoman. Geneviève's body has been pushed to the side of the passageway, out of the melee. Arthur and his four are standing back-to-back with us, fighting the numa coming from the other end of the passageway. Louis stands behind me, weaponless.

Are you with us? I ask him silently.

Nodding, he sweeps his long brown hair behind his ear. I scoop his sword from where Vincent had kicked it aside, and meet his eyes as I hand it to him. With the slightest of smiles, he moves to my side and we advance on two numa. "What in the . . . ," says the one directly in front of me, gaping when he sees Louis beside me.

Louis's sword skills aren't very good, but thanks to the split second of surprise his kindred experience when they register his defection, he's given the advantage, and together we take out our opponents. As more rush in to take their place, I see that two in Arthur's group are down. Ambrose smashes away at an

348

opponent with one arm, the other dangling uselessly by his side.

We have formed a small circle facing outward as we fight off numa that number twice our ranks. "What do we do?" I yell to Vincent as I strike at a dusky-skinned numa with a mustache.

He pulls a second sword from his belt. "We do our best," he answers. "And if we die, we hope that our backup arrives to rescue our bodies."

I ready myself for my next opponent when, from behind the line of numa, I see the worst possible thing: More fighters approaching. Another ten at least. My mouth fills with a metallic tang. I can taste our defeat. We are lost.

These newcomers are like no numa I have seen before. Their punk hair is bleached and dyed in every possible color, and their skin is covered with tattoos. And as they stride through the arched gateway, the noise of battle is suddenly drowned in a wave of speed metal. One of them actually carries a boom box on his shoulder, which he swings down and places near the entrance of the passageway. He pauses to turn the music up to maximum volume before straightening and positioning himself with his compatriots, hands on waists, across the width of the entrance.

The fighting stalls as everyone looks their way. And then I notice their auras. Not red. Gold. *They are bardia!* I realize with astonishment. They draw their weapons, and one of them steps forward.

His long hair is black, tipped in red, and stands on end like a lion's mane. His eyebrow and lip are pierced and his eyes are lined with kohl. He scans the fighters until he spots Charlotte, and one side of his mouth turns up in a grin. "Hey, sis," he calls.

Charlotte is stunned, her sword hanging by her side and her eyes wide with shock. "NO WAY!" she yells, and then with a whoop of joy she springs back into action, swinging at her enemy with such intensity that she beheads the distracted numa with one blow.

Chaos descends. Charles's kindred shout some kind of battle yell in German and plunge into the fight, swinging curved sabers and battle-axes.

The numa facing Arthur and his men fight fiercely for another minute, pushing us forward into a tight band of flailing limbs and flashing weapons. But as our defensive circle widens, confusion takes over. A couple of numa run toward the passageway's exit. They are quickly followed by more, one or two pulling wounded kindred with them, but most thinking only of their own escape.

In five minutes it is over. The blaring music mixes with the moans of our wounded foes, who are quickly dispatched. The owner of the boom box marches over and turns the music down. He shrugs when he sees me staring. "Hey, noise pollution elicits fewer phone calls to the police than screaming and battle sounds. At least, that's the case in Berlin," he says.

"Are you okay?" Vincent asks, and seeing that my worst wound is a slice on my shoulder, kisses me quickly. We gather to assess the bodies. Ten numa lie dead on the ground. A couple of others were carried out by those who escaped. Nicolas's body is still here, his fur coat a gory mess, soaked in blood. Three of Arthur's team are dead. And Ambrose sits propped up against a wall, his arm bleeding profusely as Charles and Charlotte attend to him.

Someone is missing, I realize with alarm. Scanning the passage again, I yell, "Geneviève! Where's Geneviève?" Our group scrambles around, looking for her. "She was just over here," I say, pointing to the place I last saw her body.

Charlotte raises her hands to her mouth in horror. "NO!" she screams, and runs to the end of the passageway with Charles close on her heels. They frantically scan the street on the other end, but it is clear that whoever took Geneviève is long gone.

The twins stand together, dark silhouettes under a black arch, their bodies backlit by the illuminated street beyond. As Charlotte begins to cry, her brother wraps his arms around her.

FORTY-SIX

WITHIN FIVE MINUTES, AN AMBULANCE HAS pulled up to the passageway and the bodies are loaded on. "No, man, I don't need an ambulance," says Ambrose, resisting Vincent's efforts to have him ride with the dead and wounded.

"Well, you can't walk home like that, and you're going to bleed all over a taxi," Vincent says, helping him up to a standing position.

"I'll ride with you," says Charlotte in a small voice.

Ambrose looks over to where she stands with Charles's arm around her. She smiles a sad smile at him, and he nods his head, defeated. "Yeah, okay."

Vincent turns to where I shelter Louis with my body as Charles's German clan eyes him suspiciously.

"You're still here," he says darkly.

"I am," says Louis. He lifts his chin slightly, but looks like a scared adolescent in spite of his bravado.

"Kate, will you please tell me what went on back there?" Vincent asks.

It looks like volant revenants aren't the only ones I can communicate with telepathically. I lob the thought toward him, and he starts in surprise.

"Okay," Vincent says, shaking his head in confusion. "So you telepathically offered this numa amnesty?"

"Louis told me his story on the boat, Vincent. Violette wasn't the only one unhappy with her status. And Louis is still new."

"Six months," Louis clarifies. He's staring at his shoes, his face beet red.

"What he did sounds bad," I say, "but he doesn't want to follow that path."

Vincent looks at the ceiling as if the solution lies above the plate glass. "Kate, what do you expect me to do? I don't understand what you're asking for."

"I don't know either," I admit, "but taking him in is the right thing to do. You just have to trust me."

Vincent stares at me, not knowing how to respond. "Kate. I trust you. But I don't trust him," he says, throwing his gaze toward Louis, who scowls and pushes his hands into his pockets.

"I take full responsibility for him," I say. Vincent raises his hands to his head, like he wants to tear his hair out. A strangled sound escapes his throat as he walks away. He says something to Arthur as he passes him.

Arthur walks over to us. "I've been told I'm 'on you like glue,'" he says to Louis, and waits, making it clear he's not leaving the numa's side.

As we walk toward the exit, Arthur is very obviously checking Louis out. "What?" Louis asks finally.

"So you're Violette's new consort," the older revenant says, amused. "You're with her for six months and you want to run away? Try five hundred years." Louis's jaw drops.

I leave them to follow Vincent, who is talking to the head of Charles's group. "We'll stay as long as you need us," says the girl in German-accented English. She looks like Lisbeth Salander's tougher little sister, her wiry body painted with tattoos, face dotted with piercings, and blue hair cropped short and sticking out as if she used a live electrical wire to style it.

"There's not enough space at La Maison to give everyone a room, but across town . . . ," begins Vincent.

"We don't need beds," the girl says. "No one's dormant this week."

"But space to put your things . . ."

"We share everything, including personal space," she says, amused by Vincent's concern. "Seriously, it's better to keep everyone together. Plus, you say the big battle's about to go down. Well . . . just consider us inseparable," she says, crossing her middle finger behind her index.

"Regrouping at the Frenchie's house," she yells to her crew in English and then repeats herself in German. The group has been busy cleaning up the passageway, stowing dropped weapons and mopping up blood with T-shirts that are summarily thrown into trash cans outside. When we leave, the space looks like nothing ever happened. Charles's kindred bare their ink-decorated chests like medals beneath their leather jackets, jostling one another and joking in German as we begin the walk home.

We make two stops on the way to join up with our groups that were attacked by numa. There were no deaths within their ranks. Whether it was because they were too exposed to fight for long or if the numa were only distracting our backup from supporting us, they had engaged quickly and then had run off.

As Vincent rounds everyone up and sweeps them along with us toward home, the German leader keeps close to me, studying me unabashedly from beneath her blue shorn spikes.

"I didn't get your name," I say finally, looking her straight in the eye.

She doesn't flinch, seeming to like the direct attention. "Uta," she says. "You're the Champion."

"I guess so. Not that that did us much good tonight," I concede. "I'm glad Charles got Charlotte's messages. Otherwise, we'd be toast."

"Charles didn't get Charlotte's messages," Uta says, lifting a pierced eyebrow. "At least, not until we were halfway here. We were on a wilderness motivational retreat. No cell phone service."

"Then . . . how did you know to come?" I ask, confused.

She smiles widely. "I'm a Seer. Saw your light. Brighter than anything I've ever seen. Spotted it from hours away. Knew it was something we had to check out. It just took us a while to get here." Uta laughs at my bewildered expression.

"Gotta be weird being the Champion," she says. "What are your powers?"

I feel kind of embarrassed. As if she asked me to list the things I like best about myself. I focus on the things I'm most worried about. "The prophecy says I'm supposed to have 'preternatural levels of strength.' Not sure if you noticed back there, but I'm no stronger than anyone else."

Uta nods and thinks for a second. "Maybe in your case it's not physical strength. Seems like you've got a lot in here," she says, thumping her chest with her fist. "Doesn't always take muscle to be mighty."

I think about the hippy-dippy in-touch-with-their-feelings label that Charlotte had used for Charles's kindred, and try not to grin.

"You know, we had a Champion in Germany," she continues. "A few hundred years ago. There was a load of political and social infighting—lots of chance for betrayal. Numa had overrun the place. Champion came in. He led a battle against our enemies."

"What happened? How did he do it?" I ask, my pulse accelerating. This is the first thing I've heard about a German Champion.

Uta shrugs. "Don't know. He succeeded. I mean, the numa were wiped out and our region started with a clean slate. But how he did it? Meaning what kind of powers he had—I can't tell you."

"Why not?" I ask.

Uta hesitates and then says, "Because he didn't survive the final battle."

I try to keep my face emotionless. No wonder Vincent doesn't want to talk about what I am. Being the Champion doesn't mean I'm going to win. Uta's just confirmed that.

But I don't regret what I've become. I could be dead right now. If I hadn't been a latent revenant when Violette stabbed me, that would have been it. This is a second chance, not only for me but for Paris's bardia and its unsuspecting human population.

I try to imagine what the city would be like overrun by numa. Evil would reign supreme. Images of Nazi Germany, Fascist Italy, and Francoist Spain come to mind. Of Third World countries run by dictators or generals who seize the resources and let their population starve. Genocide. That is what can happen when the balance of good and evil is disturbed. In this light, it seems impossible to me that I can make a difference.

But I was given the chance to see my grandparents and Georgia again. Not to mention Vincent. I look over to where he is talking with Louis, and his eyes meet mine before returning to the young numa. Even when he's involved in something else, Vincent's attention never leaves me. I know I'm lucky to have been given more time with him.

And I decide that if this is all I have, if we all die today, well then these precious extra minutes will have been worth it. Excusing myself to Uta, I hurry to catch up with Vincent.

Without slowing his pace, he flings an arm around my shoulders and pulls me close to him, bending down to kiss the top of my head before continuing his conversation with Louis. As the newly formed numa finishes telling his story, Vincent looks troubled.

"All I have wanted since I transformed into this monster is to go back and erase what I did. To turn back time so that I could do things differently. I want out," the boy concludes.

"There is no out," Vincent says just loud enough for me to hear.

"Even so, you should know that I will do anything to escape that fate," Louis says fervently.

As we walk past the Louvre and onto the bridge to cross back to the Rive Gauche, Vincent nods to Arthur, who takes Louis by the arm. They drop back to let us talk alone.

"Okay, Kate. I see why this guy made you think," says Vincent. "But that doesn't change the fact that he is numa. His destiny has been decided, and nothing can change that."

"Vincent, I know this doesn't make sense. But there's something different about him. Not only in the feeling I get from him, but his aura is different."

"His aura?" Vincent says incredulously. "Doesn't he have a numa aura?"

"Yes," I admit. "But it's not the same. There is this golden kind of glimmer inside. I think it means something. Like there's some good in him. Some hope. I know this goes against everything you've learned—what you believe is right. But . . . Louis has to come with us."

Vincent slows and then stops to face me, and the others flow around us like a tide. He touches my face, and then laces his fingers through my hair. He holds me like that for a full minute, studying my face like I am a book written in a foreign language. Then he leans forward and presses his lips to mine.

When he steps back the sparkle has returned to his sapphire eyes. "Okay," he says.

"So, you agree with me?" I ask.

"No. But . . . well, Kate, you're the boss." He takes my hand and we resume walking, bringing up the tail end of the procession.

"Yeah, right," I sputter. "You're the head of France's kindred."

"Yes, but you're the Champion," he says with a wry smile. "And I've never seen an actual leadership flowchart, but I presume that means you're the boss of me."

My mouth drops open in amused dismay. "I don't want to be the *boss* of anyone."

"Too late," he says with false flippancy. "You're already talking directly to people's brains, persuading the enemy to untie you while in captivity, and attracting help all the way from Germany with your billion-watt aura. It's not like you can take it back now and just be a regular revenant." He's doing his best to joke, but I know he is just as overwhelmed by what I have become as I am.

"Too bad I didn't get everything that was promised. I did okay back there, but some superstrength would have come in handy," I say.

"Prophecies are always spotty at best," he says. "Maybe the strength bit will kick in later." He pulls me closer, as if his proximity alone can shield me from what is to come.

FORTY-SEVEN

JEANNE IS WAITING WHEN WE GET BACK TO LA Maison. "Is everyone okay?" she asks as we walk through the door.

"What are you doing here? It's three a.m." Vincent places a hand on her shoulder, and she looks at him, abashed.

"I couldn't sleep," she admits. "Something is happening. I can feel it. And I've been with you lot long enough to know I can trust my intuition. I've got some bread in the oven and have put on a stew. Now, did anyone get hurt?" she asks, hiding her emotion behind practicality.

"Ambrose will need medical attention," Vincent says. And then in a lower voice admits, "Geneviève was killed and taken."

Jeanne's hands fly to her mouth. "No," she gasps, tears springing to her eyes.

Vincent nods grimly, suddenly looking tired. We are distracted by the ambulance pulling in through the gates. Jeanne dabs her eyes and moves purposefully toward the vehicle. Charlotte hops out of the passenger seat and opens the door to the back for Ambrose and Charles to get out.

"I don't care if they *are* in body bags," Ambrose is saying. "That's the last time I ride in the back of an ambulance with a half-dozen corpses." He shudders and supports his wounded arm as he steps down to the ground. "I don't mind killing them, but I don't feel like cozying up with them once the deed is done."

Charles jumps down and Jeanne stares curiously at him for a moment before a light goes on in her eyes. She runs down the steps and flings herself on him. "*Mon petit* Charles, you're back!" she coos, standing on her tiptoes to energetically kiss his cheeks. "I am so happy to see you."

"Ditto," Charles says with a broad smile.

"Just look at you," she says, leaning back and inspecting him in all of his tattooed and punk-haired glory. "You know, I'd never believe I would actually say this, but that look really suits you. Of course, if I hadn't cared for you longer than I have my own son, you'd scare my pants off. But you'll always be *mon petit* Charles *à moi*." She hugs him once again and then turns to Ambrose.

"How bad is it, dear?" she asks.

"Bad enough to need a doctor," Charlotte responds, unclipping the weapons from Ambrose's belt and shoulder strap. She hands a battle-axe to Charles and they head down to stow everything in the armory.

"I just need a few stitches," Ambrose says.

"Show," Jeanne commands, and he holds his jacket open.

Cringing, she orders, "You go straight to your room. I'll phone Docteur Dassonville and then come clean you up. Everyone else," she calls to the rapidly filling foyer, "weapons go downstairs in the armory. There's a first aid station there if anyone else needs it. Otherwise, help yourself to the food in the kitchen."

Amid the mass confusion a cell phone rings. Louis pulls a phone out of his pocket and looks at the number on the screen. His face turns ashen.

"Who is it?" Arthur asks.

"Her," he says, pressing a key to send the call to voice mail.

A second later Vincent's phone rings. He clicks speakerphone and holds it up for everyone to hear. "*Oui*," he says.

"You've killed my second and kidnapped my consort," comes Violette's furious voice.

"I plead guilty to one count, but as for the other, Louis came with us of his own free will," responds Vincent. Louis shudders and crosses his arms protectively around his chest.

"That is a lie," Violette spits. "Let me talk to your pitiful excuse for a Champion."

"I'm here," I say.

"I will give you one hour to meet me at the Arènes de Lutèce. Bring me my consort and I will give you Geneviève's body in exchange."

"Why the arena?" I ask. "Why not come here?"

"Not enough open space," she replies. "I will not tolerate any trickery. Meet me in the center of the arena. One hour. Our transaction will be finished by sunup." There is a click, and then a static silence.

"It's a trap," Arthur says.

"Of course it's a trap," Vincent concedes. "Violette will bring her men. And she knows Kate would never come alone." He turns his gaze on me, "She wants another chance at you, Kate."

"What should we do?" asks Charlotte.

"We can't go. We'll all be killed," Arthur says.

"But we have to get Geneviève's body back," argues Charlotte.

"No, actually, you don't," comes a voice from above us. Bran makes his way down the stairway, gripping the marble banister as he descends. "At least it's not what Geneviève would want," he says.

"How do you know that?" asks Charlotte, aghast.

Bran remains silent until he finally stands among us. "Because she told me so," he says simply.

"What do you mean, she told you so?" Vincent asks.

"Geneviève came to me when we returned from New York," Bran explains. "She said you had explained to her about how we flame-fingers work. And she asked if there was any way for me to disperse her spirit while she was dormant."

"Why would she do that?" I ask.

"She told me that without her husband she didn't want to exist. That all she desired was to go to whatever afterlife he has passed on to. She felt she had done enough in her time as a revenant."

"But . . . ," Charlotte begins.

"She was very determined to have her way," Bran says. "I had not yet decided what to do, but now the decision seems to have been made for us. And I would advise that we let her go."

Everyone is silent, processing Bran's story.

"We still need to get her body back in order to burn it," says Vincent finally. "That is, if this isn't just a ruse and Violette actually brings the body with her. In any case, Kate will not be going."

"What do you mean, not going?" I exclaim.

"I'm not saying that to protect you, Kate. I'm saying it to protect us. Violette's goal has not changed. She wants to trap you in order to get the Champion's power. As things stand now, she could defeat us even without that extra strength. Her men at least double our numbers. But for her, the desire for power trumps common sense. She wants you and will risk an on-the-spot, unorganized battle in order to get you. You can't go."

I shake my head, furious. "You can't make that decision for me," I say.

"Could everyone please leave us?" Vincent asks tersely. He is determined to have his way. Too bad I am too.

The room empties until it is only me and Vincent and Charlotte standing in the dappled light of the crystal chandelier.

"If we are making a tactical decision, I need to be here," Charlotte explains apologetically.

We stand in a solemn triangle, no longer lovers and friends. Our feelings don't matter anymore. We must be rational; a decision needs to be made—one that will affect everyone we know.

"I am one of you now," I begin. "And I will not hide here to protect myself. I became the Champion for a reason. And whatever the prophecy actually means—whether I am to lead the bardia against the numa to my peril or to a victory that I actually survive—I know I am supposed to do this. I have to face Violette.

I feel it here," I say, and place my hand on my chest, inadvertently pressing the *signum* into my skin. I look into sad blue eyes. "Vincent, I have never felt more certain about anything."

He continues to meet my gaze, as if waiting for me to change my mind. And then suddenly his shoulders slump and his head drops. He shuts his eyes and touches his fingers to his forehead.

"You win," he murmurs, not looking at me. And then, all business, he says, "Charlotte, call everyone together. Tell them to phone the kindred they contacted earlier this evening. Everyone will assemble, fully armed, at the northeast corner of the park surrounding the arena." Charlotte nods and goes to inform the others.

Vincent and I are left alone in the foyer. He looks at me like I'm a stranger. As if he is seeing me for the very first time. The three feet between us feels like a mile. "This could be it, Kate. It could be the end of all of us. It could very likely be the end of you."

"I know," I say, raising my chin.

He is quiet. "My first feeling when I heard you had animated was joy," he says finally. "I thought that this was the answer to all of our problems. That we could be together forever. Even though I ached that you would be forced to follow such a difficult path, I thought that together we could make it something good and beautiful."

"Vincent, I . . . ," I begin, but he holds a hand up, asking me to let him finish.

"Then Bran told us you were the Champion. And I lost that joy. Because I knew you would never be allowed to be yourself again. You would always carry a great responsibility—the survival of our kindred as well as the protection of the city. The country. That is . . . you would carry that responsibility until the day you were called into action against the numa. And I knew that when that day came, the victory you led us to might prove a tragedy for you. For me and for your family. You can so easily be destroyed. You are the target."

I take a deep breath, knowing he is right. "My grandparents and sister know what a revenant is and the dangers that go with it. They have had a couple of days to accept that." I pause. "It's as if my country were at war and I was going to defend it in battle. Mamie and Papy wouldn't want me to be a soldier. But now that I am one, they will understand any sacrifice I make."

"And me?" Vincent asks. "Does what I feel count for anything? The girl I love is offering herself up like . . ." He sighs, looking miserable as he searches for words. "Like a virgin to the dragon."

"No, the girl you love isn't offering herself to the dragon. This *virgin*"—a smile forms on my lips as I say the word—"is heading out to kick some dragon ass, not to swoon and perish."

Vincent throws himself on me, enveloping me in his arms. "No self-sacrifice," he breathes into my hair. "You won't die for us."

"Not on purpose," I promise. "Plus, Vincent, I'm not going anywhere without you. If we go down, we're going down together." I lean back and attempt a smile.

His eyes are red and glassy. "Together," he agrees, and leans down to kiss me.

* * *

"*You* aren't going anywhere," Vincent says, as Ambrose struggles to get up off the bed.

"I have one good arm," Ambrose retorts, and then grunts in pain as Charlotte pushes him back down.

"See? You can barely move," she says. "You'll only be a liability."

"The fight of the decade—maybe even the century—and I won't be there? You have got to be kidding me," he moans.

The doctor leans over and gives him an anesthetizing shot in the arm. "We'll give it a couple of minutes to get numb," he says, and goes to the other side of the room to dig through some instruments.

"I'm your leader and I say no," Vincent insists, and leaves the room.

Charlotte begins to stand, but Ambrose catches her hand before she can walk away. "Wait," he pleads.

"You're not going to talk me into it," she says, giving him a warning look.

He glances at me. "Katie-Lou, you'll give it to me straight. This is the real deal, isn't it? What's going to go down with Violette is happening now, right?"

I meet Charlotte's eyes, and she gives a slight shake of her head. I exhale. "Yes."

"Aww, man," Ambrose groans, and closing his eyes, he lays his head back against the pillow.

"Listen, Ambrose," says Charlotte, "we're going to do our best to get Geneviève's body back, if that's what you're worried about. You'll just slow us down if you go along. I promise we'll do everything we can."

Ambrose's eyes narrow. "That's why you think I want to go?" he asks. "Because of Geneviève?"

Charlotte gives him a confused look.

"Listen, baby." He rubs his thumb nervously up and down the back of her hand. "You guys are walking straight into one of the most dangerous fights we've seen. It could be *the* Fight. Besides being extremely upset that I can't have a piece of that, it's going to make me crazy knowing you are there, possibly getting yourself killed. Possibly getting yourself destroyed."

"Vincent and I will . . . ," Charlotte begins to argue.

"I'm not worried about Vincent," Ambrose says, cutting her off. "I'm worried about you."

Here it comes, I think, and grinning, I inch slowly backward toward the door so neither of them notice I'm fleeing the scene. Not that they would anyway; they're totally wrapped up in each other.

"I can fight as well as the rest of you," Charlotte retorts, pulling her hand away from him and pushing her fists to her hips.

"I never said you couldn't," Ambrose insists.

"Then why—"

He interrupts her again. "I will stay without complaining . . ."

"You have no choice!"

". . . if you'll do two things." The teasing has long left his face. He is dead serious.

I should leave but I can't. I know I'm about to witness a historic event, and I lurk next to the door, my eyes glued to Charlotte and Ambrose.

"Okay," Charlotte says, matching his gravity.

"Promise me you'll come back."

Charlotte is silent.

"And give me a kiss good-bye."

"What?" Charlotte blurts.

"You heard me."

She stands stock-still for a good couple of seconds before raising her fingertips to her mouth. Her eyes glitter with tears as she sits back down on the side of his bed. And taking his good hand in hers, she leans forward and kisses him. It is a slow kiss. It is a lingering kiss. It's the kiss she's been waiting for for years.

FORTY-EIGHT

GEORGIA IS WAITING IN THE HALLWAY AS I CREEP out of Ambrose's room. "What's up?" she asks, making me leap a foot into the air.

"I didn't see you there," I say, holding my hand to my racing heart.

"So, where's the party?" She folds her arms across her chest.

"Why are you even awake?" I ask.

"Couldn't sleep. And then I look out my window and see the Sex Pistols parking their cars in the drive. So I figure something's up."

I look at Georgia, the bed-tossed condition of her short strawberry-blond hair making her more beautiful than ever. I realize there's a chance that after tonight I might not see her again. Throwing my arms around her neck, I squeeze her to me.

She pats my back. "What, Katie-Bean? What's wrong? I mean, besides the fact that you are supposedly the undead Wonder Woman or something . . . I mean, is that why you're crying?"

"I'm not crying," I say, sniffing and surreptitiously wiping my eyes before letting her go. "I just want you to know that I love you."

Georgia's eyes narrow and she stares at me suspiciously before pointing her finger at me. "You guys are going to do something dangerous. What is it?"

"It's nothing you need to worry about, Georgia."

She makes a disgusted noise and says, "Oh, don't give me that. You wouldn't be acting like this unless you were worried you weren't going to come back. It's why Jeanne's here in the middle of the night and half of punk Berlin is hopping around the house like it's some kind of zombie mosh pit? Right?"

I just look at her and bite my tongue.

"Fine, I'll go ask Arthur," she says, and stalks off.

Charlotte steps out of Ambrose's room and closes the door behind her. Her face glows and her naturally rosy cheeks are flushed scarlet. She takes my hand and we make our way down the stairs. "Did you know?" she asks me.

"Yes," I admit. "But just recently. I think Ambrose only loved Geneviève when she wasn't available. Once it was actually possible, I think he realized she wasn't the one he wanted."

She smiles like a girl whose five-decade wish has finally been granted and, skipping down the rest of the stairs, heads toward the armory.

Back in my room, I throw some water on my face and brush my hair back into a long ponytail. Then, fishing a piece of paper and a pen out of the desk, I sit down to write a note to Mamie and Papy. My pen hovers above the page as I agonize over what to say. But before I can write anything, there is a knock at my door.

Mamie sticks her head in and asks, "Can we talk with you?"

"Yes," I say, covering the unwritten note with my hand and then, seeing her concerned expression, give up the pretense. It might be the last time I see my grandparents, and I'm grateful they came to find me.

"I was writing you a note, but I'm glad you're here. I'd rather talk to you in person."

"Where are you going?" Papy asks, walking in to stand behind my grandmother.

"We're going to battle against Violette," I say honestly.

"And do you plan on coming back?" Mamie asks, her voice catching for a second before she stops herself and puts on her brave grandmother mask.

I rise and walk to them. My grandparents. Besides Georgia, they are my last remaining family, and I love them fiercely. But our struggle against the numa is not just for them as people—as residents of a city that can easily be overrun by the evil undead—but as targets of Violette's wrath. If I fail, I know she will not hesitate to go after them. She won't pass up such an enticing chance for vengeance.

"This is something I need to do," I respond, avoiding Mamie's question.

"We know that. Reassure me again, though, that you're really hard to destroy," Papy says with a forced smile.

"I'm a revenant now, Papy. If I die, I will resurrect." *Unless the numa have a giant bonfire blazing at the battle site or kidnap my dead body and take it somewhere else to burn.* I don't speak this thought, but I don't have to. Papy knows the rules as well as I do.

Mamie gives me a hug. "I brought these from your dresser," she says and holds out my parents' wedding rings. "You know the importance I place in symbols. Take these with you as a reminder of your parents' love and support. They would be very proud of you right now, Katya."

My eyes filling with tears, I pull out my necklace and add the rings to my *signum* and the empty locket that I've kept even though it no longer has a purpose. Jeanne had snipped off more of Vincent's hair as soon as we got back from New York, and I gave her a sample of mine after my bath today. It was a little bit of insurance—in case the worst happens.

I slip the cords back under my shirt and pat the rings to feel that they are there. "Thank you, Mamie," I whisper.

She nods and smiles, wiping a tear away and moving aside so Papy can have his turn. He clasps me tightly in his arms and whispers, "Take care of yourself, *ma princesse.*"

"I will, Papy," I promise, now gulping back the tears.

My grandparents give me one last look-over, nod at me proudly, and then leave. I grab a tissue off the bedside table and take a minute to compose myself. As I start out of the room, I catch a glimpse of my reflection in a full-length mirror and, not recognizing myself, I pause. In my black leather pants, knee-length boots, thin chain-mail-like body armor overlaid with a black suede top, and long leather coat, I look like an action hero.

My cheeks are flushed from fear and anticipation, but my eyes shine like dark stars and I look older with my hair pulled back. I don't know what will happen, but I know beyond any doubt that this is my fate: Facing Violette. I am ready.

As I reach the grand foyer, I see Jean-Baptiste and Gaspard step through the front door.

"You're here!" I cry.

"I had planned on taking a couple more hours to rest up," Gaspard explains with a grin, "however, we received this almost indecipherable text message on our mobile telephone . . ."

Jean-Baptiste holds up his cell phone like it's a piece of alien machinery. "And I quote, 'Dudes, it's going down now. Get your sorry asses over here stat.' With such an eloquent request, how could we resist?" he remarks drily. But there is a ghost of a smile at the edge of his lips, and I know that he and Gaspard wouldn't miss this for anything in the world.

"Woo-hoo, I knew you'd come!" whoops Ambrose from the landing at the top of the stairs.

"You get back in bed this minute," Jeanne scolds, scurrying out from behind him, and pointing imperiously back toward his bedroom door, "before you hemorrhage all over my nice clean rug."

Ambrose grins widely and throws us all a salute, before turning and being ushered back to his bedroom.

"So . . . shall we?" I say, placing my hands on JB's and Gaspard's arms and stepping with them out the door. In the courtyard, I see a stream of cars and motorcycles lined up in front of the gate, motors idling. Two figures stand beside the fountain, bodies pressed tightly together, desperately kissing before stepping back and becoming Georgia and Arthur. Georgia walks away from him and, passing me without slowing her stride, she says, "You better the hell come back, Katie-Bean." And entering the house, she slams the door behind her.

FORTY-NINE

IT IS JUST BEFORE FOUR A.M. WHEN WE PULL INTO the Place Monge neighborhood. Vincent parks the car, and I step out onto the sidewalk as Arthur, Charlotte, and Louis scramble out of the backseat. Jean-Baptiste and Gaspard park nearby and join us. My stomach is in knots. But the calm that comes with the focus of a fight begins to settle over me, infusing me with the confidence I'm going to need. And the fact that Vincent has taken my hand and is holding it firmly in his doesn't hurt.

A few dark figures across the road shine with golden bardia auras, and one raises a hand in greeting. Groups that assembled in Paris over the last few hours have been waiting for us to arrive. We have sixty revenants in all.

But when I glance toward the park hiding the Roman arena, my vision burns with at least a hundred red columns flaming up toward the predawn sky. We are outnumbered. As we feared.

Vincent sees it on my face. "That bad?" he asks.

I nod. "Yep. More than a hundred, I'd guess—some within the park and others scattered around the neighborhood."

He turns and cups my face with his hands, gliding his thumbs over my temples. "You don't have to do this," he says softly enough that the others don't hear. "We can bring the fight to them without you ever having to face Violette. You heard Bran. Geneviève wanted to die."

"There's always the chance that they'll keep her until she's volant and then destroy her, like they did you. She wants to be free. Not trapped as a wandering soul."

"If that actually happens, Bran can disperse her."

"Okay, you're right," I admit. "But I have to face Violette, Vincent. I know it. We both do. And I'd rather do it now, when we know she's not going to slip through our fingers, than living our lives wondering when she's going to turn up next and do something even worse."

"I know." He leans down to kiss me briefly. Firmly. We stand locked in each other's gaze while small groups begin to move into place around us.

"If I should die . . . ," I begin to say.

Vincent cuts me off. "Stop, Kate!" And then he sighs and his shoulders hunch slightly. He knows it's dishonest to pretend we're all going to make it out alive. He shuts his eyes and, when he opens them, he looks resolute. "Whatever happens, remember that I will love you forever," he says. "Even if my spirit is dispersed and my consciousness released to the universe . . . whatever is left of me will never stop loving you."

Vincent won't possess me like he did when I fought Lucien. And there's no sign of whatever superstrength was mentioned in the prophecy. But I am suddenly unafraid, knowing I will face Violette with a powerful but invisible weapon: love. The complete and unconditional love of another being. That is something Violette does not have. It won't win me the battle against her. But it has already made me the victor over my fear.

"This isn't good-bye, Vincent. Because we're going to win." Although my voice is steady, I don't quite believe my own words. I take his hand and we walk toward the park.

The trees are surrounded by a tall iron fence, and as we near the gate we see that it's guarded by four large numa dressed in police uniforms. They nod to Vincent as we approach, glancing apprehensively at the windows of the apartment buildings across the street. While outside of the park, we are in public. Nothing will happen here.

"Only the girl goes in. With him." One of them points to Louis. "Our kind is staying out of the arena, and so will yours."

Vincent shakes his head. "You're lying. There is a large group of your kind already inside the park. And there's no way Kate's going in alone."

The numa eye him suspiciously, and one places a call. He muffles his voice with his hand and then hangs up. "Our leader admits that her security detail guards her within the park. Therefore, you may bring your kind inside, but no one goes within the amphitheater's arena except your Champion and her hostage."

Hostage? I think. Vincent told Violette that Louis sided with us voluntarily. And the numa who escaped the fight in the Passage du Grand Cerf must have told her about how he fought against them. Either she's in denial or she's faking ignorance in order to protect him from her clan.

Vincent makes a signal, raising two fingers high into the air, and suddenly bardia pour in from side streets, parked cars, and darkened doorways, grouping behind us. To my Champion eyes they are a sea of golden flames flowing toward a wall of glowing red columns. We walk through the gate and down a long corridor. High stone walls rise on either side of us as we move en masse toward the ancient Roman amphitheater, Vincent and Jean-Baptiste leading the crowd with Charlotte and Arthur flanking Gaspard just behind.

Louis glances over at me as we follow them. "Don't worry, we won't let them take you back," I say. "You're only here so I can get close enough to Violette to fight her. As soon as you're able, go back and regroup with Vincent and the others."

"I won't let you down," he swears.

"I know," I say, and, taking his hand, squeeze tightly before letting go.

We emerge from the corridor into a large open space. Monumental stone bleachers in a broken arc encircle a plot of dirt as big as a circus ring. There is another tunnel-like corridor identical to the one we just emerged from directly across from us. And around its opening and spilling over into groups sitting on the fanned bleachers are a hell of a lot of numa.

On the floor of the arena itself, Violette stands alone in front of a recently lit bonfire, flames licking one corner of a stack of wood as big as a semitruck. By her feet is a body bag, unzipped and lying open. Geneviève's long platinum-blond hair drapes over the sides. I unconsciously pat the sword hilt at my waist, reassuring myself that I am ready for battle.

Seeing us approach, Violette's face transforms into a mask of victory. Vincent and Jean-Baptiste hesitate, and then lead the bardia away from us, arranging them on the stone steps directly across from the numa. Only Louis and I continue down the path.

Entering the arena, we walk across the dusty ground until we're within five feet of Violette. The fire shoots up high behind her. Its blazing backlight gives her the appearance of a lovely young demon, her eyes dark coals and long black hair whipped up by the early-morning wind.

"Now, just look at us," she says. "How civilized. You have what I want, and I have what you want. So why all the backup?" Violette tilts her head to one side and crosses her arms across her chest like a pouting child.

"Same reason you've got yours," I say, nodding toward the forty-some numa positioned on the bleachers. "Except I'm not hiding most of mine behind the wall. Which is a bit unsports-manlike, I would say."

"It would be if I were expecting any sport," says Violette, with exaggerated calm. I have surprised her.

"They are merely my security detail," she explains. "I can't help it if I have more loyal followers than Vincent does."

She pauses, then unable to resist, says, "You can see my men from afar?"

I nod.

"Aura columns?" she asks, intrigued.

I nod again, reassured that she didn't already know the specifics of my powers.

Satisfied, she gestures toward the body bag. "There is your corpse, now give me my consort."

"I don't want the corpse. And your consort isn't going with you. He's chosen to side with us."

"What?" Violette exclaims in feigned shock. "Why else would you come here tonight?"

"To fight you."

A wide smile spreads across her face. "I was kind of hoping you would say that. I did so want a second chance at absorbing the Champion's power." She peels off her cloak and lays it gently on the ground.

"I assume that's what the fire's for," I say. "Unless this is just a ruse to invite us all to a monster-marshmallow roast."

"You were always a smart girl," Violette retorts. "I've got to give you that." Her gaze moves to the young numa standing next to me. "Louis, you've been such a good boy. It's time to cut the act. Do something useful." Her eyes flick to me and back to him.

Louis hesitates, not knowing what to do. *Think quickly,* I command, *Grab me and pretend to hold me for her. Do it now!*

He lunges for me and grabs me by the upper arms. I thrash wildly, trying to break his hold. To make this look real. But he's fighting me as hard as I am him and within seconds has me trapped, both arms pinned behind my back. *Ow!* I think, and hear him whisper, "Sorry!" He loosens his grip slightly.

"Louis, how could you? You swore to side with us!" I berate him loudly. He says nothing, just continues to pin me, but his grip gets increasingly tighter.

And for a second I feel a twinge of apprehension and wonder if he *has* been playing the double agent and that this charade had been planned by Violette. *You're still with me, right?* I ask worriedly. He responds with a slight squeeze on one of my arms, relieving my doubt.

I hear a roar from the bleachers on my left, and see Vincent and our kindred pouring down the steps toward the arena floor. They don't know about our act and think that Louis has betrayed us. *It's okay*, I think, glancing at Vincent. He nods at me, looking confused, and holds up his hand to try to stay his troops.

"Stop!" yells Violette, and crosses the space between us before I can draw my weapon. Her sword tip grazes my neck: I feel its razor-sharp edge slice my skin and blood drip from the nick she's given me. "Anyone moves, and your Champion is dead!" I feel Louis's grip on me loosen and realize he's about to let me go. *Don't move*, I order him, and he readjusts his hold, pulling me tighter against him. I can feel his heartbeat racing against my back and know he must be scared witless. *Just wait*, I say.

Violette glances over to where Vincent and the others have frozen in place, then shifts her gaze back to me. "You stupid, gullible girl. Louis can join you but he can't ever become one of you. Numa are damned! They can't change into bardia. Everyone knows that."

"So I've been told," I respond. "But I don't believe it. The flame-fingered *guérisseurs* recorded it as happening: I've seen it depicted in one of their paintings."

There is a gleam in Violette's eye—her curiosity is piqued, I can tell—but she lifts her sword tip to place it just beneath my chin. She either isn't buying it or doesn't care.

"There's still time for you to change too, Violette," I continue. "I don't subscribe to all this fixed destiny crap. We have a *guérisseur* who can actually disperse revenant spirits. Who can ease the pain of withstanding death. And I think there's a reason for that. It's the way things were supposed to be before everything went wrong in the revenants' history. No one is really forced to continue existing as something they don't want to be. Geneviève wanted out. And she will have her peace."

"I have been around for half a millennium," Violette responds. "I think I know more than you. You are a waste of the power that is within you."

"Tell me, Violette, what would you do with it?" I ask.

"With the Champion's powers of persuasion, I could convince heads of state to follow me and command great forces of numa. If what you said about aura-sight is true, I could see my kind— and maybe even yours—from far away with enhanced powers of perception. What better way to build a numa army or wipe out a bardia population? And with the Champion's strength? Well, that's the one thing it seems I won't get since even as the Champion, you are a pitiful compassion-crippled weakling."

She is done talking and ready to deal the deathblow. I can

tell by the look of premature victory on her face, the flex of her biceps, and slight lean backward that she is about to pivot to the side and swing with all her might.

Louis, as soon as she starts to swing, drop me and move out of the way, I think.

I meet her gaze. "You want my power, Violette? You can come and get it."

A wicked smile curves her lips, and she takes the sword in both hands. In my peripheral vision I see both bardia and numa surging down from the bleachers, yells erupting as they charge into battle.

I feel Louis release me and I duck into a crouch as Violette's sword flashes forward, whistling through the air where my neck had been. I have just enough time to leap aside and draw my own weapon before she recovers and her blade comes crashing down on me once again.

Violette's sword clashes loudly against mine, and I pull up with all my might until her blade slides off and she stumbles back. She finally has a second to see where Louis went. He stands a few feet away from us, paralyzed, watching our fight and looking lost. "You traitor!" she screams. "What could you be thinking by helping them? They can't change what you are!"

The lost look disappears from Louis's face, replaced by one of despair. *Don't believe her*, I say.

Violette turns her attention back to me. I am matching all of her moves, but barely. If I slow down at all or make one false move, she will win this fight. "I am faster and stronger than you," she spits as she lunges toward me, slashing at my sword arm.

I leap out of her way. "Maybe. But you don't have a heart," I say, meeting her sword with my own mid-swing and knocking her back a step. Our armies have now stopped a few yards on either side of us, not daring to move while we are in the midst of mortal combat.

"A heart makes one feeble," she says, glaring. "In order to wield true strength, one must be merciless." She spins and swings her sword two-handed in a horizontal arc, coming mere inches from my face as I skip backward.

"I disagree," I say, my breath ragged. "Mercy is the key. You can force people to follow you but you will never have their respect or love." I begin to swing, but Violette anticipates my move and knocks my sword out of my hands onto the ground. I reach for it, but her blade is once again lifted—she is too close this time—and I choose to face her weaponless rather than be cut down as I scramble for my sword.

"Love is for the weak," Violette says, her face distorted with scorn. With a grunt of effort she brings her steel down for the deathblow. My instinct is to duck, but I force myself to hold my ground.

Now's your time, Louis, I call to him. *Your chance to control your own destiny.* There is a flash of metal and Violette is stumbling sideways. She drops her sword and throws her hands forward, catching herself from landing face-first on the ground.

Trembling with effort, Violette props herself up on her elbows and turns to Louis, who is staggering backward, watching her with horror. "What. Have. You. Done?" she wheezes, staring at the boy, her eyes wide with pain.

"The right thing. Finally," he says, and stands tall, banishing his fear.

"You are numa," she gasps. "We don't change sides. Once a betrayer, always damned." Slumping, she rolls over to her side. And pulling the knife out of her chest, she studies it as if she's never seen a dagger before. The arena erupts in a riot of battle cries, but no one dares approach.

I look around our tragic triangle, and in a flash of clarity, I am finally convinced of something I've suspected since talking with Uta. The Champion's strength isn't a physical thing. It's not in my body. It is in my spirit. It is an inner strength—one that will inspire loyalty. One that will help me lead my kindred back to the way things were meant to be before revenants were condemned to suffer while carrying out their fate.

And with the gift of perception—the ability to see auras reflecting not only what destiny has dealt a numa like Louis, but that he holds the capability to transform himself and even change sides—maybe I am not only the Champion of the bardia but of all revenants.

I am suddenly and irrevocably certain of it. "You know, Violette," I say, lifting my sword and crouching into an offensive stance. "I'm here to change all of that."

The flames have risen to their full height behind her. The fury in her eyes echoes its blaze. Gesturing to one of her numa sentries fighting nearby, she points to Louis and screams, "Kill him!"

I step forward, sword lowered, ready to strike. Violette makes a lightning-fast movement; metal flashes midair, the knife reflecting the golden red of the bonfire, before sinking deeply into my flesh. I clench my sword tighter in my right hand and try to ignore the knife embedded in my other shoulder, swinging back as powerfully as I can and aiming my blade for Violette's neck.

In the same second, a whistling noise comes from the direction of the numa. Louis falls to the ground, an arrow clean through the center of his forehead.

Around us the battle rages in a tumult of screams, flailing bodies, and clashing of metal, but my focus remains steadily on my foe. The white-hot pain in my shoulder drives me to do what I know I must. My blade meets her neck and slices cleanly through and Violette falls backward, dead.

FIFTY

I STAND STARING AT THE BLOODY MESS THAT was Violette, paralyzed by horror and relief. But I can't afford the luxury of reflection since there is a battle-axe swinging danger-ously close to my head. I leap out of the way and feel strong hands grab me. I begin to struggle, and then hear Vincent say, "It's me." He grasps my hand, and we make a run for it, sprinting past the concentrated area of fighting to the edge of the arena.

We crouch down behind the fire, the ear-splitting clang of clashing metal almost deafening, and I drop my bloody sword to the ground. Vincent turns me toward him and grasping my head in his hands, kisses me quickly and firmly. I never thought sweat and smoke could taste so good.

"Had to do that first," he says with a ghost of a smile. He turns me carefully to the side and inspects the knife in my shoulder. "Does it hurt?" he asks, as he grasps the bottom of his T-shirt, rips off a wide band of cloth, and drapes it over his arm.

"No, I can't feel it at all," I admit.

"Okay, Kate, close your eyes and clench your teeth," he says. Then bracing my upper arm with one hand, he uses the other to wrench the knife from where the blade enters my shoulder and exits my back, just a hair's breadth outside the edge of my Kevlar vest.

I muffle my scream with my hand, but it doesn't matter—it is swallowed by the noise around us. Vincent whips the cloth off his arm and binds it tightly around the wound, under my armpit, and back around, twice. "Can you move that arm?"

I try, and a piercing pain shoots from my hand to my shoulder, causing me to cry out.

Vincent tears another strip off his shirt. Bending my useless arm in front of me, he secures it to my chest. "All the entrances are blocked," he says as he works, "so I can't get you out of here without fighting."

"We're not leaving," I say, scanning the arena. Although the numa began with more than double our number, they are falling fast. The Germans are acting like tag teams: fighting single numa in pairs, slaying them, and then quickly tossing them onto the fire. I count ten corpses already aflame, and the punk contingent isn't slowing.

A shrill whistle comes from next to the bonfire and Vincent and I turn to see Uta gesturing toward us. She holds Violette's head by the hair, brandishing it like Perseus did with Medusa's. "You are witnesses," she yells, and with a nod her men toss Violette's body onto the pyre while she releases the head to the flames.

My feelings are mixed as I see my enemy's body ignite. The broken, bitter girl is gone and I am awash with both pity and relief. Vincent grasps my hand. "You okay?" he asks, second-guessing my emotion. I breathe deeply and nod once. That story is over.

I turn away to look for our kindred and spot Jean-Baptiste and Gaspard fighting back-to-back, their movements synchronized so well they appear to be one person: the deadliest of warriors, bringing death to all it touches.

Not far from them, Charlotte has elevated herself above the fray, perched with her crossbow atop a broken stone column in one corner, steadily picking off our enemies one after the other. Her firing hand moves to her quiver, sweeps out fresh bolts, loads, and shoots them with deathly speed. Arthur stands below her defending her position, slashing away at anyone who nears.

We leave our shelter behind the fire and start in Charlotte's direction.

Although I can't see much of the battlefield, there are fewer red columns surrounding the area. More of our enemy is down, and two bardia with spiky Mohawks pass us, pulling another numa corpse toward the fire. A glimmer of hope flashes in my mind. We are doing it, evening the odds. We may actually win.

Vincent and I are a few yards away from Charlotte, when I see the arrow hit her chest. Shocked, she looks down at the projectile and then crumples and falls to the ground. Vincent pinpoints the numa archer and takes off after him while I throw myself into the fray to get to Charlotte. But before I reach her, a numa girl begins dragging her toward the fire.

"Drop her!" I yell. The girl looks up. In an instant she has drawn her sword and crouches in a defensive position. I raise my sword, but before I can move, Charles leaps in front of me, swinging his sword forcefully against hers. "I've got this one," he yells. "Just get my sister's body away from the fire."

Trying not to look at my friend's sightless eyes and gaping mouth, I tuck her feet under my good arm and begin pulling her toward the arena wall. An arrow whizzes past my ear, and I lunge to my left to dodge another three or four projectiles that are unleashed on me.

A noise erupts from the edges of the battle, and the fighting pauses as all turn to see what is happening. Pouring through the corridors on both sides of the arena is a tidal wave of armed strangers. I recognize their auras at once; they are kindred. My heart soars. Victory is ours. Or will be soon.

Suddenly, Charlotte is jerked out of my grasp. Someone has grabbed her hands and is pulling in the other direction. "Don't touch her!" I scream, and fumble for my sword. Whipping around toward my opponent, I find myself gazing into familiar chestnut brown eyes.

"Jules!" I gasp, and throw myself into his arms.

"Nice to see you too," he responds, "but this isn't the best place for a hug." An arrow whizzes by our heads and we duck back down. "Take her feet," he says. And then, seeing my wounded arm, he says, "Just take one foot," and we begin dragging her toward the wall.

"You're here!" I say, blinking as I am momentarily blinded by sweat from the fire's blistering heat.

"And you're the Champion," Jules replies with a sly grin. "Sorry I'm late. A dozen of us just arrived from New York. Jeanne sent us straight here."

"Just a dozen?" I scan the arena, which teems with new arrivals. "But who are all the other bardia?"

"I don't know," he admits.

We reach the wall and stow Charlotte safely under a stone overhang. Turning, I see Louis's corpse just yards away, lying where he had fallen with the arrow through his head.

"Help me get him over here with Charlotte," I say, and head toward the body, crouching as I run to avoid a barrage of arrows.

"Um, Kates. Isn't that a numa?" Jules asks, looking confused as he arrives beside me and sees Louis.

"No . . . yes," I stammer. "I don't have time to explain. Just help me get his body to safety."

Jules hesitates for a moment, and then, as a firebomb explodes nearby, he leaps over to help me. As we pull Louis to safety, Jules glances up and gives me a funny look.

"What?" I ask as I kick aside a dropped battle-axe.

"Not that I knew any revenants before they animated," he says, pausing to wipe off the sweat dripping into his eyes, "but Kates, you look exactly the same as before." He grins. "Figures."

I return his smile and give Louis one last tug as we arrive at the outer wall, then tuck the arm I was pulling gently over his chest.

We hear a shout from Vincent. We look in the direction he

is running. I see a squadron of giant numa dressed in matching uniforms marching into the arena. There must be two dozen of them, and they are armed to the hilt.

"Who the hell are they?" I cry, my heart dropping as I realize my optimism about our chances has been way too premature. These guys look lethal.

"Lucien's elite fighting squad," Jules answers. "We've been wondering where they were. It looks like Violette has been hiding them away, keeping them fresh for the decisive round of the battle. In our previous war with the numa, they were always called in to do the sweeping up."

He points to the blond hulk of a man leading the pack. "Their captain, Edouard, the last of Lucien's hierarchy, if you can even call it that." I shudder as the man scans the battlefield and calls out an order that has his men fanning out and running with swords raised.

They are upon the bardia in no time. One group has surrounded a handful of Paris kindred and are cutting them down in quick succession. Among those trapped within their circle are *our* kindred: Arthur, Jean-Baptiste, and Gaspard.

Vincent is sprinting in their direction, and Jules and I race to join him. When the numa see us coming, their circle splits. Those nearest us turn to engage: one each for Jules and me, four for Vincent. They weren't there for my showdown with Violette, so they don't recognize me. But they know who he is: the new leader of France's bardia. The prize.

Vincent has drawn his second sword and swings both

powerfully as he battles them solo. He is outnumbered and injured, and the numa Jules and I are fighting are intentionally keeping us from coming to his aid.

The captain, Edouard, moves forward. His soldiers remain motionless, letting him advance. I am guessing that he will deliver the deathblow, and the others will transport his body to the bonfire before we can rescue it. It's a strategy that was obviously planned.

I won't let it happen. I won't lose him again. I run toward Vincent, but before I can reach him someone else has pushed his way through the ring of numa and in front of the blade that is already thrusting its way toward Vincent's chest.

Jean-Baptiste stands with the numa's sword run through his chest and out his back, the blade tip just inches from Vincent's own heart. I hear a cry from Gaspard and see him rush toward Jean-Baptiste's body, only to be fought back by a wall of numa.

With a feral roar, Vincent takes on Edouard, making quick work of the numa captain, while I engage the two enemies to his right. Bardia and numa rush in from all sides, and the battle escalates into a fevered blur of metal and wood and arrows and spurting blood and screams and cries; and I have forgotten my injury and am fighting like a machine, without thinking, until the frenzy of battle clears and the only ones left standing are bardia.

Those numa who are not slain have run off. I can see red vertical beams moving quickly away from the arena grounds. *Let them run*, I think. *It will be easy enough for me to find them later*, and

I realize that that is exactly what I will do. Lead my kindred to destroy any numa who remain. *Except for those like Louis*, I think. Although I saw no red auras tonight containing that golden glimmer of hope, I suspect others exist.

I rush to Vincent, and help Arthur lower him to the ground. "I'm fine," he says.

"You're bleeding like a stuck pig," I retort, as Arthur gingerly pulls his T-shirt over his head and wraps it around his torso to staunch the blood loss from a deep cut to his ribs. I use my good hand to help straighten the improvised bandage, and he smiles at me. "Who was bandaging whom about a half hour ago?" he comments, glancing at my sling.

"I'll be fine in, what, three weeks?" I ask, and marvel again that this is my destiny. A never-ending cycle of life, death, healing, and awakening.

As scattered cheering begins to rise from the survivors, Uta moves to the center of the arena, the blood and grime on her face making her look like a barbarian warrior. Putting her fingers to her teeth, she gives another ear-splitting whistle. "For Vincent Delacroix, the leader of Paris's kindred, we claim victory!" she yells and thrusts a wicked-looking battle mace above her head. "Victory," shouts the crowd, and a forest of weapons are waved in the early-morning air.

Vincent raises a hand, accepting the honor with grace.

"And more importantly—sorry, Vincent—" Uta says with a joking grin, "victory and glory to the Champion, who has more than proven her strength tonight." She presses her fist to her heart again as if to remind me, *your strength is in here.* I smile and mimic her gesture.

"Champions are rare," she continues, "and it has been an honor to fight with one. To the Champion!" she yells, and the place goes berserk, with people cheering and dancing around. Charles's clan do some kind of battle chant in German and throw themselves on one another in wild victory hugs.

I am overwhelmed—my heart is in my throat as I realize that these immortal beings are all ready to follow my lead. To help me fight whatever battles the future holds. As I look around, I notice a lone figure kneeling beside the bonfire. Leaving Vincent, I make my way over to him. His hair has escaped its ponytail and sticks out around his head like a black halo.

"What's wrong, Gaspard?"

"Before . . . before I could get to him . . . ," he stammers, looking up at me with vacant eyes. "The numa. They threw his body onto the flames before I could get to him. Jean-Baptiste. He's gone," Gaspard says.

And lowering his head to his hands, he begins to weep.

FIFTY-ONE

THE BATTLEFIELD IS A SCENE OF DESOLATION. A low wind blows acrid smoke in a sickly yellow haze across the arena. Body parts and weapons are strewn everywhere, and the ground is sticky with dark red mud. Everyone works quickly to clean the mess before the sun rises so that no evidence remains that a massacre has occurred in the middle of Paris.

Everything that can burn is thrown onto the fire. As ambulances begin to arrive, Vincent and Arthur direct volunteers to carry stretchers with bardia corpses to the vehicles waiting at the park gates. Medics—all bardia, I notice—begin to attend to those whose injuries are light.

A medic approaches me, but I nod toward Vincent. "Do him first," I say.

"Gallantry?" Vincent asks, raising an eyebrow.

"No, cowardice. I hate needles," I confess, with a smile.

I watch as Vincent's small cuts are washed and bandaged and

the larger wounds to his arm and side sewn up. He doesn't even wince when the needle threads through his skin, but watches me calmly from where he sits a few feet away. The bardia are used to flesh wounds, as I too will soon be.

"Geneviève is gone. The numa tossed her on early in the fight," Vincent says, as the medic works on him. He pauses and looks thoughtful. "This probably sounds bad, but I'm glad I wasn't forced to make that decision."

There is a pang in my heart as I watch the fire rage, knowing my friend is within the flames. But in my heart I am relieved for her. "She got her wish, then. She's with Philippe."

Another medic approaches where I sit with my good arm around Gaspard, who has stopped crying and is very still. His normal twitchy nervousness has been replaced by a calmness that is more dead than numb, as if a part of him has traveled to the grave with his partner.

My injured arm hangs uselessly in its Vincent-made sling and blood still trickles from the knife wound. Helping me shuffle out of my jacket, the medic rips the sleeve off my shirt and begins silently cleaning and then stitching up my shoulder. Gaspard repositions his head on my shoulder, seemingly unaware that mere inches from his forehead someone is piercing my skin with a needle and yanking a thick black thread through it.

My eyes are already clouded with tears, and my heart so full of hurt for my friend's loss that the pain to my body seems little more than an annoyance. The medic bandages my shoulder, puts my jacket back on over it, and sets my arm in a new, clean sling.

"Are you injured, Monsieur Tabard?" the man asks.

Gaspard shakes his head numbly, and the medic moves on to the next group of injured. Vincent meets my eyes. I know he's asking me to take care of Gaspard. *I will*, I say without speaking. *Go do what you need to do.* Vincent stands and starts to round up the remaining troops and herd them to the fire.

As we watch people assemble, I ask Gaspard, "How long were you and Jean-Baptiste together?"

"One hundred forty-nine years," he answers.

"I'm sorry," I murmur. There's really nothing else I can say. I can't say that I know how he feels. It wouldn't be true. I know how it feels to lose parents, to become orphaned. But I can't put myself into the place of this man who lost the partner he has loved for a century and a half. All those years of living the same experiences, knowing the same victories and defeats, sharing lives. It must be destroying him. I feel a shudder pass through his body as he leans on me. It *is* destroying him.

"Kate, Gaspard," I hear Vincent call, and we stand to join the assembled bardia before the bonfire. Eight of the twelve New York bardia remain, two having been taken away in the ambulances and two lost to the flames. Charles stands with Uta and four of their kindred. Three have been transported back to La Maison and will be fine once they reanimate. One is gone forever. And of three dozen other bardia who fought with us, six were fed to the bonfire.

Near the flames the air is putrid and thick with the noxious smell of burning flesh. People hold their hands over their noses and mouths as Vincent stands with his back to the fire, facing us.

"We don't have long before sunrise, and I want all traces of battle gone and our kindred out of the park by the first rays of dawn. But first, we must honor those who sacrificed themselves today."

He meets my eyes. He is struggling not to cry. Trying his best to stay strong until he finishes his duty. "Among Paris's kindred," he continues, "we lost our beloved Geneviève Emmanuelle Lorieux. She died in 1943, executed by firing squad for having smuggled food and medicine to the detainees at the Drancy detention camp. Geneviève was a loving and dedicated wife to Philippe Lorieux, who died barely four months ago. We will miss you, Geneviève."

Vincent gestures toward Gaspard, who steps forward to face us. "We say good-bye to our longtime leader, Jean-Baptiste Alexandre Balthazar Grimod de la Reynière," Gaspard says in a wavering voice. "He died sacrificing his life for another on the battlefield in Borodino, September 7, 1812. Jean-Baptiste was dedicated to the preservation of his kindred, willing to do anything to ensure their survival." Gaspard's face twists with emotion when he says this, but he forces his shoulders back and raises his chin.

He pulls something from his belt, and I recognize Jean-Baptiste's beloved sword-cane topped with its carved wooden falcon's head. Facing the fire, Gaspard says, "My dear Jean-Baptiste. My love. I will mourn your loss until we are reunited in the next life." And he throws the cane onto the fire. With that motion, his arms drop to his side, and his head to his chest, and he begins once again to weep.

Arthur is by his side in a flash. Putting an arm around the older revenant's shoulders, Arthur leads him in the direction of the waiting vehicles and out of the arena.

One by one, the leaders of the other groups stand and honor the kindred they lost. Finally Vincent speaks up. "We thank you all for coming to our aid today, and pledge you our assistance in return." The assembly breaks up, and I am approached by a middle-aged man who looks to be Gaspard's age, and has the same noble bearing that Jean-Baptiste did. He steps up to kiss my cheeks. "I am Pierre-Marie Lambert from Bordeaux. It has been an honor to fight alongside the Champion."

I ask him the question I've been wondering since he and his kindred appeared. "How did you know to come here—just in time?"

He smiles sadly. "I would say that we were actually a little bit late. If we had arrived on time, there may have been fewer of our kind lost."

"Even so, how did you find us?"

"I am the Seer for my clan," Pierre-Marie explains. "I saw your light two days ago. When it persisted, I decided to come with my kindred. We met up with the others on the way." He steps aside to let the next person approach.

It's as I thought. Jean-Baptiste and Uta weren't the only Seers to receive the Champion's signal.

"Esteban Aragón, Seer of my clan in Barcelona," says a dark-haired boy, and after him a Seer from Belgium introduces herself.

They had all seen my light and followed it to help.

"If you are here, it means the beginning of an era," says Uta. "Your work has just begun. Who knows—in these modern days, maybe your influence won't be limited to your region, as were history's previous Champions. I, for one, look forward to what the future brings with the bardia's new Champion." She bobs her head in a playful bow, while her fellow Seers make noises of agreement.

Vincent asks Uta to lead everyone to La Maison to clean up and find fresh clothes. Finally only Vincent and I and a handful of Paris bardia are left in the deserted arena.

"Where's Jules?" I ask, suddenly alarmed. I haven't seen him since the memorial ceremony.

"He left. He said it's too painful to be with us here in Paris. That he needs time away before he can come back for a visit. Or more," Vincent says softly.

I understand it, but I don't like it. I wish we could all be together like before: best friends, not heartbroken strangers.

But Jules will never be a stranger. I am sure he will be back. Feelings change with time—or at least pain lessens with time; I know that from experience. I can think about my parents now without crippling sadness. I can let myself remember them with gratitude for the time I had with them, even though the parent-shaped hole in my heart will never be filled.

Vincent leads me away from the fire. He begins to put an arm around my shoulder and then, seeing my bandage, hesitates. "Are you okay?" he asks, touching my shoulder gingerly.

"I don't know, am I?" I say it as a joke. But once the words are out, I realize their multiple meanings, and suddenly I'm exhausted. Am I okay? Will I ever feel normal again? I want to hug Vincent, but it feels like he's holding back, and not just from fear of hurting me.

"Let's get back to La Maison," he says. And taking my hand, he leads me down the high-walled corridor and through the gate. The car is parked where we left it. Vincent begins to open the passenger door for me.

"I don't want to go home yet," I say.

Vincent looks surprised.

"I mean, we don't have to, do we?" I ask. "I think I want . . . no, I need . . . to walk." My stomach is in knots and my body is exhausted, but all of the emotion—the fear and pain and despair followed by relief and exultation—of the last hour is bottled up inside me and makes me feel like running instead of walking.

Pressing my hand to his cheek, Vincent brushes my fingers across his skin, closing his eyes as he savors my touch. He locks my hand in his and we begin walking.

As we approach the river, the sky lightens from velvety black to the steel gray of predawn. We cross the street to walk along the quay above the rippling surface of the water. "Look at where we are," I say, and nod toward the Île Saint-Louis in the middle of the river just across from us.

The tree-lined terrace where we sat and talked last summer juts out into the waves, parting the Seine into two rivers that skirt either side of the island. Two parallel rivers that reunite at the far tip of the Île de la Cité, once again becoming one.

I stop walking and Vincent peers at me, a hundred questions in his eyes. "Can you tell me what you're thinking about?" I ask.

He looks out over the water. "I was so afraid when you were in that arena with Violette," he says with a tremor in his voice. "When she stabbed you, it felt like I was being stabbed. I wanted to protect you. And then for the first time I realized that even if she killed you, you would come back. As long as I kept your body away from the fire you would reanimate. That you were like us now—like me. It felt like a revelation."

"But you've known that for days," I say.

"I know. But it hadn't really sunk in until I saw you there, facing death."

"And the fact that I'm like you now makes you feel different about me?"

"Yes."

A stab of apprehension makes me look away toward the water. "Do you think it will be a problem for us?"

"No, Kate. You don't understand," Vincent says, resting his hands very carefully on my shoulders. "My *feelings* for you aren't different. But everything else is. Like I said, what happened to you is something I never hoped for. I don't want you to bear the burden of life as a revenant. I don't want to see you subjected to our fate—the obsession, the craving, the pain of injury and death."

He brushes back a wisp of hair that has escaped my ponytail. "But what I want doesn't matter. It is your destiny. Now you're here. Now you're one of us. And now that we are well on our way to destroying our enemies—thanks to you—there's nothing standing in our way.

"I'm being given my heart's desire, and I just don't know what to do with it. I'm almost afraid to believe it's true, in case someone shakes me and tells me I'm dreaming."

"It's not a dream. I'm here with you," I say. "For what looks like a really long time."

Over Vincent's shoulder an orange glow burns the edge of the sky. I take a step closer, until there is no space left between us and my chest touches his.

And as we kiss, the sun breaks over the horizon and sets the river on fire, its waves flickering an incendiary red in the first light of dawn.

Life changes so quickly. Not long ago I was mourning the death of my parents and wondering if I could make it through another day. Now I have been handed eternity. And not on a silver platter, either, but down a path lined with pain and bloodshed.

But I will walk it with my kindred. With this boy I love. Together we will do something worthy and good. We will give our lives for others. Over and over again.

I don't have answers to all the questions that lie before me. But Vincent and I have time to figure them out. All the time in the world.

ACKNOWLEDGMENTS

ONCE AGAIN, I WOULD LIKE TO THANK MY EDITOR extraordinaire Tara Weikum for her guidance with this book, as well as her unending patience as I struggled through it. Much gratitude to my fabulous team at HarperTeen: Chris Hernandez, Christina Colangelo, and Casey McIntyre. I was truly lucky to have them on board, supporting the final book in the series.

I am endlessly thankful for my UK Little, Brown/Atom team, who have done an amazing job with the promotion of my books in the UK. Thanks especially to Sam Smith, Rose Tremlett, Maddy Feeny, and Kate Agar for their enthusiastic support.

My super-agent Stacey Glick loved this project enough to find the perfect home for it and to cheer me along the whole way. And Laurent E. Abramo has done a bang-up job of finding homes for the Die for Me series in so many foreign countries and languages. Merci, Dystel & Goderich!

For the third time, Mark Ecob and Johanna Basford have

worked their magic with the cover. I couldn't have wished for a more beautifully packaged series, and my readers never tire of telling me how the gorgeous covers made them fall in love with the books before even reading a word.

As with the first two books, Claudia Depkin, friend and tireless beta reader, read every single word of *If I Should Die*. Several times. And gave me the support, encouragement, and feedback I needed to keep me centered and motivated. You were a huge part of this series, Claudia, and I'm so grateful.

Thanks and love to Kim Lennert for listening to me read the manuscript out loud as she drove me from New York to Lexington, Kentucky, to Birmingham, Alabama, to Nashville, Tennessee, on my Revenant Road Trip book tour. A girl could never wish for a truer friend.

I am much indebted to copyeditors Valerie Shea and Melinda Weigel. Without their continued corrections, *If I Should Die* would be embarrassingly jam-packed with mistakes. From fixing my scary punctuation to pointing out that people don't wear heavy coats in July, they have made Die for Me a series I can be proud of. And thank you to all of my friends and readers for the enthusiasm, support . . . and forgiveness for leaving you hanging for an entire year after *Until I Die*'s monumental cliff-hanger ending. I told you everything would turn out in the end.